THE MAN WHO RISKED IT ALL

ALSO BY LAURENT GOUNELLE

The Man Who Wanted to Be Happy

Please visit:

Hay House UK: www.hayhouse.co.uk
Hay House USA: www.hayhouse.com®
Hay House Australia: www.hayhouse.com.au
Hay House South Africa: www.hayhouse.co.za
Hay House India: www.hayhouse.co.in

THE MAN WHO RISKED IT ALL

LAURENT GOUNELLE

TRANSLATED BY ALAN S. JACKSON

HAY HOUSE

Carlsbad, California • New York City • London • Sydney
Johannesburg • Vancouver • Hong Kong • New Delhi

First published and distributed in the United Kingdom by:
Hay House UK Ltd, Astley House, 33 Notting Hill Gate, London W11 3JQ
Tel: +44 (0)20 3675 2450; Fax: +44 (0)20 3675 2451
www.hayhouse.co.uk

Published and distributed in the United States of America by:
Hay House Inc., PO Box 5100, Carlsbad, CA 92018-5100
Tel: (1) 760 431 7695 or (800) 654 5126
Fax: (1) 760 431 6948 or (800) 650 5115
www.hayhouse.com

Published and distributed in Australia by:
Hay House Australia Ltd, 18/36 Ralph St, Alexandria NSW 2015
Tel: (61) 2 9669 4299; Fax: (61) 2 9669 4144
www.hayhouse.com.au

Published and distributed in the Republic of South Africa by:
Hay House SA (Pty) Ltd, PO Box 990, Witkoppen 2068
Tel/Fax: (27) 11 467 8904
www.hayhouse.co.za

Published and distributed in India by:
Hay House Publishers India, Muskaan Complex, Plot No.3, B-2,
Vasant Kunj, New Delhi 110 070
Tel: (91) 11 4176 1620; Fax: (91) 11 4176 1630
www.hayhouse.co.in

Distributed in Canada by:
Raincoast, 9050 Shaughnessy St, Vancouver BC V6P 6E5
Tel: (1) 604 323 7100; Fax: (1) 604 323 2600

Copyright © 2014 by Laurent Gounelle

The moral rights of the author have been asserted.

Cover design: Shelley Noble • *Interior design:* Jenny Richards

The information given in this book should not be treated as a substitute for professional medical advice; always consult a medical practitioner. Any use of information in this book is at the reader's discretion and risk. Neither the author nor the publisher can be held responsible for any loss, claim or damage arising out of the use, or misuse, of the suggestions made, the failure to take medical advice or for any material on third party websites.

This is a work of fiction. Names, characters, places and incidents are the product of the author's imagination or are used fictitiously. Any resemblance to actual events or locales, or persons living or deceased, is strictly coincidental.

A catalogue record for this book is available from the British Library.

ISBN: 978-1-84850-858-3

Printed in Great Britain by TJ International, Padstow, Cornwall.

MIX
Paper from
responsible sources
FSC
www.fsc.org   FSC® C013056

Life is a risk.

If you have not risked, you have not lived.

It's what gives . . . that champagne taste.

Sœur Emmanuelle

The soft, warm night enveloped me. It was taking me in its arms, carrying me. I could feel my body melting into it, as if I were already floating in the air.

One more step . . .

I wasn't afraid. And I didn't want fear to arise suddenly and hold me back, spoiling everything.

I had imagined hearing the hubbub of the city, so I was surprised by the peace and quiet. Not silence, no, but peace and quiet. All the sounds that reached me were gentle, distant, soothing.

One little step . . .

Slowly, very slowly, I walked along the steel beam that the lights had transformed into dark gold. That night, the Eiffel Tower and I were as one. I was walking on gold, breathing in air that was warm and damp, with a strange scent that was enticing, intoxicating. Beneath me, 360 feet below, lay Paris, offering herself to me. Her twinkling lights were so many winking, calling eyes. Patiently, aware she was irresistible, she was waiting for my blood to come and fertilize her.

One more step . . .

I had thought it all out and carefully prepared for what I was about to do. I had chosen it, accepted it, made it part of me. Very calmly, I had made up my mind to end a life that was devoid of purpose or meaning, that no longer offered anything that was worth the trouble.

1

One step . . .

My life was a string of failures that had begun even before my birth. My father—if that's what you can call the vulgar progenitor—had not even judged me worthy of knowing him. He had left my mother as soon as she told him she was pregnant.

Was it with the intention of getting rid of me that she had tried to drown her despair in a Paris bar? The many drinks she had consumed with the American businessman she met there did not, however, cloud her mind. He was 39; she was 26. She was anxious; his relaxed air reassured her. He seemed well off; she was struggling to survive. She gave herself to him that night, calculatingly and with hope. The next morning, she was tender and loving, and I will never know if it was sincerely or out of weakness that he said yes, of course, if ever she became pregnant, he wanted her to keep the child and stay by his side.

She followed him to the United States, and in the land of excess, nobody was surprised that I came into the world at seven-and-a-half months already weighing nearly six-and-a-half pounds. I was given an American name, and so I became Alan Greenmor, an American citizen. My mother learned English and managed as best she could to adapt to life in her adopted country. But things took a tragic turn. Five years after they arrived, my new father lost his job, and, unable to find another one during the pre-Reagan economic crisis, he spiraled down into alcoholism. He became bad-tempered, uncommunicative, and depressed. My mother was disgusted by his lack of initiative and constantly criticized him for his spinelessness. Deeply resentful, she continually looked for ways to provoke him, using the slightest transgression as an excuse to criticize him. His lack of reaction led her to increase the attacks, heaping on more and more insults. She seemed to derive some satisfaction when he at last got angry, preferring his anger to his apathy. I was terrified by her game. I loved my parents and couldn't bear to see them destroying each other. My father's fits of anger were rare but explosive, and I feared them as much as my mother desired them. When she at last got a reaction from him, she had an adversary, a man who could stand up for himself. She finally had an outlet for her built-up resentment, and she really lashed out with her tongue. One evening, my father beat her, and I was less traumatized by his violence than by the perverse pleasure I read on my mother's face. One night, during a particularly terrible argument, my mother flung in his face that I was not really his son—a fact that I became aware of at the same time. He left the house the next day and was never seen again. My second father had left me as well.

My mother struggled to keep us alive. She worked long hours, six days a week, in a laundry. She brought its chemical smells home every night. When she came to kiss me at bedtime, I no longer recognized my mother's much-loved scent, the scent that before had reassured me, inviting me to sleep as it enveloped me in tenderness.

One step, then another . . .

After my father left, my mother went from one low-level job to another, believing each time that she could rise up through the ranks, get a promotion, and earn more. She also went from lover to lover, with the hope of keeping one and setting up a home. I think one day she realized that all these hopes about her life were futile, and that is when she focused everything on me. I would succeed where she had failed. I would earn so much money that she would be wealthy, too. From that moment, my education became her absolute priority. I was ordered to bring home good grades. At meals, our conversation revolved around school, the teachers, my results. My mother became my trainer; I was her colt. Speaking French with her and English with the rest of the world, I had been bilingual from birth. She repeated endlessly that this was a major asset. I was sure to become an international businessman or a great interpreter. She even imagined me as Secretary of State. Only losers have no ambition, she said. I was very afraid of disappointing her, so I worked as hard as I could in school, getting good marks. But my success only increased her expectations of me; it confirmed that her strategy was working.

It was a terrible blow the day my mother learned that in the United States a college education isn't free. It costs money, and top dollar at that. It was the first time I ever saw her downcast. All her plans were destroyed. Perhaps she really was cursed, but it didn't take long for her natural character to regain the upper hand. She made an appointment with the principal of my school to convince him that a young American citizen shouldn't be left by the wayside when his high grades were evidence of how he might serve his country if he were given access to the lofty positions a college education would ensure. There must be a solution, she said. Weren't there scholarships or grants or something? She came home from the meeting all fired up. It was very simple, she said. There was a six-letter answer: *sports*. If I was very good at sports, there was a good chance a college would waive its tuition, just to get me on its team and increase its chances of winning tournaments.

And so, without ever daring to admit to my mother that I loathed sports, I was subjected to an intensive training regime. She pushed me, motivated me, encouraged me, continually scrutinizing my results. Now she seemed unconcerned about my grades. "Where there's a will, there's a way," she would repeat nonstop. In the end, it was baseball that I turned out to be least bad at. From then on, I lived for baseball. To motivate me, she pinned posters of the stars on

4

the Detroit Tigers to my bedroom wall. I drank my breakfast milk from a mug with a picture of the Tigers on it. There were Tigers everywhere: on my key ring, my T-shirts, my socks, my bathrobe, my pens. I ate Tigers, I wrote Tigers, I washed Tigers, I even slept Tigers. Baseball haunted my dreams. My mother had succeeded in sponsoring my brain, sliding billboards into my thoughts. She enrolled me in Little League and worked overtime to pay the dues. I spent three hours a day minimum, five on weekends, playing baseball. The coach's shouts still ring in my ears, all these years later. I hated the sport but I loved my mother, and I would have done anything not to disappoint her. She had spent her life keeping her hopes up, and I had the impression she would stop living the day she had nothing more to hope for.

The future proved me right. My mother died several years later, just after my graduation from business school. I found myself alone, holding an MBA that I hadn't really wanted, having spent my school years rubbing shoulders with young people whose tastes and aspirations I didn't share. I was offered a job as deputy head of the suppliers' accounts department of a large company. The salary was good, but the work soon turned out to be uninteresting. I wasn't really disappointed, however, as I wasn't expecting anything. My mother's life had taught me at an early age that hopes were futile.

One more step . . .

After a few years of an empty, pointless life, I left for France, almost on a whim. Was it an unconscious desire to reconnect with my origins, or was I trying to undo the legacy of my mother's miserable life by going in the opposite direction? I don't know. At any rate, I found myself in Paris and decided to stay. The city is beautiful but that wasn't the reason. There was something else: an intuition or a premonition that my destiny lay there.

At the time, I didn't know that I would want to die there so soon.

I looked for a job, and got an interview at Dunker Consulting, a recruitment agency that searched for accounts managers for big companies. The interviewer told me I was unemployable in France, as French accounts were kept according to very different regulations than American ones. "You might as well start qualifying again from scratch," he had said, laughing at a joke only he could see. On the other hand, he said that my overall knowledge of accounting, along with my American background, made me a desirable candidate to become a recruitment consultant in their firm. Their main clients were large American companies that would appreciate having their recruitment handled by an American. "Impossible," I told him. "Recruitment is not my thing. I know absolutely nothing about it." The interviewer gave me a knowing smile, like the experienced older man faced with the embarrassed young woman who admits at the last minute that she is still a virgin. "We'll take care of that," he said.

So I was hired and spent the first two weeks in intensive training, along with other young recruits who were going to contribute to the firm's sustained development. Our average age was 30, which seemed to me extremely young to be practicing this profession. Evaluating the qualities and aptitudes of a candidate amounted to judging a human being, and I was nervous at having to assume such a responsibility. Apparently my fellow trainees didn't share my fear; they obviously enjoyed slipping into the respected role of the recruiter. The shared feeling in the group was of belonging to a certain elite. Pride left no room for doubt.

For two weeks, we were taught the tricks of the trade: a simple but sensible method for conducting recruitment interviews, as well as a string of gimmicky techniques that

I think of today as so much nonsense. I learned that after welcoming a candidate, you were to stay silent for a few moments. If the applicant started speaking on his own, you were probably dealing with a leader. If he patiently waited to be asked a question, his reserve fit the profile of a follower. We were to invite the recruit to introduce himself in a very open way—"Tell me about yourself"—without asking specific questions from the outset. If the candidate launched off on his own, it showed he was independent. If he asked us where we wanted him to begin—should he start with his education, for example, or go back in time from his most recent employment—then he lacked initiative.

We practiced applying the techniques in role-playing exercises conducted in pairs. One of us played the role of the recruiter while the other put himself in the place of the candidate, inventing a background and a career so that we could practice holding interviews and asking questions to expose the "truth" about the candidate. What was most surprising to me was the competitive atmosphere that prevailed during these exercises. Everyone tried to trap their partner, who was seen alternately as a liar to be unmasked or an enemy to be deceived. The funniest thing was that the trainer, a salaried consultant with Dunker Consulting, entered into the competition as well, taking particular pleasure in highlighting omissions or blunders. "You're being had!" was his favorite phrase, spoken in a mocking voice, as he supervised the role plays, gliding among the pairs as we practiced. The insinuation was that he would have known how to handle the situation.

At the end of two weeks, we were pronounced fit for service.

I found myself spending my days behind a desk listening to timid men telling me about their careers, their faces red with fright as they tried to make me believe that their three main shortcomings were perfectionism, too much accuracy, and a tendency to work too hard. They were miles away from suspecting that I was even more timid than they were and even more ill at ease. I was just a bit luckier than them because my role gave me an advantage that was far from insignificant: I got others to speak rather than speaking myself. But each time I undertook a search, I dreaded the moment when I would be forced to tell nine candidates out of ten that their applications didn't fit the required profile. I felt like I was pronouncing a prison sentence. My unease increased theirs, which reinforced mine, in a hellish vicious circle. I was suffocating in the role, and the atmosphere within the company did nothing to lighten my mood. The human values on display were only a façade. The daily reality was tough, cold, competitive.

It was Audrey who allowed me to survive in this situation. I met her one Sunday afternoon at Mariage Frères on the Rue des Grands Augustins. I only had to set foot in this place to feel soothed. As soon as I opened the door, the first step on the old oak flooring plunged me into the refined atmosphere of a tea merchant's shop in the days of the French colonial empire. I was bewitched by the mixed fragrances of the hundreds of teas stored in immense antique jars; their scents transported me in a flash to the Far East of the 19th century.

It was while I was ordering a quarter of a pound of Sakura from the young man behind the counter that a voice whispered in my ear that the Sakura Impérial was finer. I turned around, surprised that a stranger was talking to me in this city where everyone seemed to be encased in their own bubble, haughtily ignoring everyone else. Her exact words were: "You don't believe me? Come and taste for yourself." Taking me by the hand, she led me across the room, weaving through the customers and the displays of teapots from faraway places to the little staircase that climbed to the tasting room. Here the ambiance was intimate, elegant. Waiters in colored raw silk suits glided silently between the tables with a ceremonious attitude. In my casual clothes, I was an anachronism. We sat in a corner at a little table with a white cloth, set with silver cutlery and china cups bearing the Mariage Frères crest. Audrey ordered two teas, hot scones, and a coup de soleil, or strawberries-and-cream tart—the specialty she said I absolutely had to try. (I immediately enjoyed our conversation. She was a fine arts student and lived in a garret in the Latin Quarter. "You'll see, it's really nice," she told me, thereby indicating that our meeting would not stop at the door to Mariage Frères.)

Her room was indeed charming—minute, with a sloping ceiling made of old beams and a skylight that looked out on a succession of gray roofs angled in every direction. All it needed was a crescent moon to be something straight out Henry James's novel, *The Aristocrats*. She undressed with a natural grace, and I immediately loved her body, which had a delicacy I was not used to. Her shoulders and arms were exquisitely slender, nothing like those of American girls brought up on cornflakes and intensive sports. Her white, white skin contrasted with her dark hair, and her breasts— my God, her breasts were sublime, simply sublime. Fifty times during the night I thanked her for not wearing perfume, as I delighted in the voluptuous scent of her skin at every point of her body, intoxicating like a drug. That night will remain engraved in my memory beyond my death.

We woke up the next morning entwined. I ran to fetch croissants and breathlessly climbed back up the six stories to her room. I threw myself into her arms, and we made love again. For the first time in my life I was experiencing happiness. It was a new, strange sensation. I was far from suspecting that this happiness foreshadowed the fall from which I would not get up.

For four months my life was centered on Audrey. She occupied my thoughts during the day and my dreams at night. Her schedule at art school was full of openings that left her available. During the week, we would often meet during the day. I would use a client meeting as an excuse and spend an hour or two with her in a hotel room that we rented nearby. I felt a bit guilty. Just a bit. Happiness makes you selfish.

One day, I was in my office when Vanessa, the departmental secretary, called to say that my candidate had arrived. I was expecting no one but as my organizational skills left room for improvement, just to be safe I asked her to send the candidate up. I would rather see someone for nothing than give Vanessa proof of my lack of organization; my boss would have known in less than half an hour. I waited at the door to my office and nearly fainted when, at the end of the corridor, I saw Vanessa escorting Audrey, who was dressed as a caricature of an accountant, in a skimpy suit and metal-rimmed glasses that I'd never seen on her before, with her hair in a ponytail. A real cliché, borderline grotesque. As I thanked Vanessa, my voice stuck in my throat. I closed my door behind Audrey. She took her glasses off with a suggestive look, her lips in a slight pout. I immediately knew what she intended. I swallowed hard and felt a wave of fright pass through my body. I knew her enough to know that nothing would stop her.

That day the conference table became a piece of furniture that I would never see in the same way again. I was scared stiff that someone would find us. She was crazy, but I loved it.

When Audrey left me four months later, my life stopped at once. Without the slightest suspicion beforehand, one evening I took a little envelope out of the mailbox. Inside was one word, just one, in her very recognizable handwriting: *Good-bye.* I stood rooted to the spot in the hall of my apartment building, in front of the mailbox. My blood froze in my veins. My head was throbbing. I was nearly sick. I collapsed into the old wooden elevator, which discharged me at my floor, where I entered my apartment in a state of shock. Everything was swaying around me. I fell onto the sofa and sobbed. After a long while, I sat up and told myself it was impossible, quite simply impossible. It must be a practical joke or something. I grabbed my phone and tried to call her. I listened to her voice mail a hundred times and, each time, her voice seemed a little more neutral, more distant, colder. I gave up when her machine reached saturation point and stopped taking messages.

Slowly, a distant but familiar feeling emerged from deep inside me, gradually rising to the surface. *It was natural,* the feeling said, *quite natural that I should be left. That was the way it was. You don't fight your destiny, Alan.*

It was at that moment that I realized my death was self-evident. It wasn't an impulse. I wouldn't have jumped under a train. No, it was just something obvious that imposed itself on me. I was going to pass to the other side, and everything would be fine. It was up to me to choose the place, the time; there was no hurry. It wasn't a morbid, masochistic desire. Not at all. And it wasn't just a desire to put an end to my suffering, however great that was. No, the beyond was drawing me, gently, irresistibly, and I had the strange feeling that my place was there, that my soul would flower there. My life on earth had no reason to be. I had had the conceit to cling to it, to pretend that all was well, and life had sent me Audrey to make me experience an unbearable pain and in this way to face my destiny at last.

The place was suggested to me by my memory, and it's no doubt not pure chance that it had been kept there, in one of my memory's mysterious compartments. Some time before I had read, in a magazine left behind by Audrey, a controversial article by someone named Dubrovski. In it, the author laid out his theory on the right to suicide, and his idea that, if you were going to commit suicide, you might as well do it properly. He described a suitable place for what he poetically called "the flight of one's life"—the Eiffel Tower. It is totally secure, he explained, except at one point that it's useful to know. You have to go up to the Jules Verne, the luxury restaurant on the second floor, go into the ladies' room, then open the little door marked *Private* to the left of the washbasin. It leads to a tiny room that serves as a broom cupboard. The window in there is not barred and opens directly onto the girders. I remembered these details as though I had read them that very morning. Dying at the Eiffel Tower had something grand about it. Revenge for a mediocre life.

One more step . . .

I had to walk far enough along the beam to reach a suitable point where there was no metal structure below me to impede my fall.

I was leaving nothing behind me, not a friend, not a relative, not a pleasure, nothing that could make me regret my action. I was ready, in my head and in my body.

One last step . . .

That's it. The *right place*. I stood still. Consciousness was already beginning to leave me. I took a deep breath and slowly pivoted on my heels to the right, toward the abyss that I didn't look into but whose presence, whose beauty, I could feel.

I was on a level with the flywheel of the Jules Verne's private elevator. Three yards of nothingness separated us. From where I was, I could see only the grooved edge holding the cable, as it circled the wheel, then plunged into the void. The void. The windows of the restaurant were on the other side of the tower. Nobody could see me. No noise from the restaurant reached me. I heard nothing but a gentle humming, the sound of the night. Those shimmering lights in the distance were drawing me, hypnotizing me. The warm, intoxicating air was flooding me with supernatural well-being. Most of my thoughts had left me. I no longer inhabited my body. I was no longer me. I was merging with space, life, death. I no longer existed as a separate being. *I was life.* I . . .

A cough . . .

In a flash, it brought me out of the state I was in, just as the snapping of a hypnotist's fingers breaks his patient's trance.

To my right, at the end of the girder, stood a man looking me straight in the eyes. About 60, with silver-gray hair, wearing a dark suit. His eyes, lit by the reflection from one of the tower's lights, seemed to emerge from a void. All my life I'll remember those eyes, a steely blue to freeze your blood.

A feeling of anger mixed with my surprise. I had taken every precaution not to be seen. I was certain I had not been followed. I felt as if I were in a bad film, in which a rescuer miraculously arrives at just the right moment to prevent a suicide.

I had made a mess of my life. Others had taken control of it, but my death belonged to me. To me alone. There was no question of me allowing someone to hold me back, to convince me with soothing words that life was beautiful all the same, or that others were unhappier than me, or I don't know what. In any case, no one could understand, and what's more, I wasn't asking for anything. More than anything in the world, I wanted to be alone. Alone.

"Leave me alone. I'm a free man. I'm doing what I want. Go away."

He watched me in silence, and right away I had the feeling that something wasn't right. He looked relaxed. Yes, that's it, *relaxed!*

He raised his cigar to his mouth, calmly.

"Go on. Jump!"

I was stunned by his words. I was expecting anything but that. Who was this guy? A weirdo? He wanted to see me fall and get off on it? Shit! It had to happen to me! But this can't be! What had I done to God, for crying out loud? I was incensed. It was not possible, not possible, not . . .

"What are you waiting for?" he asked in a terribly tranquil tone. "Jump!"

The situation left me completely at a loss. My thoughts were knocking into each other without managing to come together. Struggling, I managed to say few words.

"Who are you? What do you want from me?"

He drew on his cigar and held the smoke in his mouth for a while, before exhaling it in thin coils that vanished before they reached me. His eyes riveted on mine paralyzed me. This guy had enough charisma to bend the Eiffel Tower.

"You're angry. But you are suffering a lot deep inside yourself," he said in a very calm voice, with a light accent that I didn't recognize.

"That's not hard to guess."

"You're atrociously unhappy and can't bear to go on living."

His words troubled me and made me feel my pain. I nodded. The silence weighed on me.

"Let's say I've had big problems all my life."

A slow, very slow puff on the cigar.

"There are no big problems. There are only little people."

A wave of anger rose up in me. I could feel my blood beating in my temples, which were burning hot. I swallowed hard.

"It's easy to take advantage of my situation to humiliate me. Who do you think you are? Of course, I suppose you know how to solve all your problems?"

With incredible self-assurance, he replied: "Yes, I do. And other people's problems as well."

I was beginning to feel ill. Now I was fully conscious of being surrounded by the void. I was beginning to be afraid. Fear had finally found me and was worming its way inside. My hands were moist. I absolutely mustn't look down.

He went on: "It's true that by jumping your problems will disappear with you. But the situation isn't as fair as that. . . ."

"What do you mean?"

"Once again, you're the one who's going to suffer. Your problems won't feel anything. As a solution, this is not very balanced."

"You don't suffer jumping from a tower. The collision is so violent that you simply stop living without having time to feel anything. No pain. I've informed myself."

He quietly laughed.

"What's making you laugh?"

"That's true—if you start from the hypothesis that you are still alive at the moment you hit the ground. That's where you're wrong. Nobody arrives down there alive."

A long draw on the cigar. I felt more and more ill. Dizzy. I needed to sit down.

"The truth is," he went on, taking his time, "they all die during the fall from a heart attack provoked by horror, the abominable horror of the fall and the unbearable vision of the ground coming nearer at one hundred and fifty miles an hour. They are struck down by an atrocious fright that makes them spew out their innards before their heart explodes. Their eyes are bulging out of their sockets at the moment of death."

My legs were shaking. I nearly fainted. My head was spinning. I felt extremely sick. *Don't look down,* I told myself. *Definitely not. Stay standing straight up. Concentrate on him. Don't take your eyes off him.*

"Perhaps," he said after a silence, speaking slowly, "perhaps I have something to propose to you."

I stayed silent, hanging on his words.

"A sort of deal between us," he continued, leaving his words floating in the air.

"A deal?" I stuttered.

"Here's how it is: You remain alive, and I'll look after you. I'll set you back on the right road, make you a man capable of leading his life, of solving his problems, and even being happy. In exchange . . ."

He drew another puff on his cigar.

"In exchange, you'll do everything I tell you to. You promise on your life."

His words were highly disturbing and added to my unease. I had to make a considerable effort to concentrate, collect my wits, and think.

"What do you mean by 'promise on my life'?"

Silence.

"You must respect the contract."

"Otherwise?"

"Otherwise you will not remain alive."

"I'd have to be mad to accept a deal like that!"

"What have you got to lose?"

"Why would I place my life in the hands of a stranger in exchange for a hypothetical happiness?"

His face showed the confidence of a chess player who knows that his opponent is in check.

"And down there, what will you obtain in exchange for your certain death?" he said, pointing to the void with the tip of his cigar.

I made the mistake of looking in that direction and was gripped by violent vertigo. The vision terrified me, yet at the same time, the void was calling to me, as if to free me from the awful anguish that was overcoming me. I wanted to lie down along the girder and stay there without moving, waiting for him to help me. Uncontrollable nervous shivers went up and down my limbs. It was awful, unbearable.

Rain . . .

Rain was starting to fall. Rain. My God, the metal girder was going to be like a skating rink. There were five yards between me and the man, the window, safety. Five yards of narrow and slippery girder. I had to concentrate. Yes, that's it, concentrate. Above all, stay upright. Breathe in. I had to turn gently to the right, but my legs wouldn't move. It was as if my feet were stuck to the metal. Staying too long in that position had frozen my muscles, and now they weren't responding. Vertigo was an evil sorcerer that had bewitched its victim. My legs started trembling, at first imperceptibly, then more and more violently. My strength was abandoning me.

The wheel . . .

The wheel was turning. The noise of the elevator beginning to move. The wheel began to throw off water. The rotation accelerated, and I could hear the elevator going down, faster and faster. The water hit me, cold and blinding. Deafening. I lost my balance and found myself crouched down, clinging to the girder, still attacked by the cascading water. Through the din I heard the man shouting in a commanding tone:

"Come over here! Keep your eyes open! Put one foot in front of the other!"

I obeyed, submitting to his authority, forcing myself to only listen to his orders and forget my thoughts and my emotions, even though they were overwhelming. I took a step, then a second, like a robot, mechanically executing each of his commands. I managed to extricate myself from the waterfall, then to walk, in a trance, until I was level with him. I lifted a foot to climb over the horizontal beam that separated me from him, but he gripped the trembling, dripping hand I was holding out and stopped me in my tracks, pushing me back. I nearly staggered into the void, unbalanced by his force. But his iron grip held me immobile.

"Right. Is it a deal?"

The water was streaming down his face, guided by his wrinkles. His blue eyes were fascinating.

"Yes."

THE NEXT DAY I woke up in my bed, nice and warm in my dry sheets. A ray of sunlight was coming through the blinds. I rolled over to reach the bedside table without leaving the welcoming cocoon of the bedclothes. I stretched out my arm and took the calling card I had left there as I went to bed. The man had given it to me before leaving me. "Come tomorrow at eleven o'clock," were his final words.

Yves Dubreuil
23, Avenue Henri Martin
75116 Paris
Telephone: 01 47 55 10 30

I really didn't know what to expect and was rather worried.

I grabbed my phone and called Vanessa to ask her to cancel all my appointments for the day. I told her I was unwell and didn't know when I would be back. That chore done, I dashed into the shower and stayed there until the hot water tank was empty.

I lived in a one-bedroom apartment I rented in Montmartre. The rent was high and the space limited, but I had an unobstructed view over the city. When I was feeling down, I could sit for hours on the windowsill, allowing my eyes to wander to the horizon over the multitude of buildings and monuments spread out below me. I imagined the millions of people who lived in all those buildings: their stories, their occupations. There were so many of them that at any hour of the day or night there was bound to be some working, some sleeping, some making love, some dying, some arguing, some waking up. I would say "beep" and wonder how many people, at that precise moment, had burst out laughing, had said good-bye to their partner, had burst into tears, had breathed their last, had given birth, had been struck by lightning. I tried to imagine the very different emotions that each one could be feeling at the same moment, at the same time.

I rented my apartment from an elderly woman, Madame Blanchard, who, unfortunately for me, lived in the apartment just below mine. She had been a widow for the last 20 years but gave the impression she was still in mourning. A fervent Catholic, she went to mass several times a week. I sometimes imagined her kneeling down in the old wooden confessional at Saint-Pierre de Montmartre church, confessing through the grill in a low voice the malicious gossip she had proffered the day before. Perhaps she confessed the harassment she subjected me to as well. As soon as I made the slightest noise above the accepted norm—that is to say, complete silence—she would come up and knock vigorously on my door. I would open the door partway and see her infuriated face formulating exaggerated criticisms and inviting me to show more respect for my neighbors. Unfortunately, age had not made her lose her hearing, and I wondered how she could hear such insignificant noises as a ball rolling or a glass set down a little clumsily on the coffee table. I imagined her perched on an old stepladder, with a doctor's stethoscope held against her ceiling, frowning as she listened for the slightest trace of noise.

She had agreed to rent me the apartment reluctantly and not without alerting me to the favor she was granting me. Normally, she didn't rent to foreigners, but as her husband had been freed by the Americans during World War II, she had made an exception for me that I had to show myself worthy of.

It goes without saying that Audrey had never stayed over. I would have been afraid to see the agents of the Inquisition burst in, in their dark robes, faces hidden by the shadow of their hoods, and put us to the question, then hanging Audrey naked and chained hand and foot, from the hook in the ceiling for a chandelier, as the flames of a crackling fire began to lick at her body.

That morning, I went out—without banging the door—and ran down the five stories of my apartment building. I hadn't felt so light since my separation from Audrey. And yet I had no objective reason for feeling better. Nothing had changed in my life. Wait, yes, it had: Someone was interested in me, and whatever his intentions, that was perhaps enough to soothe my suffering. Admittedly, I did have a little knot in my stomach, like the stage fright I experienced before going to the office on those rare occasions when I would have to speak in public.

As I went out, I came across Étienne, the neighborhood vagrant. From the entrance hall, a small flight of stone steps went down to the street. Étienne was in the habit of hiding underneath it. He must be a real matter for Madame Blanchard's conscience, no doubt divided between her Christian charity and her passion for order. That morning, Étienne, his hair unkempt, had come out of his hole and was leaning against the wall of the building, sunning himself.

"Lovely day," I threw out as I went past.

"If ye says so, sonny," he replied in his rasping voice.

I ran down into the Métro, and the sight of all those depressed faces going to work as though they were going to the abattoir almost brought back my melancholy from the day before.

I got out at the Rue de la Pompe station and came up into the smart part of Paris. I was immediately struck by the contrast between the fetid smell of the dark underground corridors of the Métro and the fresh air, the green scent of this luminous district. The few cars on the street and the proximity of the Bois de Boulogne were no doubt the reason for the clean air. The Avenue Henri Martin is a wide avenue, with four rows of trees down the center and on either side, and sumptuous mid-19th-century houses in carved stone, set back behind high, ornate railings of black and gold.

I was very early for my appointment, so I went into a café to have breakfast. It smelled of hot croissants and coffee. I sat down near the window and waited. The waiter didn't seem particularly busy, but when I gestured to him I had the impression he was pretending not to see me. Finally, I called and he came over, grumbling. I ordered a hot chocolate and bread and butter, and while I waited, leafed through a copy of *Le Figaro* that was lying on the table. When the steaming chocolate came, I threw myself on the deliciously buttered slices of fresh baguette, overhearing bits of local gossip being passed around at the bar. Parisian cafés have an ambiance and smells that you don't get in the States.

I set off again half an hour later. The Avenue Henri Martin is quite long, and as I went along I thought about Yves Dubreuil. What had led the man to propose this strange deal? Was his intention really positive, as he assured me it was? His attitude had been ambiguous, to say the least, and it was difficult to trust him. Now, as I drew close to his house, I felt a growing anxiety.

I counted off the numbers as I went past apartment

buildings, each more handsome than the last. I reached number 25 and looked for 23, which should be next, but here the series was interrupted. Thick foliage behind the railings hid the building. I arrived at the gate. Number 23 wasn't an apartment building but a magnificent stone mansion. Immense. I got out the visiting card to check. Very impressive. Was this really his house?

I rang. The little camera behind the glass in the videophone went into action, and a woman's voice invited me to go in, as a door next to the gate opened electronically. I had scarcely walked a few steps into the garden when an enormous black Doberman launched itself in my direction, barking, its eyes threatening and its fangs lubricated by saliva. I was getting ready to leap to one side when the chain around its neck suddenly tightened. It was held back at the last moment, its front paws in the air, the strangulation this provoked propelling from its mouth a stream of slobber that hit my shoes. The dog immediately turned around and went silent, as if the fright it had just inflicted on me was enough to satisfy it.

"Please forgive Stalin," Dubreuil said as he welcomed me at the front door. "He is hateful!"

"He's called Stalin?" I stuttered, as I shook his hand, my pulse at 140.

"We only let him out at night, so during the day he stretches his paws from time to time, when we have a visitor. He terrorizes my guests a bit, but that makes them more conciliatory! Come on, follow me," he said, going before me into a vast marble hall where his voice immediately rang out.

The ceiling was impressively high. On the walls hung gigantic old master paintings in frames of antique gold.

A liveried servant took my jacket. Dubreuil started up the stairs, and I followed. It was a monumental staircase in white stone. Above it was an imposing chandelier with black crystal prisms that must have been three times my weight. Reaching the first floor, Dubreuil swept along a wide corridor, its walls lined with tapestries and more paintings, lit by crystal sconces. It was like a château.

Dubreuil walked with confidence and spoke in a loud voice, as if I was ten yards away. His dark suit contrasted with his silvery hair. Stray locks of hair made him look like a fiery conductor. His white shirt was open at the neck, showing a silk cravat.

"Let's go into my office. It'll be more private."

Privacy was exactly what I needed in this place, which, although magnificent, was not really conducive to intimate conversations.

His office did indeed seem cozier. The walls lined with antique bookcases full of books, most of them old, warmed the room. The parquet floor was partially hidden under a thick Persian rug. Heavy dark red curtains completed the muffled atmosphere. In front of the window was an imposing mahogany desk inlaid with gold-tooled black leather. The top was piled with books and files and, in the center, a large, threatening, silver paper knife, its tip turned toward me, like a murder weapon carelessly left behind by the killer in his haste to quit the scene. Dubreuil invited me to sit down in one of the two large, brown leather armchairs that faced each other on one side of the desk.

"Would you like a drink?" he asked me as he poured himself a glass of bourbon.

"No, thanks. Not at the moment."

He sat down calmly and took a sip while I waited to learn what, exactly, would be my fate.

"Right, listen. Here's what I propose. Today, first and foremost, you will tell me your life. You said you had had plenty of problems. I want to know everything. Let's not play the timid maiden; don't be afraid of confiding in me. In any case, rest assured that I've heard enough sordid things in my life not to be shocked or surprised by anything. But, conversely, don't feel obliged to lay it on to justify the act you wanted to commit yesterday. I just want to understand your personal history."

He fell silent and took another sip.

There is something shameless about telling your life story to a stranger, when you go beyond the trivial details of your existence, such as work, everyday encounters, and daily routines. I was afraid of confiding in him, as though exposing myself amounted to giving him power over me. After a while, I got started and no longer questioned what I was doing. I accepted revealing myself, perhaps because I didn't feel judged. And then I must admit I was hooked. After all, it's rather pleasant, when you've passed the barrier of propriety, to have an attentive ear at one's disposal. You don't often get the opportunity in life to be really listened to—to feel that the other person is trying to understand you, to uncover the twists and turns of your thoughts, the depths of your soul. Making myself transparent was liberating and even, in a certain way, exciting.

I spent the day in the château, as I got into the habit of calling it. Dubreuil spoke little and listened to me with extreme concentration. People capable of sustaining their attention for such a length of time are rare. We were interrupted an hour or two after the start of our conversation by a woman who must have been in her 40s. He introduced her as "Catherine, in whom I have total confidence." Lean, with dry hair tied back clumsily and drab, inelegant clothes that suggested a contempt for feminine finery. She could have been Madame Blanchard's daughter, without the violence. She asked Dubreuil his opinion, pointing to a short written text on a piece of paper. Impossible for me to know what it was about. She looked a bit too cold to be his wife. Was she a colleague? His assistant?

Our conversation—I should say my monologue—resumed until it was time to eat. We went down to have lunch in the garden, under an arbor. It was hard to believe we were in the heart of Paris. Catherine joined us but did not have much to say. Dubreuil tended to do both the questions and the answers, as if to make up for the silence he had observed during our meeting. The meal was served by a different servant from the one who had buzzed me in. Dubreuil's natural, if refined exuberance contrasted with the reserved and mannered style of his staff. His outspokenness tended to reassure me, unlike the absorbed, unsettling expressions I occasionally saw on his face as he listened to me.

"Would you mind if Catherine stayed with us this afternoon? She is my eyes and ears, and sometimes my brains as well," he added with a laugh. "I have no secrets from her."

A clever way of informing me that, in any case, everything would be repeated to her.

"I have no objections," I lied.

He suggested I go for a stroll in the park to stretch my legs before we started again. I think he took advantage of this to summarize what I had said during the morning.

All three of us went back to his office. I felt less at ease for the first few minutes, but Catherine was one of those people whose extreme neutrality means that you quickly forget them.

It was nearly 7:00 P.M. when we had exhausted the subject of my tormented life. Catherine discreetly withdrew.

"I'm going to think about all this," said Dubreuil in a

pensive voice. "And I'll get back to you to tell you your first task. Leave me all your contact details."

"My first task?"

"Yes, your first mission, if you prefer. What you're to do while you wait for further instructions."

"I'm not sure I understand."

"You have experienced things that, in a certain way, have engraved themselves upon you, conditioning the way you see the world, the way you behave, your relations with others, your emotions. The result of all that is that things aren't working, to be quite frank. It's causing you problems and making you unhappy. Your life will be mediocre as long as you live it this way. So we need to bring about certain changes."

I had the impression he was going to brandish a scalpel to operate on my brain straightaway.

He went on: "We could talk about it for hours but it would do no good, apart from informing you of the reasons for your unhappiness. But you'd stay unhappy. Look, when a computer malfunctions, you have to install new programs that work better."

"The problem is, I'm not a computer."

"You grasp the philosophy, at any rate: You must live a certain number of experiences that will make your point of view change and lead you to go beyond your fears, your doubts, your anxieties."

"And how do I know you know how to program properly?"

"You've given your word. So, no point asking the question. It would only feed your fears, which are already numerous, if I've understood properly."

Silently, I looked at him for a while. He met my gaze without saying anything. Seconds that seemed like hours went by. I finally broke the silence.

"Who are you, Monsieur Dubreuil?"

"Now that's a question I ask myself every now and then!" he said, getting up and walking before me to the corridor. "Come on, I'll show you out. Who am I? Who am I?" he declaimed as he walked, and his powerful voice resounded in the vast staircase.

THE FOLLOWING NIGHT I had a nightmare such as I hadn't had since childhood.

I was in the mansion. It was dark. Dubreuil was there. We were in an immense, dark drawing room. The very high walls were as black as those of a dungeon. The room was lit only by the flickering flames of chandeliers that gave off a smell of old wax burning. Dubreuil was staring at me intensely, holding a sheet of paper in his hand. Catherine, a little farther on, was wearing only a black leotard and high-heel shoes, her hair in a ponytail. She was holding a big whip that she regularly cracked on the floor with un-suspected violence, grunting like a tennis player who has just served. Stalin was opposite her, furiously barking after each crack of the whip. Dubreuil didn't take his eyes off me, displaying the calm air of someone who knows he is all-powerful. He held the sheet of paper out to me.

"Hey! It's your mission!"

I took the paper with a trembling hand and tipped it toward the flames to read it. Names. A list of names and next to each one, an address.

"What is it?"

"You've got to kill them. All of them. It's your first mission. The first."

Catherine's whip cracked very loudly, setting off a flood of barking.

"But I'm not a criminal! I don't want to kill anyone!"

"It'll do you good," he said, separating each word.

A wave of panic came over me. My legs were shaking. My jaw was trembling.

"No, it won't. I don't want to. At all. I don't want to."

"You need to, believe me," he said in a wheedling voice. "It's because of your history, you understand. Your past is in darkness that you'll learn to come out of. Don't be afraid."

"I can't," I panted. "I can't."

"You have no choice."

His voice was insistent. His eyes were boring through me as he slowly advanced toward me.

"Don't come near me! I want to leave!"

"You can't. It's too late."

"Let me go!"

I rushed to the great drawing room door. Locked. I rapidly turned the handle in every direction.

"Open up!" I screamed, banging with my fists. "Open this door!"

Dubreuil was getting closer. I turned around, my back to the door, and crossed my arms in front of my chest.

"You can't force me! I will never kill anyone!"

"Remember: You gave your word!"

"And if I took it back?"

My reply brought an immense laugh from Dubreuil. A demonic laugh that froze my blood.

"What's the matter? What's making you laugh?"

"If you break your word . . ."

He turned toward Catherine, a snarl on his lips. Catherine looked at me and gave a broad smile that was a grimace, a hideous smile that made me want to be sick.

"If you break your word," he went on in a slow, sardonic voice, as the flames gave a diabolical glow to his face. "If you break your word, then I'll put your name on a list, a list that I will give to someone else."

At that moment, behind me, I heard the lock activate. I turned around, opened the door, pushed the servant aside, and fled across the hall.

"You gave your word! You gave your word! You gave your word!"

I woke with a start, panting, in a sweat. The sight of familiar objects around me brought me back to a universe that was known, controlled.

I was both reassured to realize that it was only a dream and disturbed at the thought that reality might be just as I had imagined it in my nocturnal ravings. After all, I knew nothing about Dubreuil and his real intentions. I had entered a game of which I knew neither the rules nor the purpose. The only certainty: I couldn't get out of it. That was the rule of the game that I had been mad enough to accept.

It was 6 A.M. I got up and slowly got ready to go to the office. Life was reasserting itself, and I really had to get back to work, even if the very idea of going back to that vipers' nest was enough to undermine my morale.

Vanessa leapt on me as soon as I arrived, pursuing me down the corridor leading to my office.

"I didn't know if you were coming in today or not, but until I heard from you, I let your appointments stand. To be frank, Fausteri wasn't too pleased about your absence yesterday. But I stood up for you. I told him that you sounded like death on the phone and that you'd looked really ill the day before. I don't mean to boast, but if I hadn't been there, he'd probably never have believed you."

Vanessa loved situations that gave her an opportunity to show she was indispensable, even if she had to make them up. I would never know if Fausteri had even noticed my absence. Indeed, Vanessa had such a need for recognition that she was quite capable of killing two birds with one stone, covering for me while at the same time earning congratulations for bringing my unjustified absence to our boss's attention. I trusted her no farther than I could throw her.

Luc Fausteri, the head of the Accounting and Financial Sector Recruitment Department, in turn reported to the director of the recruitment side of the company, Grégoire Larcher. Dunker Consulting was a European leader in human resources, with two big internal divisions: Recruitment and Training. The company had been floated on the stock exchange two months after my arrival. This was a matter of pride for our CEO, Marc Dunker, who now saw himself as a captain of industry, despite the fact that the company had only a few hundred employees, admittedly spread over three countries. The first decision Dunker took after our stock market flotation was to purchase a luxury car with a chauffeur. The freshly garnered money had to be used somehow. His second decision was to appoint a bodyguard, as if listing the company on the Paris stock exchange made its boss a prime target for the local underworld. The bodyguard followed Dunker everywhere, in a dark suit and shades, constantly looking around as if to locate snipers hidden on the roofs.

But the real change when the company went public was of a cultural nature: The atmosphere changed overnight. All eyes were now riveted on the share price. At first, everyone was caught up in IPO frenzy, filled with enthusiasm as we watched the price climb. But this quickly became an obsession for all our managers. It's true that the company now had to publish its results every quarter, and mediocre figures would make the share price fall at once. The management regularly issued press communiqués, but it was difficult to keep on announcing good results. In a business, you don't have hot news to reveal every day, and yet we had to "keep up the pressure on the press," as our CEO said. Feeding reporters positive results quickly became a form of slavery.

Over the years, the company had grown through its professionalism, its reliability, and the quality of the services it rendered to its customers. Special care was given beforehand to each recruitment undertaken for a client. We did everything to find the rare pearl, the candidate who had not only the right skills and abilities but also the character and temperament to fit in well, get along with their new boss, and be successful in handling the responsibilities entrusted to them.

Since the stock flotation, all that had become of secondary importance. Of primary importance now were the turnover figures announced to the press at the end of the quarter, and therefore the number of recruitments entrusted to us by clients. Apart from their recruitment role, the consultants now had to seek out new business. Not really my cup of tea. But we absolutely had to bring in new clients, new contracts, and increase "turnover." The orders were to spend a minimum of time on interviewing candidates and a maximum on looking for new business. The job was being emptied of its substance, losing the noble meaning it had had in my eyes.

Relations between colleagues had also changed entirely. Any camaraderie, any team spirit I had known in the first two months had given way to frenzied selfishness, every man for himself, stimulated by competitive challenges. It was obvious that the company was the loser since to survive, each member of the team put obstacles in the way of the others, to the detriment of the common interest. Admittedly, we no longer wasted time around the coffee machine as we used to, gossiping about candidates' slips and lies, but those moments of relaxation had contributed to developing a feeling of belonging, to making us love the company and motivating us to serve its interests.

Besides, what is a company if not a group of people

with whom you share emotions while working on a project? Making an abstract number like turnover go up is not a project. And making us compete with each other did not create positive emotions.

The phone rang. Vanessa announced that my first appointment had arrived. A glance at my diary showed that seven were scheduled. A long day ahead.

I rapidly scanned my e-mails: 48 in just one day off. I immediately clicked on the one from Luc Fausteri. As usual, the subject field was blank. A laconic message:

> You must catch up with the work lost as a result of your day off. I must remind you that you are already behind with your monthly target.
>
> Regards,
> L.F.

The *Regards* in the automatic signature stuck out like a sore thumb. Copy circulated to Grégoire Larcher and all my colleagues in the department. What a pain!

I met my candidate and the interview began. It was difficult to concentrate, to get involved in my duties. I had left the office the night before convinced that I would never set foot in it again. In my mind, this job had been wiped out of my future. In the end I had remained alive, but it was as if all the data had not been updated in my brain. Now this place seemed almost foreign, and my presence here had no real meaning.

I managed to get away around seven o'clock. A miracle. Outside the building I had barely set foot on the sidewalk of the Avenue de l'Opéra, when a man in a navy blue blazer came up to me. A real hulk of a man with pale, expressionless blue eyes, flat cheeks, and no cheekbones. Instinctively, I took a step back.

"Monsieur Greenmor?"

I hesitated a second before replying.

"Monsieur Dubreuil is waiting for you," he said, discreetly pointing to a long black Mercedes parked half on the sidewalk.

The tinted glass windows prevented me from seeing inside. Somewhat apprehensively, I followed the man, who opened the back door for me. I slid inside with a twinge of anxiety. A faint smell of leather. Dubreuil was sitting next to me, but the width of the car allowed us to keep a certain distance. Before the driver shut the door, I had time to catch the intrigued look of Vanessa, who was just leaving the building.

Dubreuil remained silent. A minute later, the Mercedes pulled away.

"You're going home late," he finally said.

"Sometimes I stay a lot later, occasionally as late as nine o'clock," I replied, pleased to be able to fill the silence, which fell again right after.

Eventually, he broke the silence. "I've thought a lot about your case. In fact, you've got several problems fitted inside each other. The kernel is your fear of people. I don't know if you really realize it, but you not only do not dare impose on anyone or really express your wishes, you also have great difficulty going against someone else's wishes and expressing a frank refusal. In short, you're not really leading your own life.

"The first tasks I'm going to give you will teach you to overcome your apprehensiveness so that you can accept being in disagreement with others, can dare to contradict them, and can express your desires and get what you want.

"Then, you must accept not necessarily conforming to

other people's expectations, not always meeting their criteria or values. You must dare to display your differences, even if it upsets them. In short, you will have to let go of the image you want to project and learn not to care too much about what others think of you.

"When you fully assume your differences, then you will be able to examine other people's ways and, if necessary, adapt to them. You will thereby learn to communicate better and interact with strangers, so you can create relationships based on mutual confidence and be accepted by people who don't work like you. But first you must accept what makes you unique. Otherwise you will continue to be controlled by other people.

"I will also teach you to be persuasive, so that you will know how to get what you want. And then I will get you to dare to have new experiences, implement your ideas, make your dreams real. In short, I'm going to blow apart the shackles that are binding you today, that without you even realizing it are completely imprisoning you. I will liberate you so that you can live your life and live it to the fullest."

"And you're going to make me do certain things so that I can learn all that?"

"Do you think that by continuing to lead your little life as you've led it till now, things will change for you? Besides, you saw where it led you."

"Thanks for reminding me. I'd forgotten."

"Even if it doesn't drive you to such an extreme, life is long and boring, Alan, when you don't live it as you'd like."

"No point trying to convince me, since you've got my agreement in any case."

The Mercedes had turned onto the Boulevard Haussmann and was driving fast down the bus lane, past all the cars caught in rush-hour traffic.

"It's by rubbing up against reality that you'll realize it's not so dreadful," Dubreuil said. "And then you'll be able to do things that you're not permitting yourself to do at present. I also want to make you change your relationship to the events of life. Listening to you yesterday, I was often surprised by the way you function on a day-to-day basis. I think you frequently adopt the role of the victim."

"The role of the victim?"

"It's just a figure of speech to indicate a sort of posture that certain people adopt without thinking. It consists of living as though what happens to us has been imposed on us, that it's something we experience despite ourselves."

"I don't think I'm like that."

"You probably don't realize, but you put yourself in a victim position when you use expressions like 'I'm not lucky,' 'Things aren't as I would have liked,' 'I would have preferred . . .' When you describe your daily life, as soon as something doesn't turn out the way you want, you tend to say 'Too bad,' or 'That's a shame,' or 'I don't care,' but you don't say it with the wisdom of someone who is calmly accepting a situation. No, you say it with regret in your voice. It's a resigned acceptance, and, what's more, you sometimes remind yourself that it wasn't your choice. And then you also tend to complain at times. All these are indications that you revel in the role of the victim."

"Perhaps I adopt the role without being aware of it, but I certainly don't revel in it."

"Yes, you do. You inevitably find advantages to it. Our brain works that way. In each moment, it gets us to opt for what it considers to be our *best bet*. That is to say, in each situation you experience, your brain is going to select, from all the things you know how to do, whatever seems to be the most appropriate thing, the most opportune—whatever is going to bring you the most advantages. We all function like that. The problem is that we don't all have the same array of choices. Some people have developed a variety of attitudes and behaviors, so that when they encounter a given situation, their brain has a wide range of possible reactions at its disposal. Others tend to always do more or less the same thing, and in that case, their range is limited, and the choice they make is seldom appropriate.

"I'll give you an example: Imagine a discussion between two strangers in the street. One is unjustly criticizing the other. If the other has lots of strings to his bow, he will be able to prove that the criticism is wrong perhaps, or make light of it with a joke, or even ask pointed questions to force his accuser to justify his position. He can also put himself in the other person's place and try to understand the origin of the criticism, in order to be able to put his critic right while staying on his good side. Alternatively, he could choose to ignore his critic altogether and simply go on his way. If he is capable of all that, then the instant he hears the criticism, his brain has numerous possible responses at its disposal, and there is a high probability that it will select one that is really appropriate to the situation—that optimizes his interests and is the most advantageous. Now imagine the same situation involving someone who doesn't know how to do any of that. It's probable that the only choice his brain has is to insult his critic or passively accept the criticism, no matter how unjustified it may be. Either way, that will be his *best bet*."

"You're saying I'm a bit limited, is that it?"

"Let's say that when things don't go your way, then yes, you don't have many choices available, and you tend to put yourself in the position of the victim."

"Supposing that's true, what are the advantages I get from it?"

"From what I discovered yesterday, you like to be seen as someone who puts himself out for others, and you hope that in return you will be valued for your so-called sacrifices. And then you also enjoy being pitied and arousing people's sympathy. Between you and me, that's a load of bull. All the research shows that we are attracted to those who take responsibility for their choices and live with the consequences. In the end, you're the only one who's moved by your lamentations."

"Even so, objectively—really objectively—I think I've had less luck than others in life so far, beginning with my social background. I'm sorry, but it's much easier to be happy when you're born into a wealthy family where you've gotten all you want."

"Stop! That's bullshit, all that."

"Absolutely not. Any sociologist will tell you that statistically, children from privileged social backgrounds are far more likely to go to college than children from underprivileged backgrounds and therefore to have access to better jobs."

"But that's got nothing to do with happiness! Besides, don't forget you are an executive. Unfairness derives from the love and education a child receives from its parents; this, indeed, contributes to future happiness. In that regard, I agree, there are underprivileged people. But it's unconnected to social background. Being rich doesn't mean you know how to give love to your children, or the right dose of authority to bring them up successfully. Look around you."

"Okay. But you can't say I was lucky from that point of view either. I didn't even have a father!"

"Yes, but now you are an adult, and you can learn to move beyond moaning and crying over your fate."

The Mercedes turned onto the Boulevard Malesherbes and drove toward Rue des Batignolles. I was very annoyed by what he had said.

"Alan . . ."

"What?" I snapped.

"Alan, there is no such thing as a happy victim. Do you hear? They don't exist."

He fell silent for a few seconds, as if to allow his words to sink in. I felt his phrase go like a knife to my heart, and now his silence was pushing the blade deeper into the wound.

"Right. So what do you do to stop yourself from slipping into the role of the victim? Because if, on top of everything else, it's unconscious, I don't see how I'm going to extricate myself."

"In my opinion, the best way is to learn to do something else. Again, if pretending to be the victim is your best bet, it's clearly because your brain doesn't have many other possibilities. Therefore, you must develop some. You know, nature abhors a vacuum. So if you simply try to suppress the victim role and don't know how to do anything else in its place, it won't work. You'll resist the change. The best thing is to discover that you *can* do something different. Then, I'm confident, your brain will quickly choose the new option of its own accord, if it brings you more advantages."

"And what will this new option be?"

"Well, I'm going to teach you to get what you want on a daily basis. If you succeed, you won't need to pretend to be the victim. Listen, I know it was only an anecdote, but you staggered me yesterday when you told me your lack of luck pursued you even in an insignificant act of everyday life like buying bread at the baker's. You said you regularly get bread that's got a hard crust but you prefer it soft!"

"That's right."

"You must be kidding! That means you're not even capable of saying, 'The crust on this one is overdone. May I have that one next to it?'"

"Of course, I'm capable of it! It's just that I don't want

to put the baker out when there's a shop full of customers waiting. That's all."

"But it would take only two seconds! You prefer eating crusty bread that you don't like to taking two seconds of the baker's time! No, the truth is, you don't dare tell him. You are afraid of annoying him to get what you want. You're afraid that he'll think you are demanding and unpleasant, that he won't like you. And you're afraid that the other customers will be annoyed."

"It's possible."

"On your deathbed you'll be able to say, 'I made nothing of my life. I got none of the things I wanted, but everybody thought I was nice.' Brilliant."

I was beginning to feel decidedly ill. I looked away from this man with his upsetting words and allowed my gaze to wander over the buildings, shops, and people we were passing by.

"I have some great news," he went on.

Skeptical, I didn't even bother to look at him.

"The great news is that all that is in the past. What's more, you'll never again eat crusty bread. Never," he said, looking around. "Vladi, stop."

The chauffeur stopped the car and turned on the hazard lights. Cars passed us, sounding their horns.

"What do you want from in there?" Dubreuil asked, pointing to a bakery.

"At this moment, nothing. Absolutely nothing."

"Good. So you're going to go in, ask for a loaf, a cake, anything, and when it's given to you, you'll find a reason to refuse it and ask for something else. Then you'll invent another reason to refuse the second item, then the third and the fourth. And then you'll say that, after all, you don't want anything, and you'll leave without buying a thing."

"I can't do that."

"Yes, you can. In a few minutes, you'll have proved it."

"It's beyond me."

"Vladi!"

The chauffeur got out, opened the door for me, and waited. I looked daggers at Dubreuil and then reluctantly got out. A glance at the bakery: the crowd before closing time. I felt my heart beating at top speed.

Inside, it was a hive of activity. I stood in line as if I were waiting for my turn to mount the scaffold. It was the first time since my arrival in France that the smell of fresh bread had repelled me. The shop assistant repeated the customers' orders to the woman at the cash register, who repeated them out loud as she took the money. Meanwhile, the assistant was already taking care of the next customer. It was like a well-rehearsed ballet performance. When it was my turn, there were already eight or ten customers behind me. I swallowed hard.

"Monsieur?" she asked me in her very high-pitched voice.

"A baguette, please."

My voice was muffled, as though stuck in my throat.

"A baguette for monsieur!"

"One euro ten cents," said the cashier.

The shop assistant was already talking to the next customer. "Madame?"

"A *pain au chocolat.*"

"A *pain au chocolat* for Madame!"

"Excuse me, would you have one less well done, please?" I forced myself to say.

"One euro twenty for Madame."

"Here you are," said the assistant, holding out another loaf. "Mademoiselle, it's your turn."

"A sliced sandwich loaf, please," Mademoiselle said.

"Hmm, excuse me. I'll have a bran loaf, actually," I squeaked.

The slicing machine drowned out my voice. She didn't hear me.

"A sliced sandwich loaf for the lady!"

"One euro eighty."

"Madame?" the shop assistant asked the next customer.

"No, excuse me," I said, slightly louder. "I'll have a bran loaf, actually."

"And a bran loaf with the baguette for monsieur!"

"That'll be three euros fifteen then," said the cashier.

"Young man, it's your turn," the shop assistant said to the next in line.

"No," I said. "It was *instead of* the baguette, not in addition."

"Two loaves," the young man called out.

"Right, that's two euros five cents for the gentleman, and two euros ten for the young man."

"Madame?" said the shop assistant.

I felt awful. I didn't have the heart to carry on. A glance toward the car. The chauffeur was standing beside it, his arms folded. He wasn't taking his eyes off me.

"Half a baguette, well done," said an old lady.

"Excuse me," I said to the assistant, "I've changed my mind. I'm sorry, but I'd rather have a half-baguette as well."

"Make up your mind," she said in her very high-pitched voice, taking the other half of the baguette she had cut for the old lady.

I was very hot. I was sweating under my suit.

"Sixty cents for the old lady and the same for the gentleman."

"Madame?" the shop assistant asked.

"I'm still thinking," said a young woman who was looking at the cakes with an obvious feeling of guilt.

She must be counting the number of calories in each one, I thought.

"Another problem, monsieur?" the assistant asked, suspiciously.

"Look, I'm really sorry. I know I'm out of line, but a sandwich loaf. I think I want a sandwich loaf. Yes, that's it! A sandwich loaf!"

She stared at me with obvious annoyance. I didn't dare turn around, but I had a feeling the customers stuck behind me were about to grab me by the collar and throw me out. She sighed, and then turned around to get the sandwich loaf.

"Hang on! Stop! No, actually . . ."

"Yes?" the assistant said in a choked voice, no doubt on the verge of hysterics.

"I want . . . nothing. Actually, I don't want anything. Thank you . . . sorry . . . thank you."

I turned on my heels and walked past the line of customers, head down, without looking at them. At the door, I broke into a run, feeling like a thief.

The chauffeur was waiting with the car door open, as if I were a VIP, but I felt as ashamed as a little boy who has just been caught trying to steal a sweet from a stall. I dived into the Mercedes in a sweat.

"You're as red as an Englishman who's just spent an hour in the sun on the Riviera," said Dubreuil, visibly amused.

"It's not funny. Really not funny."

"Anyhow, you see, you did it."

I didn't answer. The car moved off.

"Perhaps I went a bit far for a first time," he acknowledged. "But I promise you that in a few weeks you'll be able to do it and treat it as a joke."

"But it doesn't interest me! I don't want to become a pain in the neck! I can't *bear* people who are a pain in the neck, who are too demanding and piss everyone off. I don't want to be like them!"

"It's not about you becoming a pain in the neck. I won't make you go from one extreme to the other. I just want you to know how to get what you want, even if you have to put people out a bit. But he who can do more, can do less. I'm going to push you to do a bit more than necessary, so that later you'll be quite at ease asking for what it's normal for you to want."

"So, what's the next stage?"

"For the next few days, you will visit at least three bakeries a day, and you will ask for two changes of what you're given. It'll be easy."

Compared with what I'd just done, that did indeed seem acceptable.

"For how long do I have to do this?"

"Until it becomes quite natural for you, requiring no effort. And remember, you can be demanding and still remain nice. You don't have to be unpleasant."

The Mercedes pulled up in front of my apartment. Vladi got out and opened the door for me.

"Good evening," said Dubreuil.

I didn't answer.

Étienne emerged from under the staircase and stared at the car.

"Well, someone's doing all right for himself," he said, coming up to me. He took off his hat and pretended to sweep the sidewalk in front of me, backing up as I advanced. "Monsieur le Président," he said with an extra flourish.

I felt obliged to give him some money.

"His Highness is too kind," he said in his hoarse voice, executing an exaggeratedly reverential bow.

He had the crafty look of someone who always gets what he wants.

• • •

Yves Dubreuil took out his cell phone and pushed two keys.

"Good evening, Catherine, it's me."

"Well?"

"For the time being, he's obeying. Everything's as planned."

"I don't think it'll last very long. I have considerable doubts."

"You always have doubts, Catherine."

"He'll rebel in the end."

"You say that because if you were in his place, you'd rebel."

"Perhaps."

"At any rate, I've never seen anyone so frightened of his own shadow."

"That's what worries me so much. That's why I think he will never have the courage to do all you're going to demand of him."

"On the contrary. His fear can help us."

"How come?"

"If he doesn't want to go on, we'll make sure he does . . . out of fear."

Silence.

"You're formidable, Igor."

"Yes."

AFTER A WEEK, I knew all the bakeries in my district, the 18th arrondissement. In the end, I observed that the best bread was to be had in the bakery I usually patronized, next to my apartment. Now I was buying three baguettes a day and off-loading my surplus stock on Étienne. Delighted at first, he had the cheek to tell me after five days that he was fed up with eating bread.

Human beings are made in such a way that we get used to almost anything. I have to admit that what had demanded a superhuman effort to begin with needed mere resolve by the end of a week. All the same, I had to consciously prepare myself for the bakery routine. One evening, I met my neighbor at the baker's, and we talked as we stood in line. When my turn came and I was served an overcooked baguette, I didn't have the reflex to refuse it. Being distracted by my conversation was enough to make me revert to my old habit of automatically accepting what was given to me. In short, I was being well looked after, but I was still not cured.

My office life carried on, more dismal than ever. Was it to try and make up for the deterioration in the atmosphere that Luc Fausteri suggested that the consultants on his team join him every morning at 8 A.M. for a run? I was sure this ludicrous idea wasn't his. He must have found it in a team-building book under a heading like *How to change your employees into winners*. The plan had obviously been approved by those higher up, however, since his boss, Grégoire

Larcher, had okayed the installation of communal showers in the building.

So it was that most of the consultants found themselves every morning inhaling exhaust from the Avenue de l'Opéra and the Rue de Rivoli, or the scarcely less polluted air of the Tuileries Gardens. They ran without saying a word, my boss being about as talkative as a funeral director. In any case, the purpose of the exercise was no doubt to stimulate everyone's ardor, not to develop camaraderie. Fausteri kept his distance from us as always. I had managed the feat of declining his offer, and no doubt the shop assistants in the bakeries of the 18th arrondissement had a share in this achievement. My painful experience at baseball had turned me off sports, and mixing with a group of out-of-breath men feeling virile because they're exercising was more than I was capable of.

I arrived at the office each day at 8:55 A.M. so that I would already be hard at work when the team returned from its morning exploits. That way, the message was clear: While you're prancing about, some of us are slaving away. That way, I was beyond reproach. Even so, the level of reproach had risen perceptibly. Having had an original idea for once, Fausteri was no doubt vexed that I wasn't falling in line. He began to pick on me, to make remarks incessantly about anything or nothing, from the color of my shirts to the amount of time I spent on each interview.

But the crucial point was the number of recruitment contracts signed. Since our role as salesmen had taken on more importance than searching for candidates, we had been allocated individual business targets, with commissions tied to our sales. Now our department had a business meeting every Monday morning. The decision probably hadn't come from Fausteri. Very introverted, he hated mixing with us. Larcher must have forced him to do it. But Luc Fausteri was very clever and had succeeded in evading the thankless task of leading the weekly meeting. Larcher managed it himself, which suited him; he liked to be involved in everything. Fausteri made do with remaining silently at his side, playing the role of the aloof expert who only opened his mouth when absolutely necessary. He would regard us with a mildly condescending gaze, wondering no doubt why the simple-minded always repeat the same idiotic remarks.

That particular morning, I met Thomas, a colleague, in the corridor.

"Well, we thought you'd died the day before yesterday," he said, sarcastically.

If only you knew, my friend. "I must have picked up a virus going around," I lied. "Fortunately, it didn't last."

"Right. I won't get close to you then," he said, taking a step back. "Even if it would suit you all if I was so ill I couldn't give you the usual hiding at the end of the month!"

Thomas was the consultant who got the best results, and he never missed an opportunity to remind us of it. I admit his figures were fairly impressive. He was a workaholic who put in impossible hours, regularly went without lunch, and was so focused on his targets that he sometimes forgot to say hello to people he walked past in the corridors. At any rate, he never stopped to chat, except when he had an opportunity to blow his own horn, either by announcing his quarterly results or by telling you that he had just bought the latest fashionable car or had eaten the night before in the trendy restaurant that all of Paris was talking about.

Everything about Thomas was calculated to serve his image, from the brand of clothes he favored to the *Financial Times* tucked casually under his arm when he arrived in the morning. Each gesture, each word, indeed everything he owned and did was an element of the persona he had carefully constructed and identified with. I would sometimes imagine Thomas naked on a deserted island without his Armani suit or Hermès tie or Weston loafers or Vuitton bag, without personal targets to reach or glory to obtain or anyone to impress. I could see him sliding into an infinite torpor, as unable to live without others' admiration as the rubber plant in our waiting room could survive without Vanessa's weekly watering.

But in fact, he would probably become the archetypal Robinson Crusoe, adopting the appearance and behavior of the exemplary shipwreck as diligently as he had cultivated that of the dynamic executive. Once he had been rescued by fishermen—amazed by his capacity for survival—he would have returned to France a hero, recounting his exploits of survival on every TV channel, while carefully preserving his eight-month beard and wearing a loincloth like nobody else. The context would change, but not the man.

"Having a chat, are we, then?"

Mickaël was another of my colleagues. He didn't take himself seriously, but he did think he was cleverer than everyone else.

"It doesn't matter for some of us," retorted Thomas, quick as a flash.

Mickaël just laughed and walked away. Slightly tubby, with jet-black hair, he always wore a crafty look. His re-sults were perfectly decent, although I suspected he took it fairly easy. Several times I had gone into his office unan-nounced. Each time he had given the impression he was absorbed in a candidate's tricky case on his computer, but the images on his screen, reflected in the glass doors of the bookcase behind his desk, made you wonder if candidates were so desperate for employment that they were sending naked photos of themselves in the hope of increasing their chances of getting a job as an accountant.

"He's jealous," Thomas said in a confidential tone.

Every week, companies contacted the firm with their recruitment needs and inquired about our terms and conditions. Vanessa took the calls, made out a file card for each query, and passed it on to a consultant. It goes without saying that we welcomed these leads. It was much easier to sign a contract with a company that had contacted us than to cold-canvass strangers by telephone. Vanessa was supposed to distribute the file cards evenly among us, but I had recently discovered that in fact she favored Thomas. Visibly fascinated by the image of a winner that he projected, she must take pleasure in the idea that she was vital to his success. I was sure I was the least favored member of the team, even though, on the rare occasions she passed a contract on to me, she did it in a way that suggested she was giving me alone a chance to profit from the only call that Dunker Consulting had received that month.

TWO WEEKS AFTER our first meeting, Dubreuil reappeared in circumstances similar to the previous time. When I came out of the office, I saw his Mercedes parked in the middle of the sidewalk.

Vladi got out, walked around the car, and opened the back door for me. I ground out my cigarette, frustrated because I had just lit up after spending the whole afternoon without smoking. I was less anxious than the previous time, but slight apprehension still tightened my stomach, as I wondered what fate lay in store for me today.

The Mercedes pulled away from the curb, making a U-turn on the Avenue de l'Opéra and heading toward the Louvre. Two minutes later, we were speeding along the Rue de Rivoli.

"So, were you physically thrown out of the Paris bakeries?"

"I'm going to eat sandwich bread from the supermarket for a month, the time it'll take for people to forget me."

Dubreuil gave a sadistic little laugh.

"Where are you taking me today?"

"See, you're making progress! Last time, you didn't even dare ask. You allowed yourself to be driven like a prisoner."

"I *am* a prisoner of my promise."

"That's true," he confirmed with a satisfied air.

We arrived at the Place de la Concorde. The muffled silence inside the luxurious sedan contrasted with the agitation of the drivers changing lanes in every direction and accelerating in spurts to try and overtake one or two cars. Big black clouds scudded across the sky above the Assemblée Nationale, as we turned onto the Champs-Élysées and the avenue opened up in front of us. The sky above the Arc de Triomphe was clear.

"So, where are we going?" I repeated.

"We're going to test your progress since the last time, to make sure that we can go on to something else."

I didn't like the wording. It reminded me of certain tests that my firm made the candidates take.

"I never told you, but I have a distinct preference for theoretical tests, the ones with pieces of paper and boxes to check," I said.

"Life isn't a theory. I believe in the virtue of experience lived in the raw. That's the only thing that really changes someone. All the rest is waffle, intellectual masturbation."

"So, what have you cooked up for me today?" I asked, putting on an air of self-confidence, whereas in fact my heart was in my boots.

"Well, let's say we're going to bring this chapter to an end by taking our business elsewhere."

"Elsewhere?"

"Yes, instead of the local bakery, you're going to a prestigious jeweler."

"You're joking?" I said, suspecting that unfortunately, he was doing nothing of the sort.

"Indeed, there's not much difference between them."

"Of course, there is! There's no comparison!"

"In both cases, you're dealing with someone who's there to sell you something. It's the same. I don't see what the problem is."

"Of course you do! Don't play the fool!"

"The main difference is located in the head."

"But I've never set foot in a big jeweler's. I'm not used to that sort of place."

"You have to start someday. There's a first time for everything."

"The place will make me feel awkward before I even open my mouth. Your dice are loaded . . ."

"What's troubling you, exactly?" he said, an amused smile on his lips.

"I don't know. Those people aren't used to dealing with people like me. I won't know how to behave."

"There's no special code. It's a shop like any other, except that it's more expensive. That gives you the right to be harder to please!"

The Mercedes stopped at the top of the Champs-Élysées. Vladi turned on the hazard warning lights. I stared straight in front of me, guessing that my scaffold was on my right, just over there, within eyeshot. I plucked up my courage and slowly turned my head to the right. The stone building was imposing, with an immense shop window more than two stories tall. Above it, in gold letters, was the name of my executioner: Cartier.

"Imagine," Dubreuil said, "what your life will be like when there is no longer any situation in the world that can make you feel awkward."

"Great. But as things stand, I'm a long way away from that."

"The only way to get there is to rub up against reality—to go and face the object of your fears until the fear disappears, not hide somewhere, which only heightens your fear of the unknown."

"Perhaps," I replied. But I wasn't convinced.

"Come on, tell yourself that the people who are going to serve you are people just like you—wage-earners who probably can't afford to buy jewelry at Cartier's either."

"What do I have to do exactly? What's my mission?"

"You're going to ask to be shown watches. You must try on a good dozen or so, ask lots of questions, and then leave without buying anything."

My stress went up a notch.

"And there's something else."

He took his cell phone, dialed a number, and a discrete ringing went off in his inside pocket. He got out a small, flesh-colored device, pressed it, and the ringing stopped.

"Put this in your ear. That way, I can listen to your amazing feats, and you can hear me if I have things to say to you."

I was dumbstruck.

"What's all this about!"

"One last thing . . ."

"*What?*"

"Have fun. It's the best piece of advice I can give you. If you manage to do that, it's in the bag. Stop taking everything seriously. Step back and see this test as a game. That's what it is, isn't it? A game. There's nothing to lose, just things to find out."

"Hmm."

"You know, one can see life as a series of pitfalls to be avoided, or as a vast playground that offers enriching experiments at every street corner."

I didn't answer but opened the car door and got out. The traffic noise hit me, and a warm wind woke up my dulled brain.

I took a few steps, lit a cigarette and smoked it, taking my time. With a bit of luck, the police would come and tell the Mercedes to move on.

Dubreuil had spoken of a test. He wanted, he said, to test my progress. That probably meant he would set other unpleasant tasks for the weeks ahead. To free myself,

I absolutely had to pluck up my courage and manage a satisfactory performance. I had no choice, in any case. He wouldn't let go; I was sure of that.

I tossed my cigarette on the sidewalk and vigorously ground it out, turning my foot from side to side longer than necessary. As I looked up at the glass window of this temple of luxury, a shiver ran down my spine. *Come on, chin up,* I told myself.

Swallowing hard, I pushed the revolving door. An image of my mother exhausting herself in the laundry flashed across my mind. Three young men in dark suits were standing in the spacious entrance hall, their arms by their sides. One of them opened the second door into the shop. I tried to assume a confident air, even though I was being dropped into a universe that was totally alien to me.

The door opened into a vast space with a high ceiling, dominated by a monumental staircase. The room was furnished with display counters in precious woods, sparkling like mirrors. A great, glittering chandelier hung overhead. Walls hung with velvet absorbed the light. I detected a subtle perfume, barely a scent, calming and captivating at the same time. A thick dark red carpet muffled the noise of my footsteps. Then a pair of woman's shoes, very beautiful, extremely feminine with stiletto heels, was coming toward me, one after the other, delicately. I looked up at slim legs that went on forever, then a short black skirt, tight, topped by a narrow-waisted jacket. Very narrow-waisted. When I finally lifted my head, I was looking into the ice blue eyes of a glacial beauty with blonde hair, perfectly smooth, done up in a chignon.

She looked straight at me and spoke in a very professional voice: "Good evening, sir, what can I do for you?"

She didn't smile in the slightest, and I wondered, paralyzed, whether she was behaving as usual or she had already marked me as an intruder, someone who would never be a customer. I felt unmasked, stripped bare by her confident gaze.

"I'd like to see your men's watches," I managed to say.

"Our gold collection or our steel one?"

"Steel," I replied, pleased to be able to choose a range less distant from what I was used to.

"Gold! Gold!" Dubreuil screamed in my earpiece.

I was afraid the sales assistant would hear his voice, but she didn't seem to notice. I remained silent.

"Follow me, please," she said in a tone of voice that immediately made me regret saying *steel,* a tone that meant *I knew it.* Hateful.

I followed her, looking down at her shoes. You can tell everything about a person by watching the way they walk. Her walk was definite, studied, nothing spontaneous. She led me to the first room and headed for one of the wooden vitrines. A tiny golden key moved between her fingers, with their perfectly manicured red nails, and the glass top rose up. She took out a tray lined in velvet, on which the watches were enthroned.

"Here we have the Pasha, the Roadster, the Santos, and the famous Tank Française. Each has a self-winding mechanical movement."

I wasn't listening to what she said. Her words resounded in my head without me trying to give them a meaning. My attention was caught by the precise gestures accompanying her words. She pointed to each watch with her long fingers, not quite touching them. Her gestures alone seemed to increase the prestige of these inert assemblies of metal parts.

I was supposed to ask to try the watches on, but her words and her gestures revealed such perfection that I feared sounding like an idiot. Then I remembered that Dubreuil was listening. I had to take the plunge.

"I'd like to try this one on," I said, pointing to a watch with a steel-and-rubber band.

She put on a white glove, as if her fingerprints might spoil its beauty, then grasped the watch with her fingertips and held it out to me. I was almost embarrassed to take it in my bare hand.

"It's one of our latest creations. A quartz movement in a steel case, with chronograph function and three counters."

A quartz watch. Not even a real clock mechanism. You could find thousands of quartz watches on the market for less than ten euros.

I was about to slip it on when I suddenly realized that I was wearing my own watch on my wrist. A wave of shame washed over me. I couldn't show her the novelty plastic watch that was hidden under my jacket sleeve. So I took it off with a gesture that was no doubt grotesque, shielding it with the palm of my hand as I stuffed it in my pocket.

"You can put it on the tray," she said.

I was convinced that she had seen my unease and wanted to increase it. I declined her offer. My face was burning. Rattled, I said the first thing that came to mind: "How long does the battery last?"

Instantly, my embarrassment increased tenfold. I must be the first customer in the history of Cartier to have asked such a question. Who among their clientele would be bothered about the life of a battery?

The sales assistant gave herself several seconds to reply, as if to give me time to realize how out of place my question was and to allow my shame to work its way deep down. Sheer torture.

"A year."

I barely heard her. I had to calm down, refocus. I tried to relax, examining the watch with false interest. I quickly slipped it on my wrist, anxious to show how much I was used to handling this sort of luxury item. I tried to fasten the watchband just as quickly but was brought to a dead halt when the folding deployant clasp jammed. I must have tried to close the wrong part first. I began again, but still couldn't close it properly.

"The clasp opens the other way," she said. "May I?"

I was overcome with shame; my face was crimson. I was afraid the beads of sweat on my forehead would drop on the tray. To avoid this supreme humiliation, I stepped back from the counter a few inches.

Now I was holding out my wrist like a fugitive surrendering to a policeman to be handcuffed. The ease with which she closed the clasp only increased my feeling of clumsiness.

I pretended to evaluate the aesthetics of the costly watch, waving my arm around in the air to look at it from different angles.

"How much is it?" I asked, as casually as possible, as if it was merely a routine question.

"Thirty-two hundred and seventy euros."

I thought I caught a hint of satisfaction in her voice, the sort certain instructors evince when they tell you you've failed your driving test or scored at the bottom of the curve on your SATs.

Was she serious—3,270 euros for a quartz watch with a steel-and-rubber band? I would have liked to ask her the difference between that and a 40-euro Swatch. Dubreuil would no doubt have appreciated the question, but it was beyond me. As yet. On the other hand, bizarrely, the price, which struck me as outrageous, helped me loosen up a bit. It freed me from the pressure I was inflicting on myself, as the magic of the luxury universe—and the awe it had elicited in me—vanished.

"I'd like to try that one on," I said, pointing to another watch and taking off the Chronoscaph.

"The Tank Française, designed in 1917," she said. "Mechanical movement, automatically self-winding."

I put it on, this time without fumbling with the clasp, and turned my wrist this way and that.

"It's not bad, but . . . " I said, pretending to hesitate.

That made two watches. How many was I supposed to try on? Didn't he say fifteen? I was beginning to relax a bit, just a bit, when I heard Dubreuil's voice, more discreetly this time.

"Tell her you think they're ugly and you want to see the gold watches!"

"I'd like to see that one," I said, pretending not to hear.

"Tell her they're . . ."

I coughed to cover the sound of his voice. What would she think if she heard? The idea crossed my mind that I might look like a thief connected to an accomplice outside. For all I knew, the security cameras had already detected my earpiece. I started to sweat. I had to hurry up and accomplish my mission, so I could get it over with and get out.

"I'm not sure. Actually, perhaps I'll have a look at your gold models," I said reluctantly, afraid of not being credible.

She skillfully slipped the tray into the display case.

"Please follow me."

I had the unpleasant impression she was making no effort to serve me, just the bare minimum demanded by her professionalism. She must be feeling she was wasting her time with me. I followed her, furtively looking around. My eyes met those of one of the men in dark suits. No doubt a security guard. I had the impression he was looking at me strangely.

We went into another, bigger room. The few customers here were not at all like the tourists and office workers passing by outside on the Champs Elysées. Sales assistants glided around the room like silent phantoms, preserving the calm of the store.

Instinctively, I located the little cameras placed at strategic points. I felt as if they were all pointing at me, slowly turning to follow each of my movements. I wiped my forehead with the back of my sleeve and tried to breathe deeply to ease the tension. I had to contain my mounting stage fright, as each step brought me closer to a collection of watches for the super rich that I would have to pretend to be interested in and pretend to be in a position to buy.

We took our places on either side of an elegant counter.

The gold collection was more extensive, and the assistant showed me the models through the glass top.

"I like this one," I said, pointing to a rather large watch in yellow gold.

"It's the Ballon Bleu model, with an eighteen-carat yellow gold case and fluted crown in yellow gold, with a sapphire cabochon winding stem, for twenty-three thousand, five hundred euros."

I had the distinct feeling that she had announced the price with the intention of informing me that this model was beyond my means. She was toying with me, gently humiliating me.

I felt cut to the quick, and that pushed me to react, to come out of my lethargic state.

She was far from suspecting that she was doing me a service by annoying me.

"I'll try it on," I said in a curt voice that surprised me.

Watching her obey my command and remove the watch from the case, I felt for an instant a very new emotion for me, a tiny pleasure that had been quite foreign to me until now. Was this what a taste for power was?

I slipped the watch on, looked at it for a few seconds without saying a word, and then delivered a final verdict.

"Too heavy."

I took it off and casually held it out to her, already look-ing at the other models.

"This one!" I said, pointing to a second watch without giving her time to put away the first one.

She sped up the movement of her nimble fingers, the red varnish on her nails reflecting the light from the spot-lights subtly angled toward the counter to accentuate the natural brilliance of the watches.

I was carried along by an unsuspected force. Affirming myself was suddenly becoming intoxicating.

"And I'll also try on that one!" I said, pointing to an-other, forcing her to follow the rhythm I was imposing.

I didn't recognize myself. My timidity had completely vanished, and I was becoming more and more dominant in the relationship. Something unheard of was taking place in me. I felt an indefinable sense of jubilation.

"Here you are, monsieur."

I had the sad feeling that she had started to respect me since I had become demanding. I was displaying an author-ity that was totally new to me, and she stopped looking down at me with her haughty gaze. She kept her eyes down on the watches, as she carried out the tasks I dictated. I stood straighter than ever, as her expert fingers briskly manipu-lated the objects.

I don't know how long the scene lasted. No longer quite myself, I slightly lost contact with reality. I was in unknown territory, discovering a singular pleasure, inconceivable an hour before. A strange feeling of omnipotence came over me, as if a heavy lid had fallen off all at once.

"Come back, now."

Dubreuil's deep voice suddenly brought me back to earth.

I took my time in leaving, and she insisted on showing me out, following me as I walked back across the shop with a confident step, my eyes sweeping the place like a general surveying conquered land. The rooms seemed smaller now, the atmosphere more pedestrian. The men in black opened the doors for me, thanking me for my visit. Everyone wished me a good evening.

I came out on the street, and my senses were at once attacked by the noise of the traffic and the luminosity of a sky that had gone white. Coming to my senses, I fully grasped the meaning of what I had just experienced: Other people's attitude toward me was conditioned by my own behavior. I was the one who caused their reactions. I couldn't help questioning myself about a number of past relationships.

I had also discovered unsuspected resources somewhere inside myself, resources that allowed me to behave differently. I certainly didn't wish to repeat what I had just experienced. I was not a power person and didn't wish to become one; I was too fond of cordial relations between equals. But I had discovered that I wasn't doomed to play the role of follower. Above all, I had found I was capable of doing things I wasn't used to doing, and that alone was what counted in my eyes.

The narrow tunnel of my life was beginning to widen a little.

"WHAT MOTIVATES YOU about a job in accounting?"

My candidate's eyes moved rapidly in every direction as he searched for the best possible answer.

"Hmm . . . I like figures."

I could feel he was disappointed with himself. He would like to have said something catchier, but nothing had come to mind.

"What do you like about figures?"

I had the impression I'd slipped another coin in the slot: The lottery balls began to turn around, as his cheeks became more flushed. He had obviously made an effort with his clothes for the interview. He clearly wasn't used to wearing the gray suit and very sober striped tie he had on, and this was adding to his unease. His white socks contrasted so strikingly with the correctness of his outfit that they looked almost fluorescent.

"Well, I like it when it comes out right. I mean, when the columns balance, and I'm sure I'm going to land on my feet. It's very satisfying, you know. As a matter of fact, I like it when things are straightforward. What's more, when there's an error, I can spend hours looking for it, until everything's straightened out. Well . . . not hours. I mean, I don't waste time. I know how to get to the heart of something. But I mean I'm very precise."

Poor young man. He was struggling to try and prove that he was the perfect candidate.

"Do you consider yourself to be an independent person?"

I had to concentrate on his face to stop my eyes from being drawn to his socks.

"Yes, I do. I'm very independent. No problem. I know how to sort things out by myself without troubling anyone."

"Can you give me an example of when you've shown independence?"

It was a technique well known to countless recruiters. When someone states they have a quality, they must be able to give examples of occasions when they've shown it. More precisely, they must be able to provide a context, a behavior, and an outcome. If one of the three is missing, then they are bound to be lying. It's logical: If they've really got that quality, they must be able to give an example of a situation in which they applied it, specifically what they did, and the results.

"Hmm . . . yes, of course."

"What was the context?"

The lottery balls were spinning furiously as he tried to remember—or imagine—such an event. The slight redness of his complexion intensified, and I thought I could make out a bead of sweat on his brow. I hated making the candidates uncomfortable, and it really wasn't what I intended. But I had to evaluate whether they did or didn't match the post on offer.

"Well, look, I regularly show independence, there's no doubt about it. You can take my word for it."

He uncrossed his legs, twisted a little in his chair, and then recrossed them. His socks really could have been in an ad for Tide.

"I'm just asking you to give me an example of the last time it happened. Where was it? What were the circumstances? What was the occasion? Take your time to remember. Relax, there's no hurry."

He began to fidget in his chair, wiping his hands, which were probably damp, on his trousers. Long seconds went by, seeming like hours, but still he could find nothing to say. I felt mounting embarrassment submerge him. He must hate me.

"Right," I broke in, to put an end to his torture. "I'm going to tell you why I'm asking you this question. The vacancy is in a small company whose accountant has resigned. He had built up so many days off that he didn't have to give notice. He left overnight. There is nobody in the company who can train his successor. If you take the job, you will have to manage on your own, going through his papers and his computer files. If you're not *really* independent, there's a risk it will turn into a nightmare for you, and it is my duty not to put you in such a situation. I'm not trying to trap you; I'm just trying to ascertain if you would be up to the task that needs to be done. From that point of view, your interest is the same as that of the company that's offering the job."

He listened carefully and, in the end, recognized that he preferred working in an environment with a clear structure, where he knew precisely what was expected of him and he could find answers to his questions if he wasn't sure. We spent the rest of the interview clarifying his career plan and defining the sort of position that would best suit his personality, his experience, and his skills. I promised to keep him on file and contact him again as soon as there was a vacancy that matched his profile better.

I walked him to the elevator and wished him the best of luck for the future.

Back in my office, I looked at the missed calls. I had a text from Dubreuil:

Come and meet me at the bar of the Hotel George
V. Take a taxi and during the ride, contradict EVERY-
THING the driver says. EVERYTHING. I'm waiting for
you. —Y.D.

I reread it twice and couldn't suppress a grimace at the
thought of what awaited me. Everything would depend
on what the taxi driver said. It could quickly become very
unpleasant.

A glance at my watch: 5:40 P.M. I had no more interviews, but I never left the office before 7:00 at the best of
times.

I looked at my e-mails. A dozen or so, but nothing
urgent.

I grabbed my raincoat and looked into the corridor. Nobody in sight. I headed for the emergency stairs. No point in
standing around waiting for the elevator. I reached the end of
the corridor just as Grégoire Larcher charged out of his office.
He must have seen my embarrassment instantly.

"Taking the afternoon off?" he asked with a mocking
smile.

"I've got to go. An emergency."

He walked off without answering, no doubt pleased
to have caught me red-handed. I rushed down the stairs,
slightly disgusted at the way things were turning out. Dam-
mit, I worked incredibly long hours every day, and the one
day I left early, I got caught.

Irritated, I charged into the Avenue de l'Opéra. The fresh
air helped me refocus—unless it was the prospect of the task
I had to accomplish, which was even more worrying than
running into Larcher. I walked to the taxi stand. Nobody. I
had a little time to spare and felt almost relieved. I lit a cigarette and puffed on it nervously. As soon as I was stressed,
I had to smoke. What a filthy habit! I'd never get rid of it.

As I walked, I had a strange feeling. The impression of being . . . followed. I turned around but just saw lots of people. Difficult to be sure. I walked on, feeling uneasy.

I thought back to the last few times I had taken a cab. The drivers were for the most part out-and-out chatterboxes, openly expressing their opinions on all the topics in the news, and I had been careful not to give a different opinion. Okay, Dubreuil was right. But perhaps it was just a form of laziness. After all, there's no point to trying to put people right. In any case, you won't convince them.

I looked in the distance. A fair amount of traffic. It was rush hour. I might have to wait a long time for a taxi.

Suppose it was cowardice, more than laziness? Besides, not saying anything was not that restful either. I was often raging inside. So what was I afraid of then? Of not being liked? Of setting off a bad reaction in the other person? I didn't know.

"Where you goin'?"

The cabby's thick Parisian accent brought me out of my torpor. Caught up in my daydreams, I hadn't seen him drive up. The driver was leaning out the window, staring at me impatiently. Fiftyish, thickset, bald, with a black moustache and a nasty look—why did I have to get a live one today of all days?

"Hey! You goin' to make up your mind? I haven't got all day!"

"The George the Fifth, please," I stammered as I opened the rear door.

Bad start. I had to get the upper hand. *Come on, chin up—the opposite of everything he says. Everything.*

I leaned back in the seat and immediately the smell in the cab made me want to vomit: stale tobacco mixed with a supermarket car deodorant. Awful.

"I'll give it to you straight," the driver was saying.

"The hotel might be close, but we're not there yet! I tell you, I don't know what people are up to today, but traffic's at a stand-still."

Hmm . . . Difficult to say the opposite. How should I reply?

"With a bit of luck, it'll free up, and we'll be there quicker than you think."

"Ha, that's right, still believe in Santa Claus, too?" he said. "I've been doing this job twenty-eight years. I know what I'm talking about. Goddammit, I'm sure half these people don't even need their cars."

He was talking loudly, as though I was in the back of a bus.

"Perhaps the cars really are useful. We don't know," I ventured.

"Yeah, that's right! Most of them don't go more than a few hundred yards in their cars! They're too lazy to walk and too cheap to take a taxi! There's no one tighter than a Parisian!"

I had the feeling he wasn't even noticing that I was disagreeing with him. It just fed the conversation. Perhaps, in the end, my task wouldn't be as hard as I thought.

"I think Parisians are rather nice."

"No joke? Well, you can't know them very well. I've been studying them for twenty-eight years. And I can tell you, they're getting worse each year. I can't stand them anymore. I've had it up to here!"

His big, hairy hands tightened on the wheel, which was covered in artificial fur, and I could see the tension spreading to the muscles of his equally hairy forearms. Under the black hair was a huge tattoo that made me think of a giant frozen French fry. When I was little, American television used to show a cartoon ad with dancing French fries. In my whole life, I'd never seen such a ridiculous tattoo.

"I think you're mistaken. People just send back a mirror of the way we talk to them."

He slammed on the brakes and turned around to face me, his eyes wild with rage.

"What the hell do you think you're saying?"

I wasn't expecting such an intense reaction. I recoiled, which didn't stop me from smelling his disgusting breath. Was that the smell of alcohol? I had to defuse the bomb, play at being the bomb squad a bit.

"I was just saying that perhaps people are uncommunicative, but if you take the time, accept the idea that they may have reasons for being stressed, talk to them gently"—I underlined this point—"they may open up and become more pleasant when they feel you're interested in them."

He stared at me wordlessly, his eyes narrowing like a bad-tempered boar's. Then he turned around and set off again. All of a sudden, dead silence in the cab. I took a few deep breaths, trying to release the tension in my body. As we inched forward in the traffic, the silence became oppressive. I had to break it.

"What's your tattoo?" I said, with the vague hope of applying the idea I had just put forward.

"Oh, that," he said, in an almost tender tone of voice that told me I had hit the mark. "That's a childhood souvenir. It's vengeance."

I suppressed a smile. I was dying to ask him how a frozen French fry could symbolize vengeance, but I wasn't that suicidal.

We were arriving at the Place de la Concorde.

"I'm not going down the Champs-Élysées. Too much traffic. I'm going along the river to the Pont de l'Alma, and then we can come back up Avenue George the Fifth from the bottom."

"Hmm . . . I'd prefer it if we went down the Champs Élysées, if you don't mind."

He didn't say anything, sighed, and carried on with the conversation.

"I love tattoos. There aren't two the same. And it takes guts to have a tattoo done. 'Cos it doesn't come off. It's for life. So it takes guts, it sure does. I love them on women, as well. There ain't nothing sexier than a tattoo where you're not expecting it—in hidden places, if you see what I mean."

Suddenly, in the rearview mirror, I could see his eyes, full of lust. *Calm down, Granddad,* I thought. *Calm down.* I mustered all my courage and said, "I don't like tattoos very much."

"Yeah, nowadays youngsters don't like them because they all want to be the same."

"Perhaps they don't need a tattoo to be different."

"Different? Pfft! We didn't give a damn. We just wanted to have some laughs. We got bikes or cars and took off. No traffic jams then!"

The man didn't know how to talk at anything less than a bellow. And the smell . . .

Okay, one more try. "Yes, but today, young people know you can't carry on polluting the planet just to have fun."

"Ha! That's right! More of that ecology bullshit! Global warming, load of bull. It comes from people who want to sell you intelligence, when they ain't got any to sell."

"What would you know?"

I said it without thinking. He braked violently, bringing the car to a standstill. I was thrown against the front seat and then bounced back. The driver exploded. "Fuck off, you hear? Fuck off! I've had enough of little jerks like you preaching at me! Get out!"

I opened the door and threw myself out, then ran off like a shot, before he thought of catching up with me.

I dodged between the cars until I reached the Champs-Élysées, running through a fine drizzle, which cooled my face. The fright passed, but I kept on running. I was running because nothing was holding me back. I had loosened my shackles, unlaced a few knots. For the first time, I had dared to say all I was thinking to a stranger, and I was beginning to feel lighter and, above all, free. The fine mist lashed my face as if to awaken me to life.

THE UNIFORMED DOORMAN pushed the revolving door, I slipped in, and there I was, in the majestic entrance hall of the George V, one of the most beautiful luxury hotels in Paris. Pale marble covered the floor and columns. The reception desk was faced in darker marble, and behind it hung a large tapestry. The atmosphere was a mixture of great distinction and silent efficiency. Valets were busy moving gilt trolleys piled with trunks and suitcases, most of them covered in leather and bearing the stamp of a prestigious brand. Smiling receptionists handed over keys or street maps or information to guests who were probably used to a high level of service. A customer in shorts and Nike sneakers, a vision as unexpected as a rapper crossing the platform of a symphony orchestra, walked across the hall with the casualness of someone used to this sort of place—or a lot more chutzpah than I possessed, at any rate. Probably an American.

I went up to the concierge.

"Good evening, I'm looking for the bar, please."

I was afraid he'd ask if I had a room there. I must have cut a sorry figure with my wet hair, damp suit, and water trickling down my face. Fortunately, the vision of the tourist in shorts had made me feel a little more at ease.

"Yes, Monsieur. Turn right after the three steps, and you'll see the bar a little farther on," he replied, his tone pleasant but rather grand.

I climbed the three steps and found myself in a vast,

glass-enclosed gallery running along one side of an interior courtyard filled with orange trees in magnificent carved pots. I walked through the gallery into the bar, an elegant wood-paneled room with red brocade chairs that invited intimate conversation. The George V bar is one of the most famous meeting places in Paris. Not many people were there when I arrived. A man and a woman of a certain age sat opposite each other at one of the marble-topped tables, and a little farther on, two men were involved in a quiet but obviously heated discussion. No trace of Dubreuil. I headed for a table at the back and sat facing the door, so I could see him arrive. Passing by the couple, I smelled the woman's heady perfume. Shalimar, a classic.

Some newspapers had been left on my table—*The International Herald Tribune*, *The New York Times*, *Le Monde*—and some decidedly less serious magazines, including a well-thumbed copy of the gossip rag *Closer*. I was checking out the lives of the stars when I spotted Dubreuil coming toward me. I quickly got rid of the incriminating magazine. As he crossed the room, everyone turned to look at him. He was one of those charismatic men who can't help but attract attention.

"So, tell me about your exploits!" he said, as he sat down in the chair across from me.

I noticed that he never said hello. Every time I saw him, it was as if he was resuming a conversation interrupted a few minutes earlier.

He ordered bourbon, and I settled for Perrier water.

I described the scene in the taxi in detail, and he was greatly amused by the driver's behavior.

"You got a ripe one there! If I'd wanted to set up a meeting like that myself, I'd never have found one like him!"

I told him of the difficulty I had had expressing opinions that were in opposition to the driver's, and the feeling of freedom in the end after I had succeeded.

"I'm really pleased you went through that. You know, you talked to me a lot about your life at work, about your feeling of being trapped at the office, of being under surveillance and constantly judged."

"Yes. In that company, I'm prevented from being myself. I'm given very little freedom. I feel like a prisoner. I feel as if everything I say and do will be commented on. Even this evening, when I left a little early, I was on the receiving end of an unpleasant remark from my section head. It's true it was earlier than usual, but I leave work very late *every* evening. It was especially unfair to criticize me on the only day I've left early! I'm suffocating in that place."

He looked at me with a piercing eye, while savoring a mouthful of bourbon. I could smell its bouquet.

"Look, when I hear you say 'They prevent me from being myself,' I want to say that, on the contrary, they're *allowing* you to be yourself. They're even *pushing* you to be more and more yourself. That's what's suffocating you."

I was perplexed.

"I don't follow at all."

He leaned back in his chair.

"You talked to me about some of your colleagues. I remember one of them, in particular, who's rather arrogant."

"Thomas."

"Yes, that's it. A bit of a show-off, from what you said."

"That's a euphemism."

"Imagine that Thomas had been in your place tonight, that he had left his office at four or five o'clock and had met his boss in the corridor."

"It wasn't our immediate boss. It was Larcher, the section head."

"Fine. Imagine the scene: Thomas leaves exceptionally early and meets his section head in the corridor."

"Okay."

"You're a little mouse, and you watch them as they meet."

"Right."

"What do they say to each other?"

"Hmm . . . I don't know. Well, that's funny, I imagine Larcher smiling at Thomas, a friendly smile, almost an indulgent smile."

"Interesting. You think that's how your section head would have reacted if he had met Thomas tonight instead of you?"

"Well . . . yes, it's likely. I imagine him like that, at any rate. It would be very unfair, I think, but there's a certain favoritism around there. The rules are not the same for everyone."

"Right. What's the name of your other colleague, the one who seems to be making fun of everyone?"

"Mickaël?"

"Yes, that's the one. Now visualize the same scene, but this time between Larcher and Mickaël. It's Mickaël who's leaving at five o'clock. What happens?"

"Let's see. I imagine Larcher makes the same remark to him as he did to me!"

"Yes?"

"He says, 'So, taking the afternoon off?' perhaps even more sarcastically than he said it to me. Yes, that's right! Larcher is really baiting him."

"And how does Mickaël react?"

"It's hard to imagine, but I think Mickaël's got the nerve to rib him back and say, 'You should know!' or something like that."

"Right! And how does Larcher take that?"

"They both laugh as they carry on walking."

"Interesting," Dubreuil said, draining his glass. "And what do you think about that?"

"I don't know," I replied. "If it really happened like that, it would indeed be the sign of favoritism."

"No, Alan. That's not it."

He signaled to the waiter, who was beside us in a flash.

"Another bourbon."

I took a sip of Perrier. Dubreuil leaned toward me, his blue eyes looking into mine. I felt naked.

"That's not it, Alan," he went on. "It's a lot more complicated than that. Thomas is full of himself, and his attitude induces in Larcher a certain respect. Mickaël teases everyone, and Larcher knows he's a smart aleck who thinks he's smarter than the rest. So Larcher teases him to let him know that he's even smarter than Mikaël. You . . ."

He paused.

"I don't play games like the others," I interjected. "I'm natural, and so he takes advantage."

"No, it's trickier than that. Alan, what characterizes you is precisely that you're *not* free. You're not free, so he locks you up even more in the prison you're in."

A thick silence, as I digested the blow. Then I saw red, and I could feel the anger rising in me. What the hell was he going on about?

"No he doesn't. It's quite the opposite! Absolutely the opposite! I can't bear anyone infringing my freedom!"

"Look at what happened with the taxi driver. You said you had to force yourself to express opinions contrary to his. Yet people like him are strangers you will never see again. Your life, your future doesn't depend on them, agreed? And yet, you feel the need to say what will make them like you. You are afraid of disappointing people and being rejected. That's why you don't allow yourself to really express what you feel or behave according to your wishes. You make every effort to adapt yourself to others. And that's on your own initiative, Alan. Nobody's asking you to do it."

"But that seems quite natural to me! Besides, if everyone made efforts for others, everyone's lives would be improved."

"Yes, except that in your case, it's not a choice. You don't say, in a detached way, 'Okay, today I'm going to do what people expect of me.' No. Unconsciously you force yourself to do it. You think that otherwise you won't be liked, you won't be wanted. So, without even realizing it, you impose lots of restrictions on yourself. Your life becomes *very* restricted, and as a result, you don't feel free. And you hold it against other people."

I was bewildered. A real smack on the head. I was expecting anything but this. Ideas, emotions, everything was rushing around in my head. I felt dizzy. I would have liked to violently reject Dubreuil's analysis, but part of me felt it contained some truth. A disturbing truth. Having spent my life feeling pain at the slightest attack on my freedom, at being dominated by other people, I was now being told I was the architect of my own suffering.

"And do you see, Alan, that when you force yourself not to disappoint others, in order to fulfill their expectations of you or to respect their way of doing things, then, believe it or not, it encourages certain people to become very demanding of you, as if they feel it is your duty to submit to their desires. It seems quite natural to them. If you feel guilty about leaving the office early, your boss will make you feel even guiltier. And no doubt it's unconscious. He senses that to you, it's not acceptable to leave early, so *he* decides it isn't. You induce his reaction. Do you understand?"

I said nothing. I remained silent, absorbed by the subtle movement of his hand that for some time had been making circles in the air with his glass, the ice cubes swirling in the bourbon, knocking on the walls of their crystal prison.

"Alan," he went on, "freedom is inside us. It must come from us. Don't expect it to come from the exterior."

His words resonated in my mind.

"It's possible," I finally admitted.

"You know, there are stacks of studies that have been carried out on survivors of the concentration camps in the Second World War. One of the studies shows that what nearly all of them had in common was the desire to remain free in their heads. For example, if they only had a little piece of bread to eat for the day, they said to themselves, 'I am free to eat this bread when I want. I am free to choose the moment to swallow it.' With the help of choices that can seem as pathetic as that, they kept a feeling of freedom inside themselves. And it would appear this feeling of freedom helped them stay alive."

I listened to him carefully and couldn't help telling myself that had I been in that situation, I would have so violently resented the domination and the abuse of power by my jailers that I would never have been capable of developing such a frame of mind.

"How can I become . . . freer in myself?"

"There is no ready-made recipe, no single way of getting there. One good way, however, is to choose to do for a certain time what you would usually carefully avoid."

"I feel as if everything you've advised me to do since the beginning consists of doing what I don't like doing. Is that how you move on in life?"

He burst out laughing. The old lady with the heady perfume turned around to look.

"It's more complex than that. But when in life we arrange things in order to keep whatever frightens us at arm's length, we prevent ourselves from discovering that most of our fears are inventions of our mind. The only way to know whether what we believe is false or not is to go out and verify it in the field! So it's sometimes useful to take ourselves by the hand, even if it means doing violence to ourselves, in order to experiment with what is worrying us and give ourselves a chance to realize that we've perhaps been making a mistake."

"So, what are you going to ask of me this time to solve my problem?"

"Right. Let's see," he said, settling into his armchair, visibly pleased to be in a position to pronounce his sentence. "Since you believe—mistakenly—that people won't like you if you don't behave according to their criteria, since you feel the need to correspond to the image they expect of you, you're going to practice disorienting yourself."

I swallowed hard.

"Disorienting myself?"

"Yes, you're going to train yourself to do the opposite of what you feel you absolutely must do. For example, you're going to start by taking to the office every day that magazine that interests you so much, until we're sure everyone has seen you with it."

To my dismay, he grabbed the *Closer* that I had turned facedown when he came in.

"If I do that, I'm done for."

"Ah! Your image, your image! See how you're not free?"

"But it would have consequences for my credibility at work. I can't do that!"

"You forget that you've told me over and over that in your company, people don't matter, all that matters are their results. So they won't give a damn about what you're reading."

"But I can't. I'd be ashamed!"

"There's no reason to be ashamed of things that interest you."

"It doesn't interest me. I never read this magazine!"

"Yes, I know, nobody reads it. And yet it sells hundreds of thousands of copies every week. But it interests you, since you had it in your hands when I arrived!"

"It was just out of curiosity."

"Precisely. You're allowed to be curious. It's a positive quality, and you don't have to be ashamed."

I could already imagine the faces of my colleagues and my managers when they saw me with it.

"Alan, you will be free the day you can't even be bothered to wonder what the people who see you with a copy of *Closer* under your arm are thinking."

That day was a long, long way away, I couldn't help thinking.

"It won't be easy," I protested.

"Each day, you're to commit, let's say, three mistakes—mistakes over common things. Specifically, I want you to behave in an inappropriate manner three times a day. It can be about anything, even small things. What I want is for you to become imperfect for a while, until you realize that you're still alive, that it doesn't change anything, and that your relationships with others haven't gotten worse. Finally, you're going to refuse at least twice a day to do what others ask of you, or else contradict their point of view. It's up to you."

I looked at him in silence. My lack of enthusiasm didn't affect his. He seemed delighted by his ideas.

"When do I start?"

"Right away! You must never put off till later things that can make you grow!"

"Fine. So, in that case, I think I'll leave without saying good-bye and without even offering to pay my share of the bill."

"Perfect! That's a good start!"

He was visibly pleased, but the mischievous look in his eye didn't bode well.

I got up and left the table.

I had gotten all the way across the bar and was at the door to the gallery when he called out to me. His loud voice broke the muffled silence of the place, and everyone turned around to see what he was waving at arm's length.

"Alan! Come back! You've forgotten your magazine!"

I HATE MONDAY mornings. That must be the most trite and widespread feeling in the world. But I had a special reason to feel that way: It was the day of our weekly business meeting. Every Monday, my colleagues and I were told that the targets hadn't been met and were asked what we were going to do about it. What decisions were we taking? What actions were we going to implement?

My weekend had been rich in emotions, as had the week following my meeting with Dubreuil. The first few days, I had forced myself to come up with the assigned number of inappropriate behaviors and refusals to do what others asked. After that, however, I had bravely grasped all the opportunities that came up.

Thus it was that I had driven two miles an hour down a narrow street with cars behind me, devoured by the desire to pull over and let them pass or speed up in order not to look like an old man. I had made noise in my apartment and been called to task twice by Madame Blanchard. I had hung up on a telemarketer trying to sell me windows. I had gone to the office wearing two different colored socks. I had taken my coffee break each day at the café across the street during the peak period when everyone at the bar is complaining about the country's economic problems and proffering obvious solutions—why didn't the government do something about it? And I, of course, had disagreed with everyone about nearly everything. Behaving like this had been very trying, even if a part of me was beginning to feel a certain pleasure at overcoming my fears.

As soon as my first interview with a candidate had finished that Monday, I ran to the accursed staff meeting. It was 11:05 A.M., so I was late. I went into the room with a notepad in my hand and *Closer* under my arm. All the consultants were already sitting at the tables, which were arranged in a circle. They were all waiting for me.

Luc Fausteri threw me an icy look. On his left, Grégoire Larcher maintained his unchanging toothpaste smile. I sat down in the empty seat. Faces turned toward me. I placed the magazine on the table, face up with the title showing, and then avoided meeting anyone's eyes. I was too ashamed.

On my left, Thomas was pretending to read the *Financial Times*. Mickaël was joking with the woman next to him, who was trying to scan *La Tribune* while chuckling from time to time at Mickaël's idiotic remarks.

"The week's figures are . . ." Larcher liked to speak, then leave the end of the sentence suspended in the air, assuring himself of our complete attention. He got up, as if to ensure his domination over those present, and went on, still smiling: "The week's figures are encouraging. We're up four percent on the number of recruitment assignments compared to the previous week, and up seven percent over the same week last year. With regard to this indicator, I remind you that our objective is to be up eleven percent. Of course, individual results are uneven, and I must again congratulate Thomas who remains at the top of the group."

Thomas adopted a relaxed and absentmindedly satisfied look. He loved appearing to be the victor who's too cool to care. In fact, I knew that compliments had the effect of cocaine on him.

"But I have an excellent piece of news for the others,"

Larcher informed us, and then paused. As his seductive gaze swept over the group, he allowed the silence to make what he was about to reveal seem more dramatic.

"First of all, I must say Luc Fausteri has worked hard for you. For nearly a month, he has been analyzing all our data to understand in a rational way why some of you have better results than the others, despite all of us using the same working methods. He has cross-checked in every direction, done the stats, studied the graphs. And the results are pure genius. We've got the solution, and each of you will be able to profit from it on a daily basis. However, I'll leave it to you, Luc, to present your conclusions yourself!"

Our section head, more serious than ever, began speaking in his usual monotone. "Going through all your time sheets, I saw an inverse correlation between the average length of interviews per consultant over the past twelve months and the average monthly sales of that consultant, corrected for any vacation he took."

The room remained silent for a few moments, everyone looking questioningly at Fausteri.

"Can you translate that into French?" said Mickaël, bursting into laughter.

"It's very simple!" said Larcher, immediately taking over. "It's the ones who spend the most time on their recruitment interviews who get the fewest recruitment contracts from businesses. It's quite logical, if you think about it. You can't be in two places at once. If you spend too much time interviewing candidates, you have less time to canvass companies and sell our services, and so your results won't be as good. Irrefutable."

The team remained silent as the information sank in.

"For example," Larcher went on, "Thomas, the best of you, spends on average one hour and twelve minutes on an interview, while you, Alan, at the bottom of the group—sorry, Alan—spend on average one hour and fifty-seven minutes. That's almost twice as much!"

I sunk into my chair, while continuing to look at the table in front of me with what I hoped was a relaxed air. But there was nothing on the table but my *Closer*. I felt the weight of their eyes.

"No doubt we can reduce the length of our interviews," said Alice, a young consultant. "But we're going to bring down the success rate for our recruits. I always think of the guarantee we give businesses. If the recruit isn't suitable or resigns within six months of being taken on, we must provide a replacement candidate. Excuse me, Thomas," she said, turning toward her colleague, "but I recall that it's *your* clients who have made the greatest call on that guarantee. For me, it happens very rarely."

"I don't want to leap to Thomas's defense; he has no need of it," said Larcher. "But the cost of renewing his defective candidates is tiny compared to the gain in turnover he contributes."

"But that's not in our clients' interests!" said Alice angrily. "And therefore, in the long term, it's not in ours either. It damages our image."

"Clients don't hold it against us, I can assure you," Larcher countered. "They know we can't control human nature. Ours is an inexact science. Nobody can be sure of choosing the right candidate all the time."

We were careful not to reply, as Larcher's smiling face swept the room.

After a moment, David, the longest-serving member of the team, dared to remark, "What's not so obvious is that our interview process is long, and we can't help it if our candidates don't always get to the point in the shortest possible time. We can scarcely cut them off, can we?"

"That's where I've got good news for you," said Larcher, triumphantly. "Luc, tell us your second conclusion."

Luc Fausteri spoke without looking at us, his eyes fixed on his papers. "I've said that the average length of Thomas's interviews is noticeably less than that of the less commercially successful consultants. Analyzed more precisely, the figures reveal something else: The duration of the face-to-face interview is especially short for the candidates who don't go through to the final phase."

"In other words," Larcher interrupted, "if you spend less time with the dead losses, you'll have more time to spend canvassing. Shorten the interviews as soon as you realize that the person doesn't fit the vacancy. There's no point in going on."

An embarrassed silence around the table.

"In any case, you won't be giving them the job, so there's no need to have scruples," Larcher said.

Embarrassment gave way to general unease.

"I don't quite agree."

All eyes turned toward me. I didn't often speak in meetings, and never to express my disapproval. I decided on a soft approach. "I think what you suggest is not in the interest of our firm. A candidate who doesn't suit a post that's to be filled today will perhaps fit one we have tomorrow. We have everything to gain, in the long run, from developing a pool of candidates who value our interviews and have confidence in us."

Larcher moved to regain the upper hand. "As far as that's concerned, no need to worry, my friends. I can reassure you that in this climate—and it's not about to change—there are far more candidates than vacancies to be filled, and we don't need to run after them. Rattle a dustbin and ten fall out. You only have to bend down and pick them up."

A wave of sniggering went around the room.

Summoning all my courage, I said, "As far as I'm concerned, I'm attached to certain ethics. We're not a company that recruits for its own benefit. Our job is to fill others' needs. Therefore, our mission goes beyond the simple selection of a candidate, and I think it's our role to advise those who don't fit the profile of the moment. It's our social responsibility, you might say. In any event, it's what makes my job one I like."

Larcher listened, still smiling, but as happened every time his interests were threatened, his expression changed imperceptibly; his smile became a little carnivorous.

"I think, my friends, that Alan has forgotten he works for Dunker Consulting and not for Mother Teresa."

He started to laugh, quickly joined by Thomas, then Mickaël. "If you're in any doubt," he went on, "look at the little box at the bottom of your pay slip, and you'll realize that a charity wouldn't pay you like that."

A few people chuckled.

Larcher's eyes narrowed as he zeroed in on me. "Now, Alan, you're going to have to keep your nose to the grindstone to earn that salary. And it's not by playing at being a social worker that you're going to do it."

"I earn the firm money," I countered. "My salary is highly cost-effective, and therefore it's deserved."

Deathly silence in the room. All my colleagues were looking at their feet. The atmosphere was oppressive. Larcher was obviously very surprised by my reaction; that's probably what disconcerted him the most.

"It's not for you to judge," he said finally, in an aggressive tone, no doubt convinced that it was vital to maintain his authority by having the last word. "It's for us to fix your targets, not you. And so far, you haven't met them."

The meeting finished quickly. It was clear that Larcher was very annoyed by the direction it had taken, which had lessened the impact of his message. The one time I'd had the courage to disagree, I might have been better advised to keep quiet. And yet, I was happy to have expressed my convictions and not let my values be trampled on.

I left the meeting room and went back to my office, preferring not to see Larcher. I didn't want to see anyone, in fact. I waited for everyone to go to lunch before leaving myself. I opened my door a crack. Silence. I walked down the corridor. Just as I passed Thomas's office, his phone rang. The switchboard was closed. Someone must be calling his direct line.

I don't know what came over me. It was neither my habit nor office procedure to answer someone else's phone, but the ringing was so insistent that I decided to go ahead. I opened the door to his office. Everything was tidy. His files were in a neat pile, and his Mont Blanc pen was placed just so. A very slight perfume floated in the air. Perhaps his aftershave . . . I picked up the phone, a much more elegant model than we had in the rest of the department.

"Al . . ." I was going to say my name to let the caller know I was not Thomas, but he didn't give me time, cutting me off and talking at top speed with a voice full of hatred. "What you've done is shitty. I clearly told you I hadn't resigned yet and was counting on your total discretion. I know you called my boss to tell him his head of administration was going to resign and that you were offering to find his replacement."

"Please, I'm not . . ."

"Shut up! I know it's you because I haven't sent my resumé anywhere else. You hear? Nowhere! It can only be you. It's disgusting."

I WAS COMING out of the building when Alice suddenly appeared. She had obviously been waiting for me since the
end of the meeting.

"Are you going to lunch?" she asked.

She was smiling, but I detected some uneasiness. Was
she afraid to be seen with me?

"Yes," I told her.

She waited a second, as if she wished the idea would come
from me, and then said, "Shall we have lunch together?"

"Yes, let's."

"I know a really nice restaurant that's a bit out of the
way. That way, we can talk freely."

"What's it called?"

"Le Repaire d'Arthus."

"Never heard of it."

"It's rather . . . original. I won't say any more about it.
I'll let you discover it for yourself."

"As long as they don't eat strange animals, it'll be fine."

"You Americans! You're so squeamish."

We walked down the Rue Molière and at the end ducked
into a vaulted passageway connecting with the arcade that
runs along the interior garden of the Palais Royal. What
a haven of peace the garden is, in the midst of this busy
district in the heart of Paris! Rows of chestnut trees, paths
of packed earth, and the massive old building itself, loaded
with history. Under the arches, we could smell the faint

musty odor of centuries-old stone, as the click of our heels resounded on the worn flagstones.

At the north end of the garden, we climbed a staircase with a pretty wrought-iron handrail. We passed a shop selling old music boxes then turned into the Rue Croix des Petits Champs. The sidewalk of this busy old Parisian street is so narrow we had to walk single file. Each of the little shops we passed seemed unique, light-years from the big chain stores that sell the same things in every city of the world. An umbrella seller stood next to a pork butcher's, next to a hat seller, followed by a tea merchant, then a specialist in craft jewelry. Food shops, shoe repairers, an antiquarian bookshop—I wanted to stop and look at them all.

"Do you know the Galerie Vivienne?" Alice asked.

"Not at all," I told her.

We crossed the street and went under an archway squeezed between two shops, emerging in one of Paris's famous covered passages. A beautiful relic of past centuries with a vaulted ceiling of glass and wrought iron, the gallery had been restored to its former glory. Upscale boutiques and restaurants lined the passageway. Our footsteps echoed like castanets as we walked along the mosaic floor. Away from the crowds and hustle bustle of the city, the gallery is an oasis of almost religious calm. Bathed in soft light, it has a melancholic serenity.

"The gallery dates from early in the 19th century," Alice explained. "It was a fashionable gathering place during the Restoration. I come here when I need to take a break and forget the office for a bit."

Back on the street, we noticed the smell of warm bread coming from a nearby bakery. It made me very hungry all of a sudden.

"Here we are!" said Alice, moments later, pointing to a restaurant with a deep gray painted facade.

We entered a small room with just 20 tables. The décor was baroque, and the walls were hung with pictures made up of quotations in carved wood frames. The owner—short, fair-haired, 40-ish, with a silk scarf knotted at the neck of his pink shirt—was in the midst of a conversation with two customers. He broke off as soon as he saw Alice.

"Here's my recruiting sergeant!" he said in a mannered voice that if it hadn't been accompanied by a knowing smile, would have seemed obsequious.

"I've already told you not to call me that, Arthus," Alice said with a laugh.

He kissed her hand.

"And who is the handsome prince accompanying you today?" he asked, eyeing me intensely from head to toe. "Madame has good taste . . . and she's taking risks, bringing him to Arthus."

"Alan is a colleague," Alice told him.

"Oh! You're one as well! Don't try and seduce me. I warn you: I'm quite unemployable in a company."

"I only recruit accountants," I replied.

"Oh," he said, simulating great sadness. "He's only interested in number-crunchers."

"Have you got a table for us, by any chance, Arthus? I haven't booked."

"My astrologer told me that an important person would come today, so I've kept this table. It's for you."

"You're too kind."

He handed us the menus with great elegance. Alice put hers down without a glance.

"You're not looking at it?" I asked.

"No point."

I shot her an inquiring look, but she merely gave me an enigmatic little smile.

The menu was fairly extensive, and everything looked

appetizing. Not easy to choose from such a fine variety of dishes. I hadn't even finished reading when our host came to take our order.

"Madame Alice."

"I'll leave it to you, Arthus."

"Oh, I like it when women submit to me! Henceforth, you're mine. Has my handsome prince made up his mind?" he said, leaning toward me slightly.

"I'll have a *mille-feuille,* a napoleon with tomatoes with basil, and . . ."

"No, no, no," he muttered.

"Sorry?"

"No, no, that's not a starter for a prince. Let me choose. Let's see. I'm going to make you chicory with Roquefort."

I was a little put out by his attitude.

"What's Roquefort?"

Arthus's jaw dropped in mock surprise.

"What? My prince is joking, isn't he?"

"My colleague is American," explained Alice. "He's only been living in France for a few months."

"But he has no accent," Arthus said. "And he's cute and not too big for a Yank. You weren't brought up on cornflakes and Big Macs?"

"His mother was French, but he's always lived in the States."

"Right. We'll have to educate him. I'm counting on you, Alice. I'll look after him from the culinary point of view. So let's start with Roquefort. You know that France has more than five hundred cheeses?"

"We've got a number in the States, you know."

"No, you haven't," he said vigorously, with mock exasperation. "We're not talking about the same thing! Not at all. What you have isn't cheese, it's plastic wrapped in cellophane. It's gelatinous gum flavored with salt.

"We're going to have to teach him everything!" Arthus continued. "Right. Let's start with Roquefort. Roquefort is the king of cheeses, and the king of cheeses—"

I interrupted him. "Okay, let's go with the chicory and Roquefort. Then, I'll carry on with—"

"We don't *carry on,* here, my prince. It's not a pantomime."

"Right. I'll follow it up with—"

"No, we don't follow anything up here, either. We're not policemen on a case."

I started again, choosing my words carefully: "Then I will have boeuf bourguignon with boiled potatoes."

"Oh no," he said very firmly. "That's not you at all. You can't go slumming with a boeuf bourguignon. No, I'll bring you, let's see, turkey forestière cooked in yellow wine from the Jura region, with oyster mushrooms from Sologne."

I was a little lost. "Am I allowed to choose my dessert?"

"You have every right, my prince."

"Then I'll have the tarte Tatin."

"Fine! So that's"—he was concentrating on what he was writing down—"a chocolate mousse. Thank you and *bon appétit!* Arthus is delighted to be able to serve you."

He disappeared into the kitchen.

I burst out laughing. "What's all that nonsense?"

"The menu is a load of bull. In fact, there is only one menu, the same for everyone. But it's very good. All the produce is fresh. Léon cooks all the dishes," she said, pointing to a tall man I could see through the round glass window in the door to the kitchen.

"I'm dying of hunger."

"The service is fast. It's the advantage of having only one menu. Their customers are all regulars. Except, once, there was a German tourist. He reacted very badly to Arthus's little game. He kicked up a fuss and left in an uproar."

Arthus came back out almost right away, twirling the two appetizers in the air.

"And here's your chicory with Roquefort!"

I was preparing to throw myself on my starter when I looked down and saw something disgusting. "Alice," I murmured, "my cheese is rotten. It's moldy. It's disgusting!"

She looked at me for a couple of seconds in silence and then burst out laughing.

"That's how it's supposed to be!"

"My cheese is supposed to be moldy?"

"That's how it's eaten, it's . . ."

"You expect me to eat rotten cheese?"

It felt like another task imposed by Dubreuil.

"It's not rotten, it's just moldy and . . ."

"Rotten, moldy, it's all the same."

"No! This is *healthy* mold," she insisted. "I swear you can eat it without risk. Besides, without the mold, the cheese would be of no interest."

"You're making fun of me."

"No, I assure you! Watch."

She skewered several pieces of cheese with her fork and popped them in her mouth, chewed, and swallowed with a smile.

"It's foul!" I protested.

"Try it, at least!"

"Certainly not!"

I made do with the chicory leaves, carefully choosing the few that hadn't been in contact with the cheese.

Arthus looked distraught when he came to remove our plates.

"I'm going to have to hide this from Léon. He'd shed tears if he saw you hadn't honored his appetizer. I know him; he'd be inconsolable."

He disappeared into the kitchen with our plates. Alice rested her forearms on the table and leaned toward me.

"You know, you really surprised me at the meeting. I never would have imagined that you'd stand up to Larcher. You were taking a risk."

"I don't know about that. At any rate, I was sincere. I'm convinced it's not in the firm's interests to neglect candidates who don't immediately fit a vacancy."

She looked straight at me for a few moments. I had never noticed before how pretty she was. Her light chestnut hair was tied back, revealing a slender, very feminine neck. Her blue eyes were both gentle and assertive, shining with intelligence. There was something very graceful about her.

"I'm more and more convinced," I went on, "that Larcher, Dunker, and the other members of the management team are deliberately making decisions that aren't in the interests of the firm."

"Why would they do that?" she asked.

"The decisions are dictated above all by the financial markets. By the stock exchange, in fact."

"You mean by our shareholders," Alice said.

"So to speak."

"I don't see what difference that makes. It's in the shareholders' interest, too, for the company to prosper."

"No, it depends . . ." I hesitated.

"Depends on what?"

"On their motives for being shareholders. You know, we have all sorts of shareholders: small investors, banks, investment funds. Do you think that the majority of them are interested in the healthy, harmonious development of our company? There's only one thing that counts, or rather there are two: that the share price keeps going up and that we cough up dividends every year."

"That's not so shocking," Alice said. "The principle of

capitalism is that those who take a financial risk by invest-ing in a company are the ones who earn the most if it suc-ceeds. It's the remuneration for their risk-taking, thanks to which the company is able to develop. The value of the shares goes up, you know, if the company develops success-fully, because then the risk seems weaker and the number of people wanting to invest increases. As for the dividend, it's just the distribution of profits to the shareholders. For there to be dividends, the company has to be in good health."

"Yes, in theory," I agreed. "But in practice the system is completely distorted. Now the shareholders who are really concerned about investing in the long-term development of the company are few and far between. Most of the share-holders either want to make a killing fast by selling their shares as soon as the value has gone up enough, or they hold enough shares to influence the company's decisions. And believe me, even the large shareholders aren't really interested in the company's development but only in mak-ing sure it can pay fat dividends, even if that jeopardizes future growth."

"And you think that's the game Dunker and his henchmen are playing—serving the shareholders' inter-ests at the expense of the company's?"

"Yes."

"Even so," Alice argued, "it's Dunker's firm; he was the founder. I find it hard to imagine he'd favor a course of ac-tion that would slowly destroy it."

"It's not really his firm anymore. Since he took it public, he only holds eight percent of the shares. It's as if he had sold it."

Alice pulled a face. "Yes, but he's remained at the head of the company. So he must love it all the same."

"He's not a sentimental person," I reminded her. "No, I think his staying at the helm is part of an agreement between him and the two major shareholders, who bought stock at the initial public offering."

Arthus set down our turkey and left us to greet another regular customer.

"Countess, at your service!" we heard him say.

Alice shook her head. "Poor Arthus. However far back my family tree may go, there are only peasants, yokels, servants. And, you know, the nobility was abolished in 1790."

"Yes, but Arthus seems to have reestablished it!"

The turkey in yellow wine was delicious. This type of dish was enough to keep even the most cornflakes- and Big-Mac-fed American on French soil.

"Did you know Tonero?" asked Alice between two mouthfuls.

"The man who resigned shortly after my arrival?"

"Yes. He was the best consultant. A very clever guy. And a salesman without equal. He knew his worth and tried to negotiate a raise."

"They refused, if my memory serves me right."

"Yes, but he didn't back down. He prepared a dossier to prove that if they refused, his resignation would cost them more than his raise. He calculated the cost of recruiting and training his replacement, how long the replacement would be paid before he was really operational, and so on. In fact, it was a no-brainer. It would cost them less to give Tonero a raise than to let him go. And yet, that's what they did. Do you know why?"

"A question of pride? Not to back down on their decision?"

"Not even," Alice said. "They coldly explained that, if they started to let wage costs go up, it would show up right away in the projected budget, and the share price would be affected. On the other hand, most of the cost of recruiting his successor would appear under *Fees* and *Training,* and the stock exchange is far less sensitive to those cost centers."

"That's ridiculous."

"In the Training division, it's not much better. Before, the courses used to finish at 6 P.M. Now they're over by 5."

"Why?" I asked her.

"You want the reason given to the client or the one dictated by business?"

"Go on . . ."

"On a pedagogical level, it's fundamental, 'Mister Client, sir. Our research shows that a slight reduction in hours improves the training by optimizing its absorption by the course participant.'"

"And the reality?"

"The trainer has to be on the phone by 5:05 P.M., canvassing new clients. Understand, by 6 P.M. nobody is available anymore."

I took a sip of wine. "Talking about unfair practices, quite by chance I discovered that one of our colleagues ratted on a candidate, telling his company he was leaving before he had resigned."

"Oh, haven't you been informed?"

"What do you mean?"

"It was the day you were absent. Dunker came along to the weekly business meeting. He hinted that there was good business to be done that way."

"You're joking."

"Not at all."

"Mark Dunker, our CEO, is inviting his consultants to indulge in that sort of practice? It's revolting!"

"He didn't explicitly tell us to do it. But he made it understood."

I looked at the gray sky through the window. The rain was beginning to fall.

"You know, even if it does us good to get it off our chest," I said, "it still depresses me. I need to believe in what I'm doing. To get out of bed in the morning, I have to feel that my work serves a purpose, even if it's not directly connected to some noble cause. At the very least, I want to be able to feel the satisfaction of a job well done. But if we're supposed to do any old thing, at top speed, just to enrich shareholders, who aren't even interested in the company, then it doesn't make sense anymore. I need my work to have meaning."

"You're an idealist, Alan."

"Yes, probably."

"That's all well and good, but you're living in the wrong times. We're surrounded by cynics, and you have to be a cynic yourself to survive."

"I . . . I don't agree. Or rather, I refuse to give in to that view. Otherwise, there's no point to anything. I can't accept the idea that my life amounts to working just to buy food, put a roof over my head, and go out every now and then. It would be absolutely meaningless."

"How are my little turkeys?" asked Arthus, looking at our plates, confident of the success of his dish.

"Don't be so familiar," Alice told him, pretending to be offended.

He walked away laughing.

"I need a job," I continued, "that brings something to others, even if it doesn't change the face of the universe. I want to go to bed at night telling myself that my day has been useful, that I've made a contribution."

"You'll have to face facts, Alan. You can't change the world."

I put my fork down. Even my turkey with yellow wine didn't tempt me anymore.

I saw Arthus kissing a woman's hand. He lived in a world he had created himself.

"Yes, we *can* change the world," I said emphatically. "I'm convinced each one of us can. As long as we don't throw in the towel, don't give up on what we think is right, don't allow our values to be trampled on. Otherwise, we're party to what happens."

"Fine words," agreed Alice. "But in practice, they're not much use. It's not because you decide to maintain your integrity that you'll stop others from behaving badly."

I looked at Alice. It's strange; I had the feeling that even if she was trying to prove that my efforts were futile, deep down, she wanted me to be right. Perhaps she no longer had hope, but all she wanted was to hope again.

I started to daydream, letting my eyes wander over the restaurant walls. They came to rest on one of the maxims that Arthus had put up. It was a quotation attributed to Gandhi: "We must be the change we want to see in the world."

"WHAT'S CERTAIN IS that change won't come from others!"

Yves Dubreuil leaned back in his armchair and put his feet up on his desk.

I like the smell of leather and old books, smells I associated with this place where, for a whole day, I had confided in him when we first met. The soft evening light filtering through the trees of his garden accentuated the English atmosphere of the room. Dubreuil was swirling the ice cubes around in his bourbon, as was his habit.

"It's my conviction," he went on, "that all change must come from inside oneself, not from outside. Neither an organization nor a government nor a new boss nor a trade union nor a new partner will change your life. Besides, look at politics: Every time people have counted on someone to change their life, did it work? Think of Mitterrand in 1981, Chirac in 1995, Obama in 2008. Every time, people were disappointed. Afterward, they thought they'd been mistaken about the man, that they'd made a bad choice. In fact, that's not the problem. The reality is that nobody but you will change your life. That's why you've got to take control yourself.

"Mind you," he continued, "I think Gandhi's thought went beyond individual considerations, personal expectations of change. I think he was referring to the changes that everyone would like to see in society generally, and he probably meant that it is much more powerful to embody the path oneself and be a model for others than simply to denounce and criticize."

"Yes, I understand," I said. "The idea is interesting, but my becoming a model of equilibrium won't change anything at all with regard to what my company demands of me, nor will it make my boss start to respect me."

"Yes it will, in a way," Dubreuil countered. "If the fact that your boss doesn't respect you makes you suffer, then don't wait for him to change of his own accord. You've got to learn how to make him respect you. See what you can change about yourself that will make you more respected: your relative positioning, perhaps; the way you talk; the way you communicate your results. Perhaps by not letting inappropriate remarks go unchallenged. Managers who go in for moral bullying don't attack all their employees, and their choice of victim isn't random."

"You're not going to say it's the victim's fault if they're bullied!"

"No, I'm not saying that. It's not their fault, of course, and you can't even say they bring it on without realizing. No, I'm just saying they have a way of behaving, a way of being that makes the bullying *possible*. Their torturer feels that if he attacks this person, he will succeed in having a really negative impact on them, whereas it wouldn't necessarily work with others."

"That's horrible!"

"Yes."

"What makes a person end up in this category?"

"It's complicated. There may be several elements, but the most decisive, no doubt, is that they lack self-esteem. If they aren't sufficiently convinced of their value deep down, they present a flaw that certain types spot at once. Then the bully only has to press where it hurts."

I suddenly needed air.

"Could we open a window?"

He got up and opened the window wide. The soft, warm air, full of moisture from the tall trees, filled the room, bringing us the calming scents of summer evenings. I could hear the gentle cheeping of birds hidden in the foliage of the tall plane trees, while the majestic branches of the century-old cedar calmly swayed.

"I wonder if . . . I think that . . . I'm perhaps a little lacking in self-esteem. In fact, it's not that I don't like myself, it's not that, and in any case I feel . . . normal, but it's true that I'm easily thrown off when I'm being blamed or criticized."

"I think so, too," Dubreuil said. "Next time, I'll give you a task to develop your self-esteem, your self-confidence, so you'll be stronger deep down."

I wondered if I wouldn't have done better to keep quiet.

"To get back to the point, I believe that you can change your manager's opinion and attitude by changing yourself, but that's not going to change the course of events in the company. That would require you to know how to communicate well. But I'm convinced that you could convince your managers, who you complain about all the time, to change their opinion on certain points. You should be able to influence them and gain progress on certain fronts."

"It won't be easy."

"You say that because you don't as yet know how to go about it. And don't forget that when a situation really doesn't suit you, you can always move to a different company. If you knew the number of people dissatisfied with their job, who complain about it and stay put. Human beings are afraid of change, of novelty, and they very often prefer to remain where it's familiar, even if that's very unpleasant, than to leave it for a new situation that they don't know.

"It's Plato's cave," Dubreuil said. "Plato described people who had lived all their lives in a very dark cave that they had never left. The cave was their universe, and despite it being murky, it was familiar and therefore reassuring. They obstinately refused to set foot outside because not knowing the exterior world, they imagined it to be hostile, dangerous. Consequently, it was impossible for them to discover that this unknown space was, in fact, filled with sun, beauty, freedom.

"Lots of people today live in Plato's cave without realizing it. They are scared stiff of the unknown and refuse any change that affects them personally. They have ideas, plans, dreams but never carry them out, paralyzed by a thousand unfounded fears, bound hand and foot by shackles they alone have the key to. The key is hanging around their neck, but they'll never grab hold of it.

"I believe life itself is made up of change, of movement. There's no sense in clinging to the status quo. Only the dead are immobile. It's in our interest not just to accept change but to initiate it, so that we can evolve in a way that suits us."

Dubreuil poured himself a splash of bourbon and added some ice cubes that clinked in his glass.

I had a sudden inspiration. "Speaking of change, there is one I would really like, but I can't make happen, even though I'm the only one concerned: I want to stop smoking. Could you do something?"

"It depends. Tell me a bit more. Why do you want to stop?"

"For the same reasons as everyone: It's filthy, and it slowly kills you."

"Right. So what's stopping you from giving it up?"

"To be honest, I like it. It's difficult to give up something you enjoy. I would miss it, especially in times of stress, when it helps me unwind."

"Okay, then imagine there exists something else that's

really good, that's nice to take and relieves stress into the bargain. You can use it whenever you like. Imagine. In those circumstances, you'd easily stop smoking?"

"Perhaps. . . ."

"That's not a very convincing reply. Imagine: You've got this magic substance that brings you pleasure and helps you unwind whenever you need it. Do cigarettes give you anything else?"

"No."

"So, what's to stop you giving up in those circumstances?"

As hard as I imagined a miracle substance that would give me pleasure and relaxation on demand, something upset me about giving up cigarettes. What? What could it be? It was as if I could vaguely feel the answer without being able to express it. It took me a long time before it came out, and then it seemed self-evident.

"Freedom."

"Freedom?"

"Yes, freedom. Even if I want to give up tobacco, there is such social pressure to give it up that I feel as if it wouldn't really be my choice anymore, so I'd be losing my freedom if I stopped smoking."

"You'd lose your freedom?"

"Everyone's rabbiting on about smoking, saying 'You should stop,' so that if I did, I would feel like I'd given in to pressure, submitted to the will of others."

A smile crossed his face.

"Okay. I'll send you my instructions. You must follow them to the letter. As usual."

I felt a draft behind me and turned around. Catherine had opened the door partway and slipped into the room. She sat down in a corner silently and gave me a little smile.

That's when it caught my eye—a gray notebook, quite

big, laid on the desk. On the cover, I could read my name upside down, written in block letters in black ink and underlined with a rapid but firm stroke. Did Dubreuil have a whole notebook on me? I had a burning desire to read it. What did it contain? The list of the trials he was going to impose on me? Notes about me, about our encounters?

"Right," Dubreuil resumed. "Let's take stock of where you are overall. You've learned to show disagreement, to express your wishes and desires, and to assert yourself in your relations with others."

"In sum, yes."

"Now—and this goes back to what we were just saying—you must learn to communicate better with others. It's fundamental. We're not alone on earth. We inevitably relate to others and interact with them, and we don't always set about it very well. There are useful things to know in order to be appreciated and respected by others, and have good relations."

There was something I didn't like about the way he put it.

"I don't want to apply techniques to communicate better. I want to stay myself and not have to say or do special things to have good relations."

He looked at me, taken aback.

"In that case, why did you agree to learn language?"

"Pardon?"

"Yes, you speak French, even English. Why did you agree to learn those languages?"

"That's different."

"How? You weren't born speaking them. You learned them. You learned the rules, and now you apply them in order to express yourself. Do you have the feeling of not being yourself when you speak?"

"No, of course not."

"Are you sure? To remain really natural, perhaps you'd prefer expressing yourself in onomatopoeia, in sounds that stand for words—plop, splash, bang—or by making bellow-ing noises."

"But I learned language when I was a child. It makes a big difference."

"So does that mean that what we learn before a certain age is part of us and what is learned after that age is artificial and we're not ourselves when we use it?"

"I don't know, but I don't feel natural when I don't do things as they come to me spontaneously."

"Shall I tell you what I think?"

"What?"

"It's still resistance to change! That's the main difference between the child and the adult: The child wants to evolve. The adult does all he can not to change."

"Perhaps."

"I'll tell you my opinion."

He leaned slightly forward and spoke in a confidential tone.

"When you don't want to change anymore, it's because you're slowly beginning to die."

I swallowed hard. Catherine started to cough. Outside, a bird gave a cry that sounded like mocking laughter.

"I have realized a disturbing fact," he went on. "In most people, the will not to change their behavior appears some-where between twenty and twenty-five. Do you know what that age corresponds to biologically?"

"No."

"It's the age at which the brain finishes developing."

"So perhaps it's not by chance," I said, "that that's the age when we don't want to change anymore. Perhaps it's natural."

"Yes, but that's not the end of it. For a long time we

thought that the number of brain cells diminished from then on, until the end of our life. But it has recently been demonstrated that we can continue to grow them as adults."

"You've cheered me up. I was beginning to feel old."

"Specifically, the process of regeneration can happen as a result of many factors, including apprenticeship. In short, if you decide to carry on learning and developing, you stay young. Body and mind are closely linked. Do you want proof?"

"Yes."

"Official statistics from the Department of Health show that the moment most people retire, their health declines sharply. Why do you think that is? As long as they're working, they're more or less forced to adapt, to develop at least a bit in order not to be thought of as has-beens. As soon as they retire, they stop making an effort. They are fixed in their ways and decline sets in."

"That's cheerful."

"To stay alive, you have to stay *in life*—in other words, to follow the movement of life, to develop. I know a woman who started playing the piano at eighty-one. That's wonderful! Everyone knows it takes years of study to play piano properly. That means that at eighty-one, she thinks it's still worth investing a few years to learn to play a musical instrument! I'll bet you any amount that she'll live a lot longer.

"If you want to stay young all your life, continue developing, learning, discovering, and don't imprison yourself in habits that cause sclerosis of the mind, or in the numbing comfort of what you already know how to do."

"Right. So what did you want to tell me about relationships?"

"Well, I'm going to tell you a secret. A secret that will allow you to relate to anyone, even someone from a different culture than yours. It will immediately make that person want to engage with you, listen to what you have to say, respect your point of view, even if it's different from theirs, and talk to you sincerely."

He took a sheet of ivory-colored paper and a black-laquered pen and started writing with a sweeping movement, the gold nib noisily scratching the paper. When he finished he held the paper out to me. The wet ink shone as if the paper refused to soak up a secret that was not meant for it.

Embrace your neighbor's world, and he will open himself up to you.

I read it, reread it, and remained lost in thought. I liked the formula; it was like a magical inscription whose meaning still eluded me.

"Do you have the operating instructions that go with that?" I asked him.

He smiled. "If we were remaining on a purely mental level, I would express the secret differently. I would say something along the lines of 'Try to understand the other person before trying to be understood.' But it goes beyond that. You can't sum up the communication between two people as a simple intellectual exchange. It takes place on other levels as well, at the same time."

"On other levels?"

"Yes, in particular on the emotional level. The emotions you feel in the presence of the other are perceived, often unconsciously, by him. If you don't like him, for example, even if you succeed in hiding it perfectly, he will feel it one way or another. Your *intention* is also something that the other feels."

"You mean what we're thinking about during the conversation?"

"Yes, but not necessarily consciously. An example: office

meetings. Most of the time in those meetings, when some-one asks a question, he doesn't really have any intention of getting an answer."

"What do you mean?"

"His intention can be just to show that he can ask intel-ligent questions. Or to make the person he's talking with uncomfortable in front of the others, or to prove that he's interested in the subject, or to claim a leadership role in the group. And quite often, it's the intention behind the question more than the question itself that we pick up. When someone's trying to trap us, we know it, don't we, even if there's nothing in their words we could objectively reproach them for?"

I nodded.

"I think things also happen on a spiritual level," Du-breuil said, "even if it's more difficult to demonstrate any-thing in this area."

"Okay, so what do I do with your beautiful magical for-mula? How do I apply it?"

"Embracing your neighbor's world involves, first of all, ripening your own wish to enter into his world. That means becoming interested enough in him to want to experience what it is to be in his skin. It means taking pleasure in try-ing to think like him, to speak like him, to move like him, to believe what he believes. When you manage that, you'll be in a position to feel quite accurately what the other is feeling and to really understand that person. You will seem to be in sync with each other, on the same wavelength. You can, of course, return to your own position. But you will still preserve a quality of communication that is beneficial to you both. And you will notice that the other will try to understand *you*. He'll start to take an interest in *your* world, moved in particular by a desire to make such a quality re-lationship last."

"This is all a bit weird. Don't forget I trained as an accountant. It's not by chance, you know, that I'm very rational."

"I'm going to try and make you feel this for yourself. We're going to try an experiment that relates to one of the aspects I've just listed. I need to prepare a few things," he said, getting up. "I need to go and get two chairs. We can't do anything in these armchairs; we're too cramped."

He left the office, followed by Catherine. I heard them walking down the corridor. I felt divided: Part of me, drawn to these rather mysterious things about human relationships, was hopeful. Another part of me, more down to earth, was rather dubious.

My eyes suddenly alighted on the notebook. The notebook . . . It was so tempting to grab hold of it and glance inside. The noise of their footsteps died away. They must have gone into another room. It was now or never. I jumped up. The floor creaked under my feet. I froze. Silence. I went around the desk and stretched out my hand. Voices, footsteps. They were coming back! Damn! I went back to my chair, but the floor creaked so loudly that they must have heard. *Don't sit down,* I thought. *Pretend to be looking at the bookcase, the books.*

They came in. I remained focused on the bookshelves.

"We'll put them there," Dubreuil said.

I turned around. They were placing the chairs facing each other, less than a yard apart.

"Sit down here," he said, pointing to one of them.

I sat down. He waited a second, and then sat down on the other chair.

"I want you," he said, "to tell me how you feel when I'm opposite you like this."

"How I feel? Well, nothing special. I feel good."

"Right. Then close your eyes."

I did as he asked, wondering what he was going to do to me.

"When you open them again in a few moments, I want you to be aware of what you feel and to tell me how that has changed. Go on, open your eyes."

He was still sitting on the chair, but he had changed position. Now both his hands were on his knees, which wasn't the case before. What did I feel? Slightly strange, but difficult to say exactly.

"I would say I feel strange."

"Do you feel better or not as good as before?"

"What do you mean exactly?"

"When you get on the elevator with someone you barely know, you generally feel less comfortable about talking with them than if you met them on the street, agreed? That's what I'm talking about. I want you to evaluate your communicational comfort in relation to my position."

"Right. That's clearer."

"So, I'll ask the question again: If you had to hold a conversation with me, would you feel more or less comfortable since I've changed my position?"

"Less."

"Okay. Close your eyes again. There you are. Now open them."

He had changed position again. His chin was resting in the palm of his hand, his elbow resting on his thigh.

"I feel . . . how shall I say? . . . observed. Not very pleasant."

"Right. Close your eyes again . . . Okay, you can look. How do you feel now?"

"Much better!" This time he was slumped down in the chair with both his forearms resting on his thighs.

"Let's start again."

He took up a dozen or so positions in succession.

With two or three of them I felt decidedly better than with the others.

"Catherine?" he said, turning toward her.

"It's quite definitive," she said to me. "Each time Yves adopts the same position as you, you say you feel better. As soon as he assumes a different position from yours, you feel less at ease."

I became aware of how I was sitting. "You mean that each time I felt good, it was because he sat like me?"

"Yes," she said.

"This is crazy! Is it like this for everyone?"

"Yes. To be precise," added Catherine, "it's like that for the great majority of people but there are a few exceptions."

"Stop quibbling, Catherine! It makes no difference."

"But how can it be explained?" I asked.

"It's a natural phenomenon that was discovered by some American researchers," Dubreuil explained. "I think they began by showing that when two people are communicating well, when they're getting along, they unconsciously synchronize with each other and end up adopting similar postures. We all notice it. For example, when you see two lovers in a restaurant, it's not unusual for them to be in the same position, whether it's with their elbows on the table, or their heads in their hands, or leaning backward or forward, or fiddling with the cutlery."

"That's astonishing."

"And then these researchers showed that you could re-create that feeling of resonance by reversing the process. If you consciously synchronize yourself with someone, it will help both of you feel good with each other, which increases the quality of communication. But for this to work, it's not enough just to use it as a technique. You have to sincerely want to embrace the other's world."

"Obviously, it's unsettling," I said, "and you're going

to think I'm putting up resistance again. But if you have to study the gestures of the person you're talking to and adapt yourself accordingly, you'll lose all sense of naturalness!"

He gave a little amused smile.

"Can I tell you something?"

"What?"

"You do it already—naturally."

"Not at all!" I insisted.

"I can assure you, you do."

"Come off it! I knew nothing about all this five minutes ago!"

His smile broadened. "What do you do when you want to relate to a young child of two or three?"

"It doesn't happen every day."

"Remember the last time."

"Well, I talked to the super's son, perhaps a couple of weeks ago. I asked him to tell me what he had done during the day at nursery school."

As I replied to Dubreuil, I became aware of a truth that was all the more astounding for being fresh in my memory: In order to talk to little Marco, I had crouched down, bringing myself down to his height, and I had naturally adopted a soft voice and chosen the simplest words possible, the closest to his vocabulary. I had done all this *naturally.* I had made no special effort. I had just had a sincere desire to get him to tell me what a French nursery school was like.

"And do you know what the most incredible thing is?" Dubreuil continued. "When you manage to create that quality of communication and maintain it for a period of time, it's such a precious experience that each person unconsciously does everything to make it last. Just consider the gestures, for example. If one person changes position even slightly, the other follows suit without realizing it."

"You mean that if I mirror someone's posture for a while and then change position, the other person will change to match mine?"

"Yes. But remember, the main thing is to be sincere in your intention to relate to the other person."

"This is absolutely staggering!" I was so excited by this revelation. I felt as if until now I had been deaf and blind to aspects of my exchanges with others. It was amazing to discover that beyond our words there are heaps of things going on that we aren't even aware of, messages exchanged by our bodies. And Dubreuil had hinted at even more levels of communication.

I begged him to tell me more, but he said I had seen enough for today. He and Catherine accompanied me to the door. I was still having difficulty figuring out Catherine's personality and the role she played for Dubreuil. She was one of those people who says little, wrapping themselves in a cloak of mystery.

I had already left the château and walked a few steps across the garden toward the gate, watching Stalin out of the corner of my eye, when Dubreuil called me back.

"Alan!"

I turned around.

"Come back! I almost forgot to give you your mission."

I froze. No, there was no escape.

I went inside and followed him across the hall, our steps ringing out on the cold marble. We went into a room I didn't know. It had the atmosphere of an old London club. Bookcases entirely covered the walls up to the ceiling, which had ornate mouldings. Two chandeliers, each with a dozen lights covered by brandy-colored shades, gave off a warm, intimate glow. Mahogany stepladders leaned against the shelves. Persian rugs covered a large part of the parquet floor. There were deep armchairs upholstered in dark leather, along with a pair of padded club chairs and an immense chesterfield sofa.

Dubreuil picked up a big book. Catherine remained at the door, watching us attentively.

"Give me a number between zero and a thousand."

"A number? Why?"

"Just give me a number!"

"Three hundred twenty-eight."

"Three hundred twenty-eight. Let's see, let's see . . ."

He had opened the book and was turning the pages, obviously looking for the one with the number 328 on it.

"Here we are. Good. Now, give me another, let's say between zero and twenty."

"What is this?"

"Come on!"

"Twelve."

I looked more closely at the book. It was a dictionary, and his finger was going down the words on the page.

". . . Ten, eleven, twelve. *Marionette.* That's quite good. You could have been less lucky. It could have been an adverb, for example."

"Okay, are you going to tell me what this is about?"

"It's very simple. You told me you had two bosses at work, yes?"

"Yes. That's to say, I have one manager I report to and then his boss, who often intervenes."

"Good. You're going to go and see them both, in turn. Find a pretext to get them talking, and your mission consists of getting each of them to say the word *marionette* once."

"*What?*"

"And there is one rule: You absolutely must not say the word yourself, or point to a photo or any object representing a marionette.

"What's the point of all this?"

"Best of luck!"

I took my time leaving the château, lingering on the steps to look up at the stars. It is rare to be able to see them in Paris. The sky usually seems opaque in the glow of the City of Light.

I was a little annoyed not to see the point of the task Dubreuil was giving me. In the past, I had certainly balked at following his directives because they required considerable effort from me, but I had always understood their usefulness. This time, I couldn't see it. And I hated the way he tended not to answer my questions, simply ignoring them! It was as if, having already gotten my promise to do what he said, he wasn't going to tire himself convincing me. And when would this little game come to an end? Granted, he seemed sincere in his desire to pass on certain information, to get me to move on in life, but despite this, it was getting harder and harder to feel myself being managed in this way, even if it was by someone whose intentions were good. And were they really? He must have a good reason for taking care of me; he must be getting something back. But what?

I thought of the notebook. A notebook entirely devoted to me, probably containing the answers to my questions. It was a glaring reminder that my situation wasn't *normal*. I couldn't continue closing my eyes to what might be motivating a stranger to take an interest in me and advise me, not to mention dictate to me—all the while keeping a firm hold on me through the rules of a promise he had extracted from me under dreadful circumstances. A shiver ran down my spine.

It was really a shame I hadn't had the time to look at the notebook during the few minutes when Dubreuil was out of the room. How frustrating! I'd missed an opportunity that might not be repeated. I absolutely must find a way to get hold of that notebook. Suppose I came back one night? With this heat, the windows probably stayed open.

A metallic noise brought me back to my senses. Stalin was running toward me, dragging his heavy chain behind him. I leapt to one side, just as the chain tightened, amid a storm of barking. His eyes wild, his fangs wet with slaver, Stalin answered my question: No, I would not be coming back at night. The night was his. Once released, he reigned as master over the grounds.

• • •

Catherine sat down on the chesterfield. Dubreuil offered her a Monte Christo, which, as usual, she refused.

"So, how do you think he's doing?" he asked, picking up a cigar cutter.

Catherine's eyes turned slowly toward the nearest lamp, while she reflected. She took her time before answering. "Rather well, but I could feel he was a bit upset toward the end. To be frank, I myself didn't understand the meaning of the last task you gave him."

"Make his bosses say a word chosen at random?"

"Yes."

Dubreuil struck a large match, which burst into flame. He brought it to his cigar, which he steadily revolved as he puffed at it. He leaned back in the deep armchair. The leather squeaked as he crossed his legs.

"The problem with Alan is that it's not enough to show him how to communicate well. That's not the way to get anywhere in his firm, and that's what he'd like. There's something that would hold him back, in any case."

"What?"

"He's too used to being dominated. He's gradually learning to resist, to oppose. That's fine. But it's not enough. Far from it. Knowing how to resist and knowing how to obtain what you want are two different things. To get there, there's a precondition."

"A precondition?"

"Developing in yourself the conviction that you are capable of it."

"You mean that if Alan isn't convinced deep down that he is capable of getting something from his managers, he won't get it, even if he conscientiously applies the best communication techniques in the world?"

"Exactly! When you are intimately convinced that you can influence other people's decisions, you always succeed in the end, even if you're slightly shaky at first. You find a way. On the other hand, if you don't believe in your ability, you're going to stop at the first obstacle, and you'll interpret it as a proof of the pointlessness of what you're doing."

He lifted the cigar to his mouth.

"And so you asked him to amuse himself getting his bosses to say a specific word, just to get him to discover that he is capable of having an influence on them?"

"You've understood everything. I want him to believe in his ability to have an influence."

"Interesting."

Catherine suddenly looked up as an idea occurred to her. "You didn't really select that word at random, did you? You chose *marionette* so that Alan would unconsciously project himself into the role of the person who holds the strings, isn't that so?"

By way of an answer, Dubreuil just smiled.

"Very clever, Igor."

He took a long puff on his cigar.

Marc Dunker, CEO of Dunker Consulting, was an imposing figure. Well over 6 feet tall and 210 pounds, he was a
heavyweight in the recruitment world in France.

He came from a village in the provinces, in the heart of
the Beaujolais region. Cattle dealers, the Dunkers were not
well respected by the local inhabitants, who regarded their
profession as a necessary evil. The family had more money
than the farmers around them, many of whom felt that
this money had been made at their expense, without the
Dunkers having to suffer, like them, during the lean years
when the price of beef fell.

Young Marc went to the local school. Proud to be the
son of the richest man in the village, in other respects he felt
excluded. He didn't feel sorry for himself because of that; on
the contrary, it fed his aggression. At the slightest remark
from his schoolmates, he would pick a fight.

His mother suffered a lot more from being ostracized.
While her husband enjoyed an envied position, she was
merely subjected to its negative fallout, the subtly hostile
looks and unspoken resentment of the women she passed
in the village streets. After years of bitterness, she finally
cracked, and breaking with the tradition established by generations of Dunkers, the family moved to Lyon, far from
malicious village gossip. Marc's father had to travel miles
each day to return to the village. Marc viewed the move as

a capitulation and despised his father for having given in to his wife's unspoken demand.

Marc's mother's satisfaction with the move was only temporary. She became disillusioned the day she realized that she and her family were seen as inferior by their neighbors, who were largely white-collar workers. Preferring to be rejected out of jealousy rather than out of contempt, Marc, too, suffered from this new exclusion, and developed a desire for revenge.

He was an average student, earning a diploma from a technical school when he was 20. He worked for nearly ten years selling agricultural goods, using negotiating skills no doubt fixed in his genes. He changed companies three or four times, each time increasing his salary substantially. He used the same ploy every time—deceiving the recruitment consultant about the post he was leaving, claiming responsibilities that weren't part of his job but that he had taken on himself.

He concluded from this that consultants knew nothing about their work and were easy to deceive. One day, Marc's employer revealed the amount of the fee he had paid to recruit him. To Marc, it was an astronomical sum for a job that seemed to be very close to his father's. He decided it was easier to convince a company of the supposed qualities of a candidate than to sell a farmer on the physical attributes of a cow—assets the farmer could easily check for himself.

Six months later, Marc went into business for himself. After completing a crash course in recruitment methods, he rented a one-room office in the center of Lyon and put up a sign: *Marc Dunker, Recruitment Consultant.* What he took away from the course was that his flair was worth more than any of their techniques for selecting a candidate. And the fact is, he seldom failed. He was a natural. He had an intuitive sense of people and companies, and which candidates were going to fit a post.

The first clients were the hardest to find. Without references, he wasn't credible. When people pointed that out to him, he became strangely aggressive. He started lying, inventing prestigious clients for himself, tossing around the names of companies whose business he had supposedly turned down on the grounds that they were too small to be worthy of his services. This attitude paid off, and he got his first contracts, quickly followed by others.

Marc Dunker's new trade fitted him like a glove. The middle-class people who had looked down on his family in the past now depended on him for jobs. He felt feared and respected. People were eating out of his hand. He would have liked to control the whole recruitment market in Lyon, just to increase their dependence on him.

All his success, however, was not enough to repair his wounded ego. Something inside him was always pushing him to do more to develop his business and to gain more power and authority in his field. Always a hard worker, he redoubled his efforts to establish his company.

By the end of the first year, Dunker already employed three consultants. But instead of being satisfied, he was driven to go even further. Six months later, Dunker opened an office in Paris and immediately moved to the capital. At that point, he renamed the company Dunker Consulting. After that, he opened a new office in a provincial town every three months on average.

Dunker measured his success by the number of his employees, his obsession being to increase his staff. He derived great satisfaction from "multiplying the flock," as he liked to put it, not realizing that the colloquialisms he used revealed the provincial origins he otherwise carefully hid. His personal value seemed to be intimately linked to the number of people he had under his command, his power measured by the extent of his troops.

The meteoric rise of his company allowed Dunker to establish himself abroad, and when he opened his first office in another European capital, he felt he was conquering the world.

Two years later, in the supreme consecration, he decided to go public.

13

EVERY DAY FOR a week, I had arrived at the office with my copy of *Closer* under my arm. The sidelong glances of my colleagues, obvious to begin with, had given way to complete indifference. I had to admit that my relations with those around me hadn't changed at all. Nonetheless, I still felt a certain embarrassment, even if it was diminishing. It would take me some time to be really free, according to Dubreuil's definition.

In the apartment, I was making fewer efforts to be quiet than before. I had accepted that it was okay to make a *normal* amount of noise, which nonetheless didn't fail to provoke almost daily visits from Madame Blanchard. I no longer sought to avoid her visits, but they still managed to annoy me prodigiously. It seemed as if nothing could stop her from harassing me. Having been very patient, I now openly expressed my exasperation, opening the door just a crack to show her that she was disturbing me. But she would come right up to the opening as if to force her way in. Frowning, with an accusatory expression on her face, she would harangue me in her shrill, moralizing voice.

The day after my most recent visit to Dubreuil I had just entered my office building and was waiting for the elevator with two colleagues from another department when I received a text message from Dubreuil: *"Have a cigarette right away."*

What was that about? He wanted me to have a cigarette?

The elevator doors opened. My colleagues dived in.

"Don't wait for me," I said.

Why was Dubreuil asking me to smoke when my goal was to stop? I went back out to the street and lit up. Was he going soft in the head? As I smoked, I was gazing at the passersby hurrying to work, when I saw a man who looked like Vladi standing motionless in the crowd. I leaned forward to try and get a better look, and he immediately turned around.

"Vladi! Vladi!" I called.

The man disappeared from sight.

I felt a certain unease. I was almost certain it was Vladi. Was he following me? But why? Surely Dubreuil wasn't asking him to make sure I was keeping my promise? That would be insane. What did he care, after all. Or should I be seriously worried and try to find out why he was taking an interest in me?

I went back into the lobby, a knot in my stomach.

In the corridor on my floor, I passed Luc Fausteri's office. He was already at work, which meant that he must have shortened his morning run. Most unusually, his door was open. Generally, he preferred to shut himself in, to isolate himself as far as possible from the members of his team.

This open door was an opportunity not to be missed. I had a mission to carry out. *Be brave,* I told myself. It would be all the harder to get Luc to say *marionette* because there was nobody in the world less chatty than him.

I said hello as I went in. He waited until I was less than a yard from him before looking up. We shook hands, but that didn't elicit even the slightest smile.

I tried to strike up a conversation, reminding myself of Dubreuil's famous secret. God, how hard it is to embrace a world you don't like. "The share's at one hundred and twenty-eight, this morning," I said with false cheer. "It has

127

gone up point two percent in just one day's trading, and nearly one percent this week."

"Yes."

He was obviously in brilliant form. I must fuel the conversation, talk with enthusiasm, and show my keen interest in the subject. If he felt a meeting of minds, he would open up to me.

"What's surprising is that it's gone up fourteen percent since the beginning of the year, whereas our half-yearly results are up twenty-three percent. It's not very logical."

"No."

"The stock is obviously underpriced . . ."

"Yes."

"In fact, it's not representative of the real value of the company."

"No."

This was uphill work. But I had to carry on, come what may. I couldn't allow a break in the conversation.

"It's a real shame. It would be better if the stock price followed our results since they're good."

Fausteri didn't even take the trouble to reply but merely looked at me as if he didn't understand how someone could spout such drivel.

I felt a hint of shame. Just a hint. After all, he already thought I was a faithful reader of *Closer*. There was no risk of disappointing him. On we go.

"It's a good share. It ought to do brilliantly."

He frowned. I went on, doubling my enthusiasm. "If I were a trader, I'd put everything on it."

He began to look sorry, even distressed, shutting himself in behind his silence.

Right. Let's change tactics. *Ask questions,* I thought. "How do you explain this gap between our results and the share price?"

A few seconds of silence, during which Fausteri remained perfectly motionless. He was probably gathering his strength and courage to communicate with the village idiot.

"There are several reasons," he finally said. "First of all, the financial markets are less concerned with past results than with future prospects."

"But our future prospects are good. Larcher tells us so every Monday morning!"

"Then, too, the stock exchange is affected by psychological factors," he said with slight contempt.

"Psychological factors?"

He cast around for inspiration. He obviously derived no pleasure from being a teacher.

"Fears, rumors. And then there's Fisherman."

"Fisherman?"

"He's the business columnist on *Les Echos*"—I knew enough to know that was a business daily, France's answer to *The Wall Street Journal*—"who doesn't believe in our development and says so day in, day out in his paper. That no doubt has an effect on our investors, because his opinions are influential. It makes you wonder why."

"Suppose someone is pulling his strings? Suppose Fisherman is his . . . what's the word?"

"I can't see in whose interest that would be."

For goodness' sake, why couldn't he just answer questions?

"But Fisherman has no personal interest in putting the brakes on the rise in our share price," I suggested. "And if that's not the case, there must be people pushing him to pan us in his paper. Fisherman is just their . . ."

I pretended to fish for the right word, accompanying my efforts with gestures to indicate my memory lapse.

"I'm no great fan of conspiracy theories," Fausteri muttered.

"Oh! It's so annoying," I continued. "I hate not being able to find a word! What do you call someone who is manipulated by someone else? He's his . . ."

"Look, Alan, I've got work to do."

"Just answer this question! My day will be ruined if I can't find the word."

"Concentrate on your work, and everything will be fine."

"The word's on the tip of my tongue," I insisted.

"All right, spit it out, but not in my office."

On the one occasion he was trying to be funny, I didn't feel like laughing. Quick, I had to make him reply.

"Give me the word, and I promise I'll disappear at once."

"*Puppet.*"

I looked at him, speechless.

"No, that's not it . . . another word."

"This is beginning to be annoying."

"Give me a synonym," I pleaded.

"*Pawn.* He's his pawn. Is that it?"

"No, that's not it either."

"Anyhow, it will have to do."

"Give me another synonym."

"I'm busy, Alan."

"Please."

"Good-bye, Alan."

His tone was final, and he plunged back into his file without looking up again.

I walked out of Fausteri's office slightly frustrated. Okay, I had put up a good fight. That was something. In fact, my mistake had probably been my enthusiasm. To *embrace his world,* as Dubreuil had said, it wasn't enough to bring up a subject that interested him; perhaps I should have adopted his style of communication: serious, rational, concise.

Better still, if I had enjoyed our interaction. But would that have made him talk more? Not certain. At any rate, I had come close to succeeding all the same.

I had scarcely sat down in my office when Alice came in to talk about negotiations she was carrying out with a client. We had been together about ten minutes when I recognized Fausteri's footsteps in the corridor. He walked past my office, then took a step back and stuck his head in my door, his face as impassive as ever.

"Marionette!" he said, and then walked on.

Alice turned toward me, outraged that my boss had insulted me like that.

I was radiant.

WOULD MY TASK be harder with Grégoire Larcher, Fausteri's boss? I wasn't sure. If Fausteri didn't like conversations devoid of intellectual interest, Larcher couldn't bear any that distracted him from his objectives. Each second of his time must be invested in building his success.

Nonetheless, this left an opening. As a skillful manipulator, he would occasionally agree to exchange twaddle if he felt that it would help his colleague. A fulfilled employee is a productive employee, Larcher figured, and in the end, there was a lot to be gained that way.

So I didn't have too much difficulty getting him to talk about his children. This brought us to weekends and excursions with the children, and marionettes cropped up in the conversation as naturally as could be.

Manipulating a manipulator was rather pleasurable, actually.

I got five text messages from Dubreuil during the day, each time making me go down to the street to smoke a cigarette. I still didn't understand the real reason for it.

My day finished in Alice's office, where she again confided in me her worry about the dysfunction of the company. Thomas came to say good-bye as he left, waving under our noses the latest BlackBerry he had just acquired. An irresistible urge suddenly came over me.

"I met an impressive candidate today," I said. "A great guy."

Every time anyone said anything good about someone in front of Thomas, his smile froze, as if his value was suddenly placed in peril by the other person's achievements.

"He's an ex-finance director," I continued. "Very clever and incredibly classy. A real class act!"

Alice looked at me, a little surprised by my choice of words.

I kept on. "He got out a pen to take notes. Guess what it was?"

"A Mont Blanc?" Thomas said, thinking of the pen he was always waving around in front of people.

"Bad luck. Try again."

"Go on, what was it?" he said with a forced smile.

"A Dupont. With a gold nib! Can you believe it? A *Dupont!*"

I opened my eyes wide to underline my words. Thomas's smile looked strained. I saw from Alice's expression that she understood my little game.

"A *real* Dupont?" she asked, pretending to be incredulous.

"Really."

"Wow! What a guy!" Alice said, continuing to play along.

"One thing's for sure. You don't see one of those every day," I added.

Now Alice was unstoppable. "It really gives off the image of a winner," she enthused. "In my opinion, he's not going to have any problems finding a great job."

I wondered how far we could go before Thomas would start getting suspicious.

"I'm sure all the girls fancy him," Alice said.

"You bet!" I agreed.

Now we were going too far, I figured. But Thomas just continued to look annoyed. He was so convinced that people valued him because of the objects he displayed that he was unable to see the absurdity of what we were saying. It was too close to his vision of the world.

Finally he wished us good night and left. We waited for him to be out of earshot, then burst out laughing.

It was nearly 8 P.M., and I soon left the office myself. When I got to the sidewalk, I couldn't help glancing around. Nobody seemed to be looking for me. I went down into the Métro but had to turn around and come right out again: Dubreuil was texting me to have another cigarette. The co-incidence in the timing was disturbing. I looked carefully around again. There were fewer pedestrians passing by at this late hour, but I spotted nothing out of the ordinary.

Three minutes later, I was again in the Métro. I decided to have a go at gestural synchronization, which I had ne-glected until now. I had preferred to approach the universe of the other by trying to take on his way of thinking, his worries, and his values.

A train came into the station with a screeching of wheels as shrill as the sound of chalk on a blackboard. A homeless guy slouched on a bench grunted something incomprehen-sible, spreading a strong smell of alcohol all around him. The train came to an abrupt halt in front of me, and I got on. Dubreuil had promised that his method would allow me to create a relationship with people of very different cultures and attitudes than mine. I glanced at the few passengers in the car, spotting a tall African dressed in a tracksuit and black leather jacket. The jacket was open, revealing a fish-net T-shirt through which I could see his powerful chest muscles. I sat down opposite him, and then slouched down to adopt the same posture as his. I tried to meet his gaze, but he seemed lost in space. I tried to feel what he might be feeling, the better to enter into his world. Not easy. I was, it's true, feeling a little buttoned-up in my suit. I loosened my tie and imagined I was dressed like him, with the same heavy gold chain around my neck. It was a strange sensation. He soon changed position, and I immediately did the same. I had to keep contact.

I didn't take my eyes off him. A few seconds later, he crossed his arms. I crossed mine. I wondered how long it usually took to really create a link, so that he would start mirroring my movements. I really wanted to experience that. The man stretched out his legs. I waited a moment then stretched out mine. I wasn't used to sitting slouched like this in the Métro, though I found it quite fun. Besides, I had never tried to put myself in the shoes of someone very different from myself, to behave like them and see what happened. The man put his hands on his thighs; I imitated him. He was staring straight in front of himself, but I don't think he was really seeing me. He had a fixed expression on his face, which I tried to replicate. We stayed like that for a few moments, still perfectly in synch. His gaze remained inscrutable, but it seemed to me that something was bringing us closer. I was certain he must be feeling that we were on the same wavelength. He sat up straight in the seat, and I did the same. Then he looked me right in the eye, and I could tell he was going to say something. I was ecstatic. I had managed to create a bond with a stranger and force him to open himself to me. I marveled at the power of gesture over the unconscious, the superiority of the body over the word.

The man leaned forward, his expression serious, and with a heavy African accent said, "Ya finished taking da piss, mon?"

THE NEXT MORNING, I arrived at the weekly meeting feeling quite carefree, never suspecting that I was going to live through one of the worst moments of my life, a moment that would also be the start of the most beneficial change possible.

That's life. We seldom realize at the time that the difficult moments have a hidden function: to make us grow. The angels disguise themselves as demons and deliver marvelous presents wrapped up as foul parcels. Whether it's a failure or an illness or the vicissitudes of daily life, we don't always want to accept the so-called present, nor do we always have the impulse to unwrap it and discover the hidden message inside.

The meeting room was full when I arrived. There were far more of us than usual. Once a month, the whole recruitment department came together, not just our part of it. There was an unoccupied chair next to Alice, which she was probably saving for me. I threw my *Closer* down on the table and calmly took my place. It was nice to be the last one to arrive; you felt expected.

"Look at Thomas," Alice whispered in my ear.

I looked around and spotted him.

"What's the matter?"

"Look again."

I leaned forward to get a better look and saw nothing but the haughty air he usually had. Then I saw it. I couldn't believe my eyes. A brand-new Dupont lying on the table in front of him. You couldn't miss it. Next to me, Alice was covering her mouth with her hand to keep from laughing.

"Morning, all."

The powerful voice made me jump. Marc Dunker, our CEO, had invited himself to the weekly meeting. I hadn't even noticed him when I came in. Silence fell over the room.

"I'm not going to interfere for long with your agenda," he said. "But I wanted to tell you about a new type of assessment test that I discovered on a trip to Austria, where we've just opened our eighteenth office. I know you already have a good dozen or so tools at your disposal, but this one is different, and I wanted to introduce it to you personally."

Our curiosity was aroused. What had he gone and found?

"We all know," he went on, "that it is more difficult to assess someone's character than their skills. You have all worked in the field for which you are recruiting, so you know how to ask the right questions to discover if the candidate has the necessary know-how to succeed in the given vacancy. On the other hand, it is not always obvious how to distinguish between his real talents and those he professes. I'm not even talking about the so-called shortcomings that ninety percent of your candidates claim. They all seem to be perfectionists with a tendency to work too hard, don't they? But between imaginary talents and predictable defects, it's not easy to get a precise reading of their tendencies at work. This test allows you to assess a character trait that is fundamental to many posts with responsibility, especially those that have a management function. I mean self-confidence. It's extremely difficult to measure it during recruitment. I've known people who have had so many recruitment interviews that they are very sure of themselves in that setting, whereas if you put them in a business, they turn to jelly when faced with the first colleague who winds them up a bit. You can flex your muscles at an interview but not be able to stand up when faced with your team."

"What you say is right, Marc, but most of the time, the person who lacks self-confidence in his life also lacks it in front of the recruiter."

There was a murmur among those present. The person who had just spoken was a young consultant, freshly arrived at the firm, who had come from a rival company where first names were the norm. Of course, we consultants used first names among ourselves, but our boss had never given in to this fashion for relational pseudo-proximity and expected us to address him as Mr. Dunker. It was hypocritical, but Marc Dunker cared deeply about signs of respect from his staff.

"I didn't know we were on first-name terms," Dunker said dryly.

This was his usual putdown in these circumstances. He avoided responding to the consultant and continued: "The test I'm talking about is awkward to use because it requires the presence of at least three people. But they don't have to be consultants. In practice, you can use just about anyone," he said with a sneer.

Our curiosity was aroused.

"The test is based on the idea that real self-confidence is independent of other factors. It's a personal character-istic that corresponds to a person's unshakeable faith in their own value, in their abilities, so it can't be harmed by external criticism. Conversely, unwarranted or phony self-confidence can't stand up to a hostile environment, and the person loses a considerable part of their faculties when attacked. But I've said enough. A good demonstration is worth more than a long speech! I need a volunteer."

He scanned the group, a little smile on his lips. Eyes looked at the ground or into space.

"The ideal thing would be a member of the Accountant Recruitment team, because we need someone good at math!"

Half the people there relaxed, while the other half got even tenser. The vise was tightening around us. He took his time, and I sensed he was deriving a sadistic pleasure from the suspense he was creating.

"Who's going to volunteer?" he repeated.

It was obvious that no one was going to accept such an invitation without knowing what ordeal lay in wait.

"Right. Then I'll have to choose the volunteer myself."

I think the Nazis did the same sort of thing, inveigling prisoners to take responsibility for what their torturers were about to inflict on them.

"Let's see, let's see."

I tried to look as unconcerned as possible, glancing down at the cover of my *Closer*. You could have heard a pin drop. The atmosphere was thick with tension. I felt Dunker's heavy gaze bearing down on me.

"Mr. Greenmor."

I was the volunteer. My heart skipped a beat. I had to hang on. Not weaken. He was going to make me do his pathetic test in front of all these people. Could it be revenge? Larcher had no doubt told him about our altercation at the last business meeting. Perhaps Dunker wanted to bring me back into line and remove any desire to do it again. *Stay calm*, I told myself. *Don't give in. Don't give him that pleasure.*

"Come on, Alan."

Okay, now he's calling me by my first name. To soften me up, no doubt. I got up and walked toward him. All eyes were on me. Apprehension, still palpable a few seconds ago, had given way to curiosity. In fact, they might as well have been at the theater. Or more likely the Coliseum. I looked at Dunker. *Ave Caesar, morituri te salutant.* Hail Caesar, those who are about to die salute you. No, I'm not really the gladiator type.

Dunker pointed me to a chair two yards away from him, facing the group. I sat down, trying to appear both indifferent and sure of myself. Not easy.

"This is how it works," he said, talking to the group. "First of all, it must be pointed out to the candidate that this is a game and that none of what we're going to say to him corresponds to reality. It's just for the test. It's important to tell him this, in order not to get us into trouble. The press is giving us a rough enough time as it is at the moment."

What was going on here? I could tell it was going to be no laughing matter. I had to hang in there at all costs.

"My role," he went on, "is to give Mr. Greenmor some fairly simple mental arithmetic problems."

Mental arithmetic? That was okay. I was expecting worse. I would be able to look after myself.

"Meanwhile," he continued, "you're going to say things to him, things that are rather unflattering—criticism, reproaches. In short, your objective is to undermine his morale by saying all the unpleasant things that come into your head. I know some of you don't know Alan Greenmor well, or at all. It doesn't matter. You're not trying to say what's true, just unpleasant criticisms to try and discourage him."

What was this rubbish? I wasn't going to let myself be lynched in public.

"I don't see the point of this test," I said.

"It's obvious, isn't it? The candidate who has genuine self-confidence will not be perturbed in any way by criticism that is not justified."

I understood that Dunker had seen in me the ideal person to act as his stooge. He obviously felt that I was fairly easily unsettled. He was almost certain to make a brilliant success of his demonstration, to impress the crowd at my expense. I mustn't take part. Absolutely not. I had nothing to gain and everything to lose. *Quick: Find an excuse, anything, but get out of it*, I thought.

"Mr. Dunker, this test seems to me to be very difficult to use in recruitment. It's not very ethical."

"There's no problem as long as you are perfectly transparent. Besides, the candidate will be free to agree to it or not."

"Precisely, nobody will agree to it."

"Mr. Greenmor, you are a consultant, aren't you?"

I hate people who ask you questions they know the answer to, just to force you to confirm what they're saying. I simply looked him in the eye.

"So you ought to know that candidates are ready to do a lot to get a good job."

I wasn't going to win on this line of argument. He would always have an answer. *Find something else to say right away . . . or tell the truth.*

"I don't wish to take part in this exercise," I said, getting up.

A murmur ran through the room. I was proud to have had the courage to refuse. I probably wouldn't have had it a few weeks before.

I had already taken three steps toward my seat when Dunker called out, "Do you know the definition of grave professional misconduct in French law, Mr. Greenmor?"

I froze, still with my back to him. I didn't answer. Total silence fell in the room. I swallowed hard.

"Serious misconduct," he went on in his odious voice, "is defined by the employee's intention to harm his employer. A refusal to take part in this test would harm me because it would undermine my demonstration in front of the whole team that has met specially for the occasion. That's not your intention, Mr. Greenmor, is it?"

I remained silent, still with my back to him. The blood was beating in my temples.

No need to draw me a picture. I was perfectly aware of the consequences of grave professional misconduct: no notice, no severance pay, and loss of any accrued vacation pay. I would have to leave immediately, empty-handed.

"Is it, Mr. Greenmor?"

My body felt leaden, fixed to the ground. My head was empty.

"Make up your mind, Greenmor."

Did I really have a choice? It was horrible. To be honest, I shouldn't have refused in the first place; I wouldn't have found myself in this humiliating position. The only way out was to do his stupid test. I had to get a grip on myself. Swallow my pride. Come on. Come on. I made a superhuman effort and turned around. Everyone's eyes were on me. I went back to the chair without looking at Dunker, sat down in silence, my eyes riveted on a spot on the ground. I was on fire. My ears were ringing. I had to get back in control again. Forget the shame. Gather my wits. Find the energy. Channel it. Breathe. Yes, that's it. Breathe. Calm down.

He took his time, and then began to call out his calculations.

"Nine times twelve?"

Don't hurry to reply. I wasn't his pupil.

"One hundred and eight."

"Fourteen plus seventeen?"

"Thirty-one."

"Twenty-three minus eight?"

I forced myself to slow the rhythm of my answers. I had to refocus, gather my strength. I would need them. Zen.

"Fifteen."

He waved his arms at the group to invite them to make criticisms. I continued avoiding their eyes. I could hear coughs, an embarrassed hubbub and . . . silence.

"It's up to you, now!" he said, motioning them to jump in. "You must say anything negative that comes to mind about Mr. Greenmor."

I had become *Mr.* again.

"Don't worry," he said to the group. "Let me remind you that you're not trying to say what's true. Besides, we all know that Alan has mainly positive qualities. It's just a game, for the purpose of the test. Come on, speak your mind!"

So now I was *Alan* again. Almost his friend. And I only had positive qualities. What a manipulator.

"You're useless."

The first hostile remark.

"Eight times nine?" Dunker asked.

"Seventy-two."

"Forty-seven times two?"

"Ninety-four."

"More, more," he shouted at the group, waving his arms. He was berating my colleagues like a general urging his troops to come out of the trenches and fight under enemy fire.

"You can't count!"

Second hostile remark.

"Thirty-eight divided by two?"

I took a deep breath in order to break the rhythm he was trying to impose.

"Nineteen."

"Go on! Go on!"

It was as if he was shouting at people pushing a broken-down car until they reached the necessary speed to start the engine.

143

"You're no good!"

So far the remarks had left me indifferent. They didn't ring true; my colleagues were even more embarrassed than I was.

"Thirteen times four?"

"Fifty-two."

"Amateur!"

"Thirty-seven plus twenty-eight?"

"Buck up!"

"Sixty-five."

"Faster! Out with it!" Dunker shouted at the group.

"Nineteen times three?"

"You're dawdling!"

"Too slow!"

"Fifty-seven."

"You're rubbish at math!"

Dunker now had a satisfied smile on his face.

"Sixty-four minus eighteen?"

"Useless!"

"You can't count!"

"No good!"

The attacks were beginning to come from all over. I had to concentrate on Dunker's questions and forget about the others. Block them out.

"Forty-six."

"Second-rater!"

"Slacker!"

"Hurry up!"

"You're so slow!"

The machine was out of control now. Everybody was shouting at me at the same time. Dunker had won.

"Twenty-three plus eighteen?"

"You don't know."

Don't listen to them. Visualize the figures. Nothing but the figures: 23 and 18.

"You're no good!"

"Much too slow!"

Nasty laughter in the room.

"Idiot!"

"Halfwit!"

"Dunce!"

"No hope, you've no chance!"

"You're screwed!"

They were becoming like excited wild animals, as they entered into the spirit of the game.

"Twenty-three plus eighteen?" Dunker repeated, all smiles.

"Forty-two, no . . ."

The smile grew wider.

"You goofed up!"

"Can't count!"

"Forty-one."

"Twelve plus fourteen?"

"You won't get it!"

"You're useless!"

"You're pitiful!"

Twelve plus fourteen. Twelve, fourteen.

"Twenty-four. Twenty-six!"

"You're worse and worse!"

"Eight times nine?"

"Rubbish!"

"Sixty-two. No . . . eight times nine, seventy-two."

"You don't know your tables, moron!"

I was going under. Completely. Had to refocus. Cut myself off from what I was feeling.

"Four times seven?"

"Idiot!"

"You won't get it!"

"You don't know!"

"You're a waste of space!"

"Four times seven?" Dunker repeated.

"You dummy!"

"Twenty . . . four."

"You've screwed up!"

"Cretin!"

"Dope!"

"Jerk!"

"Three times two?"

"Ha, ha! Can't count!"

"Three times two?"

Laughter, loud and horrible. Some people were doubled over, laughing hysterically. I didn't know what I was doing anymore.

"Two times two?"

"He's forgotten his two-times table!"

"Two times two?" Dunker repeated, euphoric.

"Moron!"

All of a sudden, Dunker stopped and silenced the group.

"Okay, that's enough!"

"Waste of space!"

"Stop, that's enough! That's enough!"

I was bewildered, stunned. I felt very, very ill. Dunker had realized this and immediately became serious. It had turned nasty. He knew he was responsible and must have known the risk he was running.

"It's over," he said. "We went a bit too far. This was just practice. In a real situation, we'd stop sooner. But here we were dealing with someone strong. It was all right, wasn't it?" he said, looking at me. "I suggest we give Alan a round of applause for his courage. It can't have been easy!"

Suddenly brought out of its trance, looking disconcerted and embarrassed, the group half-heartedly clapped. I caught sight of Alice, her eyes full of tears.

"Well done, my friend! You did really well," Dunker said, giving me a big slap on the back as I left the room.

I FLED THE office, not bothering to finish the day. Nobody would dare criticize me for leaving. I left the building, turned left, and strode along the sidewalk with no particular destination. I just had to empty out the stress.

This painful experience had completely thrown me off center, and I felt violent anger toward Dunker. How could I now meet my colleagues' eyes when I walked past them? That bastard had publicly humiliated me. He would pay for it. Dearly. I would find the way to make him regret playing with people like that.

The fact that the test had shown my lack of self-confidence paradoxically put me in a strong position. Things had gone too far, in public, and Dunker was responsible for that. I was probably in a position to give him a few problems on a legal level, and he must be aware of that. I was becoming almost untouchable.

I got a text message from Dubreuil and lit the prescribed cigarette. He would know how to help me get revenge, that was for sure. If only he would stop ordering me to light up all the time! Smoking is fine when you decide to do it but not when you're made to.

Meditating on my revenge, I walked through the streets of Paris. The sky was threatening, full of big, black clouds. The air smelled of a thunderstorm. I was walking so fast that sweat began to gather on my brow. Was it the exertion or my anger? I could no doubt file a complaint and get some compensation, but then what? How could I carry on work-ing in those conditions? The atmosphere would become unbearable. My colleagues would probably no longer dare to be seen in my company. Would I last long in such cir-cumstances? Of course not.

Gradually, my anger gave way to bitterness, then de-spondency. I hadn't felt so depressed since the day Au-drey left me. She was a shooting star in my life, come to let me experience joy before disappearing in the night. If only she'd told me the reasons for her decision. If she had expressed criticism or blame, I could have blamed myself for her loss, or blamed her and thereby given her up more easily. As it was, her sudden, unexplained departure had prevented me from turning the page, from drawing a line under our relationship, and I missed her terribly. When my thoughts turned back to her, the loss tormented me. The memory of her smile bathed me in sadness. A part of me had disappeared with her. My body missed her body, and my soul felt orphaned.

It started to rain, a fine, melancholic drizzle. I carried on walking, slower now. I didn't want to go home. Turning my back to the Louvre, I left the Rue de Rivoli and entered the Tuileries Garden, empty now, the people chased away by the rain. I walked along a path, under the trees. Finally, I sat down on an isolated stump. I thought of how unfair life could be. My childhood no doubt explained the lack of self-confidence I suffered from. I wasn't responsible for it, and it tortured me. And as if that wasn't enough, it attracted all the sorts for whom I was a natural victim, punishing me all over again. Life doesn't spare those who are suffering; it inflicts a double penalty on us.

I remained like this for a long time. In the end, I got up and instinctively headed for Dubreuil's neighborhood. He alone would be able to restore my morale.

The rain was beginning to stream down my cheeks and my neck. I felt as if it was washing me of what I had suffered, cleansing me of my shame.

I arrived at the gate to the mansion at the end of the day. The windows were closed, and the place seemed lifeless. I was suddenly certain that Dubreuil was not there. Usually he gave off such energy that it seemed possible to feel his presence even without seeing him, as if his aura could radiate through the walls.

I rang the videophone.

A man told me that monsieur had gone out. He didn't know when he would be back.

"What about Catherine?"

"She is never here when he is away, sir."

I wandered in the area a bit, finding pretexts not to go home, then had a bite to eat in one of the few local restaurants. I was frustrated not to see Dubreuil. A thought entered my mind: Suppose he, too, was the sort attracted by my weakness? After all, I had met him in very special circumstances, where my fragility was totally exposed. All this brought me back again to his motives for taking an interest in me, for helping me. Why was he doing all this? I would so have liked to know more, but how? I had no means of investigating.

An image came back to me. The notebook. The notebook held clues to the answer, it was obvious. But how could I get to it without being devoured by his cursed dog? There must be a way. I paid my bill, bought *Les Echos* from the pile on the counter, and went back to the château, this time walking on the sidewalk across the avenue. I sat down on a bench and opened my paper. There were four rows of trees between me and Dubreuil's gate. It seemed reasonable to assume that I could observe it without being spotted. I had an idea that I wanted to check out. I scanned *Les*

Echos, reading news about businesses that, large or small, all had the same objective: increasing their market value. I occasionally looked up at the château. Nothing. Time went by slowly, very slowly. Around half past nine, a light came on in a ground floor room, soon followed by others in the neighboring rooms. I couldn't see the window of Dubreuil's office since it looked out onto the garden, at the back of the château. I looked closely but saw no one. I went back to my newspaper, keeping an eye on the windows. It would still be light for another half an hour. After that, it would be hard to remain credible with my newspaper open. I would have to find something else to do. I came across an article by Fisherman that once again expressed his doubts about Dunker Consulting's strategy. "The management lacks vision," he had written. Sad to say, I was pleased to read something negative about my company.

It was getting darker and darker. I was getting tired of waiting. The air, full of moisture after the rain, gave off the strong scent of the lime trees lining the avenue. In the end, I lay down on the bench, the newspaper acting as a pillow. I didn't take my eyes off the château. Fewer and fewer cars were going by. The area was bathed in a surprising calm, barely disturbed from time to time by the distant noise of an accelerating motorbike.

At 10 P.M. precisely, I made out a slight noise far off, which I immediately recognized. It was the electric lock on the little door beside the mansion gate. I looked carefully but saw nobody. Yet I was sure I had heard the characteristic noise.

The door to the house opened suddenly. I tensed. I wanted to sit up to see better, but I was afraid of drawing attention to myself. It was better to remain as I was. I saw nothing for several seconds, and then four people came out of the house together. They shut the door behind them and crossed the front garden, then exited through the little door that had been unlocked electronically from inside. It was the staff. They exchanged a few words briefly, and then separated. One of them crossed the avenue toward me. My pulse began to race. Had he spotted me? I decided to stay motionless. If he came up to me, I would close my eyes and pretend to be asleep. After all, I had called earlier in the evening and had been told about Dubreuil's absence, so it wasn't so far-fetched to have waited for him on a bench and then fallen asleep. And if he had come home in the meantime, I could very well have missed him while I was having dinner. I screwed up my eyes without losing sight of the servant. After reaching the pavement, he turned left and stopped at a bus shelter. I relaxed. I resumed my observation of the château, as the area was once more plunged into complete calm. Seven minutes later, a bus arrived. I checked to make sure that the man got on. It was 10:13 P.M. I was beginning to get stiff. Nothing more happened for a long while. My discomfort was becoming unbearable. Finally, I sat up, and at that precise moment, a powerful light came on, illuminating the garden in front of the château. I dived back down on my bench. The front door opened, and Dubreuil appeared. Immediately, Stalin began to bark, giving yelps of joy. His master went over to him. I heard his voice and saw the dog's tail wagging. Dubreuil leaned over, and a moment later, Stalin was bounding all around him, freed from his chain. Half past ten precisely.

The dog stood up on its hind legs, and Dubreuil affectionately grabbed it by the neck. They played for a few minutes, and then the master went back inside and turned off the outside light, plunging the garden into darkness again. The dog ran off to the back of the château.

I got up, racked with pain, and walked to the bus

stop. A glance at the timetable: The bus that had arrived at 10:13 P.M. was scheduled to come at 10:10. It was three minutes late.

So there were 17 minutes between the servants' departure and Stalin's release. Was that enough time for me to get into the house? Perhaps. But weren't there other employees still inside? And how to get into the garden? After that, it would be easy to get into the château, since the windows remained open at this time of year, but how was I to get into the office without being seen? It all seemed very risky. I would have to get more information.

I walked to the Métro and went home. I hadn't been back five minutes when Madame Blanchard turned up. How could she have the cheek to trouble her tenant at such a late hour? I hadn't even been particularly noisy. I don't know if the build-up of my resentment against Dunker since the morning was the reason for it, but for the first time, I allowed my anger toward my landlady to explode. Very surprised to start with, she didn't lose her composure altogether and vehemently reminded me of the house rules. She was worse than all the others put together; nothing and no one could get the better of her!

Yves Dubreuil let out a long, hearty laugh. Catherine, usually impassive, was holding her sides as well. I had just told them about my unsuccessful attempts at gestural synchronization with the guy in the Métro.

"I don't see what's so funny. I almost got beaten up because of you."

They didn't answer, still doubled over.

"I ought to be the one making fun of you!" I said. "Your trick doesn't work!"

Between fits of laughter, Dubreuil repeated what the African man had said, imitating his accent: "*Ya finished taking da piss, mon?*"

They broke out in uncontrollable laughter again, so contagious that in the end I had to join them.

We were on the terrace on the garden side of the mansion, comfortably seated in deep teak armchairs. The late afternoon sun gave a bronze color to the carved stone of the building. The stone was beginning to radiate the accumulated heat, and, along with it, the delicate perfume of the immense climbing rose that clung to the wall.

I was enjoying this moment of rest, as I was beginning to feel the exhaustion of the previous night. Three times my sleep had been interrupted to go and smoke a cigarette.

I poured myself some more orange juice, lifting with difficulty the imposing ornate crystal carafe in which ice cubes clinked together. We had eaten early, a very light Thai meal prepared by the château chef and served on a magnificently decorated table, the most astounding sight being the pyramids of spices laid out in the center of the table on silver plates.

"In fact," said Dubreuil, who was gradually becoming serious again, "you made two mistakes, which explain your failure. First, when you are synchronizing with the other's posture, you must respect a certain lapse of time before following his movements, so that he doesn't feel mimicked. Then, and this is the crucial point, you did this like a technique that you were applying. But a technique is the last thing it is! First and foremost, it's a frame of mind to get into, a philosophy for discovering the other. It only works if you *want* to enter the other's universe, to live it from inside, putting yourself in his place to feel what he feels and see the world with his eyes. Then, if your desire is sincere, gestural synchronization is the little bit of magic that enables you to establish contact and create a quality of relationship that the other will want to preserve—which explains why he may unconsciously follow your movements. But this is only the result; it can't be the goal."

"Yes, but you'll admit it's incredible enough to make you want to experience it!"

"Of course."

"I also tried something else, which more or less worked: creating a contact with my manager by synchronizing myself with his way of thinking. It was Luc Fausteri, who's very cold, very rational, and doesn't much like chatting."

"You chose well."

"Why do you say that?"

"If you're going to embrace someone else's world, you might as well choose someone very different from you. It's more interesting. It's a greater voyage. By the way, did I tell you what Proust said about this?"

"Marcel Proust, the French writer? No, not that I remember."

Dubreuil recited from memory: *"The only real journey, the only Fountain of Youth, would be to travel not toward new landscapes but with new eyes, to see the universe through the eyes of another, of a hundred others, to see the hundred universes that each one of them can see, or can be."*

Catherine nodded her head in approval.

A bird landed on the edge of the table, visibly interested in the contents of the large plate of tidbits that we had barely touched. It must be strange to see the world through the eyes of a bird. Does each bird have its own unique experience, different from that of every other bird?

Dubreuil took a small salmon canapé, and the bird flew away.

"It's not easy," I went on, "to put yourself in the shoes of someone whose universe you don't particularly like. That was what was hard for me with Fausteri. I'm not thrilled by numbers like he is, by the changes in our results or the company's share price. I tried hard to talk about these topics, but I probably lacked conviction or sincerity. At any rate, I didn't feel him opening up to me."

"I can understand not liking numbers, and the idea is not to simulate an interest in the tastes or business of the other. No, the principle is to be interested in his *person* to the point of trying to feel the pleasure that *he* can find in numbers. It's very different. So when you synchronize with his movements, when you assume his values, when you share his concerns, do it simply with the intention of slipping into his skin to live his world from inside."

"What you mean is that I don't have to try to be interested in numbers but just to put myself in his place by saying: 'Hey, what's it like? What do you feel when you're interested in numbers?' Is that it?"

"Exactly! And to enjoy experiencing what is, as it happens, completely new for you. And that's where the miracle will take place on the relational level; that's where you'll be completely on the same wavelength."

I reached out and took a canapé, a slice of delicately smoked salmon crowned by a hint of sour cream and a miniature asparagus spear sprinkled with lemon juice. "There is a limit, though," I said. "It doesn't work with everyone."

"Yes, it does. That's precisely the special feature of this approach."

"If you have to be sincerely interested in the other as a person for it to function, that's virtually impossible to do with your enemies."

"Quite the contrary. It's the best way to beat them! *I embrace my rival the better to choke him,* as the old saying goes."

"When you hate someone or he's making you suffer, you absolutely don't feel like getting inside his skin to feel what he's feeling," I insisted.

"That's true, and yet, it's often the only way to understand what is causing him to behave in this way toward you. As long as you remain where you are, you limit yourself to suffering or rejecting the other, but that changes nothing about the situation. You have no influence over him. Whereas if you put yourself in his place, you can discover why he's acting this way. If he's a torturer, then look at the situation with his torturer's eyes and you'll understand what's driving him to torture. It's the only hope you have of making him stop. You don't change people by rejecting them."

"Hmm . . ."

"When you reject someone or simply his ideas, you force him to dig in his heels and stand his ground. Why should he take an interest in what you have to say if you reject his point of view?"

"You have a point."

"If you make the effort—sometimes unpleasant—of assuming his point of view, you will grasp what is leading him to think what he thinks, to behave as he behaves. And if he feels understood and not judged, perhaps he'll be able to hear what you have to say to try and make him change his position."

"It can't work every time."

"Granted, but the opposite approach *never* works. Generally, the more you seek to convince someone, the more you generate resistance. The more you want him to change his opinion, the less likely he is to change it. Physicists have known this for a long time."

"Physicists? What's a physicist got to do with human relations?"

"It's the law of dynamics. Isaac Newton proved that when you exercise a force of a certain strength on an object, it produces an opposite force of equal strength. Well, it's the same for human relations. When you use energy to try and convince someone, it's as though you were directing a force at him that applies pressure. He feels the pressure, and this makes him push in the opposite direction. *Push him, he'll push you back.*"

"What's the solution then? Because if what you say is true, the more you want to convince the less you'll succeed. So what do you do exactly?"

"You don't push, you pull."

"What does that mean?"

"Pushing is starting from your position and wanting to impose it on the other. Pulling is starting from the other's position and gradually bringing him to you. You see, we're still in the philosophy of synchronization. Pulling involves going into the other's universe as well, but this time to allow him to change. The point of departure is still the same: Go and find the other where he is."

"Push him, he'll push you back." I repeated Dubreuil's formula under my breath, thinking of all the times I had really shown conviction in vain.

"Moreover, the opposite is true as well. When you try to get rid of someone who's a nuisance, the more you push them away, the more they will stick around."

It reminded me of my exchanges with Madame Blanchard. The more I tried to fight against her criticism and her abusive intrusion into my private life, the more she continued. The last time, when I had gotten angry, almost shutting the door in her face, she had pushed it back open while criticizing me more vehemently than ever.

I replayed the scene for Dubreuil. He listened carefully in silence, and then I saw his eyes gleam. He had obviously just had an idea he seemed proud of.

"Do you have a solution?"

"Here's what you're going to do . . ." He outlined his idea.

I felt myself getting paler and paler. The further he got into his explanation, the more detailed he became about what I had to do, feeling perhaps that he had to counter my incredulity with precise directives. What he wanted of me was quite simply *un-ac-cept-a-ble*. I had balked at several of his tasks in the past, only to finally give in. But this was impossible. Just thinking about what he was asking of me, I could feel myself fainting.

"No, stop!" I told him. "You know I'll never do that."

I glanced toward Catherine, looking for support. She looked as uneasy as I did.

"You know you've no choice," Dubreuil said.

"You're not applying your own principles," I retorted. "The more I resist, the more you're using your position of strength."

"That's true."

"And that doesn't worry you? *Do as I say, not as I do?*"

"There's a good reason for it."

"What's that?"

"I've got power, my friend. Power. So why should I worry?"

He said that with a satisfied look, smiling. He lifted his glass of white wine to his lips; it was so cold a fine mist had formed on the glass. I took a sip of orange juice. I was annoyed with myself for having confided in him my problem with my neighbor. I led him on and then resented his imposing his solutions on me. Perhaps I was a bit of a masochist, after all.

The branches of the great cedar tree were perfectly motionless, as if they were holding their breath. The mildness of the evening enveloped us. I looked over at Catherine and suddenly froze. It was there, on her knees. She was holding it with one hand: the notebook. Perhaps she saw my eyes or felt my gaze unconsciously, because she covered the notebook with her other hand.

A thought went through my mind: *What if I just asked to look at it?* After all, there was no reason to presuppose anything. Perhaps they'd say yes. Perhaps I was getting all worked up about nothing.

I carefully assumed an air of indifference.

"I see my name's on that notebook. Can I have a look?" I asked Catherine, holding out my hand. "I'm very curious about it."

She stiffened, without replying, and looked at Dubreuil.

"Certainly not!" he said in a final tone of voice.

It was now or never. I would insist. "If what's written in it concerns me, it's only natural I should read it."

"Does a film director show the audience his screenplay during the screening of the film?"

"I'm not the audience here. I'm one of the main actors, it seems to me."

"Exactly! An actor acts better when he's told at the last minute about the scene he's going to act. He's more spontaneous."

"I'm better when I can prepare in advance."

"The screenplay of your life is not written in advance, Alan."

The words remained hanging in the air. Catherine looked at her feet.

I didn't like this ambiguous reply. What did it mean? That no one can know their destiny in advance? Or that he, Yves Dubreuil, was writing the screenplay of *my* life? The thought sent shivers down my spine.

My eyes turned instinctively to the house. The window to the study, on the first floor, was wide open. Underneath was a carved cornice that ran the width of the building. At the corner, there was a stone drainpipe that went down to the ground. It would be very easy to haul myself up to the cornice and from there, to get to the study window.

I took another salmon canapé.

"On the subject of power and power relationships, I went through a dreadful experience at the office," I began.

I told them about the meeting the day before with Marc Dunker and his mental arithmetic test. Dubreuil listened carefully. I knew I risked being given another painful task, but I was ready to do anything to punish my CEO, and I needed Dubreuil's creativity. He had Dunker's strength, plus genius.

"I want revenge," I announced.

"Who are you angry with in this business?"

"It's obvious, isn't it?"

"Reply."

"Who do you think?"

"I'm asking you."

"Dunker, of course!"

He leaned slowly toward me, boring into me with his penetrating gaze.

"Alan, who are you *really* angry with?"

I felt trapped, forced to turn my attention away from an easy answer and look within, question my own emotions. What could be the real object of my anger if it wasn't Dunker? Dubreuil continued to stare at me, immobile. His eyes were a mirror of my soul. I saw the answer there, suddenly obvious. I whispered: "I'm angry with myself for having given in to his hateful pressure. And for not having passed his filthy test."

The silence in the garden seemed oppressive. It was true: I was angry with myself, angry for having allowed a deeply humiliating situation to unfold. But that didn't stop me from being angry with Dunker as well for having been the origin of all this. I absolutely hated him.

"It's his fault, though. It all came from him. I want revenge. By any means. It's an obsession."

"Ha! Vengeance, vengeance! For decades, I thought of nothing else as soon as I was crossed by anyone! How many times have I sought revenge! How many times have I rejoiced to see my adversaries suffer! How many times have I exulted as I made them pay for their deeds! And then, one day, I realized that it was all in vain, that it served no purpose and especially that I was hurting myself."

"Hurting yourself?"

"When you meditate on revenge, you feel an energy that is admittedly very stimulating, but it is a negative, destructive energy, one that pulls you down. You don't feel enhanced by it. And then there's another thing. If you take revenge on someone, it's because he has hurt you. By taking revenge, you try to hurt him back, don't you? In the end you're acting like him; you're adopting his way of functioning. So he has won. He has succeeded in imposing his way of behaving on you, even if he hasn't done it knowingly. He has forced you to join him in evil."

I had never thought of that. It was a rather disturbing way of looking at things. If I managed to harm Dunker, which is what I was dreaming about, it meant he had managed to rub off on me. How horrible! Even so, I wasn't going to let myself be treated like that without saying anything.

"You know," Dubreuil went on, "there will be a lot less wars on this earth the day men stop wanting to avenge themselves. Look at the conflict between the Israelis and the Palestinians. As long as the inhabitants of each camp want to avenge the brother or cousin or uncle killed by the enemy, the war will go on, every day resulting in more dead to be avenged. It will never end until these suffering men and women are helped to come to terms not with their dead but with their vengeance."

It was strange, almost incongruous, to talk about war in this haven of peace—the château garden, with its soothing scents, its great reassuring trees, and a calm so entrancing that it was easy to forget the nearby city. But what can seem so obvious when you're considering other people's conflicts takes on quite a different cast when they're your own. The necessity for forgiveness in the Middle East seemed self-evident; forgiving Dunker was out of the question.

"You say that you hurt yourself when you try to get revenge. I accept that idea, but I have the feeling that stifling my anger would hurt me at least as much!"

"Your anger produces an energy, a force, and that force can be redirected and used to act in your own behalf, whereas revenge contributes nothing; it just destroys."

"That's all very well in theory, but practically speaking, what should I do?"

"First of all, you must express what's on your mind,

either by simply saying to this guy what you think of what he did, or by doing it symbolically."

"Symbolically?"

"Yes, you can write him a letter, for example, in which you get it all off your chest and express your resentment—and then throw the letter in the Seine or burn it."

I had the feeling I'd missed something.

"What's the point of that?"

"It purges you of the accumulated hatred that's hurting you. As long as you remain in a state of anger, your mind is obsessed with revenge, and that prevents you from acting in your own best interests. You're brooding, you keep turning over your grievances, and you're not moving forward. Your emotions are blocking you; you must free them. A symbolic act can allow that. And then you can go on to the second phase."

"And the second phase, what's that?"

"The second phase is using the energy of your anger to take action—for example, to achieve something you would never have dared do. Something constructive that really furthers your interests."

The image that came to me was quite ambitious. I dreamed of changing things in my company, of becoming a force for making positive suggestions, rather than continuing to deplore the course of events and moan about it with Alice.

I would go and meet with Marc Dunker personally. His blunder the day before put him in an awkward position with me. I would take advantage of it. He would be careful not to reject my ideas outright and would be forced to listen to me. I would tell him my observations, my ideas about the company and would try to negotiate putting them to the test. After all, what did I have to lose?

A shadow passed over my enthusiasm. Why would

Dunker follow the ideas of someone whose lack of self-confidence he had himself proved? Given his domineering personality, he must have nothing but contempt for me now.

I told Dubreuil about my plans and my doubts.

"It's certain that self-confidence would greatly help you get what you want at work," he said.

I swallowed hard.

"You promised to work on that."

He looked at me in silence for a few moments, and then picked up a glass of water, a stemmed crystal glass of such delicacy that it seemed almost unreal. He held it over the pyramid of saffron and slowly began to tip it.

"We are all born with the same potential for self-confidence," he said. "Then we start hearing input from our parents, our nannies, our teachers."

A drop of water broke off and fell on the top of the pyramid, forming a sort of lens magnifying each orange strand of the precious spice. The drop seemed to hesitate, then slowly made its way down the slope of the pyramid, gathering speed as it neared the bottom.

"If by misfortune," he went on, "their input tends to be negative, criticizing, and blaming, underlining our shortcomings, mistakes, and failures, then the feeling of inadequacy and self-criticism inscribes itself on our way of thinking."

Dubreuil tipped the glass again slowly, and a second drop fell in the same place. It, too, hesitated at the top of the cone of saffron and then followed the same path as the first. The third drop did the same, faster than the one before it. After a few seconds, a groove had formed, and each time he poured, the drops rushed down, deepening the groove a little more.

"Eventually, the slightest clumsiness makes us feel uneasy, the most unimportant failure makes us doubt ourselves, and the most trivial criticism throws us off, leaving us completely at a loss. The brain gets used to reacting negatively; the neural links get stronger with each experience."

Clearly this described me. Everything he said spoke to me, echoed within me. So I was one of life's sacrificial victims, abandoned by my fathers, crushed by my mother for whom I was never good enough. And now, even though I was an adult, I was still paying for a childhood I hadn't chosen. My parents were long gone, but I was still subject to the harmful effects of their education. I was beginning to feel deeply depressed when I suddenly realized that the depression itself must contribute to making my lack of self-confidence even worse.

"Is there a way out of this vicious circle?" I asked.

"It's not the end, actually. But it's hard to get out of it. It requires effort."

He tipped his head to one side, and depositing another drop of water at the summit of the pyramid, he blew on it sufficiently hard to force the drop to take another direction. It slowly made another path to the bottom.

"Above all," he went on, "your efforts must be sustained over time, because our mind is very attached to our habits of thought, even when they make us suffer."

He poured a new drop onto the top of the pile, and it rushed down the old groove.

"What's needed," he said, "is . . ."

He kept on pouring drops and then blowing on them, so that they were forced to take the new route, gradually forging a groove. After a while he stopped blowing, and the drops rolled down the new path of their own accord.

"To create new habits in the mind," he finished. "To dwell on thoughts that are good for self-esteem, that are associated with positive emotions, until new neural links are created, reinforcing each other and then dominating. This takes time."

I couldn't take my eyes off the beautiful orange pyramid, now incised with two clearly marked grooves.

"You can't suppress the mind's bad habits," he said. "But it is possible to develop new mental habits and ensure that they become irresistible. You can't change people, you know. You can just show them a path and then make them want to take it."

I wondered how deep a groove my lack of self-confidence had incised. Would I manage one day to carve in myself a confidence, a serenity, when faced with criticism? Would I know how to develop that interior strength that makes us unassailable, since persecutors only seem to attack the most vulnerable of us?

"So, what do you suggest I do for my problem?" I asked.

Dubreuil put down the glass of water, poured some more white wine, and then calmly laid back in his armchair and took a sip.

"First of all, you should know that I am going to give you a task that you must do every day for one hundred days."

"For one hundred days?" I squeaked.

It wasn't the length of the task that frightened me, but the prospect of being under Dubreuil's control for such a long time.

"Yes, one hundred days. It's what I've just explained to you: You can't create new mental habits overnight. If you carry out the task I'm going to give you for a week, it will do no good. Absolutely none. It requires a long-term commitment—repeating it for such a long time that its effects take root in you."

"What is it?"

"It's very simple, but it's new for you. Every evening, you must take two minutes to think of the day that has just passed and write down three things that you have achieved and are proud of."

"I'm not sure I accomplish that many brave deeds every day."

"It's not about brave deeds. It can be really little acts, and not necessarily things you did at the office. Perhaps you took the time to help a blind man across the street, even though you were in a hurry. Perhaps you told a shopkeeper that he had made a mistake in your favor when he gave you change, or perhaps you told someone all the good things you think about them. You see, it can be absolutely anything, as long as it's something you can be proud of. Moreover, it doesn't have to be an action. You can be pleased with the way you reacted, with what you felt. Proud to have remained calm in situations where you would normally get worked up."

"I see."

I was a little disappointed. I was expecting him to give me a more important, more sophisticated task.

"But do you really think that's going to help me develop confidence in myself? It seems so simple."

"Ha! You can see that you're not pure American! You can't hide your French origins. For the French, an idea must necessarily be complex; otherwise it's suspected of being simplistic! That's probably why everything is so complicated in this country. People love getting worked up about things here!"

It reminded me that he had an accent I'd never been able to identify.

"To be honest," he went on, "there is no miracle remedy that will give you confidence in yourself overnight. You must see the task I'm giving you as a little snowball. I'm pushing it from the top of the mountain, and if you go down with it for long enough, it will perhaps grow big enough to set off an avalanche of positive changes in your life."

I was convinced of one thing: Confidence in myself was the key to my equilibrium in a lot of areas. Developing it would contribute to giving me a fulfilled life.

"This task," he went on, "will lead you to become aware of all the things you are doing well, of all you make a success of day by day. Little by little, you will learn to direct your attention to your good qualities, your values, all that makes you a good person. The feeling of your personal worth is going to be engraved in you gradually, until it becomes a certainty. From then on, no attack, no criticism, no blame will be able to unsettle you. It won't touch you, and you'll even have the luxury of forgiving your aggressor and feeling compassion for him."

I was a long way from imagining myself feeling compassion for Marc Dunker. It was no doubt a sign of how far I still had to go.

Dubreuil got up.

"Come on. I'll show you out. It's getting late."

I said good-bye to Catherine, who looked at me as if I were a laboratory rat, and followed Dubreuil. We went around the château via the garden. The fading daylight gave it a mysterious atmosphere.

"It must be a lot of work to maintain a building and gardens of this size. I understand why you have staff."

"Indeed, it's difficult to do without."

"And yet, I wouldn't feel at home with all these people in the house. Do they stay day and night?"

"No. They all go at ten o'clock. At night I am the only person who haunts the place."

We walked, without saying a word, to the tall black gate. An unsettling calm permeated the place. Stalin remained lying down but didn't take his eyes off me, probably waiting for the auspicious moment to leap. I suddenly realized that behind him ranged not one but four kennels in a line.

"Do you have four dogs?" I asked.

"No, Stalin has four kennels just for him. Each day, he chooses the one he's going to sleep in. No one but he knows which. He has a strong paranoid tendency."

I sometimes felt as if I'd stepped into a madhouse.

I turned to Dubreuil. The light from the streetlamps made him look wan.

"I'd like to know one thing, though," I said.

"Yes?"

"You're taking care of me, and I'm grateful, but I'd like to feel . . . free. When will you free me from my promise?"

"Freedom has to be earned!"

"Tell me when. I want to know the settlement date."

"You'll know when you're ready."

"Stop playing cat and mouse. I want to know now. After all, I'm the main person concerned by this thing."

"You're not concerned, you're involved."

"You see, you're still playing with words. Concerned, involved. It's the same thing, isn't it?"

"No, not at all."

"Come on! What's the difference, then, according to you?"

"It's the bacon omelet."

"What do you mean?"

"Everyone knows that in a bacon omelet, the hen is concerned and the pig is involved."

Dear Sir:

I am writing to you to tell you of my extreme annoyance at the exercise you conducted a few days ago, in the presence of the Recruitment Department teams from your company. With all the respect I have for your position, I am nonetheless obliged to tell you of my feelings since the event: I hate you. You're a schmuck! A big schmuck! I hate people like you. You're a loser, a bastard, a shitty, lowlife moron.

Thank you for taking the trouble to read my letter.

Yours sincerely,
Alan Greenmor

Nine p.m. I opened the door to my apartment building, my letter in my hand. The lime trees on the street perfumed the evening air. I walked down the steps past Étienne. Propped against the wall, he was looking up at the sky with an inspired air.

"It's mild tonight," I said.

"It is what it is, lad."

I walked along the curb and slipped my letter into the first open drain I came across. "There we are: home delivery."

I headed for the Métro, calmly walking along the streets. Montmartre has the advantage of being situated on a hill, so that you can have the special feeling of being in Paris without being *in* the city. You don't feel buried in the noise and pollution of a megalopolis whose borders you can't even see. In Montmartre, the sky is everywhere, and you can breathe. The Butte is a village and when, at the corner of some winding street, you catch sight of the city below, it seems so distant that you feel closer to the clouds than to the hustle and bustle of Paris.

I arrived outside Dubreuil's at 9:40 p.m. and sat down on my familiar bench. I had been coming for three nights now to stake out the mansion. I had given up lying down but had taken the precaution of putting on a knit cap that came down to my eyebrows. From a distance, it should be enough to make me unrecognizable.

I had barely sat down when the lord of the manor's long black Mercedes appeared. It stopped outside the gate, and Vladi nimbly jumped out. He went around the car and opened the back door. I saw a young woman get out, immediately followed by Dubreuil, who put his arm around her waist. She had short, dark hair that revealed a pretty neck. A very short skirt and infinitely long legs. She had a particularly feminine walk, probably as a result of her high heels, but wasn't she slightly . . . unsteady? She hung around Dubreuil's neck. I heard laughter that revealed the number of glasses she must have drunk.

They went into the yard, climbed the steps to the entrance, and disappeared into the house. Lights came on one after the other at the windows.

Nothing more happened for a good ten minutes, then I heard the vibration of the lock on the little gate, just as on the previous days. One minute past ten. My eyes were riveted to the entrance, waiting for the servants to come out. They appeared 55 seconds later. To within 20 seconds, that was the same lapse of time as on the previous nights. There was the same ritual of separation on the pavement, with a few words exchanged before the group broke up. The bus-taker crossed the avenue. The bus arrived at 10:09, a minute in advance of the official timetable. We were getting to the crucial moment: How long would it be before Dubreuil came to let Stalin out? I crossed my fingers that he would keep to the schedule of the previous days: 10:30 P.M. precisely.

I kept looking from the door to the château to my watch, each minute as it passed simultaneously reinforcing my hope and my fears. At 10:18, the light in the entrance hall came on, and my heart contracted. I waited, tensely, for the door to open. My eyes were glued to it. Nothing. Then another light appeared, in the library this time, and I began to breathe again. It was 10:21. The bus had left 12 minutes earlier. I relaxed. Nothing more happened. At 10:24, again nothing. At 10:28 and 10:30, still nothing. Now I wanted Dubreuil to appear as quickly as possible. My peace of mind for D-day depended on the regularity of his timetable for releasing Stalin. It was 10:31 P.M. when the door finally opened, and I gave a sigh of relief. For the third consecutive day, Dubreuil had released his dog to within a minute of the same time. The habit seemed firmly rooted.

I wouldn't check the next day. It was Friday, and it was probable that things changed on the weekend. I had to stick to the weekday timetable.

I got up to go to the Métro. I walked in silence, looking at the ground, lost in thought. A brief ring on my mobile brought me out of my reverie. A text message. It was him. Even in good company, he didn't forget me. I took out the prescribed cigarette and lit up as I walked. I would have preferred to breathe in the mild evening air. I was beginning to be fed up with having to smoke when I didn't want to.

I thought back over the events of the day. What could I be proud of today? Let's see. I needed to come up with three things. Well, first of all, I was proud of having had the courage to leave the office at 6 P.M. Before, I would have felt obliged to stay till 7 like everyone else. Then let's see, oh yes, I was proud of having given up my seat to a pregnant woman on the Métro. Finally, I was proud of the irrevocable decision I had just taken to bring to an end my incessant questioning about Dubreuil's famous notebook: On Monday evening, in precisely 108 hours, I would know what it contained.

THE FOLLOWING NIGHT was eventful. Four times, I was woken up by the order to have a cigarette. The worst was the one at 5:00 A.M. I smoked it at the window, half asleep and numb with cold, in order not to let the smell invade the apartment. It was violently disgusting. Dubreuil prescribed a cigarette some 30 times a day, and I was beginning to find smoking unbearable. I anticipated with a certain dread the text message that was going to inflict it on me. At meals, I found myself eating faster and faster, for fear of being interrupted to go and smoke. When the alarm announcing the chore went off, I immediately felt a wave of nausea, before my hand reluctantly dived into my pocket to get the cursed packet.

As it was Saturday, I slept until 11:00, catching up on my sleep deficit. Saturday had always been my favorite day, the only day off that was followed by another day off. But today was a special day. I had stage fright—a latent, underlying fear that even when I wasn't thinking about what was causing it, continued to tie a knot in my stomach. Today was the day I had chosen to carry out the mission involving Madame Blanchard that Dubreuil had assigned. I had to get it over with and the sooner the better. In an hour, I would have already forgotten about it. So before that I had to summon up all my courage.

Finally, I got up and crossed the room barefoot to my mini stereo. I nearly removed the headphones that were permanently plugged in but then changed my mind. Above all, I didn't want to give Madame Blanchard a valid reason for complaining. I could have dispensed with music altogether, but I felt I needed it to get me in the right frame of mind. I needed something a bit . . . freaky. Let's see, let's see. What could I put on? No, not that, not that. There we are: a cover of *My Way* by the former bass player from the Sex Pistols—Frank Sinatra revised and updated via hard rock. I picked up my headphones—big headphones with earpieces that really covered the ears—and put them on. Sid Vicious's deep voice sprang from the beyond, breaking into the first verse. I turned the volume up, moving with the headphone cord in my hands like a singer holding the wire of his microphone. Suddenly, the electric guitars sped up with a vengeance. I began to move in time, my bare feet slapping the floor. The singer's voice exploded in every direction, as though he was vomiting up the song. *Forget the neighbor,* I thought. *Turn the sound up higher. Higher. Let go. Close my eyes. Come on. Melt into the music. The music is in me, in my body. Move, vibrate, dance. All the way. Freedom from everything. Jump, feel everything.*

It must have been several minutes before I realized that the drums didn't seem to be keeping time with the song. The repeated beats must be coming from somewhere else, and in spite of the trance into which I had slipped, I knew where they were coming from.

I pulled off the headphones, my ears still throbbing, and the banging on my door started again, this time louder. She wasn't knocking now; she was pounding.

"Monsieur Greenmor!"

The moment I had dreaded was finally here.

Push him, he'll push you back, Dubreuil had said. And the opposite was true as well: *The more you push him away, the more he'll insist.*

"Monsieur Greenmor! Open the door!"

I remained frozen, suddenly seized by doubt. Suppose Dubreuil was wrong?

The blows doubled in strength. How could anyone be so odious? I may have jumped five or six times on the floor as I danced. She couldn't have heard much in her apartment. She really wanted to ruin my life. What a horrid woman!

Anger pushed me to act. I tore off my pullover, then my T-shirt. Now I was bare-chested, bare-footed, in jeans.

"Monsieur Greenmor, I know you're there!"

I started to walk to the door and then stopped. I felt my heart beating faster. Come on. I unzipped my jeans and let them slide to the floor. *Dubreuil was really a madman . . .*

"Open that door!"

Her voice was full of hate. I took the few steps that separated me from the door. I had massive stage fright.

Now.

Holding my breath, I slid down my boxers, stepped out of them, and threw them across the room. It was horrible being naked in such circumstances.

"I know you can hear me, Monsieur Greenmor!"

Courage.

I reached for the door handle. I couldn't believe what I was doing. I was no longer quite myself.

She gave three final knocks as I turned the handle. I had the feeling I was working my own guillotine. I pulled the door toward me, and, as soon as it was half-open, I felt a cool draft, as if to remind me I was naked. Torture.

The sentence. I must say the sentence. With enthusiasm. Go on, it's too late to back out.

I opened the door wide.

"Madame Blanchard! How lovely to see you!"

Clearly, she got the shock of her life. She must have been pushing against my door to be able to hit it with such force, because when it opened, she nearly lost her balance.

She jerked back with a start and then froze, her eyes bulging, her face flushing violently. Her mouth opened, but no noise came out.

"Come on in!" I said cheerily.

She remained rooted to the spot, her mouth still agape, staring at my nakedness, unable to say a word.

It was dreadful finding myself naked in front of my old neighbor, but I was encouraged by her reaction. It almost made me want to lay it on even thicker.

"Come on, I'm sure you'd like to have something to drink with me," I cajoled.

"I . . . I . . . no . . . I . . . Mon . . . Mon . . . Monsieur . . . I . . . but . . . I . . ."

It was as if she had turned to stone, as she mumbled incomprehensibly, her eyes riveted to my penis. It took her several minutes to come back to her senses, then stammer an excuse and back away.

She never came to complain about the noise again.

SUNDAY, 6:00 A.M. The ringing brought me out of a deep sleep. There's nothing more annoying than being woken in the middle of a dream. An immense weariness came over me. It was the third text message that night. I could take no more. I didn't even have the strength to get up. I remained lying down for a long time, forcing myself to keep my eyes open, fighting not to go back to sleep. What a nightmare!

I had immense trouble sitting up. I could no longer bear having to smoke at all hours of the day and night. It was a real ordeal. Annoyed, I reached out and pulled a cigarette from the pack on the bedside table. I couldn't face getting up to go to the window. Never mind the smell. I'd roll up the butt and ashes in a handkerchief so I wouldn't smell the foul stench of stale tobacco as I went back to sleep.

I grabbed my box of matches—a small box, decorated with a drawing of the Eiffel Tower. The first match broke in two in my numb fingers. The second one burst into flame with the characteristic sulfur smell. This was my only moment of pleasure before the dreaded chore. I brought the match to my cigarette. As the flame licked the end of it, I inhaled. The smoke invaded my mouth, attacking my palate, my tongue, and my throat, spreading its strong, acrid taste. I exhaled. My mouth felt like it was coated. Revolting.

I inhaled a second time. The smoke burned my throat, inflamed my lungs. I coughed, a dry cough that made the foul taste on my tongue worse. I wanted to cry. I couldn't carry on like this. It just wasn't possible. It was more than I could take. Stop. Have pity.

Frantic, I looked around for something that could give some relief and finally caught sight of the guilty messenger: my mobile phone. Dubreuil's text messages. Dubreuil! I nervously reached out and grabbed the phone. Pressing the keys, I scrolled through the record of messages received. My eyes were stinging, and I had difficulty reading. Finally I found the number the messages were coming from. I hesitated a few seconds, and then pressed the Send key. With a beating heart, I lifted the phone to my ear and waited. A silence, then a ring tone. Two rings. Three rings. Someone answered.

"Hello."

Dubreuil's voice.

"It's me, Alan."

"I know."

"I can't take any more. Stop sending me text messages all the time. I'm . . . I'm at a breaking point."

Silence. No answer.

"I beg you, let me stop. I don't want to smoke anymore, do you hear? I can't bear your cigarettes any longer. Let me stop!"

Silence again. Did he even understand the state I was in?

"I beg you."

He broke the silence in a very calm voice. "Agreed. If that's what you want, then you're free to stop smoking."

He hung up before I had the time to say thank you.

It was with a heart full of elation that I put the cigarette out, stubbing it directly on the bedside table, the last cigarette of my life.

Dubreuil refused to help me prepare for my planned interview with Marc Dunker. "I don't know your company, so how can I advise you what to say?" he told me when I asked. Finally, giving in to my insistence, he had offered me some tips.

"What's difficult about it for you?" he asked.

"He's shifty, he's dishonest, and he's always ready to make unjustified criticisms. As soon as you ask him something, or point to some malfunction, he tends to attack so he doesn't have to reply."

"I see. And what do you and your colleagues do when he criticizes?"

"We defend ourselves. We try to prove that he's wrong, that the criticisms are unfair."

"So you try to justify yourselves, is that right?"

"Yes, of course."

"So you're the ones who do all the work!"

"I don't understand."

"Faced with unwarranted criticism, you absolutely mustn't justify yourself; otherwise you're playing his game!"

"Perhaps, but what else can I do?"

"Torture him."

"Very funny."

"I'm not joking."

"You're forgetting one little detail."

"What's that?"

"I don't want to lose my job."

"Be like the inquisitors in the Middle Ages. What did they call the unbearable torture they were about to inflict on someone?"

"I don't know."

"*We're going to put him to the question.*"

"Put him to the question?"

"Yes."

"And what's the connection with my boss?"

"Faced with unfounded criticism, torture him by asking him questions."

"What do you mean exactly?"

"Rather than justifying yourself, ask *him* questions to make him justify himself! And don't let go. It's for him to provide proof of his criticisms, not for you to prove they're unfounded! In other words, make *him* sweat."

"I see."

"Push him into a corner. Ask him what right he has to assert what he's saying, and don't let him hide behind generalities. Ferret away, demanding details, facts. If he's dishonest, he'll have a hard time. And you know what? The best thing about all this is that you don't even have to be aggressive. If you set about it carefully, you can bring him to his knees with great gentleness, in an apparently very respectful tone of voice. In short, you'll force him to justify his criticisms while being above criticism yourself. And if you set about it carefully, there's every chance he'll never bug you again."

I phoned Marc Dunker's office and made an appointment with his secretary. Dunker's secretary was male, a rarity in the business world. He was a very distinguished young Englishman named Andrew. His hiring had surprised everyone. Dunker clearly being the macho type, we would have imagined him going for a nymphet in a miniskirt and low-cut top, who would be at his beck and call, reassuring him of his superiority as a dominant male.

But no doubt Dunker's choice was not random. I suspected him of having a secret complex about his humble origins. The English secretary, who went with him everywhere, compensated for Dunker's lack of polish with his extreme elegance, courtesy, and—the icing on the cake—his refined French, spoken with a very British accent. With all the classiness of Her Majesty's subject, Andrew by his mere presence ennobled his boss. The odd mistake in the gender of nouns only added a touch of charm.

That morning, I deliberately arrived five minutes late, just enough to send Dunker the message that I wasn't his puppet. Andrew greeted me.

"I'm going to have to ask you to be patient for a little while," he said. "Monsieur Dunker isn't ready to see you yet."

Of course. He was responding to my lateness by being even later. In France, time is an instrument of power.

Andrew invited me to have a seat on a red leather sofa. It stood in marked contrast to the perfectly white walls. One end of the spacious room was a waiting area for visitors; the other was Andrew's office. Furnished in red leather that matched the sofa, the office was impeccably tidy.

"Would you like a coffee?" Andrew asked.

I was surprised by his question. Somehow I imagined that someone straight out of Buckingham Palace would offer me tea in a china cup.

He placed the coffee on the low table in front of me, then went back to his desk and became absorbed in reading a file. From time to time, he picked up a black lacquer pen and noted something in the margin, then put the pen down in exactly the same place, perfectly aligned with the edge of the desk.

Finally, Dunker's office door flew open as if a SWAT team was bursting in, and the CEO propelled himself into the middle of the room.

"Who wrote this report?" he shouted in an accusing tone.

"It was Alice, sir," Andrew replied evenly.

"It's unbelievable!" stormed Dunker. "She makes mistakes bigger than her ass! Tell her to reread her notes before giving me this sort of crap!"

He threw down the document, scattering its pages all over his secretary's desk. Andrew gathered them neatly into a pile.

I swallowed hard.

Dunker turned toward me and held out his hand, suddenly calm and smiling. "Hello, Alan."

I followed him into his office, a vast space dominated by an imposing triangular desk positioned with a point turned toward the visitor. Dunker sat down behind it and waved me to a stylish but very uncomfortable armchair facing him.

Though the window was open, the noise from the street below seemed distant, as if it was not allowed to penetrate the top floor of the building. Looking out, I could see the tip of the Obélisque on the Place de la Concorde, and beyond that the top of the Arc de Triomphe.

"It's a lovely view, isn't it?" Dunker said, seeing my gaze lingering outside.

"Yes, it's lovely. But it's a shame the Avenue de l'Opéra has no trees," I said to break the ice. "It would smell nice, having some greenery under your windows."

"It's the only avenue in Paris without any trees," Dunker said. "Do you know why?"

I didn't.

"When Haussmann built it at Napoleon the Third's request, he gave in to the Opéra's architect who didn't want anything to intrude on the view of his work from the Tuileries Palace."

A fly came through the window and buzzed around us.

"You wanted to see me," Dunker said. "What can I do for you?"

"I wanted to tell you about a certain number of things we could improve in the company."

He frowned imperceptibly.

"Improve?"

My strategy to convince him was to embrace his world by synchronizing with his values of efficiency and profitability. He was always talking about them. All his decisions boiled down to them. I was going to try to prove to him that my requests went along with his priorities.

"Yes," I continued, "for the well-being of all, and with a view to increasing the firm's profitability."

"The two rarely go together," Dunker said, affecting a slightly amused air.

"Unless an employee who feels better works better," I countered.

The fly landed on his desk. He flicked it away with the back of his hand.

"If you don't feel happy with us, Alan . . ."

"I didn't say that."

"Don't get excited."

"I'm not getting excited," I said, trying to appear as calm as possible, despite already wanting to push him out the window. What if he was deliberately misunderstanding what I said, just to throw me off? *Stop replying. Torture him with questions. Questions.*

"Besides," I went on, "what's the link between my opinion that an employee who feels better works better and your hypothesis that I don't feel happy in your company?"

Three seconds of silence.

"It's obvious, isn't it?"

"No. What do you mean?" I asked.

"Well, bad results can't be excused by external causes," said Dunker.

"Yet my . . ." *Don't justify yourself. Ask questions, calmly.*

"Who has bad results?" I asked innocently.

An expression of annoyance crossed his face. The fly landed on his pen. He brushed it away again, then changed the subject.

"So tell me: What are your ideas about things that could be improved?"

I had just won the first round.

"Well, first of all, I think we should take on a second assistant in our department, to help Vanessa. She is constantly overstretched, and you can tell she's really under stress. The new assistant could type up our reports for us. I've calculated that we consultants spend almost twenty percent of our time typing up reports on our interviews. Given our hourly rate, that's not at all profitable for the firm. If we had a second assistant, she could take down in shorthand what we want to put in our reports and then type them up. We could use the time gained to do really useful things that we alone can do."

"No, each consultant must type up his notes. It's the rule."

"It's precisely that rule that I'm calling into question."

"When you're well organized, it doesn't take all that much time."

"But it's logical that clerical work should be done by the person whose hourly pay is the lowest. It's better for a consultant to spend his time on activities that are more profitable for the company."

"Exactly. The appointment of an additional member of the department would bring down the department's profitability," Dunker said.

"On the contrary, I . . ." *Stop arguing. Ask questions.*

"How would it bring down the profitability?"

"It would increase the overall salary expenditure for the department, of course."

"But since the consultants would free up time to look after customers and do more canvassing for new clients, it would increase turnover. In the end, we'd be winners."

"I don't think it would increase turnover."

"What makes you think that?"

"Everyone knows that the less work you have to do, the less work you do," Dunker said.

Ask questions. Gently . . .

"Everybody? Who exactly?"

He searched for words for a few seconds, his eyes moving from left to right. "At any rate, I know."

"How do you know that?" I pressed him.

The fly landed on his nose. He batted it away, with a gesture of profound annoyance. "That's what always happens, of course!"

"Oh, you've already experienced this?" I asked.

"Yes . . . well . . . no, but I know what happens."

So that he couldn't blame me for being aggressive in any way, I made sure to seem very naïve, almost the village idiot.

"How can you know, if you haven't experienced it?"

Unless it was imagination, those were beads of sweat on his forehead. At any rate, he couldn't come up with a satisfactory answer.

"Does that mean," I went on, "that if *you* had less work to do, you'd start to do less and less?"

"I'm different," he exploded, before getting a grip on himself. "Look, Alan, I'm beginning to find you rather arrogant!"

There we were at last. I took my time.

"Arrogant," I mused, settling myself calmly in my armchair. "But the other day, you demonstrated in front of everyone that I was lacking in self-confidence."

He froze. A cloud passed over the sun, and the office

suddenly went darker. In the distance, an ambulance was speeding by, its siren screaming.

Finally, Dunker had a flash of inspiration. "Look, Greenmor, let's get back to the subject. Concerning your request for reorganization: Let the department meet its targets, and then we'll talk again about appointing an assistant!"

"Yes, of course, of course," I replied. "But suppose that appointment is the thing that would allow us to meet our targets?"

"You're taking a very limited view of the problem," he said, his tone condescending. "I've got a strategic view of the company's development. And that vision prohibits me from increasing the budget for wages. You don't have all the information to make a judgment, so you can't understand."

"Indeed, it's difficult for me to take a position on the company's strategic development, since the employees don't really know what it is. But you know, I'm a great believer in common sense. And it seems to me that every business needs the means to develop. Isn't that essential?"

"You're forgetting something, Alan. Something major. Our business is listed on the stock exchange. The markets are watching us. We can't do just anything."

"Taking on staff to allow us to expand—is that just anything?"

The fly was buzzing around us. Dunker grabbed a glass of water on the desk and poured its contents into a potted plant, keeping the empty glass in his hand.

"The market can only predict the future by examining present results," he said. "Investors won't wait to see if appointments produce a positive effect in the long term. If we pay more wages, the share will drop in price. It's automatic. We are under the looking glass. He's watching," he said, pointing to a newspaper clipping. It showed a photo of Fisherman, the journalist who was Dunker's *bête noire*. The headline on the article referred to our shares: "Potential, But Must Do Better."

The fly landed on the desk. In one swift movement, Dunker turned the glass over and dropped it over the fly. A sadistic little smile crossed his face.

"It seems as if we're really slaves to the share price," I said. "But what does it matter to the company if the share price goes up or down? We couldn't care less, could we?"

"You can say that because you don't own any shares!" Dunker snapped.

I pressed on. "But what matters, even for you shareholders, is that the price goes up in the end. If the business grows, the share price will necessarily go up sooner or later."

"Yes, but you can't allow the share price to go down, even if it's only over the short term."

"Why?"

"Because it puts us at risk of a takeover. You ought to know. You studied economics, didn't you? Only a high share price protects you from a takeover bid by another company, because if the price is high, it would cost too much to acquire the number of shares needed to gain a controlling interest in our firm. That's why it's vital to have a share price that constantly goes up—and goes up faster than that of our competitors."

"If there is the risk of a takeover, why go public?"

"To develop fast," Dunker said. "As you know, when a company goes public, it immediately gets the money of all the people who want to buy in. That finances projects."

"Yes, but if it then prevents you from making decisions that allow the company to develop, just because you have to keep the share price going up, then the result will be the opposite of what you want."

"Those are simply constraints that have to be managed," he said.

"But we're not free anymore!" I protested. "Fausteri was saying that we couldn't open the Brussels office this year because last year's profits had to be distributed as a dividend to the shareholders, and we didn't want to reduce the results of the year to come."

"Yes, but distribution of dividends isn't linked to the share price. It's just a demand from our shareholders. Dividends are the return from their investment in the company."

"But we could reinvest this year's profits in our development and and then make profits again next year, couldn't we?"

"We have two large groups of shareholders who demand that we make a profit of twelve percent each year and that we pay most of it to them as dividends."

"Yes, I know. But if their demand for a dividend prevents the growth of the business they've invested in, surely they can be patient for a year or two, can't they?"

"No," said Dunker, "our difficulties are none of their business. They've invested in our company but not necessarily for the long term. They want a rapid return on their investment, and that's their right."

"But if that forces us to make decisions that are harmful to us . . ."

"That's the way it is," said Dunker. "We have no choice. The real bosses are the shareholders."

"If their goal is solely financial and short-term, with the intention of selling their shares before long, it makes a mockery of the company's destiny over time."

"That's part of the game."

"A game? But it isn't a game," I protested. "It's reality! There are real people working here! Their lives and their families' lives depend in part on the health of this company. You call that a game?"

Dunker shrugged. "What can I say?"

"So, let me get this straight: Not only are we slaves to the share price but we're subject to the absurd demands of shareholders who won't even be shareholders for long. Doesn't it all feel a little upside down? I really can't see the advantage of the stock exchange flotation. You could have developed the company without it, just by each year reinvesting the profits from the year before."

"Yes, but we wouldn't grow as quickly," Dunker said.

I remained perplexed, never having grasped our culture's obsession with speed. Why always going faster? Where does it lead? People in a hurry are already dead.

"What's the point in developing quickly?" I asked him.

"You have to establish yourself quickly and dominate the market before your competitors can take up a long-term position."

"Because if you don't?"

"If you don't, it will be harder to take market share from them so we can increase our turnover."

"But if healthy, slow development improves the quality of what we're offering—our services—that will bring in new customers, won't it?"

Silence. Had Dunker never asked himself that question?

"It would be slower," was all he said.

"Where's the problem with that? What's to stop us from taking time to do the job well?"

He rolled his eyes. "Speaking of time, Alan, you're taking up mine at the moment. I haven't got time to spend philosophizing."

He started rearranging the files on his desk, no longer paying attention to me.

"It seems to me," I said, searching for my words, "that it's always useful to step back a bit. To ask questions about the meaning of our actions."

Dunker looked up. "The meaning?"

"Yes, why we do what we do, what the point is."

The fly was buzzing around in its bell jar.

"You mustn't look for meaning where there isn't any," he said dismissively. "You think that life has a meaning? The strongest and the cleverest win, that's all. They get the power and the money. And when you've got power and money, you can have anything you want in life. It's no more complicated than that, Greenmor. The rest is intellectual masturbation."

I looked at him pensively. How could he believe for a single second that being rich and powerful was enough for a successful life? Who could lie to himself enough to believe he was happy just because he was driving a Porsche?

"Poor Alan," he went on. "You'll probably never know just how great a feeling power is!"

His words left me feeling as though I was from another planet. They almost made me curious to find out. Besides, hadn't Dubreuil told me to get inside the skin of people to try and understand what they're feeling?

"When you do all this, you feel powerful?" I asked him.

"Yes."

"And if you didn't, then you'd feel . . . ?"

Dunker blushed. I wanted to burst out laughing, although I hadn't embarrassed him on purpose. But now my imagination was running a film of a businessman busying himself with his work to compensate for his sexual inadequacies.

"As far as the assistant is concerned," Dunker said, "the answer is no. Did you have other requests?"

I presented my other ideas, but none got his okay. I wasn't surprised, now that I understood how he worked and what the rules of his game were. All the same, I had one last request—for an explanation. "I've noticed that our firm is running a lot more ads in the press."

"Yes, that's right," he said, visibly pleased with himself.

"But I'm not being given any more cases at the moment. Why's that?"

"Trust me, I can guarantee you're not being treated any differently than your colleagues. The work is being distributed fairly. Alan, I really must end this now. I have work to do."

He underlined his words by picking up a file on the desk. I didn't budge.

"But if the advertising is working, how can it be that I haven't got more recruitment cases to work on? It's not logical."

"Oh, Alan, you always want to understand everything. You must realize that in a business the size of ours, there are some decisions you don't shout from the rooftops. In this case, placing ads doesn't necessarily mean that there are real vacancies to be filled."

"You mean we're placing false ads? False job openings?"

"*False, false,* big words!"

"But why?"

"Really, you're totally lacking in strategic vision, Greenmor. I've been explaining to you for the last hour why it's vital for the share price to go up day by day. You ought to know that the market doesn't react just to objective results! There's also an element of psychology, believe it or not. And seeing Dunker Consulting job openings in the papers is good for investors' morale."

I couldn't believe what I was hearing.

"But that's dishonest!"

"We have to have an edge."

"You publish false ads just to take care of the company's image and make the share price go up? What about the candidates?"

"It makes absolutely no difference to them!"

"But they take the time to send their resumés, to fill out the application."

He sighed by way of a reply.

I went on. "You're not taking into consideration that the more they send applications that don't get anywhere, the more their morale and self-confidence will drop!"

Dunker rolled his eyes. "Alan, have you ever considered going to work for a charity for the unemployed?"

I just stood there dumbstruck, flabbergasted by all I had just heard. How could anyone could be so uninterested in other people's lives, even if they were strangers?

Finally, I got up and turned to go. Clearly, I wasn't going to get anything from him. His decisions obeyed a skewed logic that left no place for ideas based on a sincere desire to improve things.

I took two steps and then stopped. It seemed inconceivable that anyone could be satisfied with a vision of life as empty of meaning as the one Dunker had just described. I wanted to be quite clear about it.

"Monsieur Dunker, does all this . . . does it really make you a happy man?"

A strange expression crossed his face, but he didn't answer, still staring at his document. Perhaps it was the first time in his life that anyone had asked him that. I looked at him with curiosity and even a certain pity, then silently crossed the room, the thick carpet absorbing the sound of my steps. As I turned to close the door behind me, Dunker was still staring at the file on his desk and had probably already forgotten me. But he had the same strange expression on his face, as if he were lost in thought. Then slowly he moved his hand over to the glass and lifted it.

The fly immediately flew off and escaped through the window.

THAT EVENING, I took the bus to the château. I was of two minds: on the one hand, the strong desire to discover at last the contents of Dubreuil's notebook, which I was convinced would tell me more about his motives; on the other, the fear of breaking into a place at night that had daunting security even in daytime and being caught red-handed.

The bus was far from empty, despite the late hour. There was a little old lady sitting on my right and a man with a moustache in the seat opposite me. I deposited at my feet a plastic bag containing an enormous leg of lamb I had bought at the local butcher's. After a few minutes, the warm air inside the bus began to smell of raw meat. The odor, subtle at first, grew more pronounced, then frankly revolting. The little old lady began giving me sidelong glances, then turned away very conspicuously. The man with the moustache started staring at me with a look of disgust. I almost got up and changed seats, then thought again. The leg of lamb was today's *Closer*. I had to stop worrying about the way other people saw me. *After all,* I told myself, *life is extraordinary; at every moment, it gives us opportunities to grow.*

So I stayed in my place, doing my best to relax and ignore the feeling of shame that had insinuated itself inside me. I was very proud of my decision, reminding myself that each day I had to write down three things I could feel good about. Let's see, let's see . . . what could I put down today? My interview with Dunker, of course! Admittedly, I hadn't gotten anywhere, but I had had the courage to go and confront him, and I had managed not to justify myself under attack. It even seemed as if the questioning tactic suggested by Dubreuil had rattled Dunker somewhat. That was something to be proud of.

Now the man with the moustache was eyeing my plastic bag suspiciously, no doubt trying to guess its contents. Perhaps he thought I was carting body parts around Paris.

I got off at the stop before the château, in order to cover the last few hundred yards on foot. The bus set off again at once, the noise of its engine receding with it, and the neighborhood was quiet again. As I walked, I concentrated on my future mission, going over the sequence of events, minute by minute.

9:38 P.M.: Stage 1 would start in 22 minutes. I was dressed in dark sports clothes, to be free to move and go unnoticed in the night.

As I got closer to the mansion, I began to feel mounting apprehension, and a little chink opened up for doubt. Was I right to want to read the notebook at any price? Wasn't it sheer madness to try such an expedition? Fear of getting caught was eating at me, but it was dominated by an even bigger fear, more worrying still: Dubreuil was hiding something from me. I was sure of it. Otherwise, why was he leaving everything so vague, when he was normally so frank? Why not answer my questions? I had to know for my peace of mind—my safety even.

I arrived at 13 minutes before the key moment. I sat down on the bench on the other side of the avenue, my plastic bag next to me. The area was deserted. In the heart of summer, most of its inhabitants were far away on vacation, no doubt. I was trying hard to take deep breaths to relax.

The façade of the mansion was dark. The weak light from the nearest streetlight gave it a gloomy air. A haunted castle. Only the windows of the great drawing room were lit up.

At 9:52, I got up. Eight minutes to go. With a knot in my stomach, I started crossing the avenue diagonally, taking my time. I needed to stay close to the door, without seeming to be on the lookout if a neighbor saw me.

9:58 P.M.: It would be soon now. I walked past the gate, then stopped, pretending to tie my shoelaces, and then turned around. 10:00 P.M. Nothing. I was beginning to count the seconds when the electric lock sounded. My heart began to beat faster as I picked up the pace, looking around to make sure I was alone. Less than ten seconds later, I was outside the black door. I took out the little metal plate I had bought the day before and pushed the door. It opened. Bending down, I put the metal piece on the ground, propped against the doorframe. I released the door and anxiously watched as it slowly closed. It hit my rectangle, the two metals knocking together with a characteristic ping that seemed close enough to the normal sound the door made when it closed. I pushed the door again, and to my great relief, it opened. The metal plate was just thick enough to stop it from closing all the way and locking. I released the door and took a few steps back, then crossed the avenue again. I hadn't reached my bench when I could hear voices coming from the steps outside the front door. The servants were leaving the house. They didn't seem to notice anything out of the ordinary. They came out into the street and separated, one heading as usual for the bus stop. 10:06 P.M. For the time being, everything was going perfectly. The bus was due in four minutes.

A lady with a little dog on a leash appeared on the sidewalk across the street. At a distance, I could see the end of her cigarette weaving circles in the darkness. Her companion, a wheezy Pekinese, followed her very slowly, stopping every few inches to sniff something, his long hair sweeping the ground. Every time he stopped, the woman took a drag on her cigarette and waited patiently for the dog to finish delighting in the smell it had detected.

10:09 P.M. The bus was due any second, but the dog walker would prevent me from entering the grounds. Rotten luck. The only person in the area had to walk right to the spot where I needed to be alone. She was now in front of the mansion gate. She seemed to be growing impatient with the dog's dallying and gently tugged on the leash. The Pekinese, far from obeying his mistress's wishes, pulled against the leash, his grumpy little head sinking into his shoulders as he refused to move. The mistress gave in and took another drag on her cigarette.

10:11 P.M.: The bus was late. The servant was still waiting. So was I. But even if the bus arrived now, it would take at least five minutes for the lady with the little dog to move away. I wouldn't have enough time left. I was going to have to postpone my mission.

I was thinking my leg of lamb would smell even worse the next day when I recognized the humming of a motor. As the bus stopped, a miracle happened. The lady picked up the dog and started running for the bus. The peke's head nodded like those plastic bobblehead dogs that people used to put on the back shelves of their cars in the 1970s. The woman made it to the bus in time and got on. The doors closed behind her, and the bus pulled away.

Now I had a choice, but I had to decide right away. It was 10:13 P.M. Dubreuil would release his hound in 17 minutes. I ought to have enough time.

I leapt up and crossed the avenue. I paused briefly outside the door, my senses alert, then pushed it open and slipped inside. At once, Stalin stood up and ran toward me, barking. I took up a position slightly beyond the point where I knew his chain would grow taut and reached inside the plastic bag. My fingers slipped as I tried to get hold of the raw meat. I finally managed to grab the leg of lamb and get it out of the bag, brandishing it like an enormous club. I crouched down as a sign of peace and held the meat out to Stalin. Instantly, he stopped barking and closed his mouth over the leg, his fangs sinking into the flesh. I had figured he would accept this irresistible bribe; even dogs are corruptible. I crumpled up the bag and stuffed it in my pocket, then wiped my greasy hand on my trousers.

I couldn't walk close to the building without risking being seen as I passed in front of the drawing room windows. So I dodged behind the bushes bordering the garden and ran around to the back of the house at top speed. As I arrived, out of breath, an unpleasant surprise awaited me: All the first floor windows were shut, despite the mildness of the evening and the heat that had no doubt built up inside. Only a few of the windows on the ground floor were open, including the one in the entrance hall. It was a lot riskier. 10:19 P.M. Only 11 minutes left. It was still worth a try.

I emerged from the shrubbery and raced across the garden to the house, my heart beating. As I got close, I could hear music. Dubreuil was listening to Rachmaninoff's *Piano Sonata no. 1*. He had turned it up loud. Luck was with me again.

I paused to catch my breath and then, my stomach in a knot, slipped inside the window.

A heady perfume, a woman's perfume, entrancing, floated in the air. The lord of the manor was not alone tonight.

The piano sounded loud, even as far away as the entrance hall. The monumental chandelier had been switched off, but the prisms reflected narrow rays of light in every direction. I realized the door to the drawing room must be open because a beam of light shot across the marble floor in a wide yellow band. There was a high risk I would be seen passing the drawing room to get to the staircase. Was I going to have to give up so close to the goal, after going to all this trouble?

At that moment, an astonishing thing happened: a wrong note followed by a curse in a foreign language. Dubreuil's voice. Two seconds later, the music started again. It wasn't a recording; *he* was playing the piano! It was an unhoped-for break.

The perfume . . .

There remained his probable guest, who might see me crossing the hall. Yet, if Dubreuil was playing for a woman, there was a good chance she was looking at him.

It was a risk to be taken.

I took it without really thinking, obeying instinct and perhaps also under the influence of the enchanting perfume, which made me burn with desire to see the person wearing it.

I felt my way toward the staircase, each step bringing me closer to the open door that was as threatening as it was alluring. Rachmaninoff's tormented music, tumultuous, deafening, filled the space, forcing itself deep inside me. With each step, I could see into more of the drawing room. My pulse accelerated in time with the wild chords issuing from the piano.

I crept forward, staying in the shadows. From where I stood, I could see that the drawing room was a vast space with high ceilings and Persian rugs on the floor. Everything was enormous: red velvet sofas, settees as deep as beds, gilt consoles with extravagantly carved legs, tall baroque mirrors. On every surface there seemed to be candlesticks with immense candles. As I took another step forward, peering deeper into the room, I could see the light from the flickering flames dancing on the black surface of the piano.

Dubreuil, wearing a dark suit, was seated at the piano

with his back to me. I watched his hands moving up and down the keyboard as the Rachmaninoff sonata rang out. And there in front of him, stretched out across the top of the immense grand piano, was a woman with long blond hair . . . entirely naked. She was propped up on one elbow with her head resting on the palm of her hand, looking at the pianist with a detached air. I couldn't tear my eyes away from her grace, her beauty, her refinement, her extreme femininity.

Time stood still, and it took me a while to realize that the woman was looking straight at me. Alarmed, I was overcome by the situation, at once terrified at having been spotted and fascinated by those eyes that had taken possession of mine and wouldn't release them. I stood there, like a statue, looking at her, unable to move.

Having done everything in order not to be seen, having put on dark clothes to disappear into the night, here I was being looked at with an intensity unlike any I had ever before experienced. She was in no way embarrassed by her nudity in the presence of a stranger; quite the opposite. Displaying a disturbing composure, she fixed me with eyes tinged with defiance. I would have given all I possessed just to smell her perfume on her skin.

While Dubreuil's fingers continued their wild adventures on the keys, filling the house with sound, I had the feeling, then the conviction, that the woman wouldn't betray me. Even though she seemed rooted to the present, fully inhabiting her body, at the same time I felt her to be completely detached from whatever might transpire.

Struggling terribly with myself, I finally stepped back slowly, very slowly, until no doubt judging herself beaten, she looked away.

I silently climbed the great staircase, her image fixed in my mind. Gradually coming back to my senses, I glanced at my watch. 10:24 P.M.! There was a risk Stalin would be let loose in six minutes.

I went along the corridor, plunged in semidarkness, as quickly as the need to remain silent allowed. The unlit chandeliers cast their weak reflection on the walls, outlining dismal shapes on the tapestries.

Another wrong note, followed by another curse, and the music started again. The office! I opened the door and slipped inside, my heart in my mouth.

I immediately saw the notebook, lying next to the threatening paper knife with its tip turned toward the visitor. I leapt toward it, my heart pounding. Only four minutes left. It was sheer madness.

I grabbed the notebook and going over to the window to take advantage of the weak moonlight, opened it in the middle, quite randomly. The notebook was in the form of a diary, handwritten, each new paragraph beginning with a date emphatically underlined. I hastily scanned bits here and there, frustrated at not being able to read it all.

21 July—Alan blames others for restricting his freedom and doesn't realize he's the one subjugating himself. He offers himself submissively because he thinks he's obliged to respond to their expectations in order to feel accepted. He's a voluntary slave who's resentful toward his masters for his own slave mentality. Alan is subject to doubt as a form of mental fixation when he is governed by his compulsion to avoid being different.

Each paragraph was stuffed with comments about me and my personality. I felt like a laboratory animal under the microscope of some research scientist.

I flipped back to an earlier page. Suddenly my heart was in my mouth.

16 July—Alan hurriedly left the taxi in the middle of the road, slamming the door, a sign that he probably successfully carried out the prescribed mismatching task.

So I *was* being followed. My intuition was well-founded. But then the idea made me shudder. Perhaps he knew I was here now?

I rapidly scanned more pages. Suddenly, I became aware that the music had stopped playing. The house was now plunged into frightening silence.

One last time, I thumbed through 10 or 12 pages, still going backward in time. What my eyes saw next was a shock to my system. I had met Yves Dubreuil for the first time the day of my attempted suicide at the Eiffel Tower. The date was unforgettable because it was so painful, charged with anxiety and shame: June 27.

The paragraph before my eyes was dated June 11.

I WAS STILL transfixed, the notebook in my hand, when I heard a slight creaking behind me. I turned around and, overcome with fright, saw the door handle move. Leaving the notebook on the desk, I slipped behind the thick curtains, afraid that this had all been a waste of time, that my presence here was already known.

Despite its thickness, the drapery material was loosely woven, so I could see through it, which made me afraid that I could be seen.

The door opened partway and a face looked in, peering into the darkness. It was the young woman. My heart was in my mouth. What she saw must have corresponded to what she expected, because she opened the door wide and came in, quite naked, her bare feet sinking into the thick carpet.

She came straight toward me, and I held my breath. She stopped in front of the desk, and I started breathing again, half-relieved, half-disappointed. Her eyes were searching the darkness, looking for something. I was less than a yard away. She leaned over the desk, her breasts rippling delightfully, and reached out toward the notebook. Her perfume enveloped me in its sensuality, making me melt with desire. I only had to reach out to caress her skin, to lean forward to place my lips on it.

She pushed the notebook aside and leaned over farther toward a rectangular box. She opened it and took out an enormous cigar. She left the box open and, to my great regret, went straight back toward the door, her delicate fingers closed around the cigar she was taking back to the master of the house.

I waited 20 seconds before moving. 10:29 P.M. Suppose Dubreuil had taken advantage of the young woman's absence to go and free his hound? What should I do? Try my luck, or hide in the house all night and leave when the dog was tied up early next morning?

The music started again. I felt a wave of relief. No time to lose. I would leave directly by the window. I opened it and hauled myself out. The air outside was cool compared with the stuffy air in the office. I was only on the first floor, but the height of the ceiling was such that I found myself balanced on a narrow ledge more than 12 feet above the ground. I inched forward, arms outstretched, trying to push out of my mind the painful memory that was surfacing. I made my way to the corner of the building, where I slid down the drainpipe. I charged back around the outside edge of the garden. When I arrived in sight of the kennels, I gave a sigh of relief: Stalin was still tied up, gnawing away at his bone. He saw me come out of the shrubbery and stood up at once, his ears pricked. I called him gently by name, trying to defuse his aggressiveness before he alarmed the whole neighborhood. He couldn't help but growl nastily, his jowls aquiver, showing his threatening fangs before sitting back down with his bone. He never took his eyes off me. Ungrateful creature.

A light came on inside the house. I ran to the little door and pulled. Locked? My piece of metal lay on the ground at my feet. Worried about Stalin, I had let the door shut without paying attention to it. Now I was caught like a rat in a trap. It was only a question of seconds before I was discovered. Anxiety overcame me, violent and oppressive, to which was added the anger of impotence. No other way out! The whole garden was surrounded by impassable railings, ten feet high, with spikes on the top. There was no nearby tree I could make use of, no wall, nothing. I caught sight of Stalin. He was moving his head, his teeth fastened on the bone, which he was shaking every now and then, his fangs shining white in the night. Behind him, the four great kennels were perfectly lined up just under the fence.

I swallowed hard.

Dubreuil had said that in the business world, persecutors didn't choose their victims randomly. And what about dogs? Would Stalin attack me if I weren't tormented by fear as soon as I saw him? How would he react if I were perfectly calm, relaxed, and even confident?

It was the only way out.

A little voice spoke inside me, a tiny whisper telling me I had to face this trial. Doubtless, the piece of metal had fallen by chance, but chance, Einstein said, was God traveling incognito. I had a premonition that life was presenting me with a chance to change and that if I didn't grasp the proffered opportunity, I would remain forever ensnared in my fears.

My fears. Stalin terrified me. To what extent was his viciousness induced by the vision I had of him? Was my fear the fruit of his aggressiveness or the spark that set it off? Would I have the courage to confront my fear, master it, and then go up to him? *A brave man only dies once,* says the proverb, *while the coward has already died a thousand times.*

I took a deep breath and then slowly expelled all the air from my lungs. I did it again and again, deep breaths, calming myself down, freeing the slightest contraction of my muscles. Each breath helped me relax more. After a while, I felt my heartbeat slow down more.

Stalin's a good boy, a good dog, I told myself. *I'm good.*

I feel good. I feel confident—confident about me, confident about him. I like him, and he likes me, too. Everything's fine.

I started walking forward slowly, looking vaguely in the direction of the first kennel and breathing calmly, relaxing more and more. Everything's fine.

I continued walking, paying no attention to the dog, directing my thoughts to the color of the kennel, the mildness of the evening, the quiet of the garden.

I never once looked at Stalin, but out of the corner of my eye, I saw that he had lifted his head. I continued walking forward, keeping my attention and my thoughts on harmless aspects of my surroundings, maintaining my feeling of confidence and calm. I finally hauled myself up on top of the kennel. The good dog didn't move. I climbed over the fence, then dropped down on the other side before disappearing into the night.

For more than a month, I had been letting people I didn't know govern my life. I had made it a point of honor to respect my promise. What had I been hoping for, exactly? That Dubreuil would keep his promise and make me a free and fulfilled man? But how could I become free by submitting to someone else's will? I had closed my eyes, refusing to see this obvious paradox, blinded by the egocentric pleasure of having someone take an interest in me. And now I had discovered that our meeting wasn't chance. These people had hidden motives I knew nothing about.

I could understand Dubreuil being concerned about my fate after the Eiffel Tower business. Saving someone's life sets up something irresistible that makes you continue in the direction you have started. But it was impossible to explain him writing reports about me *before* our meeting. This incomprehension became a source of anxiety that was constantly with me. My sleep became disturbed, agitated. During the day I was tense and worried.

The wording of the terms of our pact was constantly on my mind: *You must respect our contract; otherwise your life will come to an end.*

My life was entirely in this man's hands.

Then there was the additional fact that now I knew I was being followed. It's difficult to live normally under those conditions. Whether you're in the Métro, at the supermarket, or even sitting quietly in an outdoor café, you're constantly aware that someone is observing you. Those first days, it made me change my habits: I would leave the Métro at the last moment, just before the doors shut, or duck out of a movie theater by the emergency exit. But far from freeing my mind, these pathetic acts simply reinforced my disquiet, and in the end I decided to give them up.

I heard nothing from Dubreuil in the following days, which instead of reassuring me, made my imagination run wild and the questions multiply. Did he know about my intrusion? Had I been tailed that night? Had the naked girl revealed my presence? And what effect would it have on the pact that bound us? Would he give me back my freedom or, on the contrary, increase the pressure on me? I didn't think he was the type to capitulate that easily.

I spent Saturday wandering around Paris, trying to forget the situation I had gotten myself into. I walked at random through the narrow streets of the Marais, where the medieval buildings sometimes lean so much you wonder by what miracle they're still standing. I lingered under the arches of the Place des Vosges. I walked along the Rue des Rosiers, where I stumbled onto a Jewish pastry shop that had kept intact the charm and atmosphere of past centuries. The smell of the cakes just out of the oven made me want to buy out the whole shop. I left with an apple strudel that was still warm, which I ate while walking along the old cobblestone streets among the weekend crowds. When evening came, I went back to my own neighborhood, exhausted but satisfied with my day, fully feeling the healthy fatigue of the *flâneur,* the stroller.

Reaching the corner of two dark, deserted streets, I jumped as I felt a hand on my shoulder. I turned around. I was face-to-face with Vladi, who towered over me.

"Follow me," he said calmly but without any explanation.

"Why?" I hurriedly replied, looking around me and seeing, to my annoyance, that we were alone.

He didn't reply but merely pointed to the Mercedes parked on the sidewalk. The rest of his body remained as motionless as a rock.

I didn't have the strength to break into a sprint. Shouting would have been pointless.

"Just tell me why," I pleaded.

"Monsieur Dubreuil order."

He could scarcely have been more laconic. I knew I'd get nothing more out of him. He opened the car door. I didn't budge. He, too, remained motionless, calmly looking at me without any aggressiveness in his eyes. In the end I reluctantly got in. The door closed with a dull click. I was the only passenger. Ten seconds later he set off.

The soft comfort of the seat transformed my fear into despondency. I felt like a fugitive, caught by the police, who is used to journeys in the police van and almost feels relieved. I found myself yawning.

"Where are you taking me?"

No answer.

"Tell me where we're going, or else I'm getting out!"

No reaction. I felt a mixture of anger and apprehension.

The car finally stopped at a light. My muscles contracted, ready to leap out. I tried the door handle on my side. Locked!

"Me put child protection so you not fall this night on highway."

"What do you mean, *highway, this night?*"

"Me advise you sleep. Car all night."

I stiffened instinctively, seized by a feeling of panic. What was all this nonsense? I had to get out of here!

We drove past Ste-Marie Madeleine and turned down the Rue Royale. There were no policemen I could try and signal through the window. The window. Yes, of course, the window! I could get out that way. Vladi's window was already down; I could feel the air rushing in. He wouldn't hear me opening my window if I did it while he was accelerating.

I waited nervously, my finger on the switch. We arrived at the Place de la Concorde. For a second, Vladi turned his head toward the Fontaine des Fleuves, where some teenagers were shouting and splashing each other. Conscious of playing my final card, I pressed the switch and the window came down. I held my breath. We passed in front of the Obélisque, and then the light turned red at the corner of the Champs-Elysées. The car stopped.

I dived out.

I was immediately gripped by the ankle, very hard, and felt myself being pulled back inside. I screamed, grabbing the door to keep my chest outside the car. I waved in the direction of some nearby cars, but the passengers were all turned the other way, admiring the lights of the Champs-Elysées. I struggled, shouted, banged on the body of the car.

Vladi managed to get me completely back in the car, almost ripping an ear off in the process.

"Calm down, calm down," he said. There is nothing more annoying than hearing that. Especially coming from a man whose pulse is 25 while yours is 200.

I continued to struggle, landing a few blows in vain. Finally, I swallowed my anger, resigned myself, and the car set off again. Then, everything happened very quickly. We sped across the Seine and past the Assemblée Nationale, then along the Boulevard Saint-Germain toward the Luxembourg Gardens. Ten minutes later, the long, black Mercedes was speeding along the highway to the south, a bird of prey cleaving the night.

THE JOLTS WOKE me up. I opened my eyes and sat up, totally panicked, not knowing where I was. Seeing the back of Vladi's head brought me back to earth. The Mercedes was climbing a very steep, stony track. Vladi didn't even bother to avoid the many potholes, and the beams of his headlights bobbed up and down in the night, lighting up stone ruins, then getting lost among the stars.

I had tried to remain awake, but the long, monotonous hours on the highway had gotten the better of me. My mouth was dry.

"Where are we?" I said with difficulty.

"Soon there."

The car was climbing a barren hillside. No houses in sight, only the dark silhouettes of scrawny trees with tortured trunks that stood out against the stones and clumps of dried grass. I felt like I was on the way to prison.

The car stopped on a ledge near the top of the hill. The path was strewn with boulders from a wall that had partially collapsed. Vladi switched off the engine and suddenly everything was totally quiet. He remained motionless for a few moments and then got out. Warm air wafted into the car. My pulse began to race again. What were we doing in such a place?

Vladi stretched a few times to relax his back. A giant in his black suit, he resembled a huge scarecrow blown by the night wind. He opened my door. I shivered.

212

"Get out, please."

I got out, pain stabbing me all over my body. The *please* reassured me a little, but when my eyes got used to the darkness and I could make out more of where we were, my anxiety level shot back up.

In front of us, tall and imposing, stood the ruins of an abandoned castle. The partially collapsed walls, lit from afar by the Mercedes' headlights, were silhouetted against the black sky. A medieval tower with battlements was still standing, as if by magic, since its base was missing stones, leaving dark, gaping holes.

A deathly silence haunted the spot, broken only by the occasional gloomy call of a barn owl.

"Come," he said.

He made a way for us through the scattered stones and weeds. The brambles tugged at our trousers, slowing us down.

My final hour had come. It was obvious that he would finish me off, in the middle of nowhere, with no one to see or hear us.

After a few yards, he turned around.

"Arms up."

"What?"

"You, arms up, please."

The bastard was going to shoot me like a dog, and he had the gall to be polite about it. I felt the blood beating in my forehead.

I raised my arms.

He came over and frisked me from the shoulders to the knees. Twice he stopped and searched my pockets, emptying out their contents. He took my wallet with my ID, my money, my credit cards, and my Métro tickets, stuffing them in a black bag that he carefully zipped shut. No one would be able to identify my corpse, and as I had no family, no one would claim it. I would end up in a communal grave.

He glanced around furtively to check that there were no witnesses and then reached in his pocket.

I looked around us one last time, hoping to take with me some final images of the world, but the place was so dreary I shut my eyes.

"Take this," he ordered.

I half-opened my eyelids. He was holding something out to me. Surely he wasn't going to ask me to do the job myself?

"Here!"

I leaned forward, unable in the darkness to see the small object he was holding out. A coin. A one-euro coin.

"What am I supposed to do with that?"

At that moment, a guttural noise made me jump. In a horrible rustling of wings, a flock of bats flew out of a narrow slit in the tower.

Imperturbable, Vladi went on, "Take, please. You allowed this. It's all."

"But . . . I . . . don't understand."

"Monsieur Dubreuil say you learn cope all alone. All alone. One euro, it's all. Monsieur Dubreuil expect you for dinner tonight seven o'clock. You be on time. Monsieur Dubreuil hate late dinner."

His mission accomplished, he turned around.

An enormous weight lifted from my shoulders, from my whole being. I felt . . . empty. My legs shook. I couldn't believe it. I would have hugged him if I had had the strength.

"Wait!" I called out.

He didn't even glance back but got in the car and started the engine. He did a risky U-turn, stirring up a cloud of dust that seemed to catch fire in the headlights, then the Mercedes pulled away, shaken in every direction by the ruts in the track. It disappeared and silence fell again, a heavy, leaden silence. The darkness was almost total. I turned toward the castle and shivered. In the weak light of the waning moon, the ruins were even more frightening. The place gave off a deep malaise, not just the natural fear that you might legitimately feel in this sort of place. I had the inexplicable feeling that these ruins were charged with heavy emotion, past suffering. Horrible things had happened here, and the stones bore their invisible marks. I could have sworn it.

I ran down the slope, in a hurry to leave this frightening spot as quickly as possible. Several times, I nearly twisted my ankle on the loose stones. Out of breath, I came to some old, gray stone houses with roofs covered in strange round tiles. I slowed down.

Hunger was beginning to overtake me. I mustn't think about it. I hadn't eaten anything earlier that evening, waiting to get home to have dinner. Now I bitterly regretted it.

Walking on, I came to an old village, clinging to the side of a hill. There was nothing I could do before sunrise. I sat down on a stone bench worn smooth by time and took deep breaths, allowing my hands to run over its coarse surface. I imagined, behind the thick, stone walls of the houses, the slumbering villagers, sleeping peacefully in beds with rough sheets smelling of the sun that had dried them. I was glad to be alive.

Day finally broke and, along with it came the scents of nature at dawn. Before my eyes, an enchanting view unfolded. The village I was in was perched on the side of a small mountain with steep slopes covered in trees. A few hundred yards away was another small mountain, rising up to more or less the same height as the one I was on. At its summit was another village made up of old gray stone houses. Everywhere, covering the sides of the hills down to the bottom of the valleys, were bushes and trees and scrub, mostly prickly, in varying shades of green tinged with blue. The sun appeared, awakening the perfume of the umbrella pine that was covering me with its protective dome.

I set about exploring the village. It was immediately apparent that there was only one main street. I walked the length of the village without meeting a soul. But here and there through the open windows, I could hear voices, speaking with a regional accent.

I had to gather, as soon as possible, the information I needed to organize my return. Rounding a bend, I saw a café that seemed to be the last house in the village before the road dropped off into the valley. The doors were wide open, so I went in.

The ten or so people in the room instantly stopped talking. The barman—mustachioed, 50-ish—was wiping glasses behind the bar. As I headed across the room, I said a timid "hello" that got no response. The customers were suddenly absorbed in their thoughts, looking down at their glasses.

Reaching the bar, I again said hello, this time to the barman, who merely looked up without responding.

"May I have a glass of water, please?"

"A what?" he said loudly, looking around the room.

I turned just in time to see the derisive smiles, before the faces looked down again.

"A glass of water. I have no money on me, and I'm dying of thirst."

The barman didn't answer but reached for a glass on a shelf, filled it from the tap, then banged it down on the bar.

I took a few gulps. The silence was heavy. I had to break the ice.

"It's going to be a lovely day, isn't it?"

No answer. I went on, "I hope it won't be too hot, though."

The barman looked at me slightly mockingly as he continued wiping his glasses. "Where are you from?" he finally asked.

A miracle. He'd said something.

"Right now, I've arrived from the castle . . . up there. I just came down this morning."

He looked up at the other customers, then back at me. "Look, we all know no one lives up there."

"No . . . but . . . well, I was left at the castle last night, and I came down this morning. That's all I meant. I'm not trying to be funny."

"You're from Paris, right?"

"Yes, you could say that."

"Are you from Paris or aren't you? It's not a question of whether or not you could say that."

His accent was so musical I couldn't work out if this was his ordinary tone or he was annoyed. I needed information, so I had to keep the conversation going.

"Actually, this castle, how old is it?"

"The castle," he said, wiping the glasses more slowly. "The castle used to belong to the Marquis de Sade."

"The Marquis de Sade?!" I couldn't suppress a shudder.

"Yes."

"And where are we, exactly?"

"What do you mean, where are we?"

"Well, what place are we in?"

Amused, he looked around the room, before saying, "You've been drinking more than water, haven't you?"

"No, I haven't!" I insisted. "It's a long story. Just tell me where I am."

"You're in Lacoste, in the Lubéron. You're on another planet."

Suppressed giggles spread around the room. The barman was pleased with himself.

"The Lubéron. So we're in Provence, is that right?"

"Well, I never! See what you can do when you try!"

Provence. I must be 500 or 600 miles from Paris.

"Where's the nearest train station?"

Again, he shot a look around the room.

"The nearest station is in Bonnieux," he said, pointing to the village perched on the opposite mountain.

I was saved. An hour or two's walk, and I would be on my way home.

"Do you know what time the next train for Paris leaves?"

Laughter in the room. The barman was jubilant.

"What's so funny?" I asked. "Has it already left? Is that what's funny?"

The barman looked at his watch. More laughter.

"But it's very early!" I said. "There must be another one later in the day. When does the last train leave?"

"The last train left . . . in 1938."

Guffaws all around. I swallowed hard. The barman was enjoying his success. While he was at it, he offered a round of drinks. Conversations picked up where they had left off when I came in.

"Here, let me offer you a drink," the barman said, putting a glass of white wine on the bar in front of me. "To your health."

We clinked glasses. I wasn't going to tell him I didn't drink on an empty stomach. I'd had my bellyful of mocking for the day.

"Look, the station at Bonnieux has been shut down for seventy years. Trains for Paris all leave from Avignon now. You'll find nothing nearer."

"Is it far to Avignon?"

He drank a sip of white wine, then wiped his moustache with the back of his hand.

"Forty-three kilometers."

Almost 37 miles. That was a lot.

"Perhaps there's a bus?"

"During the week there is, but not on Sunday. Today, apart from me, nobody is working here," he said, lifting his glass to his lips.

"You wouldn't know someone who could take me to Avignon?"

"Today? With this heat, people don't go out much, you know. Except to church. Can't you wait till tomorrow?"

"No, I absolutely have to be in Paris this evening."

"Oh! Parisians are always in a rush, even on Sunday!"

I left, saying good-bye to all present, who this time returned my greeting.

I walked along the street in the direction the barman had indicated. "The road to Avignon is on the left, at the bottom," he had said. I was bound to get a lift.

The lane meandered prettily down the hillside, which was covered in aromatic thorn bushes. I was in Provence! I'd heard so much about Provence. It was even more beautiful than I had imagined. I had pictured an arid region, beautiful but parched. But now, in front of me as far as the eye could see, was vegetation of amazing richness: Holm oaks, pine trees with their trunks glowing red in the sun, cedars, beech, cypress raising their bluish tint to the sky, and on the ground, thistles, broom, great clumps of rosemary, bushes with varnished leaves shamelessly showing off their gaudy beauty, and countless other varieties of plants. I was filled with wonder.

The sun, although still low in the sky, was beginning to beat down, and the heat revived the perfumes of nature, spreading a thousand exquisite scents that accompanied me through this paradise of the senses.

At the foot of the mountain, the road wound around the valley amidst orchards and groves of trees. I had been walking for more than an hour without seeing a single car. Hitchhiking wasn't going to be easy. I was famished and had a slight headache as well. It was beginning to get really hot. I wasn't going to be able to continue walking much longer.

Another 20 minutes had gone by when I heard the sound of an engine. A gray van came around the bend behind me, traveling at a moderate speed. It was at least 20 or 30 years old, the van version of the Citroën 2 CV, the Deux Chevaux, that I had seen in picture books of France when I was a kid. I stood right in the middle of the road, arms stretched wide. The driver jammed on its brakes with a screeching noise, and the van coughed, then stalled. The driver got out, a short man with a belly, gray hair, and a red complexion, obviously angry with me and perhaps also annoyed at having stalled.

"What a stupid thing to do! What are you playing at, for Christ's sake? It hasn't got the brakes of a Ferrari on it, you know, I nearly ran you over! And who'd pay for the repairs? You can't get spares for love or money!"

"I'm sorry. Look, I've got a problem: I absolutely must get to Avignon as quickly as possible. I've been walking two hours in this sun. I haven't eaten since yesterday afternoon, and I'm at the end of my rope. You're not going that way, by any chance, are you?"

"Avignon? What the hell would I be going there for?"

"Perhaps where you're going would bring me a bit closer?"

"Well, I'm going to Les Poulivets. It's a bit in that direction, but look here, I've got to stop on the way. I've got things to do."

"No problem! The main thing is to get me closer. Then I'm bound to find another car."

I could feel he was about to give in.

"Please . . ."

"Okay, get in the back, I've got lots of things in the

front, and I'm not going to clear it all out for you. I don't even know you."

"Great!"

We went around the vehicle, and he opened one side of the back door.

"Sit there," he said, pointing to two wooden crates that took up the tiny space inside.

I had barely climbed inside when he slammed the door shut, throwing me into complete darkness. I fumbled my way to the crates and sat down as best I could.

He had two tries at starting before the engine sputtered to life and the van moved off, vibrating all over. A strong odor of diesel surrounded me.

I had great difficulty remaining seated. The top of my crate was strangely sloped, and I nearly slid off each time he accelerated, took a bend, or braked. I blindly felt around the sides of the van but could find nothing to hold onto. The situation was so absurd I had a fit of the giggles. It was the first time in my life I had laughed by myself.

The van finally stopped. The motor choked, and I heard the driver's door slam. Then, nothing. Silence. Surely he wasn't going to leave me in here?

"Hello! Hello!" I called.

No answer.

Suddenly, I made out a slight humming noise. It seemed to be coming from under the car. Then the sound of voices outside. When you can't see, your other senses become more acute. The humming intensified. Yes, that's it, the sound was coming from . . . inside my crate! But, good God! Surely it wasn't . . .? Yes, a BEEHIVE!

I stood up at once and banged my head on the roof. At that moment, the front door slammed, the engine coughed, and the van leapt forward. I was thrown against the back door and fell down, stuck between the door and the hives.

We must have been going down a dirt track, as the ride was so bumpy. Staying where I was seemed the best thing to do. I had only one worry: being stung by my thousands of traveling companions. Could they get out of their hives?

We finally stopped again, not without a final shake from the engine. The front door slammed. I waited. The back door opened suddenly, and I fell to the ground at my liberator's feet.

"Yes, I thought I smelled wine on you! You don't eat anything, but you have to have your little drink, right?"

I looked up at him, completely blinded by the light.

"It's not what you think."

"I believe what I see, like Saint Thomas, or rather, what I smell!"

I got up, blinking to get used to the strong light.

The view that offered itself was dazzling. At my feet were laid out opulent rows of lavender, flooding the valley we were in with blue, caressing the bases of the fruit trees that bordered it, and rising up the hill in the distance. From this colored beauty came a delicious perfume that almost made me forget the awkward situation I was in. But the most impressive thing was the song, or rather the din of the cicadas! The chirring sound was so loud it seemed as if all the cicadas in Provence had come here to greet me.

"Come on, out of the way, I've got things to do!"

The driver leaned inside the van and grabbed one of the hives.

"Here, help me! We can take one each."

I followed him, carrying my hive at arm's length.

"We'll put them there," he said, pointing to a space in the middle of the flowers.

"You make lavender honey?" I said, marveling. "I never imagined that people moved hives to put them in lavender fields."

"What do you think? That it's enough to give them a

road map and tell them not to stop on the other flowers on the way?"

With that, he turned back to the van.

"So tell me the truth," he said. "Why are you in such a hurry to get the train in Avignon?"

"Actually, it's a bit complicated. Let's say I've been given a sort of challenge. My identification and my money were taken away, and I've got to find a way of getting back to Paris. To succeed, I've got to be back by the end of this afternoon at the latest."

"A test? You mean it's a game?"

"Sort of, yes."

He looked at me sideways, and then a light shone in his eyes.

"Ha! I've got it, you're doing the qualifying tests for a TV show like *The Amazing Race!* Is that it?"

"Actually . . ."

"Well, I never! When I tell my wife about this, she's never going to believe me!"

"Yes but—"

"And then, if you're selected, we'll see you on TV this winter."

"Wait, I didn't—"

"She'll never believe it! Never!"

"Listen . . ."

"Wait, wait . . ."

He suddenly had an inspired look.

"Look," he said, "suppose I take you straight to Avignon station? Does that mean you're sure to win?"

"Yes, but . . ."

"Right. Here's how it is: I'll take you straight to the station if you'll come back with me and pose for photos with the family. What do you say?"

"Well, actually . . ."

"Just a few photos, and we'll be off to the station! That way, you'll be selected, and we'll see you on TV!" He didn't wait for an answer. "Come on, off we go! Hurry up!"

He opened the back door again, all excited. "Stay in the back. I can't move everything. We haven't got time. You've got a challenge!"

I sat on the floor, glad to be traveling on my own this time. I could hear talking on the other side of the thin metal partition. My driver was on his cell phone.

"Hi, Josette! Get out the aperitifs; I'm bringing a contestant from *The Amazing Race*. No, *The Amazing Race*, I'm telling you. Are you there? We'll see him on TV this winter. Yes, I'm telling the truth. Go and get the camera, and check that there are batteries in it! Batteries, I said. Yes. And tell Michel; he'll never believe it. And call Babette as well and tell her to get a move on if she wants to be in the photo. There's no signal. Hurry up. You there?"

My God, he was rounding up the whole planet. Oh, no, what was I going to tell them?

After a quarter of an hour, the car finally stopped, and I heard lively conversation.

My door was opened, and once my eyes got used to the dazzling light again, I saw about a dozen people gathered in a welcoming committee.

"Hey, what's your name, by the way?" asked my driver.

"Alan."

"Alan? That's an American star's name. It'll look good on the TV."

"Alan . . ." murmured a pregnant woman in the group, looking transported.

I don't think I'd ever been photographed so much in all my life. I could already see myself ensconced on any number of mantelpieces, until the next season of the TV game show started.

My driver was jubilant. He was the center of attraction. He was drinking aperitif after aperitif and beginning to turn quite red. Three times, he ignored my request to leave for the station.

"Look, I really must go. Otherwise I'm going to miss the train, and all this will have been pointless."

"Wait, wait . . . Oh, they're so stressed, these Parisians!" He picked up his phone.

"Mom, hurry up, I said. And tell Grandpa, he'll never forgive me otherwise!"

"No," I said. "This is no good. You must keep your side of the deal. *Now!*"

He didn't appreciate my remark at all, and his red face went purple.

"Listen, I didn't make you get in my van, right? I think it was rather the opposite, wasn't it? So don't be ungrateful now, or else I'm not going to Avignon!"

Now he was really getting fired up.

Perhaps it was already too late to arrive at Dubreuil's for 7 o'clock dinner. Dubreuil. He said it was important to be able to get things from other people. But how could I do that here? What would Dubreuil do?

Push him, he'll push you back. Don't push, pull.

I immediately had an idea, but something held me back. Up till now, I had been riding along on a misunderstanding, but I didn't want to openly lie. Right. Let's put things differently.

"You know, if I end up on TV one day, I'll probably be allowed to invite a guest or two," I said.

He looked up, suddenly all ears.

"But," I went on, "I don't want to build up false hopes."

"If I take you straight to the station, you promise to invite me on the set?" the driver asked, suddenly as serious as if he was negotiating putting a hundred beehives on my lavender field.

"Yes, but I'm reluctant to break up your little party."

He turned to the others and spoke in a loud voice.

"My friends," he said. "Carry on without us. I'll be back in less than an hour. I'm taking Alan to Avignon. He's got to win his challenge."

Half an hour later, I was getting on a high-speed train for the capital, my stomach still as empty, my only euro still in my pocket.

I knew the regulations: Traveling without a ticket meant a fine; with no ID on me, it was the police station on arrival.

I had a plan, which was worth trying. I remained standing, looking out for the ticket inspector in the distance. When I saw him appear at the other end of the car, I ducked into the bathroom and shut the door without locking it. If he thought it was empty, he'd go past without stopping. I waited. The minutes went by, and nothing happened. I was alone, shut in with the continuous noise of the train and the dreadful smell of the toilet.

Suddenly, the door opened, and a surprised passenger found himself face-to-face with me. Over his shoulder, my eyes met those of an obviously very satisfied little man with a black moustache and dark, frowning eyebrows, wearing a navy blue cap and uniform.

Frowning, Catherine leaned forward slightly. "I'd like to talk about the way you helped Alan stop smoking."

Yves Dubreuil sank back in his teak armchair and swirled the ice cubes around in his glass of bourbon, a slight smile on his lips. He loved going back over his exploits and commenting on them.

"You made him smoke more and more until he was disgusted by it, is that right?"

"Not at all," he replied, with the satisfaction of someone whose actions are so clever that not even a professional can understand them.

"I thought . . ."

"No, in fact, I simply reversed the current," he said.

"Reversed the current?"

He took his time answering, savoring the bourbon as much as the wait he was imposing on Catherine. The day had been particularly hot, and now they were enjoying the mild evening in the garden, comfortably seated in front of a tray of cookies.

Dubreuil finally broke the silence. "Remember, Alan said his problem was freedom. He really wanted to stop smoking somewhere deep down, but what was holding him back was the feeling of freedom he associated with cigarettes. Everyone was advising him to stop, so he didn't feel free to choose. Stopping his habit would have made him feel he was giving up his freedom in order to submit to the will of others."

Catherine was listening closely, concentrating on his words.

"So I reversed the current," he continued. "I made it so that smoking became for him a restrictive act imposed from outside. From then on, freedom changed sides. It was by stopping that he could satisfy his thirst for freedom."

Catherine said nothing, but an attentive observer might have seen a gleam of admiration in her eyes.

THEY WAITED UNTIL the waiter from the Intercontinental Hotel had finished serving them. "Please call if you need anything whatsoever, Monsieur Dunker," he murmured before withdrawing.

The brown leather padded door to the private room closed silently. Marc Dunker looked around him at the opulent mahogany bookcases filled with books bound in red leather a little too shiny to be old. Lamps with gilt bases and emerald-green opaline shades added to the intimate, rather somber atmosphere of the room.

Dunker had chosen this place on Andrew's advice. Situated on the Place de l'Opéra, not far from the office, the hotel offered, according to Andrew, a setting that commanded respect and a certain reserve—very English qualities favorable to productive negotiations. It was the third time the trio had met there, and Dunker was still pleased with the choice. He particularly appreciated the large leather armchairs that seemed to swallow up his two principal shareholders, while his height enabled him to enjoy an advantageous position. He was convinced this arrangement had an impact on their relations that was far from negligible.

"We've reached agreement," said the pudgier of the two men meeting with Dunker, casting a glance at his colleague. He smiled as he spoke, from time to time raising his eyebrows, which created waves of creases on his nearly bald head. Short and plump, David Poupon, despite his age, still looked like a big smiling baby, with a friendly manner that Dunker was enormously suspicious of. The CEO preferred the other shareholder, Rosenblack, who was much leaner and less friendly. Never looking up from the papers he was going through, Rosenblack didn't make the slightest effort to hide the fact that he had no interest whatsoever in Dunker as a person.

Dunker screwed up his eyes, concentrating on Poupon, who was announcing their demands. "We have reached the conclusion that for both the investment fund I run and the pension fund represented by our friend here," he said, smiling in the direction of Rosenblack, who was still absorbed in his papers, "your company must produce fifteen percent profits in the next quarter, and the market price of the shares must increase by at least eighteen percent annually."

Dunker remained silent until he was sure Poupon had finished. He then gave himself a few seconds to drink a sip of cognac. He knew the power of silence.

"I can't promise an eighteen percent increase in the stock price, because I don't control all the parameters, as you know. And then . . ."

He took a second sip of his drink, keeping his audience in suspense.

"And then, there's that stupid bastard of a journalist, Fisherman, who continues to undermine our image by repeating nonsense about us. Unfortunately, his analyses influence the financial markets."

"We are convinced you are capable of managing this sort of situation," Poupon said. "It's for that very reason that at the last annual meeting we chose to keep you as CEO."

Dunker heard the barely veiled threat loud and clear. "You know as well as I do that journalists can't be controlled," he told Poupon. "Try as we might to feed him good news at every opportunity, Fisherman repeats in article after article that our teams are not productive enough, which is quite untrue. I keep them under pressure, and they work hard," he said, with the pride of a captain defending his troops.

"There's rarely smoke without fire," said Rosenblack without looking up.

"I have every confidence in your ability to find a solution," said Poupon.

After several minutes of silence, Dunker announced, "I've got an idea, but I need your agreement beforehand, because it's not without consequences."

"Ha! See what you can do when you want to?" Poupon was clearly satisfied to have been right.

Dunker ignored the dig. "My idea is based on an artificial inflating of the turnover."

Rosenblack at last raised a glum eye in Dunker's direction, like a sleepy old dog lying by the fireside, who wonders, without really believing it, whether the word *walk* hasn't just been slipped into the conversation.

"Until now," Dunker explained, "we have followed strict procedures to check the solvency of our customers before signing contracts with them. If they show financial difficulties, we demand that they pay the total fee in advance, which of course they rarely accept. If we changed that rule and closed our eyes to the financial health of new clients, we would get an immediate increase in turnover of about twenty percent."

Poupon, attentive, had a look of complicity. Rosenblack looked skeptical.

"I have calculated," Dunker went on, "that if we did this, we would risk having thirty percent of payments outstanding, which wouldn't be too problematic for two reasons. One, the stock exchange only looks at the turnover figures and couldn't care less about outstanding payments.

Two, our consultants get their commissions on the basis of client payments, not on the turnover figures as such. No payment, no commission. So we'll do all right. Overall, we won't lose too much, and the share price will go up."

"Excellent," said Poupon.

Rosenblack slowly nodded. "And what about the fifteen percent profits?" he asked.

Dunker slowly took another sip of cognac. "You can leave that to me."

Poupon smiled. "Perfect! But that's bad news for you. The golden parachute of three million euros that's provided for you in your contract in case of severance won't be coming your way this year."

Even Rosenblack made an effort to laugh, as the three men clinked glasses.

"You find us tough," Poupon told Dunker, "but that's how the world goes around: You're tough with your colleagues, we're tough with you, and our own clients are tough with us. We've always got someone above us, haven't we?"

"I DON'T BELIEVE you. Not for a single second."

The assertion came like a sentence with no possibility of appeal, followed by a heavy silence, under the depressing light cast by the old neon tube.

"But it's the truth," I protested, quite at a loss.

The policeman was walking back and forth behind his desk. I was perched uncomfortably on what looked like a little school chair. The place was really getting me down. I was hungry. Desperately hungry. And I was really pissed off.

"Let's start again at the beginning."

"It's the fourth time . . ."

I had begun by trying to reply to the policeman's questions as vaguely as possible, talking about a challenge I was supposed to meet, trying to make him believe, without overtly lying, that I was the victim of a sort of initiation rite. But the guy seemed to be taking the matter very seriously. All this for traveling without a ticket. Didn't he have anything better to do? Finally, he trapped me by bombarding me with questions, cross-examining me until I had to spill the beans and tell him all about my relations with Dubreuil. Even so, he absolutely refused to believe me. So I tried as energetically as I could to convince him of my good faith, but the more I argued, the more he questioned what I was saying.

"You say you are following the instructions given by a man you don't know, who is trying to help you but frightens you, who took your ID and dropped you off in his Mercedes at the other end of France to develop your coping skills. Is that right?"

"Yes, in a nutshell."

"And you think I'm going to swallow something like that? In all the time I've been doing this job, I've never heard anything so ridiculous!"

I would never be able to convince him. It would take me all evening, perhaps all night. I had to approach it differently. How could I persuade him I was telling the truth?

If you push, he'll resist. Reverse the current.

I had an idea.

"There's something else . . ." I said in a confessional tone of voice.

He couldn't hide the hint of a smile, thinking he was about to make me fess up.

"What?"

I waited a few moments. "Oh, no, I can't tell you."

He stared at me, a little surprised. "Why not?"

I looked him straight in the eyes. "Because I don't trust you."

Imperceptibly, his face went purple. "What do you mean, don't trust?"

I took my time. "I don't trust . . . your ability to listen."

"What are you talking about?" he stammered, getting redder and redder.

I looked down at the ground and put on a sad face. "It's a private story, and I don't want to confide in someone who can't even be bothered to sit down to listen to me."

He swallowed hard.

"And in any case," I went on, "as you won't believe me, there's no point in talking to you about it."

Several seconds went by. I wasn't looking at him, but I

could feel that he hadn't taken his eyes off me. I could hear the sound of his breathing.

He sat down.

The silence lasted a long while.

I decided to tell him everything.

"I attempted suicide, a while ago. A man was there by chance. That's what I thought, at least. He saved my life in exchange for my irrevocable promise to do all he asked. For my own good."

He listened in silence.

"It's a sort of pact," I went on. "I accepted it of my own free will."

The heat in the office was stifling. I needed air.

"And you've really done all he asked?"

"You could say that, yes."

"You realize that if he made you do illegal things, you're the one who's responsible?"

"He hasn't asked that. Besides, he didn't explicitly tell me to take the train without a ticket. That's not the problem."

"Even so, I don't understand why you followed his orders like that. You were free to end your agreement, after all. Anyone would have done so in your position."

"I've often asked myself that. I don't know, I think I attached too much importance to keeping my word."

"Come on, come on, you're not one of the Three Musketeers! Loyalty's a good thing, but here your own interests are at stake."

"Until recently, what he demanded of me was, I'll grant you, difficult to do, but at the same time it brought me a lot. I felt as if I was getting somewhere."

"I really don't see how it's brought you anything but trouble," the policeman said.

"You know, I was very alone when I met him, and it's

very pleasant to have someone take an interest in you, look after you."

"Wait. To sum up, he extorted your promise at a time when you were weak, desperate. He takes you in hand, you follow him to the letter, and you shut your eyes as to his intentions. Is that right? But that's the way religious cults operate!"

"No, that's not what frightens me. Besides, the cults are after your money. He asks nothing. Given his age and his wealth, he can't be in need of much."

"Come on. He's not doing all this just to please you!"

"You're right. That's the problem. I don't know what his motives are. I discovered recently he was having me followed and that he had begun that before the meeting at the Eiffel Tower."

"So it wasn't by chance he was there the day of your . . ."

"Suicide attempt. No, he wasn't there by chance. But I'd never seen him before, I could swear. I don't know why he had me followed before that either. I can't explain it, and it's driving me crazy."

The old neon bulb flickered. The policeman looked at me, concerned. Having pushed me hard at the beginning of the interrogation, he now seemed to be expressing a certain empathy. I felt he was sincerely worried about my fate.

"Can you help me?" I asked.

"There's nothing, absolutely nothing I can do," he said, shaking his head. "If he hasn't committed a crime, I can't even start an investigation."

"In his house, there's a notebook filled with notes on me. The notes prove he is having me followed."

"If the notebook is in his house, I don't have access to it. We'd need a search warrant, and no judge would give us one, as there isn't the slightest hint of an offense that's been committed. In any case, it's not against the law to follow people."

"You know, the most complicated thing about this affair is that I have doubts," I said. "And there's a part of me that feels guilty at having told you all this."

"I don't follow."

"I can't be a hundred percent sure that his intentions are bad. I'll admit I was frightened to discover he'd had me followed before our first meeting. But putting that aside, I can't blame him for anything. Quite objectively, he's done nothing harmful to me."

"Look, you can't rule out that he's some old madman who thinks he's God-knows-who and gets pleasure out of playing the role of a savior and mentor. The simplest thing is to tell him you don't want to continue, that you're breaking the pact. You say, 'Thanks for everything, and good-bye,' and that's the end of it."

"Impossible."

"What's to stop you?"

"I didn't tell you, but . . . I promised on my life."

"What do you mean, *on your life*?"

"I agreed to forfeit my life if I don't do what he asks."

He looked at me for a moment, completely dumbstruck.

"Is this a joke?"

"No."

"You're as mad as he is! Don't ask me to help you now!"

"But you can't leave me in danger, now that you're aware of the situation!"

I cast a glance at the clock on the wall. "Right. I've got to be going, then," I said, getting up. "I've got to be at his house at seven o'clock."

The policeman looked at me without saying anything. Deep in thought, he suddenly leapt up, bothered.

"Wait. What proof is there that all this isn't a fairy

tale? That you haven't completely invented this story to get home peacefully?"

He was frowning, his face crimson again.

"If you don't believe me, come with me to his house."

He was obviously not expecting this answer. He looked first at me, then at the clock.

"Where is it?"

I searched in my pockets and took out Dubreuil's calling card, creased and limp as an old piece of material. He grabbed it and read it with a frown.

"In the sixteenth arrondissement?" he asked, recognizing the upscale address.

He hesitated a few seconds and then crossed the room to knock softly on a door.

"Sort it out yourself!" growled a voice on the other side.

The policeman thought for a moment, obviously torn between conflicting desires, and then went and opened a little metal cupboard. He got out a car key.

"Follow me!" he said.

• • •

An hour later, the policeman carefully put the key back in the cupboard. Still locked away in his office, his boss apparently hadn't noticed his absence.

There was no time to lose. The case he had been waiting for for months had just dropped into his lap all on its own, exactly as he had hoped. The young man hadn't lied. He had indeed gone into a mansion belonging to a certain Dubreuil. What a house! The policeman had never seen one like it. You didn't find residences like that around the Gare de Lyon, the railroad station, or the other areas he was used to. Who could afford a thing like that? *No doubt more dirty money,* he said to himself.

He would have to investigate without arousing the suspicions of his boss, who wouldn't fail to stop him or to take over what, he was sure, was going to allow him to reveal at last his real talents as a policeman.

The Gare de Lyon would soon have to make do without him.

THE HOUSE STOOD out against the twilight sky, a dark building full of mysteries and secrets.

I was taken to the library. Crossing the hall, I couldn't help but glance into the drawing room where I had seen the naked woman on the piano. The piano lay sadly abandoned in the semi-shade of the immense room, without either muse or musician to bring it to life.

I found Dubreuil comfortably settled in one of the library's deep leather armchairs, smoking. I was sure he hadn't had me followed from the village of Lacoste. It would have been mission impossible. So he couldn't know I had confided in the police.

Catherine was sitting opposite me. She greeted me. On the low table in front of them, I recognized my wallet and the rest of my personal effects.

"You see, in the end, money's useless. We can do without it very well!" Dubreuil said, an enormous Monte Cristo between his teeth.

What was he hiding behind his smile? What did this man want out of me in the end? Suppose the policeman was right? Perhaps he was the guru of some sect, or even a retired former guru, enriched with money extorted from his disciples, tormenting one last stray sheep to pass the time.

"By the way," he went on, "you didn't tell me how your interview with your director went."

So many things had happened to me since then that it seemed a long way away.

"Not bad."

I had been hungry for a day and a half, but Dubreuil didn't seem in any hurry to sit down to dinner.

"Did you resist the temptation to justify yourself when he goaded you, and did you ask him embarrassing questions in return?"

"Yes, and it worked really well. On the other hand, I didn't get much out of him. I wanted to negotiate additional resources for our department. I had to forget about that."

"Did you try hard enough to enter his universe and share his way of thinking before you tried to convince him?"

"Yes, more or less. Let's say I tried to demonstrate that my ideas served his requirements of efficiency and profitability. Anyhow, I think our values are so far apart that it would be impossible for me to endorse his vision of things, even to pretend. You know, it's hard to assume the values of your enemy."

Dubreuil puffed at his cigar.

"The idea isn't to endorse to his values. If they're not yours, it's impossible. But it's useful to make a distinction in your mind between the person and his values. Even if his values are despicable, the person can always be salvaged. So what counts is to stop judging those values for an instant and to tell yourself that even if they shock you, the only hope you have of making that person change his vision is to not reject him along with his ideas. Then, entering into his universe means trying to put yourself in his place, as if you were already in his skin, feeling from the inside what it is to believe what he believes, think what he thinks, and feel what he feels, before returning to your position. Only a process like this will allow you to really understand that person without judging him, to understand what motivates him and also what makes him go wrong, if that is the case."

"Hmm . . ."

"There's a difference between endorsing and understanding. If you put yourself in your boss's shoes sufficiently to understand his way of thinking without judging him, you'll be more tolerant of him, which he'll feel. And from then on, you'll be able to entertain the hope that he'll change."

"I'm not sure that he has any idea what others think about him," I said, "or if it even bothers him! But okay, let's suppose that I manage to enter sufficiently into his universe for him not to feel judged or rejected. What is there to make him budge from his present position? Don't I risk reinforcing his position instead?"

"Remember the other day when we practiced synchronizing ourselves with the other's gestures? I told you that after a while, if you do it long enough with the genuine intention of joining that person in their universe, then when you change your posture, the other person will start to follow you, even without realizing it."

"Yes."

"I think this happens because a sort of fusion is created at a very deep, unconscious level, even if no words have been exchanged. That quality of relationship is felt in one way or another, and it is so rare that each person wants to preserve it, to make it last."

"I see . . ."

"So, to reply to your previous question, I would say that if you manage, by entering without judgment into your enemy's universe—by slipping into his skin, his feelings, and his way of thought—to create this quality of human relationship that is so rare that he has perhaps never experienced it before, deep down he will want to preserve it so much that you'll only have to become yourself again, to naturally express your own values, for him to want to take an interest in them. You won't need to ask him to change, or need to give him a lesson in morality. Being yourself will be enough, thanks to the relationship you have created. You will have unconsciously made him want to open himself up to you, to discover your values, and, in the end, to allow himself to be influenced a little by you and thereby to modify his position. To change, in other words."

"You mean that having met him on his own ground, I make him want to come and discover mine?"

"Sort of. By being yourself, you present him with another model of the world, another vision of things, another way of behaving and acting, which he will be interested in without you having to criticize him or make demands."

"It reminds me of our conversation about Gandhi . . ."

"Yes. *We must be the change we want to see in the world.*"

I remained deep in thought. This perspective seemed very beautiful and admirable and, at the same time, difficult to realize. Would I have the desire, the courage, and the patience necessary to create the relationship that Dubreuil presented as an indispensable prerequisite to changing the other?

"To live for the business seems so pathetic," I told him. "When I was in the States, I knew a guy, Brian, who used to say: 'You want to make God crack up? Tell him your plans!'"

Catherine burst out laughing. I had forgotten she was there. Dubreuil took a sip of bourbon.

"Perhaps, for your boss, it's a way of forgetting the tragedy of his existence."

"The tragedy of his existence?"

"Deep in our unconscious," he went on, "we men are wounded by our inability to bear children and give life. I am utterly convinced that the professional ambition so prevalent in most of us comes from the unresolved need to compensate for this lack, to fill this sort of existential void."

I was dumbstruck. I had never imagined anything like that, never made such a connection. To me, the mad race for power was just the result of a mixture of aggressiveness and competitive energy, common masculine traits. It was strange to hear this from Dubreuil's lips, since I had the definite feeling that he had a certain taste for power. Could he be this insightful about himself?

After all, the misogyny of some men springs from an inferiority complex.

"To get back to my situation in the office," I said. "I don't know if the managing director is jealous of his wife, but I can't get anything out of him."

Dubreuil looked rather annoyed. Was it because I wasn't succeeding in applying his teachings, or because he wasn't able to transmit them as effectively as he would like?

He tossed his cigar into a large brass ashtray.

"You have within yourself all the necessary resources to take control of your life without passively accepting what others want to force on you," he declared.

He drank the remainder of his bourbon, banged the glass down on the coffee table, and stood up.

Catherine kept her eyes down on her notes.

"Here's what you're going to do," he said with a Machiavellian smile, as he paced up and down in front of the bookcases. "It's a new task you have to carry out."

"Yes?"

"You think your managing director is mistaken, that his decisions are bad for the company?"

"That seems obvious."

"You feel that the company should be managed differently, incorporating criteria other than purely financial ones?"

"Absolutely."

"So take his place."

"Very funny."

He looked me in the eyes. "I'm not joking, Alan."

"Yes, you are!"

He frowned. "No, I assure you."

I suddenly had grave doubts. Was he really serious?

Seeing my obvious embarrassment, he looked at me in silence for a few seconds.

"What's stopping you?" he asked in a honeyed voice.

I was thrown off balance by the question; it seemed so incongruous. What do you reply to someone who kindly asks you what's stopping you from becoming a foreign minister or an international star?

"But that's obvious," I said. "Come on, let's be realistic. There are limits to what we're capable of doing."

"The only limits are the ones we give ourselves."

I could feel myself getting angry. I knew him too well to think he would let go now. I was in a mess. Obviously, the guy swung between moments of lucidity, subtle analysis, and wild ravings.

"You do realize he's not even my boss? He's my boss's boss's boss! There are three levels in the hierarchy between us!"

Catherine had looked up and was staring at Dubreuil now.

"He who wants to climb the mountain mustn't let its height impress him."

"But have you ever set foot inside a company? You can't jump the rungs like that! There are rules!"

"The person who obeys rules avoids thinking. If you think inside the box, the only solutions you'll find are those that everyone else has already thought of. You have to think outside the box."

"Fine words, but what exactly would you do in my place?"

He sat on the arm of his chair and smiled as he looked at me.

"Find out for yourself, Alan. Dig into your resources."

I got up, determined to leave. I wasn't going to stay and have dinner with a madman.

"There's no way I can do that."

He spoke slowly, in a deep voice: "It's your last mission. Carry it out, and I will give you back your freedom."

My freedom. I looked up at him. He was smiling.

"You can't make my freedom depend on an impossible task. I won't accept that."

"But you're not in a position to choose, my dear Alan. Do I have to remind you of your promise?"

"How can I keep my promise if you make it impossible to do so?"

His eyes bore down on me with a look that was imperious, demanding, pitiless.

"I order you to become the managing director of Dunker Consulting."

I met his gaze.

"I'm giving you three weeks," he said.

"It's impossible."

"It's an order. Whatever happens, meet me on August 29th. I'll be waiting for you at eight o'clock at the Jules Verne."

My heart skipped a beat. The Jules Verne is the restaurant in the Eiffel Tower. As he said it, he lowered his voice, pronouncing the name very slowly, without taking his eyes off me. The threat was clear, awful. I felt my legs go weak. My past hopes were vain. I was definitely in the hands of a madman.

We remained motionless and silent, face-to-face, then I turned around. Walking to the door, I caught Catherine's eyes. She looked as appalled as I did.

"Yves Dubreuil doesn't exist," the policeman told me over the phone.

"Excuse me?"

"You heard right: Yves Dubreuil doesn't exist."

"I was with him two hours ago."

"His real name is Igor Dubrovski."

When I heard the name, I immediately felt vaguely uneasy without knowing why.

"He's a White Russian," the policeman went on, "a nobleman. His parents left Russia at the time of the revolution. They took their fortune with them. Apparently, it was one heap of dough. Then Igor was educated in France and the States. He became a psychiatrist."

"Psychiatrist?"

"Yes, a psychiatrist. But he hasn't practiced much."

"Why?"

"I can't get that info now, on a Sunday. It would appear he was struck off the register of doctors. I was told it's very rare for that to happen, so he must have done something serious. If I were you, I'd watch out."

At that moment I heard someone bellowing in the background. Snatches of conversation: "Who are you talking to? Who is it?" Then muffled sounds. The policeman must be putting his hand over the receiver.

"Headquarters has phoned," he told me when he resumed our conversation. "They say you've been asking for records. What are you up to? I don't want any hassle. You follow me? And also . . ."

I heard the beeping noise of a broken connection. He must have hung up. I suddenly felt alone, very alone, with a rising wave of anxiety.

I put down the phone. My apartment seemed very quiet, very empty. I was dumbfounded. The simple fact that Dubreuil had lied to me about his identity made me feel deeply uneasy. The man I had confided in wasn't who I thought he was.

Something serious. How serious could it be?

The physical and nervous fatigue that had built up since my kidnapping 24 hours earlier hit me like a sledgehammer, and I suddenly felt drained. I turned out the lights and curled up in bed, but in spite of my exhaustion, sleep didn't come.

Fear slowly took possession of me as the terms of my promise to Dubreuil came to mind: *On your life.*

This guy was quite capable of carrying out his threat. I was certain of that now.

• • •

I woke up in the middle of the night, covered in sweat. An answer had come to me in my sleep, at an hour when the unconscious, now the only one in charge, can find a lost memory in the bottomless pit of knowledge, experiences, and information that we've long since forgotten. *Dubrovski* was the name of the man who had written the article on suicide I had read—the one that revealed how to reach the girders of the Eiffel Tower, presented as an ideal place for a spectacular suicide.

I SPENT THE next day in a strange state. Apart from the insidious fear that accompanied me all the time now, I again felt dreadfully alone. That was even harder to bear than the fear.

In this hostile universe, only Alice found favor in my eyes. Granted, she was just a colleague, not a friend, but I valued her genuineness, her naturalness. I felt she quite simply liked me, without any ulterior motive. That was already a lot.

I saw four candidates during the day—strangers, of course, who talked about their lives in a favorable light. I found myself envying them, wishing I was in their place, pursuing a path they hoped would lead to a career, without asking metaphysical questions about the meaning of their lives. I wanted to become their friend, forgetting that their warm expressions were simply aimed at gaining my favor as a recruiter.

I left the office early. Outside my apartment building, I lingered with Étienne on the old stone stairs. I don't know why his presence and his serene expression reassured me so much. We talked about anything and everything while eating the still-warm apple turnovers I had bought at the bakery across the street.

Later, I searched my apartment from top to bottom, going through it with a fine-tooth comb to unearth any hidden microphones. I found nothing.

Then I went on the Internet. I typed *Igor Dubrovski* into

Google and with a knot in my stomach launched the search. I found 703 results, most in unknown languages, probably Russian. I scrolled through the search results until I found one in French. The entry was a list of names, each one followed by a percentage: *Bernard Vialley 13.4%; Jérôme Cordier 8.9%; Igor Dubrovski 76.2%* . . .

The URL was societe.com, a site containing financial information on companies. The Igor Dubrovski listed there was probably only someone with the same name, but I clicked on the link to be sure. The webpage listed shareholders in a company called Luxares SA. Probably no relation to the Igor Dubrovki I was looking for.

Back to Google and the list of results. Another in French, with the words "Did Dubrovski kill François Littrec?" I shuddered. The information was published on an online news site, lagazettedetoulouse.com. My heart was beating faster and faster as I clicked on the link. *Error message. Page can't be found.* Damn. Why don't people update their links? Back to Google.

I scrolled through listings for other news sites, clicking on articles reporting on what was in all likelihood the same incident. "The Dubrovski Affair: When the accused takes control," read one post. I clicked on it. The text was a commentary on trial proceedings, but instead of revealing the charges in the case, it described the behavior of Dubrovski at the trial. He had constantly corrected his lawyer and, in the end, had spoken in his place. According to the article, the jurors had been visibly unsettled by his contributions.

The jurors . . . So it was a *Cours d'Assise,* an assize court. That's the court that hears serious criminal cases, like murder.

I looked at another article, entitled, "Will We Know the Truth One Day?" The journalist explained the reversal of the court's findings and expressed surprise that a man presented by the police as obviously guilty had managed to sow doubt in the jurors' minds.

Several other articles said more or less the same thing. All dated from the 1970s, more than 30 years ago. An article from *Le Monde* was titled "Freud, Wake Up. They've Gone Mad!" I clicked on it. It was bylined Jean Calusacq and dated 1976. A long text, it was, above all, a denunciation of the psychiatrist Igor Dubrovski's methods, described as dangerous. I shuddered. It was him. The author attacked the psychotherapeutic models, American in origin, that were preached by Dubrovski, virulently denouncing the validity of his work. The article left no doubt as to Dubrovski's guilt: Evidently he had induced young François Littrec to commit suicide under conditions that were still mysterious. Calusacq wanted his head.

I was dismayed. I was in the hands of a dangerous psychiatrist, obviously crazier than the people he was supposed to be treating when he had still been practicing. My God.

I found other articles. The word *acquitted* suddenly leapt at me. "Dubrovski Acquitted," said a headline in *Le Parisien*. "Dubrovski's acquittal raises issues for the whole profession," the article suggested. "How can the court have released a man whose guilt was so obvious?"

Another article wondered if the psychiatrist hadn't hypnotized the jurors to influence their vote, reporting the disturbing testimony of people who had been present at the hearing. Two others ran headlines about Dubrovski being stripped of his license by the Medical Board, while also denouncing the board for refusing to make public the reasons for the sanctions.

I had read enough.

With a knot in my stomach, I switched my computer off. I had to protect myself and get out of this mess. But how? One thing was sure: It wouldn't be by trying to carry out the mission impossible Dubreuil had given me.

I HAD BEEN going over all the possibilities in my head for two days without satisfaction. I had to face it: There was nothing I could do as long as the police refused to protect me. Finally I had to admit that my only hope was to convince Dubreuil to retract his demand and give up this final mission. It was the most sensible thing to do. I was going to turn his teaching to good account by using it against him, to make him change his mind.

I constructed a detailed scenario, preparing a series of attitudes, questions, and arguments, anticipating every possible objection and reaction he might have. I spent several days putting the finishing touches on my approach, until I realized that I had been ready for a long time and that my extensive preparations could be explained only as my desire to put off their implementation. Dubreuil frightened me, and I was afraid to go back into his lair and throw myself deliberately into his clutches.

I finalized the plan of action. I decided to turn up unannounced one evening after dinner, at a time when his energy would no doubt be at its lowest but before the departure of the servants.

So I reached the avenue around 9:30 P.M. I got off the bus at the stop before his house, so I could breathe deeply and relax by walking. The lime trees perfumed the air, but the warm air smelled of thunderstorm.

The neighborhood was very quiet, even though a

number of July vacationers had returned. In my mind I ran through the different possible scenarios. My chances were slim, but I remained hopeful, impelled by the pressing need to free myself from Dubreuil's control.

The shadow of the château slowly rose before me as I drew near. The windows on the front were dark. A deathly silence reigned over the place, which seemed deserted. From time to time, lightning streaked the sky.

I waited, hesitantly, before ringing the bell, peering into the darkness. Suddenly, I heard violent shouting. A woman's voice. The hall light came on.

"I'm sick of it! I've had enough!" cried the woman.

The front door opened, and her silhouette appeared against the light. I was paralyzed, seized by surprise and incomprehension. The young woman who ran down the steps toward me was none other than Audrey. Audrey, my love. Before I could make the slightest movement, the little door next to the gate flew open, and we found ourselves face-to-face. It brought her up short. I saw the amazement on her face.

"Audrey . . ."

She didn't reply, but fixed me with a distraught look.

In the darkening sky, the lightning flashes multiplied.

"Audrey . . ."

Tears came to her eyes, as she drew back to escape.

"Audrey . . ."

I took a step toward her, overcome by emotion, torn between my unchanged attraction to her and the unbearable pain of her rejection.

She put up a hand to stop me and said between two sobs, "I . . . I can't."

The she ran off without turning around.

• • •

My pain rapidly turned into violent anger. Forgetting my fear, I threw myself at the door beside the gate. Closed. I called like a madman on the entry phone, pressing the button dozens of times and then keeping my finger pressed on it.

No one replied.

I grasped the gate with both hands and shook as hard as I could, venting my anger, shouting with all my might, my voice covering the flood of barking from Stalin.

"I know you're there!" I shouted.

I called again, in vain. The storm burst at last; there was a muffled rumble of thunder. The first drops were scattered, then quickly became more intense, and the clouds burst.

Without thinking, I threw myself at the gate again. Propelled by an anger that gave me the energy of ten, I hauled myself up by the strength of my arms and managed to stand on top. I jammed my feet between the spikes and then jumped into the yard.

The bushes cushioned my fall. I got up and rushed to the heavy door, out of breath. I entered the cold entrance hall. Light was coming from the main drawing room. I strode across the hallway, my feet pounding the marble. The noise rang out in the enormous space. I entered the drawing room. The subdued lighting contrasted with my anger. I saw Dubreuil at once. He was sitting at the piano with his back to me, motionless, with his hands on his knees. I was soaked to the skin; water was streaming down my face and my clothes, dripping onto the Persian rug.

"You are angry," he said as calmly as anything, without turning around. "That's good. You must never keep your frustration or your resentment to yourself. Go on: Express yourself. Shout if you want."

His words cut the ground from under my feet. I had planned to shout at him but shouting now would be obeying his command. I felt trapped, my momentum broken. I felt like a marionette whose emotions and actions were being manipulated by someone pulling on invisible strings. I decided to thwart his influence and let my anger burst out.

"What have you done to Audrey?" I screamed.

No reply.

"What was she doing here?"

Silence.

"I forbid you to interfere with my love life! Our pact doesn't give you the right to play with my feelings!"

Still no answer. I noticed Catherine on one of the sofas in the corner of the room.

I went on, "I know you despise love. It doesn't count for you. The truth is, you're not capable of loving. You have repeated affairs with women half your age because you're afraid of abandoning yourself and really loving one of them. It's great to know how to get what you want in life, to have the courage to assert your will and pursue your dreams. I owe you that, and I acknowledge it's precious. But it's pointless if you're not capable of loving, of loving a person, of loving others in general. You smoke in public places, drive in bus lanes, park on the sidewalk. You despise other people's well-being. But what's the point of knowing how to get what you want if you cut yourself off from others? You can't live just for yourself, or else life has no meaning. All the luxuries in the world can never replace the beauty of a relationship, the purity of a feeling, even just the genuine smile of a neighbor or a passerby you hold the door open for, or the touching look of some stranger. Your fine theories are perfect, effective, brilliant even, yet you're forgetting one thing, just one thing, but it's essential: You're forgetting to love."

I turned around. When I got to the door, I looked back.

"And leave Audrey out of this!"

THE NEXT DAY, my rage gradually gave way to the incomprehension that was eating away at me.

The more I advanced, the more inexplicable were the events that followed, and the more enigmatic my relationship with Dubreuil, or rather Dubrovski. How could he have infiltrated my life to that extent? And what was he up to? He wasn't just a former psychiatrist who wronged his patients. He was dangerous, manipulative, and capable of anything.

Even so, I thought I had put my finger on his weak point: his theories about human relations. For something magical to happen in a relationship, you had to allow yourself to love the other. *Love the other*. It was the key. The key to all relations, whether friendly or professional. The key that Dubrovski lacked. And which I lacked, too, when it came to convincing my boss. I didn't like him, and he was bound to feel it. All my efforts were in vain, pointless. I should have found a way of forgiving his hateful behavior enough to like him a little, just a little. And then he might have opened up to me, to my ideas and my proposals. But how do you find the strength to like your worst enemy?

I was still deep in thought and reflections about love, when I caught sight of my old neighbor walking toward me, dressed, as always, in black from head to toe. Since her last visit to my apartment, she had avoided talking to me.

Our eyes met, but she turned away and pretended to

be interested in the nearest shop window. Unfortunately, it was the window of a particularly alluring lingerie shop. She found herself staring at G-strings and garter belts displayed on models in very suggestive poses. In the center of the window, where she couldn't fail to see it, was an enormous poster that revealed the charms of a curvaceous beauty, with the advice given by a famous brand of underwear: "Lesson number 36: Give your angular form some curves." She abruptly turned her head away and walked on, eyes on the ground.

"Hello, Madame Blanchard!" I called out gaily.

She slowly looked up.

"Good day, Monsieur Greenmor," she said, blushing slightly, no doubt remembering our last encounter.

"How are you?" I asked.

"Well, thank you."

"Lovely day, isn't it? Makes a change from last night."

"Yes, you're right. Now that I see you, I must tell you: I'm sending around a petition about our neighbor on the fourth floor. Her cat walks along the ledge and goes into people's apartments. The other day, I found it lying on my sofa. It's quite unacceptable."

"Her little gray cat?"

"Yes. As for Monsieur Robert, I've had enough of his cooking smells. He could at least close the window when he's cooking. I've already talked to the managing agent three times, but I'm the only one who's complained."

Right. Let's change the subject. I so wanted to get her onto something positive. "You're out shopping?"

"No, I'm going to church."

"On a weekday?"

"I go every day, Monsieur Greenmor," she said with pride.

"Why every day?"

"Well, why do you think? To tell the Lord Jesus of the love I have for him."

"You go to church every day to tell Jesus you love him?"

"Yes."

I hesitated a second.

"You know, Madame Blanchard, I must tell you."

"What?"

"I have . . . how shall I put it? I have doubts."

"Doubts, Monsieur Greenmor? Doubts about what?"

"Well, I don't know if you are a good Christian."

She froze, stung to the quick, and then started to shake, red in the face. "How dare you!"

"Well, I don't think you're following Jesus's teaching."

"Of course I am!"

"I'm not a scholar, but I don't remember Jesus ever saying 'Love me.' On the other hand, I'm certain he said, 'Love one another.'"

She stared at me, dumbstruck.

"However," I said, "I acknowledge that you follow Jesus's orders to 'love your neighbor as you would yourself.'"

She looked at me uncomprehendingly.

Then, very gently and sincerely, I asked her, "Madame Blanchard, why don't you love yourself?"

Two in the morning. I would never get back to sleep, end-lessly turning over the same thought in my mind. I didn't know what Dubrovski really wanted.

And that list of shareholders with his name on it that I'd seen online? Was it really just someone with the same name? Suppose it was him? I should have looked at it more closely. What was that company? Luxores? Luxares? Something like that.

I got up, crossed the bedroom, and sat down at my computer. I typed Dubrovski's name into Google. Again, the results in Russian came up on the screen. I scrolled through the entries until I came to the one with the list of names followed by percentages. I clicked on the link. *Luxares SA*—that was the company whose majority share-holder was an Igor Dubrovski. I copied the company name into the Google search box and clicked *Enter*. Just 23 re-sults: newspaper sites, financial sites, and then luxares. fr, the link for the company's site, "Restoration company specializes . . . ," I read. I opened the page.

I couldn't help recoiling, stupefied by what filled the screen. It was a panoramic photo, shot at night. In the fore-ground were those familiar metal girders and behind them, picture windows, lit from inside, revealing the luxurious interior of the Jules Verne.

I WAS FRIGHTENED. It was no longer the slight apprehension that had been with me since the beginning of our pact but a terror that gnawed at me and wouldn't leave. The man who had taken control of my life was all the more dangerous for being rich and powerful. Now I had only one obsession: getting out of his clutches.

I called the policeman again, telling him about my discovery and insisting I get police protection. He repeated that all I had was just a bundle of suspicions—worrying, admittedly, but there was not even the hint of a crime. He could do nothing for me.

I had searched in vain for all feasible ways of freeing myself. The only more or less realistic idea had been to try and negotiate with Dubrovski. Audrey's presence had squashed that plan, and now I no longer had the courage to go back there, after the scene I had caused. I had insulted him in the presence of Catherine, and he wasn't the sort to forgive easily.

I had to face reality. My only hope for ending the pact was to accomplish the final trial he had given me—a task that was impossible. I was caught in his trap, cornered.

The following two days were torture. I desperately sought a solution. My nights were disturbed, sleep impossible. At work I had terrible difficulty concentrating on my interviews. Alice said I looked like a ghost and advised me to see a doctor as quickly as possible. I was on a downward spiral.

On the evening of the second day, as I turned around to go back to the office to get my wallet, which I'd forgotten, I caught sight of Vladi, who just happened to be a few yards behind me on the Avenue de l'Opéra. My fear went up a notch.

The following night, I had a strange dream. It took place in America, on a farm in Mississippi. A frog had fallen into a vat of cream. The sides of the vat were very high, and the frog was trapped, unable to get a footing in the cream. There was no possibility of escape; its fate was sealed. All the frog could do was wait to die. But it was too stupid to understand this obvious truth, and it continued to struggle as hard as it could, without thinking how futile its actions were. The frog struggled so much that finally it churned the cream into butter. Now the frog had something solid to stand on. It leapt out of the vat and regained its freedom.

In the wee hours of the night, I made up my mind. I was going to fight tooth and nail to take my CEO's place.

I DIDN'T WASTE a moment.

I downloaded the bylaws of Dunker Consulting from the Chamber of Commerce website, along with the most recent annual reports. I had to know all the ins and outs of the organization.

Over the next two nights, I plunged into this torridly erotic literature. Why do French lawyers have such convoluted ways of expressing things? I needed help.

One of the good things about working as a recruiter is that you rapidly build up an impressive address book. I contacted a young finance director I had recruited some weeks before, mentioning the help I needed. He replied right away, sending all the documents I needed by express delivery.

We met a few days later at the end of the afternoon, at an outdoor café near the Luxembourg Gardens. He had taken the time to read everything on my company.

"Dunker Consulting is an SSC quoted on the new market of the Euronext Paris stock exchange," he told me.

"An SSC?"

"Yes, a simplified joint-stock company. That's similar to a limited liability company in the U.S. An SSC is particularly well suited to a small or mid-sized company because of the flexibility it offers in establishing the bylaws under which it operates.

"The founders of the company make up the rules, is that it?"

"To a certain extent, yes."

"And what are the specific rules that characterize it?"

"Nothing special, apart from the appointment of the CEO."

"That's precisely what interests me."

"The CEO is elected directly by the shareholders, at the annual meeting."

"So all the shareholders vote to choose the CEO, is that it?"

"No, not quite. Only the shareholders who are present at the meeting. Everyone can take part, of course, but in practice virtually none of the shareholders attend the annual meeting and vote, except the major shareholders. Dunker Consulting has two main shareholders and tens of thousands of small investors."

"Let me guess. I bet one of the major shareholders is Marc Dunker."

"No, he owns only eight percent of the shares."

I remembered then that Alice had already told me that when Dunker took the business public, he had kept only a small stake in the company. The power wasn't really in his hands anymore.

"Who are the other big shareholders?"

"An investment fund, INVENIRA, represented by its director, David Poupon, and an American pension fund, STRAVEX, represented by a certain Rosenblack, the manager of the French subsidiary. Between them, they hold thirty-four percent of Dunker Consulting. No other shareholder, apart from Dunker himself, owns more than one percent of the shares. It goes without saying that Poupon and Rosenblack have a free hand."

I decided to take an enormous risk and outline my plan to the finance director. He was kind enough not to laugh.

"I don't want to put you off, but it won't be easy," he said.

"No, I don't doubt that."

"In fact, mathematically, you have no chance. If Dunker has remained CEO, that obviously means he had the votes of the two big shareholders."

"Why? They've only got thirty-four percent of the shares, not fifty percent."

"For the reason I gave you just now: The small shareholders don't come to annual meetings. What would they get out of it? No, the only shareholders who come are a few retired people who are bored and turn up in the hope that there will be a buffet and drinks after the meeting. They have no impact on the voting.

"Let me remind you," he continued, "that there are tens of thousands of small investors, almost every one of whom would have to turn up for their votes to count. And that never happens, except perhaps when a company is on the brink of disaster and the shareholders are afraid of losing their nest eggs. Then they turn up and weep in unison."

I was the one who felt like weeping at the moment.

"If Dunker was reelected CEO," the finance director went on, "then he obviously has the support of the big two. Their thirty-four percent of the shares probably represents at least eighty percent of the voting rights of the shareholders present at the annual meeting. I don't want to jump to conclusions about your talents or your powers of conviction, but I don't see why those two would change their opinion to support a young consultant employed by the company."

I remained deep in thought, disheartened by so much good sense.

"I'm so sorry," he finally said, with great sincerity.

It's always nice to feel other people's compassion when everything is going wrong, but I wasn't ready to give up yet. I had to find a solution, a plan of attack. There must be a way.

"If you were in my place, what would you do?"

He replied without hesitating: "Give up. There's nothing you can do. In your situation, you have everything to lose and nothing to gain."

My situation. If only you knew what it was, my friend.

I paid for our Perrier waters and thanked him for his help.

I set off through the Luxembourg Gardens. I was downcast, but I didn't want to capitulate. This battle was my only hope of regaining my freedom, perhaps even of staying alive. I was going to throw myself into it body and soul, even if my chances of winning were close to nil. I had to find a line of attack.

I spent the evening walking around the city, looking at the situation from every angle, searching for the weaknesses in the system, trying out different scenarios. I had a feeling I would manage to find an entry point, an idea that would allow me to redeal the cards and be in a position to take on the CEO. But was it genuine intuition talking, or simply my burning desire to find a solution?

When I got home, I found a paper bag hanging from the doorknob of my apartment. I opened it at the kitchen table. Inside was a plate, still warm, covered in tinfoil. Taped to it was a little blue envelope with a scalloped flap. I opened it and pulled out a card of the same color. Written in classic European penmanship, with loops and flourishes that few people know how to form anymore, was the message: *Bon appétit from Madame Blanchard.*

That evening I dined on a delicious chocolate cake.

In spite of my wish to do everything I could to try and succeed at my last test, I had to take precautions. My chances of success were so slim that I had to prepare myself to face the consequences if I failed.

So I decided to begin a thorough investigation of Igor Dubrovski's shady past. If he had obtained his acquittal by hypnotizing the jurors, which we would probably never know for sure, there remained other aspects of the case that could be uncovered and would give me a certain negotiating power when I confronted him. I was driven by the conviction that the keys to my freedom lay in Dubrovski's past.

I went back on the Internet, looking for the article by the journalist from *Le Monde* who seemed to know far more than the others about the suicide affair. I remembered that the article contained such precise details about Dubrovski and his methods that it seemed very likely the journalist had known him. I absolutely must talk to him.

I found the article again, by Jean Calusacq. I picked up the phone and dialed *Le Monde*.

"Hello, I'm trying to contact Jean Calusacq, a journalist who was working for *Le Monde* in the 1970s. I don't know if he's still with you."

"Who did you say?"

"Calusacq. Jean Calusacq."

"Never heard of him. And I've been here eight years. Your friend must have retired a long time ago!"

"He's not my friend, but I absolutely must find him. It's very important. There must be someone in your office who would know how to contact him."

"How should I know? I can't go and shout on every floor!"

"Okay, but somewhere you must have the name of the editor at that time. He could tell me."

I heard a sigh.

"How long ago, did you say?"

"1976."

"Please hold."

A jazz tune on the saxophone played while I waited for the operator to come back on the line. I began to wonder if I hadn't been forgotten.

"Here it is, Raymond Verger," she finally said. "But I can't guarantee anything. We lost contact a long time ago."

I dialed the number the *Le Monde* operator gave me, concerned that it might no longer be in service. A ring tone. Phew! After eight rings, I was about to give up when someone answered. Crossing my fingers, I asked to speak to Verger.

"Who shall I say is calling?" asked a woman, in a slightly quavering voice.

"Alan Greenmor."

"Does he know you?"

"No, not yet, but I'd like to speak to him about one of his former colleagues."

"Good! That will amuse him. Speak clearly if you want him to understand you."

There followed a long silence. Finally I heard whispers, then "Hello," in a drawling voice.

I followed the advice given by his wife, enunciating clearly. "Hello, Monsieur Verger. My name is Alan Greenmor. I got your number from *Le Monde*. I'm calling because I need to speak to one of your old journalists. It's very important, and the paper thinks you might known how to contact him."

"An old journalist? I still see a few of them. What's his name? I remember every one of them. My wife would say I'm unbeatable."

"Jean Calusacq."

"Who?"

"Jean Calusacq."

A long silence.

"Monsieur Verger, are you still there?"

"It doesn't ring any bells," he admitted.

"It was more than thirty years ago," I prompted.

"No, no! That's not the problem! I'd remember. No, it must have been a pseudonym."

"A pseudonym?"

"Yes, journalists often use them to sign articles that aren't in the style of what they usually write, for example."

"And you could find his real name?"

"Yes. I've got the list of my journalists and their pseudonyms. I've kept everything. Call me back in thirty minutes, and I'll tell you."

Half an hour later, his wife passed me on to Verger, but not before she'd advised me to be brief in order not to encroach on his naptime.

"There is no Calusacq on my list," Verger told me. "Are you sure of the name?"

"Yes, absolutely."

"Then it was probably someone famous. If that was the case, we didn't write anything down in order to ensure complete anonymity."

Someone famous? Why would someone famous take an interest in the suicide of someone unknown?

"I'm sorry," Verger said, clearly disappointed. "I'm not going to be able to help you. Leave me your phone number though, in case I remember something."

THEY SAY THAT fortune favors the bold. In my case, it was a long time coming. I went from misfortune to mishap. I was trying to take on an incredible challenge, while fighting on my own against a brilliant and powerful madman. But the fates were obviously not on my side.

That morning I arrived at the office late. The day's first candidates were waiting in the ground-floor reception area. I crossed the lobby and took the stairs in order not to find myself in the same elevator as my boss, sparing us both the embarrassed silence that would have accompanied us from floor to floor.

I scarcely had time to sit down at my desk before Alice came in and closed the door after her.

"Look at this," she said, holding out two sheets of paper.

I took the documents. One was from the administration department. I recognized the black list of companies in financial difficulties that wanted to use our services. It was drawn up each month for the department heads, who usually passed it on to us. This month, we hadn't received it.

The other piece of paper contained each consultant's list of prospective customers to be contacted or followed up with during the week. A glance at it was enough to see that most of the companies were on both lists. The black list was dated August 1; the list of prospective customers, August 5.

"Do you realize what this means?" Alice was incensed. "We're being pushed to solicit business from clients we know probably won't pay! It's ridiculous! Management is making more and more senseless decisions! I really don't understand the company. And do you realize what this means for us? If the client doesn't pay, we don't get our commission! So we'll be working for nothing."

I wasn't listening anymore. An idea had just arisen in my mind and was slowly taking shape.

"Why are you smiling?" Alice asked, piqued that I wasn't sharing her outrage.

"May I keep these papers?" I asked her.

"Yes, of course, but . . ."

"Thanks. A thousand times thanks, Alice. You have perhaps just saved my life."

"Well, let's just say it'll stop you from working for nothing."

"I've got to make a call; do forgive me."

As soon as she left, I picked up the phone and called Vanessa, asking her to reschedule all my appointments. I had to take the day off. There would be repercussions, but in any case, my future as an employee was compromised whatever happened.

• • •

The annual meeting of Dunker Consulting was to take place on August 28. Igor Dubrovski had said we were to meet on the 29. So he hadn't chosen the date at random. And I had been thinking that the idea of this last test had come to him in the heat of the moment, during our meeting. But no, it was premeditated.

Back home, I called my bank and ordered them to buy me one share of Dunker Consulting, the prerequisite for running for CEO. According to the bylaws, it wasn't necessary to declare my candidacy in advance, just at the beginning of the meeting. So I could stay in the shadows until the last minute.

My idea had a 1 in 1,000 chance of succeeding. But I would present myself to the shareholders to try and convince them to vote for me. My God, just the thought of it made me shiver. I got stage fright when I had to talk in front of 10 or 15 colleagues. But I couldn't afford to ruin my chances just because of stage fright. There must be a way to learn to speak calmly in public.

I searched on the Internet for companies that offered training in public speaking. I only managed to reach one of them on the phone; all the others were closed for August. The name of the company was promising: Speech-Masters. The person who answered suggested I come and meet the tutor before I signed up. I made an appointment. Then I called Alice at the office.

"I told you, didn't I, that Dunker was putting bogus job advertisements in the papers?"

"Yes, Alan. I still haven't gotten over it."

"Listen, I need you. Could you draw up a list of them?"

"A list of bogus ads?"

"Yes, that's it."

Silence.

"It would take ages to do. How far back do you want to go?"

"I don't know. Let's say the last three months."

"I would have to check all the ads in each newspaper one by one and then cross-reference them with our internal lists."

"Could you do that for me? It's mega-important."

"I think you're a little mysterious today."

"Please, Alice."

Since I could find no trace of the journalist from *Le Monde*, I decided to go to the source—to the family whose son François was the suicide mentioned in the articles on Dubrovski's trial. It was sensitive, but that way I could probably find out a lot more about what had really happened.

The house was not very difficult to find. At the time, the newspapers had described the location. There were no other Littrecs in the neighborhood, and I easily found their address in an online directory.

Vitry-sur-Seine is a few miles southeast of Paris. I went by car. Knowing I was being followed, I kept looking in the rearview mirror. Under no circumstances must Dubrovski know where I was going. At the Porte d'Orléans, I took the highway to the south, then after a few miles, I pulled over on the shoulder, threw the car in reverse, and backed up an on ramp. A dangerous maneuver, but it worked.

It's always difficult to get your bearings in the Paris suburbs. At each red light I pored over the map I had unfolded on the passenger seat next to me. I arrived in Vitry by the Boulevard Maxime-Gorki, then made my way through streets with names like Avenue Iouri-Gagarine and Boulevard de Stalingrad. Where on earth was I? I thought the Soviet Union had been dissolved years ago! Turning my head to the right, I saw the Vitry town hall. I was so surprised, I nearly ran into the car in front of me: the building was a sort of miniature Kremlin!

All this was amusing, but I had to find my way. Now I was thoroughly lost. I finally came out on a quiet street lined with modest houses. I parked and continued on foot. Number 19 was tall and narrow with white-painted bricks. The paint was peeling in places, but the house must have been charming before time left its mark.

I went up to the wooden gate. The garden, if you could call the meager space separating the house from the street a garden, was abandoned, with weeds poking up through the gravel path. I screwed up my courage and gave a short ring on the bell.

Nothing happened for a long while. Finally, the door opened a crack, revealing the exhausted face of an old man. I knew right away that I had the right address.

"Monsieur Littrec? My name is Alan Greenmor. I've come to see you because I need to ask you a few questions. Please forgive me in advance for awakening painful memories, but I must talk to you about your son."

The vertical fold between his eyebrows deepened even more as he shook his head. "No, Monsieur," he said weakly. "I don't want to talk about him. Sorry."

I insisted. "I have reason to think I am in a situation similar to your son's at the time, and . . ."

"Let him come in!" shouted a woman's voice from inside the house.

The man looked down, sighed, and then opened the door wider, as he withdrew inside.

The interior was simple and old-fashioned but spotless, despite a slight musty smell.

"I can't get up to greet you; my legs hurt too much," said the old woman, who was propped up in an armchair. I heard the staircase creak as her husband disappeared upstairs.

"At the moment," I began, "my life is being threatened

by a psychiatrist named Igor Dubrovski. If my information is correct, you lodged a formal complaint against him at the time of—"

"My son's suicide, yes."

"And he got away with it, cleared for lack of proof. Would you tell me what you know about the man?"

"It was so long ago," she said.

"Tell me what you remember; it's important so that I can try to protect myself."

"You know, I had only met him once before the trial."

"But he was the person treating your son in therapy."

"Yes, chiefly, and we spoke to him the day my husband and I entrusted him with François. To be honest, I don't even remember what he said to us that day."

"Why do you say 'chiefly'?"

"There were two of them looking after François."

"Your son had two psychiatrists?"

"Yes. Doctor Dubrovski and another one, at the hospital."

I paused, thinking.

"What did your son tell you about Igor Dubrovski?"

"Oh, he told me nothing, Monsieur. He wasn't a talker, you know. He was used to keeping everything to himself." She sighed for a moment, and then added, "It's probably what weighed on him so heavily."

"But why did you complain about Dubrovski, if there were two psychiatrists looking after your son?"

"The world collapsed beneath us when François died. He was our only son. All the rest was of no importance. We knew it wasn't going to give us our François back. We complained because we were asked to, but we were never into revenge. There's no point fighting fate."

"But why did you press charges against Igor Dubrovski and not against the other psychiatrist? Why not both of them? And by the way, what were you accusing him of exactly?"

"It was explained to us that he was the one who had made François commit suicide. We didn't make anything up, you know. We just said what we were told to say. And even then, we went to the hearing every day reluctantly. Above all, we wanted to be left alone."

"Wait, wait. Who told you what to say?"

"The man who was advising us. He kept saying, 'Think of all the young people you're going to save.'"

"You mean your lawyer?"

"No, not the lawyer. He never came to see us."

"Who was it, then?"

"I don't remember anymore. It was so long ago. And lots of people came to the house at that time. First the emergency services, then the police, an inspector, insurance people. All of them were people my husband and I didn't know."

"And this man, you don't remember his title or his official role?"

She hesitated, delving in vain into her memory.

"No. But he was someone high up."

"Could you describe him to me?"

"No, I'm sorry. I can't remember his face. The only thing that comes back to me is that he was fanatical about his shoes. It was so odd that I remember it."

I wouldn't get far with that sort of information.

"Really fanatical," she went on, recalling the scene with a sad smile. "He kept asking us to make sure our dog didn't get near his loafers. I admit the dog slobbered a bit. And during our conversation, the man got a handkerchief out of his pocket several times to wipe his shoes. As he went out, he wiped his feet for ages on the mat. It annoyed me a little, I have to say."

YOUR ENEMIES' ENEMIES are not necessarily your friends. The man I was due to meet that morning behind the stock exchange was not my friend and probably never would be. Yet he was the only man in the world capable of keeping Dunker awake at night: Fisherman, the journalist who regularly published negative articles about our company in *Les Echos*; Fisherman, who without ever having set foot in our offices, had one day dared to write that our teams weren't productive enough, setting off a wave of internal measures worthy of the worst austerity plans, thereby ratcheting up the pressure we lived under.

We had spoken on the phone, and I had persuaded him to meet me, being sufficiently enigmatic to arouse his interest while still leaving him in the dark. I arrived early and sat at a little round marble table. There weren't many customers in the late morning, but a waiter was busy laying tables for lunch, and the barman was serving beers to a few regulars.

I had described myself to Fisherman so that he would recognize me when he arrived. But when I saw a man in a tweed jacket and open-necked shirt, with a serious face and large tortoiseshell glasses barely hiding thick eyebrows, I had a feeling it was Fisherman, even before he saw me.

He half-heartedly greeted me, without smiling. I offered to buy him a coffee, which he refused.

"As I was saying on the phone," I began, "on certain days, I will be in a position to tell you the probable movement of the Dunker Consulting share price for the next day."

"What gives you this ability?"

"From time to time I know about events before they are made public."

He looked at me suspiciously. "And how do you have access to that information?"

"I am an employee of the company."

He stared at me contemptuously. "What do you want in exchange?" he said, with the look of someone who no longer has any illusions about human nature.

"Nothing."

"You wouldn't do it if there wasn't something in it for you."

"I agree."

"So, what do you get out of it?" he asked, inquisitorially.

I met his eyes. "I hate Marc Dunker. Anything that can hurt him delights me."

He seemed to accept my answer. It fitted in with his vision of the world. He motioned to the waiter to bring him a coffee.

I went on, "Every time you print a negative notice about his firm, he's beside himself."

No reaction. Fisherman remained impassive.

"So, you'll pass on to me in advance the events you know about, is that it?"

"No, I won't reveal the events. But when I know for sure that a piece of information is about to become public, I'll warn you."

"In that case, what's the difference?"

"If you take into account an important piece of information even before it becomes public and give a negative notice on the share, it'll increase the general feeling that something is not right at Dunker Consulting. It will make matters worse. That's what I'm hoping for."

He looked at me in silence for a few moments.

"What interests me," he said, "is the information, not just the announcement that it's going to come out."

"That I'm not going to give you. You mustn't be too greedy. In any case, your job is to make predictions about the share price of companies quoted on the stock exchange, isn't it? I'm giving you the means of announcing before everyone else that Dunker Consulting shares are going to go down. That's already quite a lot."

He didn't reply, but continued to stare at me suspiciously.

"Exclusive to you," I added.

"There's nothing to prove that your predictions will turn out to be true."

"You can judge for yourself this week."

He raised an eyebrow.

I leaned toward him slightly and lowered my voice to underline the importance of my revelation. "The day after tomorrow, Dunker Consulting's shares will fall by at least three percent before the end of trading."

He stared at me for a few moments, gloomily, and then drank his coffee in silence, looking very doubtful.

"In any case," he finally said, "I can't publish a notice on the basis of a rumor from someone I don't even know."

"Do what you like. I will give you, let's say, three tips. If you don't use them, after that I'll give the others to one of your colleagues on a rival paper."

I got up, fished some coins out of my pocket, and put enough on the table to pay for my coffee. Then I left him to his skepticism.

THE RINGING OF the telephone interrupted my thoughts. I picked it up.

"Hold on, please, my husband would like to talk to you."

A long silence.

"Hello? Monsieur Greenmor?"

I recognized the drawling voice at once.

"Speaking."

"Raymond Verger here. You know, the ex-editor of *Le Monde*. I'm calling because I think I've found the name of the person hiding behind the pseudonym Jean Calusacq."

Luck was turning in my favor. I was at last going to be able to talk with the author of an article on Igor Dubrovski that was, admittedly, provocative but also so precise that it was impossible to think the author hadn't known Dubrovski personally.

"It's just what I thought," Verger went on. "It was someone famous. That's why his name wasn't on my list of pseudonyms."

I felt my heart racing. "Tell me, what's his name?"

"I'm sorry?"

I'd forgotten he was partially deaf. I started again, articulating carefully: "What's his name?"

"Well, first of all, Monsieur, please note that I am following standard practice. I'm revealing his identity only because he has been dead for a long time; otherwise I would protect his anonymity. But it's been so long, it's ancient history."

My blood froze. It was no good.

"I found his name when I remembered that some people found it amusing to create a pseudonym that was an anagram of their name. It took me a good hour to work out that behind Jean Calusacq lay Jacques Lacan."

"Lacan, the great psychoanalyst?"

"The very same."

I was dumbfounded. Why had Lacan been so angry with Dubrovski that he had written a vitriolic article about him?

I put the question to Raymond Verger.

"That I can't tell you. Only a specialist might be able to answer. You could always try Christine Vespalles."

"Who's she?"

"Christine Vespalles, a former journalist at the review *Sciences Humaines*. Psychoanalysis is her passion. She would get great pleasure from answering your questions. You will find her easily; since her retirement, she spends her afternoons at the Deux Magots."

"The café in Saint-Germain-des-Prés?"

"That's the one. You could go and see her. You'll spot her right away: She always wears extraordinary hats. Nowadays, you don't see that many hats. She's very easy to talk to; you'll see. I'll give her a call and tell her about you."

• • •

I had trouble finding the street, lost behind the Place de la Bastille in an unrenovated area that still had the old-fashioned charm of working-class neighborhoods in days gone by. Most of the apartment buildings housed a workshop or business on the ground floor. Their doors were open to the street, and the tradespeople congregated on the sidewalks, as busy with neighborhood gossip as with their work. Deliverymen were unloading their goods in the middle of the street, calling out to familiar faces and interrupting the conversations by talking louder than anyone else.

There was a shoe repairer working at his polishing machine, which gave off a smell of warm leather. His neighbor was a hardware shop with the poetic sign *Color Merchant.* A glance at his stall was enough to realize that he kept his promise. There was an incredible profusion of everyday objects: multicolored clothes hangers, sponges, tea towels; green, yellow, and blue aprons; bowls and buckets in red, yellow, and beige plastic. A fruit-and-vegetable seller was trying to nab passersby by shouting the price of his goods. Farther on was a newspaper seller's metal stand: the headlines of his papers announced various scandals. Jets of steam poured out of the dry cleaner's next door, while across the street, there was a delicatessen with sausages hanging from metal hooks.

I finally found Number 51, a building whose façade was patinated by time. Next to the entrance was a handmade plaque that announced:

SPEECH-MASTERS: STAIRCASE IN THE COURTYARD

I passed under an archway and came out in an internal courtyard. Facing me was a second building, but its door was closed and there was no sign. Finally, I spotted a staircase off to one side. A small sign was attached to the handrail by metal wire. When I got closer, I saw that the sign said *Speech-Masters*, with an arrow pointing down. I descended the stairs, which disappeared into darkness at the bottom. Not very inviting.

I rang the bell and waited. Finally, the door opened

partway, and a red-headed man of about 30 greeted me, introducing himself as Éric.

I liked the place right away. It was a vast space, with a magnificent vaulted ceiling of stone. In each corner of the room, glass bricks admitted shafts of natural light. At the far end of the room was a wooden platform. Facing it were perhaps 100 stools, arranged neatly in rows. Near the entrance was a kitchen table with a coffee machine and an impressive number of plastic cups. Beneath the table, a little fridge was quietly purring away.

"You're in the old storeroom of a family of cabinetmakers," explained Éric. "They worked here for several generations until 1975, when the last one retired without finding a successor.

"Tell me," he asked. "What makes you want to enroll here?"

"Well, I can't speak in public," I said. "I get terrible stage fright, which leaves me completely at a loss, and it so happens that probably I will soon have to speak in front of a large group of people. I would like to train first, to avoid a catastrophe."

"I see."

"What's the procedure for the lessons?"

"They're not lessons. Each member trains by diving into the deep end with a talk of ten or so minutes on a topic of his choice. After that, the others write feedback on bits of paper, which are then given to the speaker."

"Feedback?"

"Yes, information about his performance. Comments about his little defects, his tics, his imperfections—everything, in short, that can be improved, whether it's his voice, his posture, or the structure of his talk."

"I see."

"If there are thirty of us, you'll get thirty pieces of paper.

It's for you to see what crops up most frequently in the comments so you can correct yourself and try to do better the next time you speak."

He had emphasized the words *correct* and *better* with a slight frown, like a schoolteacher. In spite of that, the method seemed interesting.

"When can I start?"

"We start again on the 22nd of August. Thereafter, we meet once a week."

"Only on the 22nd? Not before?"

"No, everybody is on holiday now."

I was done for. The annual meeting was on August 28. I would have the benefit of only one session, which seemed a bit light. I told him about my problem.

"It's not ideal, that's for sure. Our teaching demands long-term effort. But you'll still get some comments that might help you a little with your performance. You should have started sooner," he said in a reproachful tone.

"Alan, darling! How are you?"

I was taken aback to be greeted so dramatically by a woman I had never seen before, as if we had been friends for 20 years. Half the customers in the Deux Magots turned around. Madame Vespalles held out her hand in a theatrical gesture, wrist bent and palm down. What was she expecting—that I kiss her hand?

I shook it as best I could.

"Dear Raymond Verger has said so many nice things about you," she gushed.

I couldn't imagine the ex-editor-in-chief of *Le Monde* lavishing compliments on me.

"Do sit down," she said, pointing to a chair next to her. "Welcome to my table. Georges?"

She turned to me as the waiter appeared at her side.

"What will you have, Alan? You don't mind me calling you Alan, do you? It's such a nice name. You're English, I presume."

"American."

"Same thing. What would you like?"

"Er . . . a coffee."

"Oh, come on, do have some champagne. Georges, two glasses, please!"

Late in the afternoon, the terrace at the Deux Magots was packed, with tourists as well as with regulars who were obviously used to talking to one another across the tables.

As predicted, Christine Vespalles was wearing a monumental hat, pale pink with a veil and a fuchsia-colored bird on the side. Dressed all in pink and very elegant despite her eccentric garb, she was a good 70 years old even if she had the spirit and spark of a 20-year-old.

"Raymond told me you were interested in Jacques."

"Jacques?"

"'Tell him all you know about Lacan,' Raymond said, and I replied, 'Darling, you're underestimating the extent of my knowledge of the subject! The whole night wouldn't be enough, and I don't know how much time Alan has.'"

"In fact, what interests me very specifically is his relationship with another psychiatrist, Igor Dubrovski." I told her about the article I'd read.

"Oh, Lacan and Dubrovski! You could write a novel about those two and their perpetual rivalry!"

"Their rivalry?"

"Of course! You have to call a spade a spade, and their relationship a rivalry! Lacan was jealous of Dubrovski, that was clear.

"Jealous, but at what period?"

"In the 1970s, when Dubrovski was becoming known."

"But Jacques Lacan was already famous and recognized, wasn't he? It was at the end of his life. How could he be jealous of someone young and virtually unknown?"

"You have to put it in the context of the time. Lacan was the key figure in psychoanalysis in France. Psychoanalysis being what it is, people thought it was natural for a patient to spend fifteen years on a couch talking about his problems. Then one day a young Russian comes along and solves his patients' problems in a few sessions. He upsets things somewhat, don't you see?"

"Perhaps the patients weren't treated in depth," I suggested.

"That I have no way of knowing. The fact remains that a patient suffering from a phobia—I don't know, fear of spiders, for example—had a choice between fifteen years on the couch with Lacan or thirty minutes with Dubrovski. Which would you choose?"

"So Lacan was jealous of the results obtained by Dubrovski?"

"Everything. One was old, the other young. Lacan was an intellectual who had a theoretical approach and published books. Dubrovski was a pragmatist preaching action and seeking results. And then, there's the origin of their different theoretical models."

"You mean the methods they used?"

"Yes. Psychoanalysis is a European invention. Dubrovski was the pioneer in France of cognitive therapies from the States."

"How was that a problem?"

"Let's say it was a period when anti-Americanism was the norm in intellectual circles. But that's not all, you know. They were also separated by money."

"Money?"

"Yes, Dubrovski was rich, very rich. A family fortune. That wasn't the case for Lacan, who obviously had a problematic relationship with money."

She took a sip of champagne.

"In fact," she went on, "I think Lacan became completely obsessed with Dubrovski. Jealous of the speed of the younger man's sessions, he began to shorten his own. At the end, when a patient arrived in Lacan's consulting room, he had barely opened his mouth when Lacan interrupted him and said, 'Your session is over.'"

"That's crazy."

"That's not all. He was so jealous of Dubrovski's fortune that he started to increase his own rates exorbitantly. Lacan was known to charge five hundred francs, a considerable sum at the time, for a few minutes' session. When one of his patients protested, he grabbed her handbag to take out the money himself. Poor Jacques: He'd really lost it."

I took a sip of champagne, savoring its delicate taste and aroma.

"The great pity," she went on, "is that if Lacan had simply ignored Dubrovski, everyone would have forgotten him."

"Dubrovski? Why? If he got better results . . ."

"Oh, my poor friend, only an American would ask that question. You value results. In France, we admire intellect. Results seem almost secondary."

She rummaged in her handbag, pink crocodile to match her outfit, and extracted a paperback book.

"Here! I brought you this. Open it at random and read a passage."

I took the book, which was signed by Jacques Lacan, and opened it in the middle. I glanced down the page.

"It's incomprehensible, but then I'm not a psychologist."

"I assure you, psychologists don't understand it either. But this is France—the less people understand what you're talking about, the more you are taken for a genius. So just imagine Dubrovski, with his very practical, pragmatic side, his tasks to be carried out. He looked almost stupid next to Lacan."

At that moment, I moved my hand and knocked over my glass. Champagne spilled on the table, then dripped onto my shoes.

"Now that's something Lacan couldn't have endured," Madame Vespalles said.

"Spilling champagne on his feet?"

"I should say. He was fanatical about shoes."

I shuddered.

"Fanatical about shoes?"

"His passion! He was capable of slipping out of his consulting room by a hidden door between sessions, leaving his next patient sitting in the waiting room while he went to buy himself a pair of shoes. Bizarre, isn't it?"

LET'S JUST SUPPOSE that young François Littrec committed suicide. He had two doctors, one of whom was Igor Dubrovski. Jacques Lacan, jealous of Dubrovski, does all he can to bring about his rival's downfall. Under a pseudonym, he writes an extremely hostile article in *Le Monde* to denounce Dubrovski's methods. He also visits the young man's parents to manipulate them into accusing Dubrovski of murder. Then, having failed to get his colleague convicted by a court, Lacan nonetheless influences the medical council to take away his license, ending a promising career that had become an annoyance. But if Igor Dubrovski really was innocent in this business, how to explain all the shady areas that remained? Why attract, through his article on the right to suicide, depressives to the Eiffel Tower, where he could then pick them up before they carried out their plan? The better to manipulate them? To obtain promises from them? For what purpose? And how to explain the notes he took on me *before* my attempted suicide? And what about Dubrovski's relationship with Audrey?

Lost in thought, I was not following the proceedings at our Monday morning business meeting. With a certain animosity, Luc Fausteri and Grégoire Larcher were reviewing columns of figures projected on a screen—figures and more figures, then graphs, bar charts, pie charts. I felt light-years away from their concerns; all these barely intelligible results were foreign to me. Their voices seemed muffled, distant, incomprehensible. They sounded like two wardens in an asylum vehemently criticizing the assembled madmen for having chosen the wrong numbers on their lottery tickets. The inmates clapped. They must be masochists.

The meeting finished late, after which everyone disappeared for lunch. Everyone but me. I went back to my office and waited to be sure that my floor was deserted. Then I opened the file perched on top of the bookshelf, pulled out two sheets of paper, and slipped them into my pocket

I went out into the corridor, glanced both ways, and listened. Silence. At the top of the stairs, I stopped again. Still no one. I crept down to the floor below and peered around. I was alone. Stage fright was beginning to mount as I snuck into the fax room, my heart beating. I put my papers in the machine, aligning them carefully in the document feeder so the machine wouldn't jam. I glanced into the corridor one last time. Still nothing. With trembling fingers I dialed the first number. Each key I pressed emitted what sounded like a deafening beep. Finally I pressed *Start,* and the machine began to swallow the first page.

It took me nearly 20 minutes to send the list of Dunker Consulting's bogus job vacancies to every newsroom in France. Every one except *Les Echos's.*

Igor Dubrovski was alone that evening in his immense drawing room. He was playing a Rachmaninoff piano sonata, his muscular fingers dominating the keyboard as the pure sound of the Steinway resounded in the vast space.

The door behind him opened swiftly. He glanced over his shoulder without stopping. Ah, Catherine. She didn't usually enter in such an abrupt manner.

"Vladi is quite sure!" she said, visibly agitated.

Dubrovski took his hands off the keyboard, keeping the right pedal down to prolong the vibration of the last chord.

"Vladi," she went on, "confirms that Alan is preparing to stand as a candidate for the position of CEO of his firm at the annual meeting!"

Igor swallowed hard. He wasn't expecting that at all. He released the pedal, and the last vibrations of the music died instantly, creating a heavy silence. Catherine, usually so calm, was pacing up and down as she spoke, visibly upset.

"He has apparently enrolled in an institute specializing in public speaking. For one session. Just one. And in three weeks he'll be standing up in front of I don't know how many people, to convince them to vote for him. He's in for one hell of a beating. It's a catastrophe!"

Dubrovski turned around, deeply moved. "You're right," he muttered.

"It'll destroy him! Can you imagine? Being humiliated

in public, there's nothing worse. He'll be devastated. Everything we've done from day one will go up in smoke. All the progress he's made wiped out at a stroke. He'll be even more weak and fragile than before."

Igor didn't reply, merely nodding in agreement. She was obviously right.

"But why on earth did you give him the task?"

He sighed and then replied in a flat voice, "Because I was convinced he would refuse."

"Well, in that case, why give it to him?"

"Precisely in order to make him refuse."

A long silence.

"I just don't follow you anymore, Igor."

He looked around at her.

"I wanted to make him rebel. Against me. I wanted to put him in such an untenable situation that the only way out would be to dare to confront me and break our pact. The moment has come for the disciple to free himself from his master. You can easily understand, Catherine, that there's a paradox in guiding someone toward freedom by leading them by the hand all the way. Strict control was necessary because it made him do what he would never have done otherwise, but now he must free himself from my control to become really free. It's not for me to free him. It's got to come from him; otherwise he'll never have really won his freedom."

Dubrovski took a swig of bourbon from the glass on the piano. The ice had disappeared.

"By ordering him to take the place of his CEO, even if it's impossible, I was giving him permission to question authority. I was sending him a metaphorical message about our own relationship."

He put the glass down. He could feel the weight of Catherine's reproachful look.

"Except that it didn't work," she said. "He didn't rebel. On the contrary, he's carrying on."

Igor nodded.

"We must help him," she said. "We must do something. We can't leave him on his own to face this situation, after having brought him there!"

A long silence followed, and then Igor sighed. "For once, I really don't see what we can do, unfortunately."

"Why don't you just tell him to drop it, that you realize what you asked him to do is too difficult?"

"Absolutely not! That would be worst of all. It would amount to telling him that I, his mentor, don't have confidence in his abilities. That would be a severe blow to his self-esteem. Never mind that it would permanently reinforce the dependency I'm trying to loosen!"

"Okay, but you've got to do something! We can't let him go like a lamb to the slaughter. Even if we can't change the course of events, we must at least stop him from experiencing his failure too violently. We absolutely must avoid a total public humiliation. Let him save face, not feel pathetic."

"I've no idea what to do. I can't see a way out. Leave me alone, please."

Catherine suppressed a response and left the room. Her steps sounded in the hall. He heard them recede, then vanish in the night.

Silence returned, empty and oppressive. He was alone with his mistake, a huge mistake, unforgiveable. A mistake charged with consequences.

He slowly placed his hands on the keyboard and joined Rachmaninoff in his tormented dreams.

COMING OUT OF the house that morning I saw Madame Blanchard's black silhouette at the foot of the staircase. She was giving something to Étienne. I recognized from its shape that it was a cake like the one she had given me. Étienne looked highly surprised.

I crossed the street to go to the newspaper kiosk, a knot in my stomach. The bakery was giving off its aroma of fresh baguettes and warm *pains au chocolat*.

I bought all the daily newspapers, then went and sat on the terrace of the café next door. I opened *Le Figaro* and turned to the business section. I could feel my heart beating as I skimmed the articles, jumping from title to title. I searched in vain, my stress level going up as my chances went down, until suddenly I held my breath.

"Suspected Malpractice at Dunker Consulting," read the headline. There followed a few lines of explanation, neutral in tone.

Excited, I grabbed *Le Monde,* and also found a brief item, followed by a feature on recruitment agencies, their methods, and the criticisms often leveled at them. *Libération* printed a relatively short but very visible article, with a photo of our company headquarters under a catchy headline, "When the Head Hunters Lose Their Heads." *Le Parisien* calculated the time a candidate would have wasted applying for all the bogus vacancies, and the estimated cost of printing and sending out his CV. *France Soir* explained the extreme competition in the recruitment sector that could have made Dunker step over the line. *L'Humanité* devoted half a page to the matter, with a large photo showing an alleged candidate circling ads in a paper with a black marker pen, under a headline that announced "The Scandal of Dunker Consulting's Bogus Job Vacancies." The article included testimonies from numerous unemployed people relating that they had never received replies to their applications. For good reason, the journalist wrote. There were no vacancies to fill.

The kiosk didn't sell provincial papers, but given that there were Dunker offices dotted around the country, I felt confident that a similar mention would appear in those local papers, too.

But most important was what the financial papers reported. From *La Tribune* to *La Cote Desfossés* and *Le Journal des Finances*, all published the information I had sent them. This meant the critical information had reached the decision makers. I had achieved my goal.

I rushed to the office. I wanted to be there before 9 A.M., to see the opening of the stock market and follow the movement of our share price. At 8:50, I was at my computer, on the *Echos* website. I had no way of knowing whether or not publishing the information about Dunker Consulting's phony recruitment ads would have any impact on the company's share price. Perhaps I was dreaming.

At 9 A.M. precisely, Dunker Consulting's opening price came on the screen. It was down 1.2 percent. I was flabbergasted, unable to believe my eyes. I suddenly felt enthusiasm, joy, extreme excitement. I, Alan Greenmor, had influenced the Dunker Consulting share price on the Paris stock exchange! It was incredible! Unheard of! Monumental!

I remembered my prediction to Fisherman. I had announced a drop of 3 percent over the day. I had plucked the figure out of thin air, of course. But to maintain my credibility, the drop had to be as close to that as possible. And in this affair, my credibility was essential; my plan rested on it.

I spent a good part of the day checking the share price on my screen. Even during my interviews, I couldn't help but glance at it every now and then.

Except for a slight improvement in the middle of the day, the downward trend continued. At the close of trading, the final price was down 2.8 percent. Luck was on my side.

Euphoric, I left my office and rushed to the staff room. I didn't exactly expect to find champagne coming out of the machines, but I drank a Perrier, savoring my first victory.

Returning to my office, I passed cubicles full of employees stressed out by the ever more dehumanizing management style, harassed by the demands of stock-market profitability, and no longer motivated by an exciting business plan. What a waste to see all these people unhappy on the job when every one of them could be fulfilled, could bloom in their work! The contrast with my enthusiasm at that moment was stark. I suddenly understood that it wasn't just my fear of Dubrovski that was making me take on my final task. Caught up in the whirlwind of an intoxicating game whose first round I had just won, I felt within me the first stirrings of a calling, a mission. Even though I risked losing everything and finding myself in the street, I had only one desire now: to go to the end.

• • •

Coming back from lunch, Marc Dunker casually glanced at his share price on the Internet. "What's all this shit?" he suddenly shouted.

Andrew's voice could be heard from the next room. "Do you need anything, sir?"

Dunker ignored him. "What's happening, for Christ's sake?" he bellowed.

Andrew appeared in the doorway. "Did you read the newspapers I put on your desk this morning, sir?"

"No, why? What's up?" Dunker asked, worried.

"Er . . . it would appear there have been leaks, sir."

Marc Dunker's heart skipped a beat. He jumped up and grabbed the pile of papers. "What are you saying?" he asked, madly searching through *La Tribune*, half-tearing pages as he went.

"Page twelve, sir," Andrew prompted.

Dunker immediately saw the article his secretary had highlighted in yellow. He read it, then closed the paper and slowly sat down.

"There is a black sheep among us," he said with a thoughtful air. He was calm, but his face had gone red. "It doesn't matter," he stated, as though to convince himself. "In a couple of weeks, everybody will have forgotten."

DUNKER WAS RIGHT: The stock exchange has a short memory. For ten or so days, the Dunker Consulting share price remained at the level it had fallen to, then slowly started rising again. The investors apparently couldn't have cared less about the fate of the unfortunate candidates replying to bogus vacancies. All our CEO had to do was publish projected accounts so optimistic they were laughable for the financial markets to regain confidence. Investors, it seems, seldom look too deeply into the real capabilities of a business. In any case, the reality matters very little, as long as everyone involved gets excited. Fortunately, I had a little surprise up my sleeve, likely to calm them down.

I called Fisherman at *Les Echos*. Had my prediction coming true put an end to his skepticism? I now had to strengthen my embryonic credibility.

"I have another piece of information for you," I said in a confidential tone of voice.

Zero reaction from Fisherman. But he didn't hang up.

"The Dunker Consulting share price will go down by more than four percent the day after tomorrow," I told him.

Once more, I had pulled a figure out of thin air. A little bird told me that the accumulation of scandalous news would amplify the stock exchange's reaction.

"The day after tomorrow?"

A miracle. He had spoken. He was licking the hook with the tip of his tongue.

"Yes, the day after tomorrow."

That way I was leaving him time to print his predictions in tomorrow's edition of the paper.

No answer.

I hung up, beginning to regret having chosen Fisherman. I had bet on him because of his constant criticism of my company in his articles, but my mistake had been to believe that he had it in for my boss personally and would leap at anything that tarnished the firm. Perhaps I'd projected my own feelings onto Fisherman. Thinking about it, he seemed totally devoid of emotion. He was critical of Dunker only because he didn't believe in his strategy.

This realization spoiled the rest of my day. My whole plan depended on Fisherman. Was I failing already? That evening, I had great difficulty going to sleep.

The next day at dawn, I went down to the kiosk to buy *Les Echos*. Not the slightest word in it about Dunker Consulting. I was disgusted. It was too late to turn to another journalist. I was probably going to use the last of my ammunition for nothing, but I had to continue counting on Fisherman. When a gambler has played red all evening in vain, he seldom has the courage to put his final bet on black, because if, as ill luck would have it, red came up, he would never forgive himself.

At lunchtime, I went back to the fax machine and sent every newsroom irrefutable proof that Dunker Consulting had knowingly decided to canvass insolvent companies.

● ● ●

It had taken me nearly three days just to choose the theme of my talk. Obviously, you can only speak well about a topic you know. That being so, I had a choice between accounting—my original training—and my present profession, recruitment. The latter was a minefield. I risked having my audience remember unpleasant personal experiences of job hunting and then projecting their resentment onto me. So I took refuge in a topic from accounting. Besides, wasn't it a hiding place for all the timid people on the earth? My talk might not be very exciting, but at least I was lessening the chance of endangering my relationship with the audience. If they fell asleep, I would feel all the safer.

I prepared my text with great care. When you suffer from stage fright, it's very useful to have a script to hang on to in order not to stand there desperately searching for words, mouth dry and head empty.

I arrived at Speech-Masters early. It would be comforting to see the associates arrive one by one rather than having to face them all at once. It would give me time to get acclimated—to master my fear and not let it grab me by the throat and rob me of my intellectual powers.

Éric greeted me kindly, putting me at ease right away. I looked at the platform like a condemned man looks at the scaffold from which he's about to hang. I was surprised to see a microphone. On my previous visit, I hadn't noticed that the room was equipped with a public address system.

People trickled in, saying hello to Éric, then joking among themselves. It was very pleasant and reassuring, even if, at the same time, I couldn't help but think that if they were regulars, they had no doubt reached a level much above mine.

Éric shut the door at the agreed time, which was a miracle for Paris, a city where everyone thinks it's normal to be 30 minutes late. I was glad to see that there were no more than 25 members present. I would be more at ease than if there had been a full house.

After a few announcements, Éric said to the group, "Today, I have the pleasure of welcoming a new member . . . "

Breathe, I told myself. *Take deep breaths. Relax.*

". . . who is going to make his first speech: Alan Greenmor."

Everyone clapped as I stepped onto the platform. My heart was pounding. All eyes were fixed on me. I took the microphone in my right hand, keeping my notes in the left so I could refer to them if need be.

"Hello, everyone," I began. My voice was muted, as if it was stuck in my throat. My lips were trembling, and my body felt stiff. "I'm going to talk to you about a topic that I'm aware doesn't have much sex appeal: American accounting practices."

General laughter, immediately followed by thunderous applause.

Hey, what's going on here? I thought. This wasn't what I had expected. I had spent nearly an hour looking for something funny to start my speech with, but I didn't think it would be so successful. Their response immediately warmed my heart. My stage fright dropped 50 percent. *Let's carry on. But I must articulate better, place my voice better.*

"I studied the subject for four years in the U.S., and, er . . ."

Damn! What was I supposed to say next? A blank. A complete blank. Yet I knew my speech by heart! Oh, right, my notes.

Reading from my notes, I continued: "When I landed in France, where I come from on my mother's side, and looked for work."

I must seem such a moron reading a cheat sheet in front of everyone. It's so uncool.

I continued, "The consultant in a large recruitment firm that you all know told me with a big smile that French accounting practices were so different from American ones that I might as well put my American qualifications in the garbage."

More laughter. They're all looking at me with broad smiles, in such a kindly way. I love them.

"He, too, laughed a lot as he told me that. I didn't."

Another outbreak of laughter, then long applause. I couldn't believe it. It's crazy how much fun it is to make an audience laugh. I suddenly understood why some people make a career of it.

"So I felt the need to study the differences between the French and American accounting systems."

No more stage fright. I feel good, light. It's wonderful.

I continued for ten or so minutes, managing to free myself almost completely from my notes. The audience looked really interested in the topic, which wasn't that easy to achieve, believe me. Apparently, I was succeeding in capturing their attention, arousing their interest. I felt astonishingly good, more and more at ease. I even allowed myself to move around the platform as I spoke, still looking at the audience.

I finished amidst particularly loud applause, mingled with cheers. Some members stood up, soon followed by others, then the whole room. *A standing ovation!* I couldn't get over it. They were chanting my name. I was deliriously happy.

Éric joined me on the stage, continuing to applaud. Then he asked everyone to take a few minutes to write down their comments.

A few moments later, Éric gave me a large envelope containing pieces of paper folded in four. I went and sat down in a corner of the room and started impatiently unfolding the messages, curious to know what little defects and points for improvement the audience had picked out. My surprise increased as I went through the comments and saw that 100 percent of them were positive! It was incredible, unimaginable. I couldn't get over it. It seemed that behind the fear that had paralyzed me lay a hidden talent, a natural gift that was just asking to express itself.

Éric came to say that after a very first session, he advised going home at once rather than sitting through the other talks, so I could remember my performance better while quietly rereading the comments. I waved good-bye to the assembled associates and left.

I climbed the dark staircase as if I was climbing the steps to a palace, carried by my success. Nourished by the new strength I had gained, I felt ready to set out, if the day came, to meet my destiny.

"WE HAVE A traitor in our midst!"

"I beg your pardon, sir?" said Andrew, appearing in the doorway.

Dunker gestured to the two newspapers lying open on his desk. Then he dropped back in his chair, with the annoyed look he wore on bad days.

Andrew came up to the desk to look. The headline on *La Tribune* read, "Dunker Consulting: After the Bogus Vacancies, the Bogus Clients?"

Le Figaro: "After the Job Vacancies without Jobs, the Clients Without Money."

"That's not good for our company!" remarked Andrew.

Dunker looked daggers at him. "Any more clever analyses where that one came from, Andrew?"

The Englishman blushed slightly but didn't reply. He should have kept quiet. When the boss was in this mood, he would take it out on you by using the slightest thing you said against you.

"Yes, a traitor on the team, it's obvious!" repeated Dunker. "The share price is going to go down more."

He turned to his computer and nervously tapped on the keyboard.

"There we are! All it takes is some idiotic news making the rounds for these wimps to panic and sell! The share price is down two percent! And the market has only just opened!"

• • •

"Oh yes, definitely! That's perfect!"

"You said smiling; I've done him smiling."

"Well, smiling he certainly is! But anyhow, it's fine. It's really good."

I paid the price we'd agreed on the day before and left, extracting myself with difficulty from the group of onlookers who were leaning forward to try and see the painting.

There was a crowd on this fine, sunny, late afternoon on the Place du Tertre. The tourists came to have their portrait done by one of the numerous painters gathered around the square, each with a wooden easel and a color palette in one hand, a brush in the other. It was fascinating to watch the artists' eyes as they examined the faces they were sketching, looking past the smiles to unearth the expressions that would best characterize their subjects.

I took the painting back to my apartment to wrap it. I had been on cloud nine since the end of trading that day. The Dunker share had lost nearly 5 percent, and I was feeling generous.

Ten minutes later, I knocked on Madame Blanchard's door.

"Who is it?"

"Monsieur Greenmor, your neighbor."

She opened the door.

"Here, this is for you," I said, holding out the parcel.

"For me?" she said, not hiding her surprise. "To what do I owe the honor?"

"To nothing. I was very touched that you gave me a cake the other day. So I wanted to give you a little present as well."

She unwrapped it, and then admired the painting for a few seconds.

"It's very pretty. Very well painted. Thank you very much, Monsieur Greenmor."

I could feel she didn't dare ask the question.

"Do you like it?" I asked.

"Yes, very much. And who is it, exactly?"

"Madame Blanchard, come on! It's Jesus Christ!"

"Ah."

She looked at it wide-eyed. I wanted to put her at ease.

"Of course, we're not used to seeing him like that."

She was speechless.

"You must admit," I went on, "that men have played a dirty trick on him, showing him on the cross, his face disfigured by suffering. Would you want to be photographed on your deathbed, in your final agony, and then have the image be circulated forever?"

I HAD PLANNED to call Fisherman at the end of the day, to leave him relatively little time before his deadline. I wanted him to react instantly, without having a chance to revise his position later. But I hadn't foreseen that my last appointment would drag on forever. The candidate had come a long way, so I couldn't cut short the interview and see him another day. It was 7:35 P.M. when he left. Fisherman's paper went to press at 8:00 P.M. I grabbed the phone, afraid I was too late.

"Hello, *Les Echos!*"

"Monsieur Fisherman in the editorial office, please. It's urgent!"

"Please hold."

The Four Seasons played ad nauseam. A version to make Vivaldi turn in his grave.

For crying out loud, pick up!

7:41 P.M.

"Hello . . ."

"Mister Fisherman?"

"Who's calling?"

I replied, and this time my ears had to put up with endless bars of "Summertime."

7:43 P.M. *Pick up, pick up.* Fisherman would never have time to write anything before the 8:00 P.M. deadline.

"Good evening."

His cavernous voice, at last.

"This is Alan Greenmor. I have another scoop for you."

Silence, which he finally broke. "I'm listening."

"In my last call, I forecast a drop in the Dunker Consulting share of three percent, and it happened."

"Almost," he corrected.

"The second time, I predicted more than four percent. It was four point eight percent."

"Yes."

I concentrated. My voice had to sound both confident and relaxed. I wasn't used to bluffing, and this was bluffing on a grand scale. There was absolutely nothing to back it up; I had no more scandals to reveal to the press.

I followed my gut. "Tomorrow, the share will experience the most breathtaking fall in its history. It will lose at least twenty percent in a single day."

"Twenty percent in a single day? That's impossible."

Don't back off, or you're screwed.

"In fact, I'm convinced the fall will be greater than that. Far greater. Perhaps trading will even be suspended to stop the price from falling to zero."

Silence.

"We'll see," he said finally.

His ambiguous reply annoyed me. What did it mean? That he was going to print a notice, then see how far the share dropped? Or stay on the sidelines, as on the previous occasions, and just watch the action? If he played the spectator again, I was done for.

We hung up.

The die was cast.

A long wait began. I tortured myself trying to predict the course of events. Would Fisherman write something? Had my earlier forecasts, which had turned out to be true, been enough to build my credibility? All evening, these questions went around and around in my mind. I was first anxious, then confident, then doubtful again. I wanted to believe, but I was so afraid of being wrong. Fisherman's market advice was so highly regarded, so closely watched in financial circles, that just a word from him was enough for the share to collapse. For good.

I had enormous trouble going to sleep, then slept fitfully. Several times, I woke and looked at the time. Finally, at 6 A.M. I got up and got dressed, making myself listen to the radio in order not to think of anything else. At 6:55 I went down to the street. The café was already open, so I ordered a coffee and asked for *Les Echos*.

"It'll be here soon. Wait a bit," said the waiter in his usual unfriendly tone.

Wait. I couldn't bear any more waiting.

My coffee was too strong. The first mouthful was bitter. I ordered a croissant to get rid of the aftertaste. I ate it without noticing, lost in thought.

The waiter snapped me out of my reverie when he tossed the paper down on the bar. I grabbed *Les Echos* and quickly turned the pages, my stomach in a knot. Suddenly a headline leapt at me, and I stopped dead. For a moment I felt nothing, absolutely nothing, as if the shock had cut off all emotions and thoughts.

"Dunker Consulting: Sell Before It's Too Late."

I wanted to shout with joy. I couldn't believe my eyes. It was crazy, extraordinary, fabulous!

I ordered another coffee and a second croissant, and plunged into the short article that followed. Fisherman, the powerful and respected Fisherman, was advising shareholders to sell! He explained that the recent evidence of malpractice, along with some toxic rumors and the strategic errors of recent months added up to a worrying picture. It was far too risky a share, and the best thing was to unload it as quickly as possible.

If he had been sitting next to me, I would have thrown my arms around him.

An hour later, I was at the office, unable to contain my impatience as I sat in front of my computer screen, waiting for trading to begin on the stock exchange. The figure I had waited for so long finally came up at 9:01 A.M.—a fall of 7.2 percent at the opening. I didn't know what to think. Would it be enough?

I spent the day with my eyes riveted to my screen.

The price went up and down all morning, but overall the trend was down. At lunchtime, the share was down 9.8 percent. I ran to buy a sandwich from the machine. When I came back it had collapsed to 14.1 percent. My heart leapt. The only possible explanation for such a movement was a massive sell-off. In the space of a few minutes, someone had unloaded a large block of shares. One of the big shareholders must have called it a day. Hurrah! I was jubilant. The 10-percent drop must have been the trigger. These investment funds make their selling decisions on the basis of criteria fixed in advance.

Just one more! If the second big shareholder sells, I will be free!

What was the stop-loss threshold the second shareholder had fixed? Was it when the share price dropped 15 percent? I hardly dared hope. We were so close.

Not much happened in the next hour. I could barely contain my impatience. I ran like a madman to get a coffee from the staff room and nearly spilled half of it as I ran back. No movement while I was gone.

The *Echos* website printed just two lines, with no further comment, saying the INVERNIA fund had sold its Dunker Consulting shares. At 4:30 P.M., we passed the 15-percent mark. I waited with bated breath.

Go on, go on, sell!

The minutes went by without anything happening. A bad sign. I waited, champing at the bit. Then it dropped to 15.3 percent. The fall was continuing, but slowly, without the sudden spurt I was hoping for. It went to 15.7 percent.

Trading ended on a historic fall of 16.8 percent. That was no doubt huge, unheard of even, but there was still one big shareholder in place, which complicated things. Together, he and Marc Dunker might hold the majority of voting rights on the day of the annual meeting. It was a tricky situation.

I had spent the whole day in a state of intense excitement, intoxicated by results that were more than heartening, and now it was all ending on an unfinished note. The machine had jammed, blocked. The sky, so bright until then, suddenly went dark. I had the feeling of a half-victory tinged with failure. My adrenaline retreated like a courtier who feels the wind change direction, and I suddenly felt weary, emptied.

What was the point of being persuasive in front of the shareholders at the annual meeting? Against the electoral weight of the biggest shareholders, what were the tens or even hundreds of votes the others brought me?

ANDREW TIPPED THE canvas bag onto his desk. The white envelopes piled up on the red leather, forming a heap as high as on the previous days. Andrew hurriedly picked up three envelopes that had fallen on the floor. He put the wastepaper basket to the right of the desk, pushed the pyramid of letters to the left, then armed with a letter opener in his right hand, he picked up the first envelope with his left hand, slit it open in a precise and rapid gesture, extracted the document inside, and placed it in front of him, throwing the envelope into the wastepaper basket before repeating this carefully choreographed sequence.

Half an hour later, he heard his boss yell. Was Dunker on the phone? A glance at his screen informed Andrew that he wasn't. He'd better go and see what was happening.

Andrew gave the usual two knocks and opened the door. Dunker immediately shouted, "A bunch of sheep! All of them! A crummy journalist sticks his nose in where it doesn't belong, and all the morons incapable of thinking for themselves follow his damn-fool advice and sell. As a result, the share price goes down a bit, and the others rush in without thinking! Without thinking!"

Andrew knew from experience that when his boss exploded it was best to say nothing and let him get it off his chest.

"And Poupon is a sheep like the others!" Dunker continued. "INVERNIA left us three days ago, and for three days

313

I've been trying to seize the bull by the horns and call Poupon to convince the dummy to reinvest now that the price
is low. Can't be reached! Supposedly. Let's say he just doesn't
have the balls! It wouldn't cost him much, either. With all
the press exaggerating our imaginary problems, the share
price has been falling for three days. Falling? I should say
crumbling, collapsing! Soon, it won't be worth anything."

Andrew waited patiently and when he thought Dunker's
anger had run its course, he tried to change the subject.

"At our next annual meeting, sir—"

"Stop talking about the annual meeting! It's the least of
my worries! I've lost my biggest shareholder, and the price is
nowhere near picking up. Nothing I say to the three people
who turn up at the meeting because they've got sod-all else
to do is going to change the situation! If it wasn't a damn-
fool legal obligation, I'd cancel the annual meeting."

"Yes, of course, sir. You're legally obligated to bring the
shareholders together once a year."

"The shareholders, the shareholders! That's a grand title
for the people with three cents' worth of savings they dump
on the stock exchange in the hope it's going to bring a better return than the savings bank. But none of them come to
the annual meeting anyway, apart from some morons who
think they're important just because they own a handful
of shares."

"I'm afraid the shareholders who will be attending the
annual meeting are rather more numerous than you think,
sir. For a few days now, we've been receiving replies to our
notification. That's what I've been trying to talk to you
about since yesterday: We're going to have to change the
venue, because the meeting room we hired at the Hotel
Lutetia will be too small."

"Too small? What do you mean, too small? What the
hell's going on?"

"I think they're frightened by the drop in the share price, sir, and are deciding to take a closer look at the company whose shares they hold. "

"But they've hardly got any shares! Each one's got five or six at the most. They've got a fucking nerve! I'm not going to talk development strategy with them. I've got nothing to say!"

"The people who don't closely follow the price of their shares, and then wake up when they've lost thirty percent, realize it's too late to sell," said Andrew. "They would lose too much. As a result, their only hope is for the situation to reverse itself. That's why they're suddenly interested in the way the business is managed, even though it was the least of their worries two days ago. We saw the same phenomenon when the Eurotunnel shares went down, sir. The small investors decided to come in droves to the annual meeting to defend their interests.

"At any rate, sir," Andrew continued, "we really will have to change the venue to be able to fit them all in."

"Change the venue, change the venue. You're not expecting me to hire a goddamned convention center, are you?"

"No, sir, a convention center would be too small. The way things are going, we're going to have to think about the Omnisports Palace at Paris-Bercy."

LIKE ALL THE shareholders, of which I was now one, I had received my notification of the annual meeting by registered mail two weeks before the meeting date.

I had been writing my speech for a week, polishing it the way a sculptor puts the finishing touches on his marble statue, smoothing away the slightest roughness. I almost knew it by heart, as a result of reciting it over and over in front of the bathroom mirror, imagining myself before the small group of shareholders who would need to be convinced. I thought about the speech constantly—walking along the street, sitting in the Métro, waiting in a line. I even spouted certain passages in the shower, visualizing an audience captivated by my words. I constantly reminded myself of my triumph at Speech-Masters, and it gave me faith in my ability.

I was rather proud of my speech, which I thought was persuasive. If I were in the small shareholders' place—which, of course, I now was—I would no doubt vote for me.

The venue of the meeting had been changed at the beginning of the week. An official letter informed us of a new address: POPB, 8 Boulevard de Bercy, in the 12th arrondissement. The location meant nothing to a newly arrived Parisian like me.

I already knew that Dunker would never forgive me for standing against him. The day after the annual meeting, I would either be CEO of Dunker Consulting or an unemployed ex-recruiter pursued by a half-mad former psychiatrist.

Fear had gone right to the core of my being.

The morning of the annual meeting went by very quickly. I reread my speech for the umpteenth time, and then went for a walk to clear my head and lower my stress level. I was in a strange state, with nagging stage fright. As I came out of my apartment building, I saw Étienne under the steps and felt the need to confide in him.

"I've got stage fright," I admitted.

"Stage fright?" he said in his rough voice.

"Yes, I'm going to speak in front of people today, to tell them my vision about certain things, and it's giving me stage fright."

He gazed at the passersby.

"Where's the problem?" he said. "I say what I think when I think it, and everything's fine."

"It's not that simple. I won't be alone. I'm going to be seen, listened to, judged."

"Look, if they're not happy, too bad! You got to say what you think. Listen to your heart, not your fear. Then you won't have stage fright."

I made myself a light lunch and then switched on a radio news channel. I had just started eating when I was suddenly stopped in my tracks. The journalist had just announced the news headlines at 2:30 P.M. My heart leapt as I checked my watch. It said 1:45 P.M. I ran to the bedroom. The alarm clock there said 2:30 as well! *It couldn't be!!!* The annual meeting started at 3:00 P.M.—on the other side of Paris!

I pulled off my shirt and jeans, threw on a white shirt and my gray suit, and grabbed an Italian tie. It took me three attempts to get the knot in the right place. My shoes were tied up in a flash. I seized the meeting notification and my speech, slipping them into a folder, then tore out of the apartment, slamming the door and rushing down the stairs.

I hit the street at 2:38 P.M. I'd never make it by 3:00. Hopeless. All that was left was to pray that the meeting wouldn't start on time. I had to declare my candidacy to the chairman at the beginning of the session. If I missed the boat, I was screwed.

I ran as I'd never run before and reached the Métro platform, out of breath, just as the doors were about to close. I jumped on the train and, panting like mad, collapsed on a seat opposite an elderly woman who was looking at me wide-eyed.

I was beside myself. How stupid for my watch to act up on the very day I had no room for error. I spent the whole journey in a terrible state.

When I came out of the Métro, my cell phone said 3:05 P.M. But was it accurate? I started frantically looking for 8 Boulevard de Bercy. Along either side of the street were huge, grass-covered berms, with openings like gaping mouths cut into the earth at intervals. No street numbers in sight. I was cursed. I ran up to a passerby.

"Excuse me, where is 8 Boulevard de Bercy, please?"

"Hey, I don't know," he said. "What are you looking for?"

I got out my notification.

"POPB. It must be . . ."

"Oh, it's there," he said, pointing to one of the gaping mouths, which had a giant poster of Madonna displayed beside it. "Don't panic," he said. "The concert's tomorrow!"

I ran as fast as I could through the gate, waving my notice at a security guard. *Palais Omnisports de Paris-Bercy* said a sign. Omnisports Palace of Paris-Bercy. I didn't know sports stadiums rented out rooms to businesses. Strange idea.

"Go to reception," said the guard, pointing to a line

of tables with bored-looking, blue-uniformed receptionists sitting behind them.

I rushed over. "I'm late!" I said impatiently, flashing my notice.

The receptionist took her time, looking up my name on a list while talking to her colleagues. She began to prepare a badge, fumbling with it as quickly as her long red-varnished nails would permit, then broke off to take a call on her cell phone.

"Yup, I'll be finished soon," she said with a laugh. "Wait for me, because after, I'm going to the hairdresser's and—"

"Please," I interrupted. "I'm very late, and I absolutely must get in. It's very important."

"I'll call back," she said, looking daggers at me as she put down her phone.

She finished writing my name on the badge and held it out to me, nodding her head in the direction I should take. "Over there, second on the left," she said.

"Thanks. I don't know if I should go the same way as everyone else, because I'm"—I could hardly say it—"running for CEO."

She looked bewildered, and then dialed a number on her switchboard.

"Hey, it's Linda from reception. I've got a visitor who says he wants to stand for CEO. What do I do? Yup, OK."

She looked up at me. "Someone will come and get you."

3:20 P.M. Time went on, and no one came.

For Christ's sake, I don't believe it! I'm screwed.

I was torturing myself so much with the idea that I was too late that I completely forgot my stage fright. Unwittingly, I had found the antidote.

I saw him approaching and swallowed hard—our finance director, Jacky Kériel. He came up to the receptionist, who pointed at me. He opened his eyes wide in amazement when he recognized me, then pulled himself together and came over.

"Monsieur Greenmor?"

Who else did he think it was?

"In person."

In his surprise, he forgot to say hello. "I'm told you . . ."

"That's right; I wish to run as a candidate for the position of CEO."

He remained silent for a moment.

"But . . . have you . . . told Monsieur Dunker?"

"'That's not a precondition, according to the bylaws."

He stared at me, obviously ill at ease.

"Shall we go?" I said.

He seemed to be thinking. Finally, he said, "Follow me."

I fell into step, advancing into one of those vast, high-ceilinged passageways found in every sports arena. We walked along for a while, then turned down a corridor watched over by a security guard who nodded to my companion. At the end of the corridor we came to a gray metal door with a red light on above it. I followed the finance director through the door . . . and had the shock of my life.

I was on the stage of an enormous hall, filled to overflowing. People were everywhere, seated in tiers in front of me, to the right, to the left, rising to the ceiling. There must be 15 or 20,000 of them, perhaps more.

I should have been overjoyed. There were enough shareholders to counterbalance the remaining big investor. Henceforth, my fate was in my own hands. But, in my stomach, a ball of anxiety was getting bigger by the second. I was going to have to speak before this immense crowd, and the very idea made me feel like I was going to throw up.

I suddenly realized that the finance director had continued walking, leaving me behind. I hurried to catch up. We headed to the right side of the immense stage, where there was a long table covered with a blue cloth—the blue of our company logo, which was projected on a huge screen at the back of the hall. At the table, facing the audience, were 10 or 12 people: Dunker in the center, the directors around him, and a few people I didn't know. Behind them were 50 or so armchairs arranged in rows. I recognized only a few of the occupants, carefully selected colleagues.

The finance director stood next to Dunker and leaned down to speak to him. I could hear none of their conversation, but it was clear my candidacy was disturbing the order of events. The finance director finally came back and motioned to me to follow him.

"Go and sit there," he said, pointing to an armchair that a hefty guy was carrying across the stage. To my surprise, the stagehand put the chair down at least five or six yards away from the rest of the group. I was being kept shunted off to one side, as if I had the plague. As I went and sat down, anger rose up in me, an anger that gave me a semblance of courage. And a desire for revenge.

A few seconds later, one of the strangers at the big table got up and came over to me, introducing himself as the company's auditor. He asked me for ID and handed me a declaration of candidacy to sign. He then returned to his seat at the table, leaving me alone at the side of the stage.

"Ladies and gentlemen, good afternoon." The voice boomed out of the powerful loudspeakers, bringing silence in the hall. "I'm Jacky Kériel, the finance director of Dunker Consulting. I am responsible for opening our annual general meeting with some legal matters. To begin with, the number of people present . . ." Droning on, he began reading a long list of figures: ratios, quotas, results, debt rates, self-finance potential, cash flow.

I stopped following what he was saying and let my eyes

and thoughts wander around the hall. I never would have imagined that the drop in the share price would make so many people come to the annual meeting. They must be bitter, anxious, and unhappy. The meeting would no doubt be stormy. I knew, of course, that I ought to be overjoyed at this huge turnout, because it gave me a chance of tipping the vote in my favor, in spite of the remaining big share-holder. But at the moment I could think of nothing but speaking in front of so many people, on this stage where I was so exposed. A nightmare.

I felt completely overwhelmed by events, out of place. Out of *my* place. Where *was* my place exactly? Was I made to fill a position without heavy responsibilities? Perhaps. That certainly seemed more comfortable. But why? It wasn't a question of educational level; there were too many ex-ceptions at both ends of the spectrum. Was it personality, then? But the directors of the company seemed very differ-ent from one another; I saw no typical profile emerge. No, it must be something else. Perhaps our family background unconsciously held us back, if, for example, we aspired to a profession that was clearly superior to that of our relatives. Perhaps we couldn't quite allow ourselves to outdo them. Or perhaps we couldn't go beyond the level our parents had intended for us, feeling deep down that to do so would be a betrayal. However probable that might be, it wasn't certain that climbing the social ladder brought greater per-sonal fulfillment.

"Now it's your turn to ask questions, and we'll do our best to answer them," I heard the finance director say. "People will be coming up and down the aisles with microphones. Please raise your hand if you want to say something."

The question-and-answer session dragged on for a good hour. The directors replied from the table. Some were concise; others were chattier, at times losing themselves in soporific details.

Finally, it was Dunker's turn to speak. "And now," Kériel said, "I'll turn the meeting over to our CEO, Marc Dunker, a candidate for reelection, who will give us his analysis of the current situation and present his strategy for the future."

Dunker got up and walked confidently to the center of the stage, where a podium had been set up. Silence fell over the hall. His speech was clearly much awaited.

"My dear friends," he began. "I must first thank you for having come in such numbers. I think it's a sign of your affection for our company and the interest you have in its future."

He was good; I had to admit it.

"We are in a paradoxical situation: The company has never been in better shape, as is shown by the results my finance director has just presented to you, and yet, our share price has never been so low."

His ease and charisma reminded me painfully of my own shortcomings. What would I sound like, coming after such a good orator?

"The practices that we have been criticized for by the press and by one journalist in particular are nothing out of the ordinary. They are common in our profession and normally no one is offended by them. But, really, I ought to be flattered by this criticism, these attacks. They are the treatment reserved for the great, who are targets for the jealousy of the weak."

Not necessarily very clever of Dunker. On which side did the people in the audience see themselves? The great, because they own three shares? Or the little people, characterized as weak?

"Unfortunately," Dunker continued, "I have to face the

facts. The origin of this disorder, apparently, is an informant inside our company, who has passed these slanderous accusations to journalists, who have had a field day with them. There is a traitor in our ranks. His harmful actions have upset our company's share price and have jeopardized your savings. But here, before you, I promise to find who it is and drive him out as he deserves."

At that moment, I wished I could teleport elsewhere, disappear into thin air. I made an effort to look impassive, while underneath, I was seething with a frightful cocktail of shame and guilt.

A wave of applause spread through the audience. Dunker was succeeding in shifting the anger of the small investors onto a mysterious scapegoat, while he passed himself off as a protective leader who was going to give them justice.

"Soon it will all be no more than a bad memory," he went on. "Even cyclones don't stop the grass from growing back. The truth is that our company is in full development and our strategy is winning."

He went on in this self-satisfied way, asserting the validity of each of his strategic choices, going through them in detail and expressing his desire to continue them in the future.

He finished to the applause of the directors and the guests, soon followed by a fair share of those in the hall. Dunker waited until they were silent and then continued speaking in a relaxed tone. "It turns out that we have a last-minute candidate for CEO. A slightly fanciful candidate, shall we say."

I sank down in my chair.

"The candidate is a young man who happens to be an employee of our company. A young recruit, I ought to say, since he's only been with us for a few months. He joined our firm directly from the classroom."

Laughter in the hall. I sank down a little farther.

"I nearly dissuaded him, to avoid wasting your time, then I said to myself that after going through these difficult moments on the stock exchange together, it would do us good to be able to smile together."

Snickering could be heard in the hall, as Dunker calmly returned to his seat, wearing a satisfied smile.

I was appalled at his shameful remarks. It was lousy of him.

He slowly turned his head in my direction, briefly giving me a contemptuous look.

Dunker had barely sat down when the finance director took the microphone and said, "So now I invite our second candidate for the position of CEO, Monsieur Alan Greenmor, to speak."

I swallowed hard while my stomach tightened as never before. I felt weighted down in my seat, cast in a block of cement.

Go on. You must. You've no choice. Get up!

I made a titanic effort to stand up. All the directors had turned in my direction, some of them with mocking smiles. The guests were staring at me as well. I felt alone, terribly alone, so oppressed I found it hard to breathe.

My first steps to the podium were the most painful. Carrying the sheets of paper with my speech, I crossed the stage toward the vast audience. If only they would turn off the lights in the hall, leaving just the footlights. Then I wouldn't be able to see the thousands of unknown, mocking faces looking at me as if I were an animal at the zoo.

I reached the podium at last. As I placed my speech on the lectern and adjusted the height of the microphone, my hand was shaking, and my heart was beating as if it was ready to burst. I could feel the blood rushing to my temples. I absolutely had to refocus before I started. *Breathe. Breathe.*

I mentally reread the first sentences of my speech. Suddenly it seemed bad, unsuitable, off balance.

Far off in the rows of spectators, right up at the top, a voice shouted, "Come on kid, out with it!" immediately followed by hundreds of scattered snickers.

It's painful when two or three people make fun of you. When there are 300 or 400 of them with 15,000 witnesses, it's unbearable. It had to be stopped. In a wild desire to survive, I gathered my strength and threw myself into the water.

"Good afternoon."

My voice, powerfully amplified by the loudspeakers, seemed hollow.

"My name is Alan Greenmor."

"Tell us more," a wit called out, setting off another wave of laughter, louder than the first. The problem was spreading.

"I am a consultant in recruitment, which is the core of Dunker Consulting's business. I have come here today to introduce myself as a candidate . . . "

No good. It doesn't sound right.

" . . . for the post of chief executive officer. I am aware of the heavy responsibilities that go with the position."

On my left, a mocking voice called out, "You already look crushed!" A new outburst of laughter. The machine was speeding up. Prepared in a Machiavellian way by Dunker's derisive words, egged on with his tacit permission and given his blessing, the small investors were being unleashed. I had been thrown to them; they were going to make mincemeat of me.

To be the laughingstock of the audience was the worst thing that could happen to me. The worst. It destroyed my credibility, crushed all hope. I would have preferred hostility to mockery. Hostility pushes you to react, mockery to run away. I wanted to disappear, to be anywhere else, but I absolutely had to stop this. Immediately! Anything, as long as they stopped making fun of me.

Impelled by the gravity of the situation, which was getting worse by the second, terrified at the idea of being booed by the whole audience, and gripped by shame, I forgot my speech, my notes, even my own best interests and looked up at the tiers of faces where the laughter was multiplying in response to my silence. I looked straight at this audience totally devoid of compassion. Meeting the mocking eyes, I finally brought my lips so close to the microphone that they touched the cold metal.

"I'm the one who told the press about Dunker's malpractices!"

My voice resounded impressively in this temple of mockery, and silence fell instantly. Total silence, absolute, deafening. The amazing silence of a hall of 15,000 people. Mockery gave way to stupefaction. The clown onstage was suddenly no longer a clown. He was an enemy, a dangerous enemy who had wiped out their savings.

Igor Dubrovski's words came back to me, no longer a technique to be applied but a philosophy to be adopted: *Embrace your neighbor's world, and he will open himself up to you.*

Embrace your neighbor's world. We weren't individuals fighting each other; we were human beings linked by the same aspirations, the same desire to live a better life. What set us apart was, at bottom, only a tiny detail, compared to what brought us together. But how was I to share this with them? How was I to explain it? And how would I find the strength to express myself?

The image of Speech-Masters passed before my eyes, allowing me to reexperience the wonderful feeling of that occasion. I possessed, somewhere deep within me, the necessary resources. I was capable, if I dared, of going toward these people and speaking to them from the bottom of my heart.

The rostrum now seemed like a barrier, a hindrance. I reached out and removed the microphone from its stand, and, leaving my notes behind, walked toward the crowd, alone and unarmed, offering my vulnerability. I walked slowly, carried along by a sincere wish for peace. I was afraid, but my fear gradually gave way to a new feeling, a feeling of confidence.

I reached the front of the stage. I could make out the grave expressions of the people nearest to me. Farther away, the faces faded until they became the vague, colored brushstrokes of an Impressionist painting. But I could feel all eyes on me, in the heavy and intense silence.

It was obvious that I couldn't deliver my prepared speech. Written a week earlier, it was disconnected from the present, dissociated from the emotions of the moment. I had to be content with the words that came to mind. "You speak with your heart," Étienne had said.

I looked at all these people gathered around me. Their sense of helplessness and their anger were palpable. I could feel them vibrating in my body.

I brought the microphone to my lips.

"I know what you're feeling at this moment," I said. My voice resounded in the gigantic space, assuming an unsuspected and impressive sonority. "I can feel your concern. You invested your money in our company's shares. My revelations to the press made the share price fall, and you're furious with me. You see me as a vile person, a traitor, a bastard."

Not a murmur in the crowd.

"That's what I would think, too, if I were in your place."

The entire hall remained in absolute silence—a tense, electric silence.

"Your hopes of financial gain have been disappointed. Perhaps you needed that money to improve your standard of living, your purchasing power, or to improve your pension, or to grow the capital you will leave to your children. Whatever your concerns, I understand them, and I respect them.

"Perhaps you think I gave this information to the press out of hatred for Marc Dunker, out of a desire for personal vengeance. It could have been the case, given all that he has inflicted on me. And yet, no, that is not the reason. I published the information with the precise goal of making the share price drop."

Some insults could be heard. I went on, "Of making the share price drop and thereby making you come to the annual meeting, so that I could speak to you face-to-face."

The tension was at its maximum, and I could feel the audience totally concentrated on my words, burning to discover my thoughts, to give a meaning to my actions.

"When it was founded, the stock exchange's purpose was to allow businesses to collect money from the public to finance their development. Those who chose to invest, whatever the amount, placed their confidence in a company and trusted its ability to develop over time. They believed in its plan. Then the lure of gain made some invest for ever-shorter periods, moving their capital from one company to another to try and tap short-term gains and thereby maximize their income. This speculation became widespread, and bankers invented financial tools that allow all sorts of betting on share movement, including betting on a falling market. The person who speculates on the share price going down makes money when the business starts to be in difficulty. That's a bit like profiting from a decline in your neighbor's health. Imagine: Your neighbor has cancer. You bet a thousand dollars that his health will decline dramatically in the next six months. Three months later, the cancer metastasizes. Great! Your investment is up twenty percent. Of course, you think there's no link between this example and the market—your neighbor is a person and not a company. But this is the heart of the problem. Since the stock exchange has become a casino, we have forgotten its prime function, and especially we've forgotten that behind the names of the companies we gamble on like we're playing roulette, there are people—living, flesh-and-blood people, who work in these companies and devote much of their lives to the company's development.

"The price of your shares is directly linked to the prospect of short-term gains. For the share price to go up, the company must publish excellent results each quarter. But a company is a little like a person in another way: its health has ups and downs, and that's quite normal. And sometimes, just as it does in a human being, an illness allows the company to step back a bit, see things differently, adjust its trajectory, and then set off again with a new equilibrium, stronger than before. As a shareholder, you have to be patient. If you deny the reality that a company's health goes up and down, then the company will deny its difficulties—it will lie to you or make decisions that will generate positive results in the short term. By publishing bogus job vacancies or by deliberately canvassing insolvent companies, Marc Dunker simply responded to the demands of a game whose rules are intolerable.

"This requirement for share-price growth brings with it enormous pressure on everyone, from the CEO to the most recent hire. It prevents people from working properly, calmly. It encourages short-term management that's good for neither the business nor the employees nor the company's suppliers who, squeezed hard, will reflect that pressure back on their own employees and suppliers. We end up with companies in good health laying people off just to maintain or improve their profitability. This threat now hovers over each one of us, pushing us into an individualism that affects the atmosphere between colleagues.

"In the end, we all find ourselves living under stress. Work is no longer a pleasure, yet I am convinced it ought to be."

A deadly silence continued to reign in the hall. We were a long way from the stimulating laughter I had experienced at Speech-Masters. But I felt carried along by my own sincerity. I was just expressing what I believed deep down. I wasn't claiming to possess the truth, but I believed wholeheartedly in what I was saying, and that gave me the strength to carry on.

"We won't remake the world today, my friends. Then again, I learned recently that Gandhi used to say, 'We must be the change that we want to see in the world.' And it's true that the world is nothing more than the sum of each one of us.

"If you want your shares to return rapidly to the price they were a few weeks ago and continue on a steep upward curve, then I advise you to reelect the man who leads the company today. If you choose to put me at the head of the company, I will not make any promises on that score. It's even probable that the share will stay low for a time. What I *do* promise, on the other hand, is to make Dunker Consulting a more humane company. I would like everyone to be happy to get up in the morning with the thought that they are coming to work to express their talent, whatever their position. I would like our managers to be responsible for creating the conditions for the fulfillment and success of each member of their team, making sure that everyone can continue to develop their abilities.

"And I am convinced that in such an atmosphere everyone will give their best, not with the goal of meeting a target dictated by external demands but for the pleasure of feeling competent, of mastering their craft, of excelling. I want to build a company in which the results are the fruit of the passion we put into our work, rather than the consequence of pressure that destroys our pleasure and equilibrium.

"I also promise total transparency in the management and results of the company. No more propaganda and misinformation. If we temporarily have bad results, why should we hide them? To keep you from selling your shares? But why would you, if you are signed on to a long-term plan? We all catch a cold or flu that puts us in bed for a week. Do you hide it from your partner for fear that they'll leave you? I am convinced that a company whose operation is based on healthy values absolutely can grow and generate profits. But those profits must not be pursued obsessively, like a drug addict after his fix. Profits are the natural fruit of healthy and harmonious management."

Igor's words came back to me: *You can't change people, you know. You can only show them a path, then make them want to go down it.*

"The choice is yours. In the end, it's not a CEO you are going to choose, but the sort of satisfaction you want to feel in the long run. On the one hand, you will have the satisfaction of having maximized your revenue and perhaps going a bit farther for your holiday at the end of the year, or buying a slightly bigger car, or leaving a little more money for your children to inherit. On the other hand, you will have the satisfaction of taking part in a fabulous adventure: the return of humanism to the business world. And each day you will perhaps feel a little glow of pride, the pride of having contributed to building a better world, the world you will leave to your children."

I looked out at all the people. They seemed close, despite being so numerous. I had told them what I had in my mind and heart; there was no point in adding anything. I didn't feel the need to finish with a well-turned formula to mark the end of my speech and set off applause. Besides, it wasn't a speech, simply the expression of my deepest convictions, of my faith in a different future. I stayed a few seconds just looking at the assembled, in a silence that no longer frightened me. Then I went back to my isolated chair, apart from the others. The directors at the table were looking at their feet.

The vote and the count lasted an eternity. It was already night when I became CEO of Dunker Consulting.

THE NEARER I got, walking along the paths through the perfumed gardens of the Champ de Mars, the more gigantic the Eiffel Tower seemed, dominating me with its immense height. Lit crimson by the setting sun, it was majestic and disquieting at the same time. Yet there was no longer any objective reason for my apprehension. The success of my final task the day before freed me from Igor's clutches, and we were going to be able to celebrate my victory in peace. But somehow, in my eyes, the tower remained a trap. I had the feeling of going back into a cage that I had escaped.

Reaching the foot of the Iron Lady, I looked up at the top. Vertigo made me reel. I felt minute and fragile, a penitent kneeling at the feet of a god-like giant, begging it to grant him mercy.

I headed for the south tower, weaving through the tourists, and introduced myself to the man who was screening people waiting to use The Jules Verne's private elevator.

"What name is the reservation under?" he asked, about to look at the list he had in his hand.

"I'm with Monsieur Igor Dubrovski."

"Right, sir, please follow me," he replied at once, without even looking at the piece of paper.

I followed him into the space at the foot of the tower. He gave a discreet sign to his colleague, who was waiting with some customers. We slipped in front of them and entered the old, narrow elevator with its iron-and-glass walls. The door closed noisily behind us like a dungeon door, and we rose among the tangle of metal that constitutes the tower.

"Monsieur Dubrovski hasn't arrived yet," he told me. "You're the first."

The elevator rushed upward. Arriving at the second floor, I felt a pang as I recognized the great wheel pulling the elevator cable. I felt my hands become moist. The man led me to a maître d' who greeted me with great distinction. I followed him across the restaurant to our table, next to the window. He offered me an aperitif while I waited. I chose a Perrier.

The atmosphere was subdued and pleasant. A restrained décor in black and white. The late-day sun reached into every corner, accentuating the ethereal feel of the place. A few tables were already occupied. I caught snatches of conversation in foreign languages.

I couldn't help but shudder when I looked out. Those beams were only too familiar. In the end, it was healthy to come back to the scene of my trauma. I experienced it as the possibility not of wiping out the past but at least of writing another story on top of it.

What a lot of ground I had covered since that day. I felt as if I had freed myself from my chains, like a boat casting off the moorings that have kept it dockside. I had discovered that most of my fears were just an invention of my mind. Reality sometimes takes the shape of a terrifying dragon that disappears when you dare to look at it head on. Spurred on by Igor, I had mastered the dragons in my mind, and it now seemed to be inhabited by benevolent angels.

Igor . . . Igor Dubrovski. Yves Dubreuil. Was he going to shed light on the shadowy areas that remained, now that our pact was coming to its end? Was I going to understand at last his motives, or would I continue to see him as an old, half-mad psychiatrist?

Time was passing, and Igor hadn't come. The restaurant was gradually filling up, and the ballet of waiters, maître d's, and sommeliers was being played out, a fluid and silent choreography. I had another drink. A bourbon this time. I never drank the stuff, but suddenly I wanted one.

Igor wouldn't come. I knew it deep down. In a confused way, I could feel it.

I dined alone, carried by the mildness of the evening, lulled by the languorous chords of a jazz-inspired pianist. In the sky, the stars were shining peacefully.

THE MAN SAT down comfortably under the arbor and placed next to him the cup of steaming coffee he had brought. He got a cigarette out of the pack and put it between his lips. He struck a match on the side of a little box, broke the match, and swore as he threw the broken end on the ground. The second match caught fire at once, and he lit the cigarette, taking a drag.

It was the best moment of the day. The sun had barely begun to rise in the still pale blue sky. It was going to be hot.

The man opened his paper, *La Provence*, and read the headlines on the front page. Not much news at the end of August. Another forest fire rapidly brought under control by the Marseilles fire department with the help of Canadair fire-fighting planes. *Must have been a pyromaniac,* he thought, *or some thoughtless tourists picnicking in the countryside despite the ban.* Another article reported on the increased numbers attending summer festivals, which nonetheless didn't always cover costs. *We're going to have to pay for the Parisians' concerts with our local taxes again,* he said to himself.

He drank a sip of coffee and opened the paper to the inside pages.

The photo leapt out at him. Underneath, the headline in bold said: "A 24-year-old Man Elected CEO of the Biggest French Recruitment Firm."

His cigarette fell out of the corner of his mouth.

"Well, I never! Josette, come and have a look at this!"

• • •

You can no more judge a man by his job title than you can judge a book by its cover. However, it inevitably changes the way others see him. My return to the office, two days after my election, was rather off-putting. There was a small crowd in the lobby when I arrived. It was as if the disbelief after the announcement of my election was such that my colleagues wanted to check the results for themselves. Each one greeted me after his fashion, but none of them addressed me as they normally would. I could already feel that personal interests were at play—I couldn't hold it against them, and some were being cautious, while others were obviously inspired by the wish to cozy up to me in order to benefit from it sooner or later. Thomas was the most flattering among them, which didn't surprise me. Only Alice was genuine in her reaction, and I felt her satisfaction was sincere.

I didn't hang around but went up to my office. I had barely been there a quarter of an hour when Marc Dunker turned up.

"Let's not beat around the bush," he began, without even saying hello. "Since you're going to fire me, we might as well get it over with. Sign here; that way it's over and done with!"

He held out a sheet of paper. It was a letter typed on company letterhead and addressed to him, indicating that his services were no longer needed. Under the signature line, it read: *Alan Greenmor, Chief Executive Officer.*

This guy was so used to deciding everything that he was sacking himself! I took the letter and tore it in two, then tossed it in the wastebasket. He stared at me, stupefied.

"I've thought about it long and hard," I said. "Rather than serve as both president and managing director of the company, I've decided to keep just the overall presidency and to appoint a separate managing director. I'm offering you the job. You worship efficiency; you have a passion for results. We'll set them to work for a noble cause. From now on, your mission, if you accept it, is to make this company a more humane business, producing high-quality services while respecting everyone from the clients to the employees to the suppliers. As you know, I am betting that happy workers will give the best of themselves, that suppliers treated as partners will rise to the trust we place in them, and that our clients will appreciate the value of what we have to offer."

"It'll never work," Dunker said. "Have you seen the share price? The day after the annual meeting, it lost another eleven percent."

"Nothing to worry about. It's just the second big shareholder selling his shares. Henceforth, the company will be made up solely of small investors who believe in the new vision for the business. We're finished with the pressure of a few big shareholders deciding everything! Now we are part of the same family."

"You'll be eaten alive. I give it six months before a competitor launches a hostile takeover! In less than two weeks he'll be the majority shareholder, and you'll be fired."

"Hostile takeovers won't work. A takeover is just an investor offering to buy the shares at a higher price than the market price. But I must remind you that the shareholders voted for me *after* I pointed out that the share price would go up less quickly than with you. So they've signed on to our business plan while giving up hope of short-term financial gain. I'm betting they'll remain faithful and won't be tempted by the siren song."

"You're not facing reality. They'll give in. The flesh is weak when money is at stake."

"You haven't understood that the situation has changed.

Your shareholders couldn't care less about your business. Their only motivation was the lure of gain. That's why you were a slave to the profitability of their investment. Those who have stayed with me are now united around a business plan, a real business plan based on a philosophy and values. There is no reason for them to go back on their values now. They'll stay."

Dunker looked at me, perplexed. I opened the file in front of me and took out a piece of paper that I held out to him.

"Take it; it's your new contract. The terms are the same, except that you are now managing director and not CEO." He looked at me, speechless, for a few seconds. Then I thought I caught a flash of malice in his eyes. He took a pen out of his pocket, leaned over my desk, and signed.

"Okay, I accept."

At that moment my phone rang.

"There's a journalist on the phone," Vanessa said. "Shall I put him through?"

"Okay, put him through."

Dunker nodded and left.

"Monsieur Greenmor?"

"Speaking."

"Emmanuel Valgado from BFMTV. I'd like to invite you to be on our program on Tuesday morning. We'd like you to tell us the behind-the-scenes story of your takeover at Dunker Consulting."

"I don't really think of it as a takeover."

"Precisely. That's what interests us. The taping takes place on Monday at two o'clock. Will you come?"

"Just one thing. Will there be an audience?"

"Twenty people at most. Why?"

"Could I invite one or two people? I have an old promise to keep."

"No problem."

• • •

Marc Dunker left Alan Greenmor's office with a slight smile on his lips. The young whippersnapper had had a vague desire for power, but he didn't have the balls to do it on his own. That's why he was keeping Marc as managing director. He was incapable of leading the business, and he knew it.

The ex-CEO was already rubbing his hands, as he ran up the stairs two at a time. He would soon gobble up this kid who was so naïve that he wasn't even careful. No sense of power, that's for sure. In the end, nothing would change. He, Marc Dunker, would control everything from the managing director position. The presidency would follow obediently. After a year, Marc would present his results to the annual meeting, and when the shareholders learned he had done all the work, he would be elected CEO hands down.

Dunker was at the door to his office when suddenly his face tensed and then went purple as he thought of something: his three million euro golden parachute in the event of severance. That was it, of course! That's why Greenmor had asked him to stay. And he had signed!

As Dunker went into his office, he walked past Andrew without even seeing him. The words came out of his mouth without him realizing: "That little jerk has just screwed me a second time!"

His secretary raised an eyebrow.

"I'm sorry, sir?"

I LEFT THE office early to go to see Igor Dubrovski. He owed me an explanation. It was too easy to hide as he had done the day before. The CEO's chauffeur, henceforth at my disposal, drove me.

Arriving at the mansion, our large car stopped outside the black gate, and I got out. Thick clouds were gathering in the sky; the air was heavy with moisture. Looming in the grayness, the château looked like a ghost ship.

I recognized the servant who opened the door for me and led me without a word to the great drawing room. The gloomy weather plunged the interior into a melancholic darkness. Contrary to the habits of the house, few lights were on.

I found Catherine on a sofa with her legs tucked under her, her shoes abandoned on the carpet.

"Hello."

She looked at me but didn't respond, making do with a slight nod. I looked around. She was alone. In the darkness, the large, closed piano looked like a slab of black marble. Through the tall windows, opened onto the garden, I could see the first drops of rain sliding off the leaves.

"Where is Igor?"

She didn't reply but looked away.

"Oh . . . you know his real name."

"Yes."

She remained silent for a long while.

"Alan . . ."

"Yes . . ."

She sighed.

"I've got to tell you . . ."

"What?"

I could sense she was tense.

"Igor is dead."

"Igor is . . ."

"Yes. He had a heart attack yesterday morning. The servants could do nothing. Help arrived too late."

Igor dead. I couldn't believe it. It was inconceivable. Even if my feelings toward him were mixed, after going through the spectrum of emotions, from admiration to hatred and fear, in the space of a summer, there remained nonetheless the man who had freed me from the shackles of my inhibitions and made me capable of fully living my life. Igor was dead. I suddenly felt very much in his debt, and . . . ungrateful. I would never have the opportunity to thank him.

Sadness slowly mounted in me, finding its place in every part of my being. I suddenly felt heavy, downcast. The old lion had left the world.

A thought crossed my mind: *Did the answers to my questions disappear with him?*

"Catherine, can I ask you something?"

"Alan, I . . ."

"The trial. The François Littrec trial. Igor was guilty, wasn't he?"

"No, he had nothing to blame himself for in that business."

"But why did he hypnotize the jurors? That's what he did, didn't he?"

Catherine gave a sad smile.

"It wouldn't surprise me, but if he did, it's probably

because he preferred exercising influence to having to justify himself. Or perhaps it was simply impossible for him to prove his innocence, however real it was. He had had very few conversations with the young man, who was being treated by others as well. Igor was not responsible for him ending his life."

"And me? Our meeting at the Eiffel Tower wasn't by chance, was it?"

She looked at me kindly.

"No, you're right."

"He deliberately drew me into his sanctuary, is that it?"

She nodded.

I swallowed hard. She was his accomplice; she knew about everything and had let it happen.

"Catherine, do you know why he knew Audrey?"

She turned her head toward the window, then spoke in a dreamy voice, her attention on the rain streaming down noisily in the garden.

"Igor knew the intensity of your relationship. He informed Audrey of . . . his plan for you. He convinced her to leave you after putting the article on suicide in your apartment."

"He asked Audrey to leave me?!"

I was disgusted. How could he have done such a beastly thing?

"She was hard to persuade, but Igor was good at that. He proved it was in your interest and negotiated with her the period of time he needed before she could renew contact with you."

I found it hard to believe that Audrey had played along with him. Her personality was too definite for that.

"And when I saw her coming out of here that one time . . ."

"She had come to tell him to get lost, that she couldn't

go on, that it was all senseless. Igor had to renegotiate the time left. Alan . . ."

This story made me beside myself. I felt a dull anger mounting in me.

"But how could he?"

"Alan . . ."

"It's really hateful to play with people's feelings like that!"

"Alan . . ."

"And if she'd met someone else during that time?"

"Alan . . ."

"It was taking an enormous risk to . . ."

Catherine shouted over my words to make herself heard.

"Igor was your father, Alan!"

Her voice resounded in the great drawing room. The vibrations went on in my head. Silence fell all around. I was stunned, bewildered. My mind reeled under the combined assault of emotions and thoughts.

Catherine remained rooted to the spot. She didn't take her eyes off me, despite her embarrassment.

"My father . . ."

I stammered, quite unable to articulate anything intelligible.

"I don't know if your mother told you," she went on very gently. "The man who raised you in the States was not your father."

"Yes, yes, she did. I knew that."

"Years after conceiving you, Igor agreed to take in the daughter of a servant who'd fallen ill. She was a single mother and had no one to look after her child during the two weeks she was in the hospital. She was a lovely little girl, about the age you would have been . . . Very bold, she was full of life, mischievous and funny. She was still very young, but she already had quite a personality. Igor fell for her. He'd never shown the slightest interest in children, but now he spent all his time looking after her. She was a revelation to him. She made him realize a lot of things. When Audrey's mother came out of the hospital and took her daughter back, Igor insisted he be allowed to continue looking after her regularly. He played the role of a godfather, a protector—a role he kept later when she became an adult, even after her mother was no longer working here. The little girl coming into his life was a trigger. Igor suddenly remembered the child he had had, who had never known its father. That idea started to haunt him day and night. He was seized with remorse and couldn't bear knowing that his only child was living somewhere without him. So he started searching on a grand scale, with all the means at his disposal. But it was like looking for a needle in a haystack. It took him nearly fifteen years to find any trace of you. And by chance you came back to live near him, without knowing it."

"Chance . . ."

"Then he waited to contact you, putting it off from day to day, week to week. A sort of reserve, no doubt. After spending all that time looking for you, once he had found you, he suddenly no longer had the courage to face you. He was afraid you'd reject him, that you wouldn't forgive him for having abandoned you and your mother even before you were born. At one point, I even thought he would never approach you, that he was going to give up forever. Then he had you followed, more and more closely. It became almost an obsession. He read the reports every night. He knew all about your life, day by day, including your fears, your disappointments, your feelings.

"Vladi was no longer enough to tail you. You would have noticed him sooner or later. So he asked his protégée to take part. She agreed. But the man who loved to control everything had not at all imagined what was going to happen. As a result of following you, observing you, the girl fell head over heels in love with you and from then on refused to give him the reports."

"Don't tell me . . ."

"Yes."

"Audrey?"

Catherine looked at me in silence, and then nodded.

My God, Audrey was Igor's protégée.

"It was then that he decided to . . . take you in hand. I think it was a way of treating his guilt for not having brought you up. Unless it was a way of regaining control of a situation that was getting away from him. He'd been looking for you for fifteen years, and just as he was getting ready to appear in your life, you threw yourself body and soul into the arms of a young woman. Perhaps, unconsciously, he wanted to keep you to himself for a while. As for me, I was very much of two minds about his idea of taking care of you. I thought there was a risk it would make your reunion even more complicated the day you found out about it, but he took no notice. As usual, he was his own master."

"But what were you to him? I always wondered."

"You could say a female colleague who became a friend. I'm a psychiatrist as well, and when I was still officially practicing, I had heard of his achievements. So I contacted him and asked to train in his presence. He agreed right away, only too happy for someone to take an interest in him and his skills. You must accept that your father was a genius, Alan, in spite of his slightly special methods."

"But you must admit it's madness to push your son to commit suicide, just to put yourself in a position to support him afterward. I could have died then and there, or even killed myself by another method than the one he had tried to suggest."

"No, you were being closely watched."

Nonetheless, something was troubling me, upsetting me profoundly, though I wasn't able to identify what. I remained like this, in this strange state, for a few moments, and then the memory came rushing back to me.

"Catherine . . . the day I met him for the first time, at the Eiffel Tower, I was in a sorry state."

"I know."

"And Igor encouraged me to jump. I swear. I can still hear him saying: 'Go on, jump!'"

Catherine gave a slight, melancholy smile.

"Ah, there you are! All Igor is in that scene! He knew enough about you and your personality to be certain that giving you the order to jump was the best way of stopping you."

"But . . . suppose he'd been wrong? He took an enormous risk!"

"Don't you see? That's why we'll never be like him. All his life, he took risks. But your father knew people better than they knew themselves. It was instinctive. He felt what had to be said in an instant. And on that level, he never made a mistake."

Outside, the rain had stopped. Now, the garden was bathed in a bright light that was reflected in the wet leaves. Some delicate scents reached us through the open windows.

We talked about my father for a long while. I finally thanked Catherine for confiding in me. She told me the day of the funeral, and I left. At the drawing room door, I hesitated, and then turned around.

"Did Igor know . . . about my election?"

Catherine looked up and nodded.

One question bothered me; I was a little ashamed to ask it.

"Was he proud of me?"

She turned her head to the garden, remained silent a

few seconds, and then answered in a voice that was slightly husky: "I came to see him that evening, after Vladi told me. He couldn't reach Igor. I came in, and Igor was at the piano. He remained with his back to me, but he stopped playing to listen. He knew why I was coming. I announced your victory, which he received in silence, without saying a word. He didn't move. After a long while, I went over to him."

Catherine left a long pause, and then went on:

"His eyes were full of tears."

MY REUNION WITH Audrey took its place in the record book that had already been full for some days. It was a great joy to be reunited, closing the painful parenthesis of our separation. I was delighted to find she still loved me. I felt light, happy, overcome with emotion to be able once more to see her, touch her, smell her, kiss her. We swore never to be separated again, whatever happened. We talked about Igor as well, of course, united in sadness, both of us in tears. She told me of her childhood with him, and I of our short but intense relationship. We laughed together at my fears about him, the tasks he had given me, the adventures that resulted.

After an Orthodox mass at Saint-Alexandre Nevsky Cathedral on the Rue Danu, the burial took place at the Russian cemetery in Sainte Geneviève des Bois, half an hour south of Paris. Most of the people present didn't know each other, apart from the assembled servants. The others didn't talk, but stood quietly or walked along the cemetery's shaded paths while waiting for the body to arrive. There were more women than men, some of them very beautiful, wearing bright colors.

Then the coffin appeared, and instinctively we all grouped together. It was carried by four men dressed in black, followed by Vladi, who was holding an astonishingly calm Stalin on a leash.

We followed them in a long, silent procession, in radiant

sunshine, through the verdant expanse of this beautiful and disturbing place filled with great birches, spruce, and pine trees, their knotted trunks standing out against the brilliant blue of the sky.

I turned down a path, and suddenly my heart felt a pang. A piano had been put there in front of us. A young man with Slavic features and pale blue eyes sat at the keyboard, looking serious. He started to play, the crystalline, melancholy notes falling in the silence. The crowd stopped moving, hanging onto the emotion of the moment. Audrey pressed against me. The melody moved into heartbreaking chords, their beauty enough to shatter the armor of the strongest man, drawing him into the realm of feelings, suffering, and meditation.

I would have recognized the music anywhere: Rachmaninoff was accompanying my father to his last resting place. Even the most insensitive among us could not hold back the tears.

Months went by. Audrey and I moved into the château one winter morning, when snow had covered the garden with a fine downy mantle and the flakes had gathered on the long, majestic branches of the great cedar. It was cold and the air smelled fresh, like in the mountains.

I was excited at the idea of living in such a vast and comfortable house. The first week, we changed bedrooms every night and had our meals alternately in the drawing room, the library, and the magnificent dining room. We were like two kids in a palace filled with toys. The daily chores disappeared; the servants took care of them for us. After a few weeks, we had gotten our bearings and established a routine. Our life gradually organized itself around two rooms.

We entertained Audrey's friends several times, but the atmosphere was tense. Although our attitude hadn't changed, they didn't feel at ease in this place that I myself had found so impressive for so long. They saw us differently, and the conversations lacked naturalness, warmth, spontaneity. Our relationships started to wither, becoming cold and distant. They knew we were rich, and some of them, without any hesitation, asked us for financial support, which naturally we couldn't refuse. After a while, we were less their friends than their bankers. Conversely, others tried to force us to be friends. Wealth attracts snobs and show-offs. We gradually got used to fending people off, and then shut ourselves away altogether.

The omnipresence of servants soon encroached on our private life. There was a risk they would appear at any moment, hindering real relaxation and intruding on our intimacy. We felt like outsiders in our own house. At the end of three months, we had lost all real joie de vivre, our slightly childish good nature. The situation was getting out of control. We were completely at a loss.

I tried to understand the meaning of what was happening to us. I had become convinced that things didn't happen to us by chance. I stepped back and asked myself why all this luxury had suddenly dropped into my life, offering itself to me. Perhaps life wanted to challenge me about my values. Perhaps I had allowed myself to be caught in a trap, no doubt confusing the need we all have to better ourselves with social mobility alone. Isn't real change inside? It's by changing yourself that you become happy, not by changing what's around you.

In a burst of lucidity, we decided to part with this cumbersome burden. We sold the mansion and divided the money among the servants. They deserved it, after loyally serving my father all their lives. Audrey's mother, who had retired the year before, received her share. Vladi, who kept Stalin, got the Mercedes, too, as we had no use for it.

Then Audrey and I crossed our fingers and called Madame Blanchard. We leapt with joy when she confided that she still had not rented my old apartment, suspecting the different candidates she had interviewed of being potentially noisy neighbors!

We took possession of the apartment again one fine Saturday in April, taking with us just what we needed to be happy. The boxes had barely been set down, when Audrey opened the windows wide and put crumbs on the sills. The radiant sun filled the whole apartment, and the Parisian sparrows were soon accompanying our move with their joyful cheeping.

That very evening, Madame Blanchard organized a get-together in the courtyard to celebrate our return. Something had changed in her, but I couldn't identify what. She put a big white tablecloth on an old table and laid out a variety of quiches and cakes that she had spent all day making, perfuming the building with tempting smells. She invited all the neighbors, who were happy to take advantage of the mildness of one of the first spring evenings, and to my surprise, she went and fetched Étienne. He stuffed himself and appropriated a bottle of Crozes-Hermitage that he hung on to all evening. An old battery-driven cassette player gave out slightly old-fashioned but very joyful French songs that we wiggled to as we laughed. Carefreeness and lightness were back.

Several times during the evening, I looked at Madame Blanchard as I tried to figure out what had changed. It was nearly midnight when suddenly the answer came to me, perfectly obvious: She had abandoned black and put on a pretty flowered dress. The biggest things are sometimes the ones that go unnoticed the most.

ABOUT THE AUTHOR

Laurent Gounelle is a personal development specialist who trained in humanities at the University of California, Santa Cruz. Besides lecturing at Clermont-Ferrand University, he is now a consultant and takes part in international seminars. His three books have sold more than a 300,000 worldwide. They are based on the principles of neuro-linguistic programming (NLP).

Hay House Titles of Related Interest

YOU CAN HEAL YOUR LIFE, the movie,
starring Louise L. Hay & Friends
(available as a 1-DVD programme and an expanded 2-DVD set)
Watch the trailer at: www.LouiseHayMovie.com

THE SHIFT, the movie,
starring Dr Wayne W. Dyer
(available as a 1-DVD programme and an expanded 2-DVD set)
Watch the trailer at: www.DyerMovie.com

• • •

THE DALAI LAMA'S CAT, by David Michie

THE FIRST RULE OF TEN, by Gay Hendricks and Tinker Lindsay

THE GOLDEN MOTORCYCLE GANG: A Story of Transformation,
by Jack Canfield and William Gladstone

THE LAST LAUGH, by Arjuna Ardagh

PUSHING UPWARD, by Andrea Adler

All of the above are available at your local bookstore,
or may be ordered by contacting Hay House (see next page).

• • •

We hope you enjoyed this Hay House Visions book. If you'd like to receive our online catalogue featuring additional information on Hay House books and products, or if you'd like to find out more about the Hay Foundation, please contact:

Hay House UK, Ltd.
Astley House, 33 Notting Hill Gate, London W11 3JQ
Phone: 44-20-3675-2450 • *Fax:* 44-20-3675-2451
www.hayhouse.co.uk • www.hayfoundation.org

• • •

Published and distributed in the United States by: Hay House, Inc.,
P.O. Box 5100, Carlsbad, CA 92018-5100
Phone: (760) 431-7695 or (800) 654-5126
Fax: (760) 431-6948 or (800) 650-5115
www.hayhouse.com®

Published and distributed in Australia by: Hay House Australia Pty.
Ltd., 18/36 Ralph St., Alexandria NSW 2015 • *Phone:* 612-9669-4299
• *Fax:* 612-9669-4144
www.hayhouse.com.au

Published and distributed in the Republic of South Africa by:
Hay House SA (Pty), Ltd., P.O. Box 990, Witkoppen 2068
• *Phone/Fax:* 27-11-467-8904 • www.hayhouse.co.za

Published in India by: Hay House Publishers India, Muskaan Complex,
Plot No. 3, B-2, Vasant Kunj, New Delhi 110 070
• *Phone:* 91-11-4176-1620 • *Fax:* 91-11-4176-1630
www.hayhouse.co.in

Distributed in Canada by: Raincoast Books, 2440 Viking Way,
Richmond, B.C. V6V 1N2 Phone: 1-800-663-5714 • Fax: 1-800-565-3770
• www.raincoast.com

• • •

Take Your Soul on a Vacation

Visit www.HealYourLife.com® to regroup, recharge, and reconnect with your own magnificence. Featuring blogs, mind-body-spirit news, and life-changing wisdom from Louise Hay and friends.

Visit www.HealYourLife.com today!